THEIR

SILENT

GRAVES

CARLA KOVACH

Bookouture

Published by Bookouture in 2020

An imprint of Storyfire Ltd.
Carmelite House
50 Victoria Embankment
London EC4Y 0DZ

www.bookouture.com

ISBN: 978-1-83888-866-4
eBook ISBN: 978-1-83888-865-7

THEIR
SILENT
GRAVES

BOOKS BY CARLA KOVACH

Their Silent Graves *is dedicated to those who have suffered loss or illness this year. I know the pandemic has affected so many people in heartbreaking ways. Being able to hug a loved one is a precious thing. Don't take it for granted. Xxx*

PROLOGUE

24 years ago

Friday, 27 September

'Hey, get my buddy here a pint and pour me another one while you're at it.' Terry sniffed, before wiping away the touch of white powder that was irritating the bottom of his nose.

He slapped me on the back, almost knocking me over as I went to sit on the bar stool. I didn't mind, not while he was dishing out the freebies like there was no tomorrow. I glanced around and nodded at the others, mostly older men. I wasn't the only one who was enjoying his drunken generosity. It looked like the party had been going on for a while now. My mouth watered as I inhaled the hoppy smell. 'Thanks, Terry. You're a gentleman.' He's far from it; I don't know why I said that. It just seemed like the right thing to say.

'I know I am. I just wish the bitch at home felt the same, my man; but that's women for you.' As the server bent over to grab another glass, I saw Terry leering. 'What you doing later, love? Maybe you and me, we could do things that would have you howling with the wind in pleasure. All the fun with no strings. You know you want to.' He stuck his tongue out several times before winking.

The woman rolled her eyes and stood, pulling her skirt down as she stepped over to the other side of the bar to pull their pints.

'Have one yourself, you always do.'

'I'm okay thank you, and no I don't.' She turned away.

'She's an ungrateful bitch just like my wife. The key is to stay ahead of them, all the time. Show them their place and if they try to step outside of it, drag them back by the hair. Be in control.' He grinned and sniffed again.

I let out a wry smile and a slight huff. My takings have been down this month – not enough people are dying. I'm just ticking by. Don't get me wrong; people are spending less on coffins than ever. I supply quality goods, the most beautiful bespoke boxes that people can rest in for eternity. Rubbing my fingers together, I flinch at the splinters and callouses. I'm not just a carpenter, I'm an artist. I sculpt the wood. I enjoy the feel of it and treat it with love.

Terry gave me a nudge. 'I mean, that bitch dared to answer me back so what did I do? I left her in the shed. She has to know that she can't get away with speaking down to me.'

He's now grinning at me as the server plonks my pint down. 'Thanks, Terry.' I take a sip.

'Might leave her in there all weekend until she learns her lesson. When I let her out, she'll be so grateful, if you know what I mean. It does wonders for our relationship.' He winked again.

He has no idea what respect is. Everyone around here knows where she gets her bruises from, but we pretend to be his buddy. Why? I don't know. A sense of unease washes over me. I should say something, tell someone, but I won't - just like no one else here will. They could call the police or social services, but they won't. We won't. We ignore other people's problems in exchange for free drinks at the pub. We live by an unwritten code of not grassing on our fellow man. That's just what we seem to do.

'I'm going to go home and see to ma bitch!' He guzzles down the pint and slams it on the bar. 'Me and her have got some unfinished business. I'm going to show her who's boss. Bye, sexy, you've got my number. Call me.' He staggers to the door and flings it open, almost falling as he leaves.

'I don't think so.' The server leans over the bar. 'Why do you all encourage him?' The others turn away and get back to their conversations and games of cards and dominoes.

I recoil, scrunching my nose. 'Encourage him? I don't.'

'Whatever. You accept him buying you drinks, you say nothing when he's rude to people, mostly women. And the way he speaks about his wife, don't get me started. You know something, you're just as bad as him. You're just as bad as them.' She points to the others, throws the beer mat onto the bar and turns away from us all. I shrug and turn to them. I can see a couple of them grinning and one of them puts two fingers up at her back.

I grip the pint and I want to throw it. As I try to swallow a gulp, it doesn't taste as it should. I could stop her suffering. I could stop it right now. I could follow Terry home and I could call the police when he goes for the woman. I imagine her, locked in a cold, wet shed, shivering. I knock my pint over as I leave.

'Thanks for that,' the server calls as I run through the fog, catching up with Terry. My heart pounds. If anyone ever treated my daughter, niece or sister in that way, I'd kill them. I'd go guns blazing, like Billy the Kid. Straight in there with a bullet to his head.

I can't stand by and do nothing…

CHAPTER ONE

12 years ago

Halloween

'Where am I? Help! Let me out.' She began to feel around in the dark, flinching as something sharp pierced the skin that divides nail and finger. 'Let me out!' Banging on her surrounds, she hoped that someone was listening. With quickened breath, she tried to turn one way, then another. With every turn she bumped her elbow, toe or knee.

As she went to wiggle, she cried out as the muscle in her neck tugged, sending a sharp pain across her shoulder. Cold - so cold - and damp, and trapped. With trembling fingers she felt the gritty rainwater that had soaked into her midriff, right through to her tights and underwear. Each muscle burned with every shiver and she couldn't feel her toes. This couldn't be happening. Maybe it was all a dream and she was snuggled up in bed.

She inhaled sharply as a tear rolled down the side of her face, then she wheezed as if someone had stamped on her chest. This wasn't a dream. She banged and kicked until the sound of her toe cracking sent a sickening wave through her body. While struggling to breathe, she grappled for anything but there was nothing to grab hold of. Even though she couldn't see, she knew her head was spinning. The constant throbbing as blood pulsated through her body threatened to deafen her. Her head was going to explode with the *boom, boom* of blood whooshing through it. Banging and kicking, this was her last chance to escape before her own lights went out. She closed her eyes – not that that made any difference – and she willed the spinning to end. Her chattering teeth felt as though they'd shatter if she didn't try to stop them.

'Stop.' She forced herself to inhale, hold her breath, and then exhale. A few moments later, her mind was beginning to clear. What did she know? She was in a box made of wood, old damp wood. She ran her fingers over the rough grain and let out a small cry as another splinter pierced her fingertip. Someone had hurt her, maybe hit her over the head, if the constant pounding was anything to go by; then they had placed her in something wooden… a box, a… a coffin. Screaming, she hit the sides and the roof.

'Help, let me out.' Tears spilled out and her nose filled. As she continued thumping everything, she felt a weak spot in just one part of the wood, the part above her belly that was leaking. Thudding and pressing, she managed to crack a piece. As she pushed at it, harder and harder, gasping for breath, she felt a tickle on her midriff that made her jump. If only there was a little bit of light, then maybe she could take a good look at where she was and what was on her now. Her mind filled with large eight-legged freaking spiders, woodlice, worms, centipedes; everything that gave her the creeps at home. She was never able to deal with creepy crawlies; her parents had often had to come to the rescue.

With trembling hands, she reached out and screamed as she grabbed a handful of earth. *It's just earth, not a spider.* Wait – wasn't that worse? She'd cracked the box and now it was filling up with mud and grit and… *water.* She could hear a drip, drip, dripping, as it seeped through the gap – the coffin would fill up and she'd drown.

Do something. Think, think. A whirl of thoughts flooded her mind in what felt like lightning speed. *Do what?* She banged on the roof and then came the thud, followed by muffled laughter. There was someone out there, watching and enjoying her misery.

She'd already called for help and they'd done nothing. They were leaving her to die. Whoever was out there wasn't there to help; they were enjoying the show far too much to end it. Running her fingers through her pockets, she pulled out a box and traced its contents with her fingers. A mighty shiver ran down her spine, causing her to jerk and kick the wood with her toes. She screamed out as one of her toenails pushed into skin with full force. The earthy smell in the little box turned into another smell she recognised. Matches – she fiddled around with the contents – there were three.

She placed a match between her teeth as she fumbled to turn the matchbox, getting the sandpaper in the right position. The match slipped from her mouth, and the other two spilled out into her hair. Why had she been so clumsy? She could barely feel around her shoulders, her fingers were too numb and it was as if the box was closing in on her. *Calm down.* It had to be there, she could find it, logic told her that. A few seconds later, she had the match that had fallen from her mouth and she wasn't going to let it go this time. With one strike, she lit it. As she'd guessed, she was in a box. The hole she'd made was miniscule but that wasn't stopping the filthy water and earth from getting in. If she pushed at it even more, would she be drowned in earth? 'Ouch.' The match had burned down and scorched her index finger. She inhaled the sulphur dioxide that filled the tiny space. She knew that fire burned oxygen; science was one of her favourite subjects. She also knew that the oxygen in the box was limited and she'd run out soon. What she didn't know was how long it took to suffocate when buried alive. Seconds, minutes, hours?

She hyperventilated as the muffled laughter came again. *Breathe in and out, slowly.* She closed her eyes and thought back to before. She hadn't been hit over the head. It was coming back to her. She'd been pushed, then she fell headfirst into a rock. From that point, she couldn't remember anything. She rubbed her forehead with her gritty hand and flinched as she brushed the sticky wound.

She let out a scream and hit the top of the box. Someone put her here. Who? She thought back to the evening but it was all a blur – only fragments of it flashed through her mind.

That was it. She'd been drinking some sort of blood red punch from a bowl. Everyone had been drinking it. The idea of the plastic floating eyeballs that had been bobbing on the top made her stomach turn as she thought about them.

Loud music.

A girl being sick in the kitchen sink while a group of boys passed around the funny smelling cigarette. They'd accused her of being a bore when she'd turned it down.

A neighbour wearing a dressing gown knocking, complaining about the noise.

People everywhere. Devils, witches, the Snow Queen, the skeleton-clad figures.

'Don't Cha' by The Pussycat Dolls playing at top volume.

Falling up the stairs while trying to look for the toilet. Then stepping over a drunken sleeping boy who had lost his shirt.

A flash of a naked bottom-half sexy cat sitting on a vanity unit, being penetrated by Freddy Krueger. Her tail and leggings strewn across the bathroom floor and her cat ears were wonky. The girl telling her to shove off before throwing a hairbrush.

The sudden urge to get out. This wasn't her scene. She'd tried, made an effort and now she wanted to go home, especially after everyone at the party had virtually ignored her, leaving her sitting alone in a corner. Her so-called friend had abandoned her as soon as they'd arrived.

Slipping down the stairs in her stripy leggings. She wished that she hadn't dressed as a sexy witch, the outfit she'd chosen on the advice of her well-meaning newest friend. The one who'd ditched her as soon as they'd arrived at the house party. Her pointy shoes had long been discarded when she'd awkwardly tried to dance. She couldn't find them. They'd gone.

A large tear began to well in the corner of her eye. Her lovely parents had told her to be safe and call them when she needed picking up. She didn't tell them that she didn't want to go to the party as she knew that she had to make the effort to fit in. Being a newbie to the area, that's all she wanted.

Another image came back to her. It was when one of the boys was looking into her eyes just before he'd kissed her – her first kiss. Then he'd laughed at her with all his friends. She was nothing but a joke to them. Where had he gone? He'd left her, like all the others had.

Why had she left the party in tears? It would take more than a couple of people teasing her to make her cry. She had no trouble holding onto her sadness in a well-practised way, often letting it all out when she was alone in her bedroom. Maybe it was the alcohol in the punch.

She tried to swallow, then she coughed as her own saliva hit her windpipe.

There it was, the muffled laughter. The fact that she could hear them was good. She wasn't buried too deep. It had to be a prank.

She let out a scream as a thud came from above. They were throwing more earth on the box.

She wanted to tell her family how much she loved them. She wanted to go back to their old house in Birmingham and talk to her best friend, Sasha, again; the same friend who'd since moved on and not answered any of her calls. She wanted to walk around the shops, breathe in the air, feel the rain dripping down her face; feel the frosty undergrowth crunching as she walked her terrier, Miffy, through the naked brambles. It was the little things she craved – even school. She wanted film night with her mum and dad, with popcorn and crisps. She didn't want to die. She wasn't ready. She hadn't even had her first proper job or boyfriend. She'd never go to university or college or experience freshers' week.

She felt the trickling earth that was now piling up on her tummy. She tried to bang again and again, barely getting any pressure behind her fists in the confines of the box. Would a group of partygoers all get her out and claim it was a Halloween prank? She forced her hand above her head and began to touch her surroundings again. Rough wood… and… wait— A piece of string was poking through the tiniest of holes. Her mind flashed back to how there used to be bells attached to string that led to the casket during historical outbreaks of cholera. That was it. This was a test, an initiation. Depending on how she handled this, she'd either be forever ridiculed or admired by her peers. The matchbox slipped from her other hand.

It was okay now. She knew how this worked. All she had to do was pull the string. A bell would ring and she'd be freed. The partygoers would be waiting for her and tell her it was just a joke.

'Okay, I know what you're doing. You can let me out now. *Ha, ha, ha.* It's not funny any more.' She'd play it cool, pretend it wasn't a big deal, but it was. As soon as she was let out, she'd run as fast as she could, all the way home. She wanted nothing more to do with anyone she'd met at the party, or the one person who had claimed to be her new best friend.

The laughter started up again, but this time she couldn't hear it as well and another spray of earth landed on the coffin. With numbing fingers, she reached for the string, taking two attempts to grab hold of it and wrap it around her wrist to gain some purchase. She began to pull over and over again, banging her elbow with each tug. The string slackened. She pulled it more and more, winding it around her two hands until the end flew through the hole with a final flick against her cheek.

All she wanted to do was cuddle Miffy and be in her bed. She dug what was left of her nails into the gap and felt the weight of the earth pressing on the wood above. She could see no way out. *Goodbye Mum, Dad and Miffy.*

CHAPTER TWO

Now

Monday, 26 October

'I'm glad you could make it.' DCI Chris Briggs sipped his coffee in their usual seat at Lucy's Café. Even sitting down, he appeared tall. His greying brown mottled hair had flopped forward, giving him that off-duty look. At this precise moment, it didn't feel like he was her boss and she was his detective inspector, they were just two friends having a coffee together.

Gina glanced at the fake cobwebs and pipe cleaner spiders that adorned the café windows, ready for Halloween. The new owners had done such a good job since taking over. 'I'm glad you asked me to come.' Gina waved a hand to the woman in the apron who was frantically cleaning the table that a family had just left.

'Have you got any plans for your break yet?' The coffee cup looked tiny in his shovel-like hand.

'I have. I've booked a spa break. I'll be away from Wednesday and, for once, I can't wait.'

'I didn't have you down as the type to enjoy relaxing.'

'I'm not. My daughter keeps telling me I need to try it.' She pressed her lips together. Having some stranger's hands kneading her back and painting her toenails fuchsia pink didn't sound altogether appealing, but she had promised she'd try it at some point and after seeing a cheap break online, she booked it on a whim.

'Is Hannah going with you? A bit of mother-daughter time?'

'I haven't told her I'm going. I've only told you. I thought, if I hate it, I can just come home and no one will be disappointed in me. If I go with her and I even look like I hate it for a second, she'll never let me forget. I suppose I should have asked her, but it really is safer this way.'

'Maybe next time?'

Gina pulled a horrified face and broke into a titter. 'You always did know how to make me laugh.'

He looked into her eyes for a moment longer than usual.

She smiled and placed a strand of hair behind her ear. For once she'd made an effort, curling her hair to frame her face rather than it all falling down in an unruly mop. 'Looks like that last lot of customers had a bit of a food fight.'

There were pieces of what looked like tuna sandwich mashed underneath the highchair, crisps all over the table and a spilled cup of hot chocolate dowsed in soggy napkins. The café owner looked up, not realising that she'd smeared cocoa dust across her forehead. 'I'll be with you in a tick.' She brushed the errant strands of dark wavy hair away from her face.

Gina smiled. 'It's okay, I'm not desperate.'

'Liar.' Briggs knew her too well, better than anyone else at the station would ever know. 'I can tell you're beyond gasping for a proper coffee, not that machine stuff or cheap instant muck at the station.'

She held her hands up, rolling her eyes as she bit her bottom lip. 'You got me.' She looked across the room and spotted Cyril and June, the elderly couple who seemed to live here. June always knitted a few rows of the scarf she was working on while Cyril tried to do a crossword. The woman who sat in the corner peering through her large glasses was always alone and always reading a classic – this time it was *Crime and Punishment*. She was a people watcher and Gina could identify with her. Gina wondered what she might think of her and Briggs. Two colleagues enjoying a coffee, or past lovers trying to hide their feelings? A woman wearing heavy black boots and a vicar's dog collar left. Gina watched her as she ran across the road towards the church, takeaway coffee in hand. Then, Gina glanced at June again, just as she was whispering into Cyril's ear while looking at Gina. Gina frowned and looked away.

'Coffee?' Lucy wiped the sweat from her brow as she placed the broom against the window and exhaled. 'Your usual… Let me guess.' She closed her eyes and clicked her fingers a couple of times. 'I make a lot of coffees but here goes: Americano with a spot of skimmed milk.' She pointed at Gina.

'That's right, thank you.' Gina smiled as the woman wrote it on an old-fashioned order pad.

'Bill.' She called across the room to the man with a slight hunch and a full head of grey hair. 'Americano, spot of skimmed.' She pointed to Gina. The man turned his back on them and set to work, making the drink. 'Bill's my dad – and you are? I hate pointing to you guys when you come in because I don't know what to call you. What are your names?'

Gina cleared her throat. 'Gina and Chris.' It was rare that she got to introduce him to someone as Chris and she almost felt a warm flutter running through her body as she said his name. They were both out together, socialising, albeit only in a platonic way while enjoying a coffee. It had become a regular occurrence where they discussed life, the news and the cases that they were working on.

The server pointed to her name badge. 'I'm Lucy.' She turned to the counter. 'The Americano's for Gina, make it snappy, Bill.'

Bill stared in Gina's direction for a second longer than she was comfortable with. Gina smiled and he looked away. When she glanced back, he was making her drink. Lucy hurried to the counter, her flat shoes slapping on the stone floor.

'There you go.' Bill winked and handed the coffee to her.

'Thanks.' Lucy took the drink from her dad. He smiled, then continued reducing the prices on the leftover sandwiches that hadn't been sold at lunchtime. 'One Americano. I've got a tab open for you both. Just flag me down when you want to pay.' She tore the duplicate copy of the order and left it on the table along with a couple of beautifully wrapped chocolates. 'New line, thought you might like to try them.'

'Thank you. They are most welcome.' Briggs reached over and his hair flopped forward, covering his forehead.

Gina noticed that he was wearing the casual shirt that she'd bought him when they were in a serious – but secret – relationship. 'What've you been up to then?'

'Today? Nothing. I've binge-watched season one of *Stranger Things* on Netflix and walked the dog, that's all. Oh, I made a chilli, there's a box of it for you in the car. I know you don't cook. How was work today?'

Gina sat back in the swirly pink armchair and enjoyed the warmth of the vintage bulbs with the quirky filaments glowing above. The furniture was a mixture of comfy and colourful, made of reclaimed metal and wood. 'As you know, we've charged someone with the assault on Hanger Road. So, all in all, a good day, not too taxing.' She unwrapped a chocolate and popped it in her mouth.

'I heard. You know me when I'm off, I can't keep my head out of my emails. I can't believe so many people stood around doing nothing during that attack. Normally some good Samaritan steps forward or calls the police before things get too out of hand.'

Gina nodded. 'It seems people just hang around recording these things on their phones. We had seven recordings and, as you know, it took twelve minutes before someone stepped in and helped the man. We had lots of videoed evidence but the poor man had his jaw broken after ten minutes. In my book, that could have been prevented.'

'I suppose sometimes people are scared to step in, just in case they get hurt. That doesn't excuse them not calling the police.' Briggs smiled at the server. 'Could I get a top up, please?'

Lucy nodded from across the room, where she was admiring the scarf that June was knitting.

Gina tapped her finger on the table. 'I know people get scared around trouble and I'd normally agree with you, but I heard the running commentaries on the recordings that were taken. There was a lot of, *look at them go* and *phwoar, what a punch* as they were watching it through a screen. It was almost like they were detached from what was happening in front of them. Bizarre. I couldn't help feeling a bit sick after watching them while mulling over what we're becoming.'

'Sounds like it's a good job that case is over.'

'This time.' Gina stared through the cobwebbed window at the old church that had been situated on the end of Cleevesford High Street for two hundred years. The giant cross was lit up on the front of the building. Several male youths and a couple of girls were hanging around in front of the Perspex bus stop.

Lucy sashayed towards Briggs and placed the large milky coffee, along with the order slip on the table. 'Extra caffeine shot, just the way you like it.'

'Thank you.' He watched as a couple of cars passed by. 'It certainly is a funny old world and we meet them all.'

'You can say that again.'

Briggs took another sip of his coffee and Gina flinched as someone burst through the door. A small gale blew a flurry of dried leaves, scattering them across the café.

The man in the long navy coat stood at the counter, pulling at the thread unravelling at one of the cuffs. 'Large black coffee and one of those reduced-price chicken sandwiches to go.' He stared at everyone in the room, one by one, before slamming his fist on the counter. 'Is anyone here serving?'

Lucy hurried to the counter. 'Ooh, sorry about that. Bill must be out the back. You're in luck, the sandwich has just been reduced. That will be three pounds and seventy pence.'

'Rude or what?' Gina shook her head but continued to listen as she watched through the reflection in the window. Her nostrils twitched; the smell of stale sweat and smoke filled them as the man fidgeted.

She felt a wash of tension working its way through her muscles. Maybe she needed this spa break more than she thought.

The man fumbled in his pockets, emptying change, keys and crumpled tissues onto the counter. He pulled his black beanie hat closer to his eyebrows, then he began counting his money and getting aggravated by a strand of wool trailing from his fingerless glove. 'That's expensive. How can you charge that for coffee and a sandwich? You said it was reduced? If it's about to go off, you should be giving it away.'

Gina turned to get a better look.

'Sorry, we have overheads to pay. We have to charge what we charge.' Lucy began to tremble slightly.

'Okay,' he leaned in and read her name tag, 'Lucy – lovely Lucy.' He stared at her before breaking into a grin. 'Forget the sandwich, just make the coffee and make it to go. Your sandwiches look shit anyway.' He shook his head. 'Go on then. What are you waiting for?' He paused and sneered. 'Why are you staring at me? Fancy a bit of rough? I could show you a good time.' He reached out to touch her.

'Okay. I'm back.' Bill shuffled through the door. Lucy swallowed as she nodded to Bill and he began to make the drink. She took the change from the counter and rang it up.

'Boo.' The man laughed as she flinched. 'Hurry up with the coffee, mate. What's taking you people so long?' He slammed his fist on the counter three times in a row, causing the charity tin to rattle.

Gina went to stand and Briggs placed his hand over hers. 'You okay?' She pulled her hand away.

'Too right. I'll show this idiot that he can't speak to people like that.'

Briggs nodded and smiled at the same time as Bill placed the coffee on the counter.

'Hey, there's no need to speak to her like that. You need to apologise.'

'Says who?'

She calmly stood and took a few steps towards the counter. 'DI Harte. I can't have you intimidating these lovely people.'

He hiccupped and belched, exhaling the stench of beer. 'Ooh, the big bad police. I've done nothing wrong. Come on, arrest me for buying a coffee!' A wide smile formed across his face. He grabbed the coffee. 'Thank you.' The rude stranger stared back at Gina. 'Better now?' He turned on the scuffed heel of his muck-coated shoe and hurried out of the shop, blowing dried leaves everywhere once again.

Gina hurried back to her seat and watched him as he walked away. Her gaze stopped on something more troublesome. 'Dammit. Your coffee will have to wait.' Gina scooped her keys, the chocolate and the order slip from the table and dropped them into her coat pocket. She left a ten-pound note to cover the bill. Briggs threw a few pieces of loose change on top of it.

'Thank you,' Lucy called as they hurried out the door.

Gina held her hand up and headed towards the commotion. It was all kicking off tonight.

CHAPTER THREE

Gina flung her bag across her chest as they ran. A group of teens – including one who resembled a younger Justin Bieber – were jeering at another boy who lay on the floor, cowering. A taller boy threw a full can of pop down at him, which made him curl up more.

'Wait up.' Briggs brushed her back with his arm as he caught up.

Pushing her way through the crowd that had gathered, Gina hurried to the victim and kneeled down beside him, then glared up at the group. 'Police.' She held her identification up and Briggs followed suit. The boys shuffled back a little and a couple of the teens scarpered. 'Are you okay?'

The boy sat up and nodded. 'Yeah. Why wouldn't I be? We were just messin'.' He glanced back and forth as he stumbled to a stand and pushed through the four boys that were left. 'Wankers.' He began to walk away.

Briggs finished his phone call to the station and chased after the boy. 'Wait, that's a nasty shiner you've got there.'

The instigator nudged his tall friend before scarpering down one of the side streets, followed by the last two. As the rest of the crowd vanished, leaving only the victim, Gina nodded at Briggs. 'Keep him here.' She ran across the road, narrowly missing a white pickup as she darted down several streets following their calls in the distance. The injured boy may have been okay but watching the Justin Bieber lookalike kicking him had fuelled her anger only a little bit more than watching the crowd stand by and gee him on.

Almost slipping on an icy step onto the next road, she listened out for more shouts and calls, but there were none. She had no chance of catching several teenagers, who were all wearing trainers and had a head start. Two women came from around the corner with a group of children wearing skeleton outfits and holding plastic pumpkins that were bursting with sweets. She bent over, panting at the roadside as she held her waist, hoping that the stitch would pass before jogging back towards the scene. The women took the children into a house with a green light glowing in the window.

With every breath she took, a white mist coiled from her dry lips and dispersed into the darkness. Several lights were on in the terraced houses, curtains shut; no doubt their inhabitants were enjoying the fact that their working days were coming to an end. She hurried past the closed bakery, taking a shortcut behind it.

Gardens backed onto each side of the path. She almost kicked the chair that had been dumped against a fence, only just making out its outline as she squinted. Grabbing her phone from her pocket, she held its torch out and managed to avoid the half-singed mattress and the old fridge. She flinched as a dog bounded against the other side of a fence, barking and snarling. She picked up the pace a little until she crashed into a man coming from the opposite direction. 'Sorry, I didn't see you coming.'

His dark clothes and silent step had concealed his approach. She stopped and waited for him to pass but he remained standing right where he was. She flashed her phone up towards his face but he turned away. He oddly went back the way he came from, back towards the high street. Her vision was almost blurred as she tried to identify him, then she inhaled. Smoke and sweat, that's what she could smell.

She pressed Briggs's number on her phone and shivered. It wasn't as if she couldn't defend herself, but he'd unnerved her. 'How's it going?'

'Harte, uniform have just arrived but the boy they attacked, he doesn't want to say anything and is claiming that they were all just joking around. He then ran off too. I suppose we now have nothing.'

Her shoulders dropped.

'Did you catch any of them?'

'No. I lost them on Bentley Street.' The man in front of her turned onto the high street and she exhaled. 'See you in a minute.' It was definitely the rude man from the café.

She ended the call and picked up the pace. As she came out onto the high street, she waved at Briggs and hurried across the road. PC Smith and PC Kapoor had joined him in the car. As Gina went to speak, she spotted the man standing at the street corner. Why was he staring at her? Like before, he was playing with the cuff of his coat, but this time he didn't have his beanie hat on. She could see that he had no hair – or did he have a bit of hair? Maybe a crew cut? She glanced back at Briggs who was poking his head through the open window of PC Smith's car. The rude man grinned before turning away and going back towards the backs of the gardens.

Briggs headed over to her. 'I hate days like this when you don't have much to go on. We'll pull the CCTV from the church but I don't think it will give us much. It's not exactly covering this area well. I suppose we tried and we can only hope the boy comes forward to tell us more about the assault. You okay?'

She tore her stare from the brick of the closed accountant's office where the man had just been standing. 'Yes.' But she wasn't. When she got home, she was going to make sure all her doors were locked to the max and she knew she'd struggle to sleep. 'That rude man in the café. I just saw him standing over there. Did you see him?'

'No, he wasn't there when I looked and I was looking for witnesses. In fact, after all the kids scarpered, there was no one around.'

That meant he'd been lurking around at the backs of the gardens, watching. She knew she'd got on the wrong side of him by the way he stared at her. The nape of her neck tingled.

CHAPTER FOUR

Now

Thursday, 29 October

As Tilly tripped over a clump of tree roots in the middle of the woods, she shrieked. 'Katie, wait. This stupid dress. I know I shouldn't have worn it and I don't know why we came this way, I'm covered in mud.'

'Don't be silly. Logan is going to love you in the dress and it's Halloween. No one else will be going as Frankenstein's bride. It's more original than my witch dress.'

Tilly rubbed the trail of blood from her knee before pulling the splinter out. 'I can't get up.' She grabbed her phone and lit up the scene. 'Why did you have to bring me this way? We should have got the bus.' A few drops of rain began to fall.

'But then we wouldn't have this.' Katie held up the bottle of cider that the old man purchased on their behalf from the corner shop.

'I still wish we'd got the bus. It's creepy out here and, besides, my mum would freak if she knew I was out here at night, especially with the flood warning out.' Tilly grabbed onto a thick branch and pulled herself up. 'I look a complete mess now.'

Katie pulled out her phone and took a photo. She batted the moth away with the other hand as it fought to reach the light on her screen.

'What are you doing?'

'Instagramming it. Send.' She laughed, wiped the rain off her screen and popped her phone back into her bag.

'Wait till later.' Tilly shook her head and laughed. 'Have you got any tissue or a make-up wipe?'

Katie nodded and began rummaging through her bag. 'Here you go.'

As she cleaned the wound that the splinter had left, Tilly noticed her phone lighting up. 'And queue the smarmy comments. Thanks, friend. I hate you sometimes.'

Katie giggled and opened the cider. 'Did you hear the story about these woods? I think it was years ago, probably fifteen years ago or twenty years ago or more, I don't know.' She took a swig and offered the bottle to Tilly.

Tilly shook her head. 'I don't want to know while we're in the woods. Tell me later when we're at the party.'

'You're going to hear it anyway. Watch where you step. I know it's a Halloween party and all, but I don't want you to turn up covered in real blood or even dog muck. Right, the story. It was Halloween night, years ago, like proper olden times. A farm boy found out that his young love had been secretly seeing his older brother and his world fell apart when she told him that she'd accepted his proposal. He loved her more than anything but she didn't feel the same. His rage built up so much that he dragged her out into the woods where he'd already dug a hole. She said she didn't love him and she also said that he was mad, so he buried her alive right where we're standing. The story doesn't end there. He not only took her life, but he slashed his own throat with a knife and died on top of her grave. Some people say that he rises every Halloween to look for another girl to bury, taking his revenge, over and over again. Logan told me that this happened only a few years ago; he's heard the stories. A girl who looked just like the farm boy's love is buried somewhere in these woods, trapped with her killer's spirit forever. She roams on Halloween, along with all the other girls he's exacted his revenge on. They don't know they're dead and search for a way out, but they can't leave the woods. Imagine those poor girls, banging and clawing at the coffin as the oxygen was sucked out of the air. They never found his recent victim or any of them. It's as if the earth they're buried in fed on them; fed on their fear and misery. They still lie buried in these woods. I can feel them.'

'Shut up! Logan never said anything to me about that. You're just making all this up to scare me.'

'I swear on my life. It was during maths. We were dossing around and he just came out with it. He was serious too, him and his friends.'

Tilly felt a tickle on her head and screamed. 'Stop it with these stupid stories. Don't you think that if someone had been murdered in these woods they would have found the body and it would have been on the news? Get the spider off me.' She tried to grab the little creature, failing and hitting her long black wig.

'Like I said, the earth soaks them up so they'll never be found. Keep still.' Katie began fiddling with the nylon strands of hair, getting it tangled around her fingers. 'Don't move, I've nearly got it.' She yanked the wig and the grips tugged at Tilly's own hair, almost ripping a clump out.

Slapping her friend's hand away, Tilly took a step back, standing in a moonlit patch of mossy earth. 'Look what you did to my hair.'

'Here, let me fix it.'

'No. You've done enough damage. I can't turn up at school looking like this.'

Katie took her phone out again and let out a chuckle.

'Don't you dare.' Tilly reached out, whacking the phone from her fingers. They listened as it crashed against a stone.

'You've broken my phone. My dad's going to kill me.'

Tilly stared open-mouthed at the ground. 'I'm so sorry. I didn't mean it. You'll have to tell him it was my fault.'

'I had a month's worth of photos on there and they weren't backed up. I've lost everything.' She fumbled for the battery, scraping the sodden earth in her fingernails.

Tilly rolled up the stupid wig and pushed it into her handbag. 'Here, let me help you. We'll find all the bits and I'm sure it will work. Your dad will never know.'

'It's got a big dink in the side and the screen is all smashed up.'

Tilly began to feel in the spiny undergrowth.

The trees in front of them rustled and the girls stopped what they were doing.

Katie went to speak and Tilly clasped a hand over her mouth. The moon disappeared behind a large cloud and a few specs of rain tickled Tilly's nose. Tilly pulled Katie deeper into the trees. They stopped when a twig snapped beneath them.

The slight shiver Tilly started out with was now a full-on tremble. She wished they'd caught the bus. There was no need to buy more drink; Logan had already told them he had enough stashed in his locker to sort them all out. They were meant to meet in the art block toilets next to the hall and have a few swigs before slinking back into the party.

Another rustle, followed by the sound of a dainty footstep close by. The clouds blew over and the moon lit up the way once again. Tilly didn't know if she wanted to see what was coming for them. She wanted to run but the stupid heels she was wearing would make that impossible. She reached for her phone. As she went to press call on Logan's number, their stalker came into the light.

'It's just a stupid fox.' Katie chuckled and stepped out from behind the tree. 'We look like a right pair of idiots. Now, let's hurry up and find my phone battery. I do want to go to this party.'

Tilly fell against the tree and took a couple of deep breaths as she looked up at the moon. Something shiny dangling in the trees caught her gaze. She held her phone up and pressed the on button, casting a strip of light on the object. A rusty looking bell hung from a branch. It appeared to have a long piece of string leading from it, further into the dense woodland. 'Look.'

'Have you found it?'

'No, it's a bell.'

Katie peered around the tree. 'So.' She laughed. 'It doesn't have a clangy bit in the middle.'

'You mean a clapper?'

'Whatever. It's just a stupid old bell that someone has left in the bushes. Why aren't you doing what's important and looking for my phone battery?'

Tilly stared at the string and held her phone up. She followed it behind another tree, once again catching her ridiculously long and straggly dress on a thorny bush. 'Oh well, the dress is already ruined.' She took another step. 'The string leads into the ground through here. Come and have a look.'

'Actually, can we just go? Forget the battery. I don't like this.'

'Is the story you told me true, about the girl who died?'

'Probably not. I think Logan just made it up to scare us. Come on, let's go. I'll tell my mum about the phone first, she'll make an excuse to my dad, maybe tell him I fell over. Let's just go.' Katie reached out and tried to grab Tilly's arm.

'Wait.'

Their gazes fell onto the heap of earth.

Tilly pulled the string. 'Nothing.'

'You know what, Logan knew we were walking, he knew we'd come this way as it is the most common shortcut through the woods from the estate to town. He did this. Him and his friends. He told me that stupid story and set this up, hoping that we'd find it. If we didn't, he was probably going to make sure we did.' She turned. 'Ha, ha, ha. You can come out now, Logan. We know it's just a trick or treat. Tilly is ready for her treat now.'

Tilly nudged her friend. 'Stop it.'

After waiting in silence for a moment, no one responded. A bird flapped in the tree above and an owl hooted. Katie gripped Tilly's hand.

'He's not there. If he isn't there, then who did this? We have to call the police.' Tilly's phone fell from her trembling hands and once again the moon's light had disappeared and the rain began to fall in icy sheets. She reached down and went to press the first nine.

'Wait.' Katie placed a hand over the phone, her face looking ghostly as the screen lit up her features, casting a stretch of light on the spidery branches behind her. The bell clanked against the tree and they flinched. 'If we call the police, we'll have to wait here for ages and we'll miss the party. I've looked forward to this for weeks.'

Tilly's fair hair began to stick to her forehead and cheeks. 'What if someone is in there, buried alive, and they need us.'

Katie shrugged. 'They'd be pulling the bell, obviously. Wait, there's no clanger in the bell. We wouldn't hear it ringing. Let's just go.'

'Wait.' Tilly began to pull the string from what looked like a grave. The end slid through the earth. She shone her phone on it. 'I don't like the look of that.' Tilly got onto her knees as rain began to plop in huge droplets and she scraped at the earth. 'No way.'

'Tilly, Tilly? Shush. There's someone there.' Katie hurried over to Tilly and cowered down beside her as the figure came towards them.

CHAPTER FIVE

Gina lay back on the couch and stared at the ceiling. It was either that or uncomfortably look at the three other women that were also sprawled out in the relaxation room, one wearing a thick grey mask that resembled something from a horror film. Whale sounds filled the room and Gina caught the scent of massage oil coming from her own shoulders. The hotel was lovely but the spa side of it seemed like a waste of time.

Her phone lit the darkened room up. 'Jacob? Everything all right?' She clasped it between her ears and pulled the cord tighter on the hotel bathrobe. It had to be important if DS Driscoll was calling her during holiday time.

'Sorry to disturb you, guv. We've just had a call and I knew straight away that you'd want in on this. Me and Jennifer were just sitting down to dinner when it came in. Are you okay to talk?' One of the other women rolled her eyes and another tutted.

'Give me a second.' She grabbed her unread book and left the room, squinting as the bright lights from the gymnasium almost blinded her. 'Okay. Go for it.'

'There's been a report of something resembling a grave in the Cleevesford Woods. Two teenagers taking a shortcut to their school Halloween party happened upon a bell hanging in the bushes. They followed a piece of string leading from it and it led them to a heap of freshly dug up earth. Are you in?'

She pulled the towel turban from her hair and dropped it into the communal linen basket before hurrying to her room. 'No, but I've had enough of this place. I was only sticking it out so as not to waste my money. I definitely won't be booking another spa break.'

'Where are you, guv?'

'Only Stratford – Warwickshire not London. I can be there in about forty minutes. Give me a chance to throw some clothes on and I'll be on the road.'

'Great. Forensics have been alerted and PCs Smith and Kapoor have left to set up the cordon and assist.'

Gina hurried to her room and was soon throwing her toiletries into a bag. 'Let's hope it turns out to be nothing more than a Halloween joke. See you there.'

Jacob cleared his throat. 'Get this. One of the girls reported that there was blood on the end of the string that they pulled. They dug a little and found what they think was a coffin.'

Gina felt a shiver run through her as she dropped the dressing gown onto the floor.

'On my way.'

'Guv?'

'Yes.'

'Drive safely. It's treacherous out there. All these sudden downpours are creating havoc on the roads with flash flooding.' He ended the call.

An image passed through her mind; that of her own nails scratching against wood as damp earth chilled her to the bone. She inhaled and shook her head. She prayed it was just a prank, but something told her it wasn't.

CHAPTER SIX

'Guv, over here.' Jacob waved at her from a distance, his raincoat flapping under the portable lighting. The sloshing of the River Arrow could be heard, along with the howling wind and the steady falling rain.

Gina squelched in a puddle along the beaten track, stepping over a fallen branch. Voices called out, people in rain macs and forensics suits bustled around. Two paramedics were gesturing as they finally managed to put the tent up.

She wished she had better footwear with her when she'd had the call. The new trainers she'd bought for the spa break would be ruined. She shivered as the cold water seeped in through the fibres, dampening her feet. She waved back at Jacob as she charged forward through the branches.

PC Smith finished wrapping the police tape around the last tree. Gina ducked underneath. 'Good night for it.'

Rain bounced off his cap and drizzled off the end of his nose. 'You're telling me.'

Her heartbeat quickened as she headed towards the crowd. The lights flickered as tree branches wavered in the light. A gust of wind turned an umbrella inside out. Everyone but her was wearing wellies and raincoats. Her light fleece and skinny jeans were no protection against this level of weather and, to top it all off, her tangled hair kept blowing into her mouth.

Jacob and crime scene manager, Bernard Small, were huddled against a tree as she slid on the mud below and smiled as she successfully righted herself and remained standing. Bernard's wiry frame arched over Jacob, their profiles silhouetted against the moon's light.

'That was close and I made it in one piece. Have you found anything out yet?' She swiped the rain from her face with her arm and wrapped her annoying hair in a bun and tucked it under the nape of her neck. It would stick like that for a while given how wet it was. Bernard's long grey beard had escaped from his beard cover and Jacob pulled the hood of his raincoat further over his extreme Action Man-shaped hairline. Despite the harsh weather, his smooth skin and clean-shaven face made him look completely unaffected by the elements. His relationship with crime scene assistant, Jennifer, had done him the world of good. Gina only wished she'd found the magic formula to such contentment and happiness.

'As you can see, this scene is a nightmare. We have, however, managed to remove some of the soil and just to confirm, what we have is indeed a coffin. There's a crack in the wood and when we shone a torch in it, we could see what looked like a hand. We prised the lid open and paramedics confirmed that we have a dead male looking to be any age from his late twenties to mid-thirties. It's going to be a long night.'

Her heart rate quickened and for a moment she didn't care that she was standing in the middle of the woods, soaked to the skin and feeling close to getting the uncontrollable shivers. It was possible that a person had been buried alive and left for dead. If that was the case, it didn't get any more sinister than that, especially in the run up to Halloween. 'What's the plan?'

'Finish getting the tent up properly to secure the scene and start working it more thoroughly. I just hope the rain hasn't ruined or washed away all the evidence. The casket was tightly sealed so hopefully we'll find something in it that can help. We have the bell and the string too. After we've photographed everything, we'll start filling evidence bags.'

Gina's shoulders slumped. It wasn't ideal weather for collecting evidence. It was more likely to be blown away and sloshed down the River Arrow than sent to the lab. 'Don't let me stop you. Have you got any forensics suits?'

He pointed to where the light stand was. 'Over there in the plastic box.'

'I'll see you in a moment.' She glanced back at Jacob. 'We best take a look. At the very least, I wouldn't mind seeing who's in the coffin. We can run the description through missing persons if there are no visible clues to their identity.'

As they pushed through the shrubbery, almost sliding as they hurried towards the lights, Gina glanced around. They were between what she'd always referred to as the wealthier end of Cleevesford and the town centre. Wealthier as the housing estates backed onto this particular area were all privately owned houses, mostly large and detached. The woods eventually came out at the back of the church where anyone walking would then arrive at the top end of the high street. In the midst of the estate there was a country club with vast amounts of land. Whoever chose this spot, knew it was a quiet one. A person could easily dig a hole that was surrounded by bushes without being disturbed. It was far enough away from the houses and the town and, most of all, prying people. With the weather being unpredictable, even dog walkers had stayed away. 'You know. There's a high chance that whoever is in that coffin was murdered here.'

'Here?' Jacob waited for more as she pulled the forensics suit over her sodden clothes. He pulled out a tissue and wiped the rain from his eyes and nose.

'There's nowhere to park close by. You'd never get a car here. The closest parking place is at the roadside to my right and that would take several minutes to walk through the thickets. It would be hard for one person to navigate their way through, let alone if they were dragging a body or a casket. I've just had a fair walk from the main road where the ambulance is parked. It took me ten minutes and that route is easier. It's the route most people take when they're walking to town. Imagine carrying a coffin and or a body all this way.'

'Maybe whoever did this used some sort of trolley.'

'Best to keep an open mind. I don't think we'll find the answers to that one here, looking at how soggy the ground is.' She looked down. If someone had parked up and used some sort of trolley to put the coffin and the body into place, any tracks in the earth would be long washed away after tonight.

'Jake.' Jennifer called him over and smiled at Gina. 'Step on the plates.' They hurried across, clunking on the metal plates and Jacob looked like he was about to instinctively kiss her, but then he stepped back. They'd been a solid couple for a while now. Her white forensics suit swamped her.

'Jennifer. How's it going? Dinner's ruined.' Jacob swiped the rain from his eyes and smiled at her.

'You mean another dinner's ruined. We should be used to it by now.' She gave him a little laugh and brushed her fringe back under her hood. 'Well, tents up. I just hope it holds. We have the casket open if you want to step inside.'

Jacob stood back and waited for Gina to step in. She stood before the shallow grave.

'We've started boxing the soil as you can see.' Jennifer placed her hands by her sides.

Another crime scene investigator nudged through the tiny gap and he began taking photos.

Gina pulled a tissue from her pocket and blew her nose, noting that the sensation in her fingertips was barely in existence, especially through the gloves. 'Can you get those emailed over to me as soon as you can?'

The man smiled and nodded before continuing to zoom in on everything. Flashes filled the tent as photo after photo was taken.

Gina bent over a little and squinted in the poor light to see the body. A hoodie was tied up at the neck and pulled over the victim's eyes. His stiff fingers were clasped around something she couldn't see. She gazed further into the box and spotted a tiny burnt stick. 'That looks like it was once a match.'

Jacob came in a little closer. 'There's another.'

The victim's mouth was open in a pained expression like he'd died terrified. Earth and muddy water had slipped through the slight gap in the coffin lid. It had seeped through the red lining and had spread into a huge dirty damp patch around the man's chest. His bloodied fingernails told a story of the torturous hours he'd lived out in this box, or had he been placed there post-mortem? Maybe the person who placed him there had killed him already and made it look like he'd died after being buried alive. Maybe they made the claw marks on the casket lining. Not likely, but something she had to consider at this stage. There was something about his shoes that were familiar. Her gaze was drawn to the scuff marks.

'What are you thinking?' Jacob almost made her flinch.

'I want to see his face.'

Jennifer leaned in and with a gloved hand, gently lifted the hood as the man with the camera took another photo. 'There we go.'

Gina scrunched her brow. 'I recognise him.'

'You know him?' Jacob got his notebook out and began writing.

She shook her head. 'Not exactly. I saw this man in the café at the top of Cleevesford High Street a few days ago. He was being really rude to the person serving and I ended up giving him a piece of my mind.'

Rain began to pelt against the roof of the tent.

'He really unnerved me. Did DCI Briggs mention the incident?'

Jacob nodded. 'He said something about a gang of kids picking on another kid after you'd been having a drink in the café.'

'That was it. I chased a couple of them and when I came back this man, here, almost bumped into me at the back of the gardens – scared the hell out of me. Then, he weirdly turned around and started walking the way he came. When I arrived back at the scene, he was standing at the other side of the road just staring at me. I thought I'd upset him when I basically told him to stop being rude to the woman serving at the café. Something's really off about this.'

Jacob closed his pad. 'Although, if he's generally that rude, maybe he had a lot of enemies.'

'Stands a chance. We need to get back to the station and work on identifying him. If we find some ID on him that would really help. If not, we'll need to cross his features with those of all missing persons from around the county and if we come back with nothing, maybe we can look to take a screen grab from some of the CCTV and release it to the press. Someone has to know him. Can you make a note to task O'Connor to chase up CCTV outside Lucy's Café and the church, dating back to Monday the twenty-sixth?' Gina remembered that the victim looked to have a crew cut. She leaned over a little and studied his features. He had blue eyes and quite dark bags under them. Two of his bottom teeth looked to be crooked.

Bernard entered the tent, the redness of his nose telling of how the chill was biting. 'Rigor mortis has set in which means he's been there over three hours but there's not much sign of decomposition yet. There is evidence of a struggle and it looks like he has bits of red cloth under his bloodied nails, suggesting the struggle was from within this box. You can see the damage to the upper part of the lining.'

Gina's shoulders tensed and she swallowed. 'How long would it have taken for him to die?'

Bernard shifted the hood of his forensics suit slightly. 'An average person would take about five and a half hours to die in these circumstances. The oxygen would run out. He looks to be pretty average in size.' He stepped around the body, avoiding Jennifer and the photographer.

'This looks to be a good quality coffin. Where would a person buy one of these?' Gina made a mental note that the wood was darker and reddish, possibly mahogany or made to look like mahogany. Brass handles finished it off.

He nodded a few times. 'That will be the problem. You can even buy coffins from eBay. I'm hoping there will be some marking that gives away the maker or the make. Maybe there will be something sewn into the lining. Who knows? When we get it back to the lab, we'll be able to pull it apart and take a better look.'

'Do you know what he's gripping in his right hand?'

Bernard shook his head. 'I haven't got a clue yet. As soon as I find out, I'll let you know. I'll email any relevant findings as they come through and as soon as I have a time for the post-mortem, you'll be the first to hear.'

Jacob stepped from foot to foot in his saturated boot covers. 'How does death play out in this instance? If it is all how it looks.'

'If he was buried alive? Not good. With every breath, the oxygen in the air is replaced with carbon dioxide. Totally harmless, say, in your bedroom when you're sleeping. But here, our victim may have sped the process up by panicking, hyperventilating and lighting matches. His breathing will have deepened. Then there would be twitching muscles, an increased pulse rate and his judgment would start to diminish. Unconsciousness and death would have followed. I'd say it would come within the top ten of most feared deaths. A post-mortem will be needed to confirm all this though.'

'Anything else you can tell us?' Gina hoped there would be something.

He scratched his ear over the top of his hood. 'The bell that was hanging off a branch. There was no clapper in it. That's all I have for now.'

'Thank you.' Gina stepped back towards the tent flap. 'And, yes, keep me updated with anything. In the meantime, we need to identify this man so if you discover any ID on him at all, call me straight away, please.'

Jacob waved to Jennifer and followed Gina out of the tent, stepping carefully on the plates. The rain had steadied to a fine smattering and was more like a damp mist. In the distance she heard the church bells chiming and that told her it was nine in the evening.

'Where are the girls who found the coffin?' Gina stepped over a puddle, determined not to fill her trainers with water all over again.

'With PC Kapoor. She took them to the station when the rain began to bucket down and then the parents were called. Hopefully they'll still be there.'

'We need to get back. I'd like us to speak to them before they go home. Are DCs Wyre and O'Connor in yet?' Paula Wyre and Harry O'Connor would definitely be needed – she couldn't see them all getting home until the early hours, if they were lucky.

'They were on their way last time I checked. They should be there now. I can talk to O'Connor about the CCTV too.'

Gina shuddered as she hurried back to the cordon.

PC Smith smiled. 'Was it a prank, guv?'

She shook her head. 'I'm afraid not. Some poor man is lying dead in that casket.' Gina tried to hide the jitter that was running from her neck to her spine. For a moment, she imagined the victim panicking, struggling for breath as he clawed away at the roof of the coffin. Had he screamed for help? Had he pulled the string at the end of the bell that contained no clapper, giving him a tiny bit of hope? Someone had set this up, knowing the distress it would cause, followed by an agonising death. That someone was dangerous and she wanted them banged up before they did this to anyone else.

CHAPTER SEVEN

Cherie dumped the overstuffed carrier bags on the table just a moment before the cucumber threatened to completely poke through a hole in the bag.

'Where have you been? Me and the kids were worried sick.' Christian rolled his eyes and his black brows rose as he waited for an answer. His dark cheeks were speckled with a few freckles.

Again, he was questioning her. Where have you been? What were you doing? Years ago, she'd thought he was sweet, now it was nothing more than annoying. He looked like a sad puppy who couldn't bear to be on his own for more than five minutes. She began to pull the food from the bags; first the carrots, then the chicken. Slapping the cucumber down, she huffed as she heard the kids running around above them. Now wasn't the time to start an argument. Bella and Oliver had already seen them shouting too many times.

'I popped to see Mum. She called to say she needed help to move a bit of furniture around the living room so I went round. I just stopped for a cup of tea, that's all. We got talking. You know how lonely she's been since losing Dad.' It had been four years now and her mother had a better social life than she did.

'I get that. You could have called or even answered your phone. The kids are just getting ready for bed and I thought you'd have at least wanted to be here to say goodnight. I kept them down for as long as possible but it's late now.' He checked his watch. 'I mean, look. You've missed the whole evening. We thought you'd only be about half an hour when you went shopping at six. It's now gone nine.' He paused and scrunched his eyes.

She wanted him to give her a break, leave her alone. This time of year wasn't her favourite and he knew that.

'What's that on your leggings?'

She glanced down and spotted the mud splats up her clothes. She knew it had been wet but she hadn't realised she'd got that dirty. 'I slipped on the path, on the way to Mum's. You know how slimy it is. It really needs a clean. Maybe we can head over at the weekend, take the jet washer.'

He shrugged his shoulders and began stroking his bristly stubble. 'Sometimes I wonder if you still love me.' He looked down and shook his head.

Not now. Why couldn't he see that she needed to unpack the shopping and check on their children? She didn't have time to go through all this again.

'Are you seeing someone?'

She shook her head. 'Not this again.'

'What am I meant to think? You tell me.'

'You really think I'm having an affair? I work all the hours I can. Mum needs me and I keep this house together. I don't have time to have an affair. Look at me; I'm wearing leggings and an old jumper. Don't you think if I was having an affair, I'd have come home for a shower, maybe done something with my hair or even put some make-up on?'

She could almost see the thoughts whirring around his head. He turned to the kitchen sink and looked out onto their drive. 'Sometimes, just sometimes, I don't bloody well know what to think. I called your mum.'

She swallowed and felt a tremble at her knees. She should have answered his calls. Now he knew she wasn't where she said she'd been. 'I was in the car. I needed time to think, time to myself. Sometimes everything is so… so loud and I can't hear myself think.'

'Why didn't you say that? You lied to me and, what's worse is, you found it easy to do. Can you see how it all looks to me?' He ran his fingers through his thick black hair, the hair she'd once enjoyed stroking as they lay in bed.

She placed a hand on his back and he flinched, shaking her off. 'I'm not feeling too good and I'm sorry.' She reached into her bag, pulled out her tablets and threw the blister pack on the draining board.

'What's this?' He picked it up and began scrutinising the packet.

'That's why I was on my own. I didn't want to tell you.' She paused and began biting her bottom lip.

He turned around and placed his firm hands on her shoulders. 'What's going on, Cherie? You can talk to me.'

A thud came from above and Cherie wiped the tears that had spilled from her eye. She hadn't told anyone about the tablets, and she hadn't wanted to. 'I just keep getting these moments where I can't breathe, like when I'm in the shops or sometimes when I'm working. I need to get out or I feel as though I might die.' He dropped one of his hands and squeezed her shoulder a little. 'Tonight, I sat in the car staring at the fields from a layby. I needed to think.' Some of that was true. She gazed up into his eyes.

'You should have said something. I can do more. I could have gone shopping or if you need time alone, you can always go up to bed or take a walk while I occupy the kids. You love lying in the bath, maybe you could try that. You love reading, maybe you should do that more. But don't shut me out.'

She gripped him in a tight embrace until the ceiling lampshade began to shake.

'Come on.' He kissed her on the nose and stroked her damp brown hair. 'The kids are coming down and you need to dry off before you catch a chill.'

Bella and Oliver burst through the kitchen door. 'Where were you, Mum? You were meant to help me with my homework.' Bella opened the snack cupboard. The ponytail on the top of her head was tufted like a black pineapple top.

Oliver began picking through the shopping bags before pulling his earphones off and looping them around the back of his neck.

'Hey, you two. It's late.' Cherie grabbed the crisps from Bella and threw them back into the drawer. 'I'm sorry about your homework, kiddo. Maybe I can help tomorrow.'

'It's okay. Dad helped me with it. I'm hungry.'

'No you're not, we had dinner not long ago.' This was the chaos Cherie was struggling to cope with. Her face began to heat up and she felt her breath quicken. She was either going to shout at them or cower and cry.

Christian could see her angst. 'Come on, kids. It's gone nine. I want you both in bed. Go up and I'll be there in a minute to say goodnight.' He smiled at Cherie.

Again, she could see that he was trying so hard.

They all stopped as the security light on the drive flashed on, followed by three loud thuds on the door.

'Don't answer it.'

'What?' Christian hurried across the kitchen floor and into the hall. After removing the chain, he called back, 'There's no one there.'

She ran to the window and stared out. The row of houses opposite were displaying nothing unusual, then three faces clad in green and bloodied make-up appeared at the window. Her heart began to thrum as blood pulsated around her body.

'Brilliant,' Christian called out as the teenagers shouted trick or treat. 'Did you buy any sweets when you were out?

Bella and Oliver ran to the front door.

Cherie almost slid on the floor tiles as she ran and slammed the door closed. 'Go away! Leave us alone,' she yelled as she leaned against the closed door.

'You're overreacting. They're just kids having fun.'

'Mum. I wanted to see their costumes.' Bella tried to push through to open the door.

'Get to bed. Get to bed, now.'

'But, Mum—' Oliver whined, his bottom lip protruding.

The hallway began to sway a little. She undid the buttons of her coat and began to gasp.

'Mum can't breathe. Mum.' Bella pushed through and held her mum's hand.

'She's okay, kids. Just go up. We'll be there in a minute.' Christian kissed his children on the head and ushered them away.

Bella let go of her mother's hand and followed her brother back up the stairs.

'Come on, love. It's okay. Just breathe.'

Chants of trick or treat came from the other side of the door. The kids outside opened up the letterbox and began feeding a worm on a piece of paper through the gap.

Cherie gasped as she ran under the stairs and cowered in the corner. 'Make them go away.'

A moment later, all was silent except for the creaking of Bella's bed.

Christian picked the worm up, opened the door and threw it out.

'No. Close it quick.' Trembling she pulled her coat around her and began to sob.

He calmly closed the door. 'Come on. I'm going to help you through whatever it is you're going through, I promise. It was just a few stupid kids playing stupid Halloween pranks. We should have given them a bag of Haribo and that would have been it.' He held his hand out and helped her up.

'They're not just being kids, they were terrorising us.'

'That's a bit over the top.' He smiled and kissed her on the head.

Still shaking, she allowed him to lead her to the kitchen where she continued to breathe in and out. As she sat at the kitchen table, her heart jumped as three eggs were hurled at the window followed by the sound of thudding feet and giggles as the kids ran away.

'They're gone now. They're little tyrants, that's for sure, but don't let them get you down. Let's think about nice things. We're going on holiday in a couple of months. Your friends are coming to dinner on Saturday. Everything will be okay. Look at me.'

She lifted her head and he kissed her gently on the lips. He hadn't changed, she had. It had been the week from hell. She always hoped that *he'd* never come back, but he had and he'd brought something unsettling with him. She needed to go out, but it would have to wait until Christian was asleep. She'd never sleep until she'd dealt with her unfinished business.

CHAPTER EIGHT

Gina pulled a wad of paper towels from the dispenser and began to pat her drenched hair. She'd changed into the old pair of shoes she kept in her cupboard and pulled her spare suit jacket around her body before glancing back at her reflection. It was as good as it would get given the circumstances.

DC Paula Wyre peered around the door to the toilets, her dark suit as sharp in style as ever and her black shiny hair straightened to perfection. They were worlds apart. 'The girls' parents are asking if they can leave. We need to hurry, guv. I hear it was a bit of a nightmare out there tonight.'

'It was indeed. I got absolutely drenched. I'm on my way.' She placed the wet towels into the mesh bin and followed Wyre out. 'Are you and Jacob okay to interview...' she glanced at her notebook '... Katie? We can compare notes after.'

Wyre nodded and smiled. That's the first time that Gina noticed the little dimples in Wyre's cheeks. 'Definitely. Tilly is with her father in interview room one. I'll head over to the waiting room and take Katie to interview room two.'

'Thank you.' Gina brushed her fingers through her hair as she hurried along the corridor. 'O'Connor, interview room one.'

He placed the last of a Chelsea bun into his mouth with his chubby fingers, his bald head shiny on top. 'Ready.' He wiped his hands on his trousers, leaving a shiny sugary smear. 'Damn.'

As they entered, the girl was hunched over the table, her gritty fair hair flopping over in a way where Gina could just about see her eyes. The girl's father removed his hand from her shoulder and fidgeted in the plastic chair. Eventually it stopped squeaking.

'Thank you so much for waiting. I know it's late and you're tired. I'm Detective Inspector Gina Harte.' The girl looked up. 'You can call me Gina. It's Tilly Holden, isn't it? Can I call you Tilly or do you prefer Matilda?'

'No one calls me Matilda.' The teenager yawned, exposing her tonsils.

'Okay, Tilly it is.' Gina smiled. 'I won't keep you or your father too long but as you know a body was found in the woods tonight after you alerted us to it. You and your friend, Katie, were so brave. You must have been really scared.'

Mr Holden undid the zip on his coat and placed an arm around his daughter. 'She was meant to get the bus.'

'We've already been through this, Dad.' Tilly nodded. 'We decided to walk in the end and when we saw the bell we thought it was a Halloween joke. I scooped a few handfuls of soil away and then I saw a chip in the wood. When I looked in with my phone light, I saw a hand. We still thought it was a joke but decided to call the police anyway, just in case.'

'Well you did the right thing.'

Tilly began tapping her feet on the floor, depositing flecks of dried mud all over the threadbare carpet tiles. 'I pulled the string, the one that dangled over the tree. It had some sort of bell attached but it didn't make a dinging noise. When it came out of the ground, it was red on the end.' Gina could see that the girl had since washed her hands and she was glad but the cut on Tilly's finger left her with a shiver.

'Did you touch it?'

She shook her head. 'I don't think so, I just dangled it in front of me and dropped it on the ground.'

Gina read through a few of the notes that had been taken by PC Kapoor. 'Tell me a little bit about where you were going?'

The girl glanced at her father, then back at Gina. 'We were taking a shortcut to school. There was a Halloween disco. We were going to get the bus but we thought it would be okay to walk as the rain had stopped.'

'And which school do you attend?'

'Cleevesford High.'

'Did you notice anything unusual while you were walking through the woods?'

Tilly shook her head. 'We heard a noise in the bushes.'

Gina sat up. 'And?'

'It was just a fox. It scared us to death.' Tilly paused. 'Whoops. I shouldn't have said that, not after we found a dead person. I didn't think.' The girl glanced at her dad and he patted her shoulder.

'It's okay, Tilly. Just tell us everything in your own words, however weird it feels to speak them.'

The girl took a deep breath and shifted a clump of hair away from her eyes, revealing a streak of mud on the side of her face. 'We were walking quite slowly. I had stupid shoes on and I remember bickering with Katie about it, then I knocked her phone out of her hand. She'd been telling me creepy stories about ghosts. She freaked me out so I lost it. I accidentally smashed the screen on her phone. Sorry, Dad.'

'Don't worry about that, Tilly. We'll deal with it later.'

'Anyway, we ended up searching for the battery. It had come apart from the phone. That's when I saw the bell and the string hanging from a branch.' The girl paused and wiped her left eye, which was going a little red from rubbing it too much.

'And after that?'

'We saw the outline of a person just back of the clearing. They came, walked around for a few minutes, then left. That's when we called you.' The girl yawned again, this time more vocally.

This was the bit Gina was interested in more than anything. 'You're doing really well. I know you're tired but this is really helping. Can you tell me anything at all about the person you saw? Height? Did it look like a man or a woman? Larger or thinner in build?'

'We couldn't see. We just stayed hidden, holding our breath. It was dark and I didn't want to flash my phone and show whoever was lurking about where we were, not after just finding the hand in the box. We then began to think there really was a murderer so we sat together, holding hands, in silence. I've never been so scared, Dad.'

The man placed an arm around his daughter. 'You're doing really well, my love.'

'You are. This is really helping us, Tilly.' Gina smiled a little, just enough to try and put Tilly at ease a little. 'You're safe now.'

She wiped her nose on her arm. 'The only thing I saw is their eyes as the clouds moved and the moon lit up the clearing. Whoever it was seemed to be looking at me. I remember toppling a little as we stooped and my dress was getting tangled around my waist. My legs started to burn and shake, then I slipped, making a noise. Then the creepy person ran away.' Tilly paused and stared open-mouthed at the grain in the table.

'What is it, Tilly?'

'It looked like they were wearing a long black coat with a hood. I could see an outline of the person's legs under as they lifted it to stop it brushing in the mud. That's all I remember. Maybe they were wearing cycle bottoms or leggings, either way, they were wearing something tight.' She shrugged. 'We were just so glad to get out of those woods. I want to go home, Dad…' The girl began poking her finger through a hole in her dress, tearing a bigger hole in it.

Gina glanced over at O'Connor. 'Tilly, what you've told us has been so helpful. And thank you for staying here to talk to us again. Just as a precaution, I'd like you to pop to the hospital. I know you say that you didn't touch the blood on the string, but I wouldn't be doing my job or looking after you properly if we didn't get you checked out. I know it all sounds scary but it doesn't take a moment.'

The girl's bottom lip began to quiver. She buried her head into her father's chest and sobbed. 'They'll make me have an injection, won't they?'

'But she didn't touch the blood,' Mr Holden said. 'Does she need to go through this?'

'Tilly, I'm definitely not saying you have anything. This is just a precaution and I'm sure you'll be fine. We'd also like someone to tend to the cut on your finger. It looks sore. We need to make sure it doesn't get infected.' Gina paused and glanced at O'Connor's notes. 'Tilly, will you be okay sitting in the waiting room with DC O'Connor? You can call him Harry by the way.'

O'Connor placed his chewed pen on the table, stood and smiled. 'I think Katie will be there too. Maybe she can go with you for support, if you'd like that.'

Tilly nodded.

'Is that okay, Mr Holden?'

'What?'

'If Tilly goes with DC O'Connor so that we can talk for a moment?'

The man nodded. 'Yes, of course.'

After Tilly left with O'Connor to meet up with her friend, Gina leaned in. 'I know it sounds like we're going over the top but Tilly has a cut to her finger. We can't be too careful and I'd like her to be examined as a precaution. I know it's been a distressing night for you as well as your daughter, but all I can say is she's been so brave and we'd be failing in our duties if we didn't get her looked at.'

He shook his head and clasped his hands on his head of thinning hair. 'I know. I just don't know what I'll do if anything comes back bad. What if she touched the blood and it got into the cut on her finger? I know how these things work, I used to be a nurse in another life.'

'So you also know how important it is to be checked out.'

He nodded. 'You're right, thank you.' He went to stand. 'Why did it have to be my daughter who found the body?'

Gina had no answer for that. She was glad someone had found the body but it did choke her a little that it happened to be two fifteen-year-old girls. She only hoped that they'd soon forget the incident and not let it affect their lives.

He scratched his head, grabbed his phone from the table and left.

Gina tried to imagine herself standing by where they'd found the body. She imagined the rain trickling through the gaps in the coffin and, in her mind's eye, she crouched by the tree and peered out at the figure wearing a long dark coat and tight trousers. Why had they come back if they'd buried the body? Maybe they'd come back to check that their victim was dead or maybe something else brought them. Had they cycled? She felt slightly light-headed, heart racing as she thought of how close those girls had come to a potential murderer. Someone had been there, lurking in the bushes. She only hoped that whoever it was hadn't seen the girls, which might make them a target. A cold tingle reached up the back of her neck and she did up her jacket as she imagined the girls being watched. She made a note to discuss keeping an eye on their houses.

CHAPTER NINE

Now

Friday, 30 October

The candle flickers, lighting up the board on the wall – my mood board. I think that's what people call them. It's nothing more than a piece of cork with push pins attaching all my research to it in an orderly fashion. I stare at the photo of him as I grab a marker pen and slash a huge cross over his face. He's gone, but it doesn't end there. This is just the beginning.

I place a sheet of paper in the printer and double-check the most important letter I will ever write before I print it up. Gloved hands, of course. I wouldn't dream of touching the paper or the envelope. I know how these things work. Not that it will matter much, once a team of journalists have had their grubby hands all over it, any evidence would probably be destroyed with layers of fingerprints.

The map to my right tells me where I go next and who will come to me. I have everything well planned. Years of preparation now finally have a purpose. Today, I'm stronger than ever and that strength will only grow. I'm more ready than I've ever been.

My body feels electrically charged as I run through the details of the next piece of the puzzle. Those nights where I'd wriggle in my sweat-drenched sheets mulling over these moments made it all worth it. The days where I'd be eating breakfast and look down at my empty plate of toast, not remembering the process of actually eating it. The only clue was the taste of molten margarine coating the back of my throat, threatening to reach further down my gullet before forcing it back up. That's no way to live. There are pleasures in life and they are there to take so that's what I'm doing. I'm no longer going to hide or deny who I am and what I want.

Staring at the little screen, I scan my words. The letter is perfect. It says everything I want it to say and, for once, people are going to want to know who I am. Maybe they will find out who I am. Who knows? A grin spreads across my face. I'm back.

Look at me, see me; open your eyes; for if you don't, I will open them for you.

Then I see you in my mind's eye, the most important cog in this wheel. I scrunch my eyes in the candlelight and focus on your features. It's an old photo of you in uniform, one of you getting presented with a tuppenny-ha'penny award many years ago. You look so young, but behind your smile lies a haunted expression. You spend all day lying about who you are, just as I do. You've been hurt too. We're so alike and I will make you see that. I need you to see.

The printer finishes chugging and spits the page onto the floor. I struggle to scoop it up and crease the corner a little as I get hold of the paper. It's not easy working in gloves. I fiddle with the new pack of envelopes until I've opened them and stuff the letter into one. It's ready to go. I blow out the candle and sit in darkness. There's nothing as soothing as a naked flame but the smell of one that has just been extinguished; that's true fear. *You'll find that out soon enough. I need you to feel it too.*

The images on my board are now in darkness and my nose is tickled by the stench of the smoking wick.

Time to close up for the night. I slam the door to the pitch-black attic, trapping my secret world behind it. That locked up world has no right to exist in my daily life and the two shall never cross. To everyone else, I'm just a standard member of the community. Not too good and not too bad. I don't stand out and I don't totally fade into the background. I'm plain old me.

The bells finish clanking on the back of the door. They have aged, like me, and the last three await their destinies. For now, I have a letter to post and my walking boots are calling. The letter I posted yesterday should reach you soon. That one's just for you.

I pick up my burner phone and see that I have a reply to my messages. Someone is lying awake. The news I gave her would keep anyone awake at night. I reply.

Be there. I have so much to tell you. You deserve to know the truth about him.

The snoring below pauses as do I. I freeze midway down the stairs and wait. Then it starts again, just as it will continue all night long. That's what normally happens anyway. The nights are mine, all mine.

I grip the letter and smile. I'd kiss it if I was sure my DNA wouldn't be trapped in the paper.

Hello DI Gina Harte. I have some news for you – Terry's back.

CHAPTER TEN

'What the hell are you doing?' Cherie flinched as Christian turned the hall lights on. 'It's four in the morning.'

He wasn't meant to wake up. He'd been sound asleep. 'I was—' She paused. Nothing she could think of was going to make any sense. 'I think I sleepwalked. It must be my new tablets. I woke up on the drive.'

'And you got dressed?'

She looked down. How to explain that one? Her mind whirred from one excuse to another. *I don't remember. I slept in my clothes.* He wouldn't believe either; he'd seen her get changed for bed.

He pushed past and padded into the kitchen, hitching his lounge pants back up a little to not trip over the hem. 'And you drove in your sleep?'

She shrugged her shoulders. She'd driven the car onto their drive and the previous evening, she'd reversed in. He was definitely more astute than she'd originally thought. She peered out through the dried up egg on the kitchen window as she tried to think of an excuse. There's no way she could tell him the truth.

'No.'

'No what?' Hands on hips, he gave her that look, the accusatory one that irritated her.

'No, I didn't drive in my sleep.' Her mind whirred. 'I sleepwalked down the stairs and into the kitchen; then I woke up confused. I couldn't relax so I got dressed and went to the all-night garage.'

He took a few paces towards her until their noses almost met. 'Really?'

She didn't want him to know about the secret in her bag, not after what she'd put them all through in the past, but it was better than the alternative. 'Yes, really.' She pushed by him and leaned over the sink. If only she'd backed in, he'd be none the wiser. She'd have got away with the sleepwalking excuse and could have explained it as being anxiety triggered.

'Okay. What did you buy?'

She kicked the cupboard. 'You're doing it again, questioning everything I do.'

'After what you've put me through in the past, I feel as though I've earned that right. You've abused my trust in you too many times. I'm trying to protect this family and last time I looked, you're part of it.' He snatched her bag.

'Give it back.' This was part of her plan. Not an ideal part but it was okay for him to see. The contents of her bag would give him something to latch onto. She tried to reach over but he kept turning his back towards her as he dropped her purse onto the floor, followed by a packet of sweets; then he dropped a few scrunched up tissues and a make-up bag. Her compact shattered on the floor and he stopped.

'You've broken it. That was my grandmother's.'

Ignoring her, he continued to rummage. 'So this is what you were up to.' He pulled the offending item out of her bag.

She swallowed and turned away. After giving it to him on a plate, shame still burned inside her. Her breath quickened and she felt the urge to sob and cry, to hit something, anything. She slammed her fist onto the table, feeling the instant burn to her knuckles as one of them cracked a little.

'I thought this,' he pointed to the unopened miniature bottle of vodka, 'was in the past.'

A tear slid down her cheek and she fell into the chair, her outburst finally passing. That tiny bottle of happy juice was only the tip of the problem that consumed her every thought, especially with what was happening. What lay beneath would shatter him; the vodka he could deal with. He unscrewed the bottle and poured it down the sink.

'I'm sorry.'

'I told you, you can always talk to me. We could've talked about this. We will talk about this and I'm going to help you. You need to get on top of this for the sake of our children. They don't need to see us go through all that heartache again.'

She'd hurt him but small sacrifices had been made. She had every intention of drinking the vodka. The very thought of the warm liquid sliding down her throat made her tingle. She loved nothing more than that initial fuzzy feeling as the alcohol seeped into her bloodstream and slowed her heart rate down. She'd have been able to sleep soundly and forget everything. That little bottle had sat in her bag for several weeks and she hadn't touched it once. Just knowing it was there had given her the comfort she'd required. Now he'd poured it away, that sense of panic had returned.

'I've got to be up in a couple of hours so we best go to bed. My class isn't going to teach itself.' He dropped the bottle in the bin and pulled her into the hall as he turned the kitchen light off.

'I wasn't going to drink it, I promise.'

He manoeuvred towards the stairs and nudged her, giving her no option but to climb them.

He didn't believe her. The absence of a reply told her all she needed to know. He was right. She may have drunk it when she'd got back from her little middle-of-the-night outing, she may have drunk it when she was at work at the nursing home the next day, or she may have enjoyed it at home. Most of all, she wanted to know it was there, that's all. After the week she'd had, she'd shown great strength in not drinking it, but she couldn't tell him that. He couldn't know what she was doing, not now, not ever.

CHAPTER ELEVEN

Gina finished yet another coffee; anything that would help her to stay awake before she addressed the team was a bonus. The chill in her office sent a shiver down her spine. A few raindrops battered the window and a gust of wind coming through the tiny vent made her blinds clatter. She pulled the tangled cord to open them and gazed out across the dark car park, wondering if daylight would actually break through the gloomy morning.

A quiet knock almost startled her. As she called out 'Come in', the young woman from administration dropped a letter on her desk. 'Thank you.' The woman smiled before leaving. She glanced at the envelope that had been marked up 'Private and Confidential'.

She yawned and rubbed her eyes as she toyed with the letter. After going home, she hadn't gone to bed, instead choosing to sit in the lounge for most of the early hours mulling over the case. Eventually, she'd fallen asleep sitting in front of her laptop, while her cat, Ebony, snuggled against her arm, waking a couple of hours later with the twinge in her neck that still persisted now. Her phone rang. It was Wyre. 'Are we all ready?'

'We're all gathering in the incident room, guv.'

She left the letter on her desk and hurried out, allowing the door to slam behind her.

'Morning, guv.' Jacob yawned. With his laptop bag in one hand and a notebook in the other, he nudged the main door to the incident room with his bottom, releasing the chatter that came from the room. She was going to tell him that his shirt flap was out at the back but she kept her mouth shut.

DC O'Connor passed around a box of croissants filled with butter and jam. 'Mrs O thought we might need these. Help yourselves.' Harry O'Connor, always a smile regardless of how gruesome or disturbing the case was.

Mrs O was right. Gina grabbed one and headed straight to the head of the room. 'I'm glad to see we have some photos on the board.' The email from Bernard had arrived in the night and she'd forwarded it to PC Smith so that he could print the photos up, ready for the briefing. She took a bite of the buttery pastry, almost salivating as her taste buds exploded. She wiped a streak of jam from her bottom lip as she took in their victim's features. Blond male, described in Bernard's email as being six feet tall. She scrunched her eyes a little. He'd had a piercing in his eyebrow at some point but it looked as though it had almost healed over. His grey, ashen skin had a bluish tinge in places. A flashback to the night she and Briggs were at Lucy's Café filled her mind. He'd been lurking around after and what had the staring been about? He'd watched her from afar. She shuddered as an uneasy feeling flushed through her. If only she'd chased him instead of their Justin Bieber lookalike. Hindsight was a wonderful thing. She had no idea he would turn up in a coffin – dead.

'We'll start with the door-to-doors from the estate at the back of the woods.' She pointed to the area on the wall map. 'Any updates?'

PC Smith wheeled his office chair closer to the main table, nudging Wyre and O'Connor to create a gap. He placed his hat on the table and ruffled his flat hair. 'Nothing of any help. We have several CCTV recordings that some of the residents have given us and we've been through most of them. Nothing so far. I spent the night watching most of them myself.' He rubbed his eyes and took a swig from his travel mug. 'There were only reports of trick or treaters playing up. Reports of eggs being thrown, kids knocking doors and running away, things like that. Someone's car had been covered in pink custard. All manner of pranks were played and there are a lot of kids hanging around the streets in these recordings, as you will see if you watch them.' He licked the crack in his thin lips.

'I don't think this murder is the work of kids but we should keep an open mind at the moment. How about the town? The woods lead to the edge of Cleevesford Town and onto the high street, in fact the church backs onto them, or should I say the graveyard does.'

O'Connor leaned in. 'PC Kapoor orchestrated the door-to-doors after bringing the two girls in and she left me with her findings when she clocked out in the early hours. We knocked at the vicarage and the vicar was more than willing to hand their CCTV over. I've watched it over and over again and all I saw was a few kids dressed as ghosts playing what looked like hide and seek amongst the graves. It would be good to speak with some of them to see if they saw anyone out of the CCTV range. As for identifying any of them, let's just say their costumes were good. Most were wearing thick make-up or masks and as soon as it started to pour down, they cleared off.'

Gina glanced back at the board and focused on the map. A pin marked the murder spot. 'I wouldn't mind speaking to the vicar. It's possible that our murderer used the church grounds to enter the woods at some point. Burying someone alive is a morbid thing to do. We are looking for someone with a thing for graves and the dead, and the graveyard would be a good place to check out. Who is the vicar or priest?'

O'Connor flicked through his notebook. 'It's a vicar, Sally Stevens.'

Gina made a note. 'There's also this road. I know it's a back road, but to get the victim and the coffin to this location' – she pointed – 'our murderer or murderers would have wanted to park as closely as possible.' She paced across the room and fixed her gaze on the squad cars parked up in the potholed car park below. A van to the one side caught her eye and a woman stepped out and began to talk into a microphone. Great, the press were about to make their job a whole lot harder. She turned back to the room. 'Unless, the coffin was placed there beforehand and the victim was lured to this location. It'd be a struggle carrying a dead weight from this position to here.' Back at the board, she traced a line with her finger from the road to the spot in question. 'On the other hand, getting a coffin to this location would be tricky too. At the very least there would have to have been two people or one person using some sort of trolley. Wyre, can I task you with looking into how easy it would be to move a box the size of our coffin around? I'm hoping that we will have the weight and dimensions soon. I checked this morning and the crime scene crew are still there and it's likely to be a long day. After the rainfall last night, they're also buried up to their knees in mud. Oh, and to top it all off, the press have arrived and I'm sure they going to make a lot of a murder that involves the victim being potentially buried alive in the run up to Halloween.'

Wyre made a few notes. 'I'll get onto it, guv.'

'Also, can you research all the funeral directors within a ten-mile radius, starting with Cleevesford and working outwards? This was a real coffin, not a box knocked together with any old wood – an actual all-singing, all-dancing, fully-lined coffin. Thinking about it, this would rule kids out. Coffins don't come cheap.' She paused. 'I checked my emails this morning and there have been no manufacturer markings found on it yet. I want to know if anything like this has been stolen. O'Connor?'

'Yes, guv.' He shook the crumbs from his hands and swallowed the last of his croissant.

'Continue with the door-to-doors. I know there was a lot of activity with kids hanging around everywhere last night and yesterday, but we need to keep at it. Someone must have seen something. The kids may have seen something. I could be convinced of a lot of things but one thing I'm totally convinced of is that this isn't the work of a ghost. So someone, somewhere, will have seen something. Whether it's a car pulling up at the side of the road or someone behaving suspiciously in the woods. When was the grave dug? Someone may have heard this happening or seen our perpetrator walking around with a shovel. Graves don't just dig themselves, coffins aren't easily transported into the middle of the woods and the same with bodies or people.'

O'Connor tapped his fingers on the table. 'There are still a lot of houses to tackle and a fair few businesses.'

Gina leaned over the table and placed both hands flat on it. 'Right, onto our victim. The basics of his description are in the file. The email that Bernard sent also confirmed that there was no identification on him. We haven't found a phone on him either. That's strange in itself. How many people do you really know who don't carry a phone around with them? We literally have no idea who he is, but someone must be missing a relative. He wasn't wearing a wedding ring but that might not mean much. He could have a partner or children; a mother, siblings, friends.'

Gina thought back to the café and remembered the smell that he brought with him when he entered from the roadside. In her mind he either lived rough or didn't look after himself. She thought back to the fuss he made about the price of the sandwich and coffee. 'As you know, on the night of the disturbance that DCI Briggs and I called in, we'd already seen this man in the café. He was giving the owner a bit of abuse. I do remember a slight smell of smoke coming from his clothes.'

Jacob leaned back in his chair and Briggs crept in and sat at the back of the room. Gina swallowed. There was a point at the café where she clearly remembered Briggs placing his hand over hers. She knew what was coming next.

'We can see if the café has any interior CCTV. Maybe a screenshot of our victim could be circulated to the press. As you say, someone has to know him,' Wyre said.

Gina nodded, her gaze shifting quickly from Briggs's. 'I'll head over there next and see what they have. It won't do any harm to talk to the owner, see if she remembers seeing him at any other time.'

'Great.' Jacob pulled his coat from the back of the chair, assuming she'd ask him to go.

It was a fair assumption. She'd tasked Wyre and O'Connor with door-to-door and undertaker research. Jacob was her usual right-hand detective. Briggs ran his thick fingers through his hair and straightened his tie before glancing at her again then quickly looking away. 'Okay. Are we all clear about what we're doing?'

A murmur of yesses filled the room and everyone turned to their notes and chatted about their plans. Gina watched as Briggs slinked off into the kitchen. She hurried out and closed the door, switching on the kettle and waiting until it began to boil. 'We could be on those images.' Gina bit her bottom lip and leaned over the worktop, allowing her tangled up hair to fall over her face.

'I was thinking that too. We'll just have to see what you come back with and hope we're not on the footage.' He paced towards the cupboard. 'It wasn't that bad, it was just a slight touch. It was nothing. I accidentally reached over to you out of concern when our victim came in and intimidated everyone in the café.'

'You shouldn't have.'

His shoulders slumped and he looked away.

Jacob burst through the door and the kettle clicked as steam bellowed from the spout. She forced a smile.

Jacob leaned over and threw a teabag into a travel mug. 'One for the road. Am I missing something?'

'No, we were just talking about the case. Nothing we haven't covered.' Briggs headed towards the door. 'Come and see me later. We can continue our conversation then. In the meantime,

I'll prepare an update for the press. Reporters are all over the crime scene and now they're beginning to camp on our car park. Anyway, with any luck, we'll have a clear image that I can send to them when you get back. That should keep them off our backs for a short while and it might lead to our victim's identity.'

Gina nodded. 'Let's hope something comes of it, then we can put a name to the face. I'm off to the café so see you later.' Jacob filled his cup. 'I'll just grab my coat.' As Jacob left, Gina exhaled and wiped the small droplets of sweat that had formed at her brow, knowing that this case could be the start of her undoing.

She hurried back to her office to get her coat and stopped as she caught sight of the letter again. Tearing it open, she began to read the words on the page. She leaned against her desk as the room began to swirl, her heart banging like she was about to have a heart attack. It was as if her breath had been sucked from her body.

CHAPTER TWELVE

Gina pulled up in the church car park, unable to recall the journey there even though she'd driven all the way. The letter in her pocket felt as though it was trying to burn its way out.

Jacob unclipped his seat belt. 'Are we heading over to the café, then coming back to speak to our vicar or is it the other way round?'

'Café first.'

As they hurried over the mound of grass dividing the church and the bus stop, the rain began to fall a little harder. A rumble of thunder filled the skies followed by the tiniest of flashes. Gina felt the hairs on the back of her neck creeping around her nape. The thunder that crashed on the night she watched her abusive ex-husband Terry tumble down the stairs to his death would always haunt her. She'd never be able to switch off that association, but things had been getting better – that was until she'd read the letter.

Gina followed Jacob across the road through the gap in the traffic, just before a lorry rumbled past. 'I don't envy Bernard and the team in this weather. They've been at it all night and are still searching the area for more.'

'I think we drew the long straw for a change. I can't think of anything worse than scrutinising mud all day for the tiniest of clues, in the rain.' As Jacob opened the café door, the gale force wind almost blew them in.

Two mothers were enjoying a hot drink while their babies slept in prams. Gina tried to hide her face as she spotted June and Cyril. The scarf the elderly lady was knitting dangled on the floor. Her chunky needles stopped clicking and she looked up. 'Hello, dear. Where's that lovely man of yours today? It's so nice that you can be happy now.'

Cyril nudged her. 'Don't take any notice. She doesn't know what day it is.'

Gina's face flushed and Jacob's brows arched. 'Who's this man?'

'No one and it's none of your business.' She concealed her angst with a jokey smile and turned away from Jacob. It's so nice that she can be happy now – what was June on about? 'He's just a friend, June.'

'Well, he's a nice man. He's definitely a looker.' She stopped clicking and poured her tea from a pot.

They dodged the chairs and waited at the counter for someone to come back in to see them.

'So, who's this friend then?'

She tutted and looked up. 'It was only Briggs. We were just having a coffee here the other day while talking about a case, that's all.' She didn't mention the other times they'd met there after work. Briggs had insisted that it was only coffee, and that two friends and colleagues should be able to talk over coffee. Gina heard Lucy humming from the kitchen. A door slammed and she approached.

'Oh, what can I get you... don't tell me your name... I should remember.' She clicked her fingers with her eyes closed. 'Gina. Is that right?'

Gina nodded. 'You remembered.'

'I aim to please. What can I get you both? I know you like an Americano with a splash of milk.'

'You've mellowed, guv. You don't normally have milk.' Jacob undid a few buttons on his coat.

Lucy began twisting her hair, as a fair few women always would when they came across Jacob. He didn't give her much of a glance. He didn't give anyone a glance any more, not since being loved up with Jennifer.

'We're on official business, actually, so no time to sit around enjoying one of your lovely coffees today.'

Lucy tightened her ponytail and redid her apron, nipping in her waist a little more. 'Is it about those kids the other day? Is that boy alright, the one they were all picking on?'

'He managed to run away from us once we'd dusted him down. It's not about that. Unfortunately, we lost them. On that same night, do you remember that man, the rude one who was moaning about the price of sandwiches?'

Her nose scrunched as she thought. 'Yes, I don't think I'd forget him in a hurry. What about him?'

'We're trying to identify him and we need your help.' Gina gulped. 'Do you have any CCTV in the café at all?'

Lucy glanced up above Gina and pointed to the camera in the corner of the room. 'That's all we have and it points straight towards this counter. I thought it was a good idea just in case we were ever robbed.'

Gina felt her heart racing. She and Briggs were sitting almost underneath it but there was a chance they may appear in the corner of the frame. 'May we take that footage? It would really help.' Gina pulled a memory stick from her pocket and passed it to the woman.

Lucy shrugged and took it. 'I can't see why not. Can you watch the shop for a few minutes while I head out the back? I just have to go through it on the computer then save it onto your stick.' She turned and poured two filter coffees. 'Here, these are on me while you wait. Take a seat.'

'Thank you.' They both sat and sipped the coffee. Gina glanced at the camera once again.

Jacob smirked. 'Fancy describing Briggs as a looker.'

'I'll tell him you said that.'

'You dare.'

'Were you on about that horrible man, dear?' June's hearing was obviously intact. She removed her glasses and placed her knitting next to her empty plate.

'Yes, do you know him?'

She shook her head. 'Not really, but I have seen him around. Always looks a scruff.'

'And he stinks.' Cyril placed his newspaper on the table. His eyes crinkled at the edges as he rolled them. 'That was cruel of me. We think he's homeless because we've seen him sitting on the streets wrapped in an old sleeping bag. June gave him a few pence to buy some food with, didn't you?'

She nodded. 'He walks up George Street. I've seen him a few times.'

'Where have you seen him sitting?' Gina bit her bottom lip.

'Just around the corner from the accountants. He's doesn't try to get attention. He just leans against the wall staring into space like he's on drugs or something. Is he in trouble?'

'No. We're just making enquiries at the moment as a part of our investigation. Have you ever—'

As Gina pulled her notebook out, Lucy came back in from around the back. 'The footage isn't very clear but it should give you something to work with. If there's anything else you need, just ask.' She placed the memory stick on the table.

'Have you seen him around or has he been in before?' Gina almost burned her mouth on the coffee as she took another gulp.

Lucy shook her head. 'Not that I can recall. I'd have remembered him, I'm sure of that.'

Gina turned back to June who had picked her knitting back up. 'Have you ever spoken to him?'

June nodded. 'I went up to him a couple of weeks ago and tried to get him to talk. I know his name. He said, call me Al, like the song by Paul Simon. I think that's why I remember. Cyril likes Paul Simon.'

'Thank you so much, June.' It might only be something small, but it was a start. She only hoped he was using his real name. Al could be an Alan, an Alex, an Ali, an Albert or an Alastair. There are probably many Als that weren't coming to mind too. 'Did he say anything else?'

'No. He ignored me when I asked him if he'd like me to make him a scarf. I thought he was cold so I offered.' June shrugged.

'That was very kind of you.' Gina smiled.

'He was definitely on something, June. I swear, she'll talk to anyone because she's got a big heart but she does worry me.' Cyril squeezed his wife's hand. 'Ah ha, four down: rotten.' He picked up his pen and went back to his crossword.

'Thanks, Lucy, and thank you, June.' The elderly lady had a sad look in her eyes as she gave Gina a parting smile.

Back out in the crisp air, Gina shivered. 'We've got time for a quick chat with our vicar, Sally Stevens, then we'll head back to the station and catch up with the investigation where I'll check this CCTV out, see if I can get a close up on his face. So, we're looking for an Al.'

Gina pulled her hood up and glanced back at the shop where she caught Cyril staring at her over his newspaper. She scrunched her brow and looked away. Why was he now acting weirdly? She felt in her pocket for the letter. It rustled, reminding her of its presence.

To the right was George Street. She pictured their angry stranger – now victim – sitting against the wall wrapped in a sleeping bag. She still couldn't work out why he'd been lurking around on the night of the incident. Maybe he wasn't staring at her, maybe it was something to do with the kids or the church behind her. Maybe a homeless man with a bit of a mouth on him made the perfect target and they'd been giving him some grief. 'We need to track those kids down, the ones who were here beating the boy up.'

'It'll be a miracle if we do that with the CCTV footage from the church. It's as blurry as hell. I don't hold out any hope at all.'

Gina glanced back at the café. Cyril's head was now concealed by newspaper. Maybe she was making something out of nothing. Why did it feel like Cyril knew something she didn't?

CHAPTER THIRTEEN

'Ms Stevens? I'm DI Harte and this is DS Driscoll. May we speak to you for a moment?'

'I literally have ten minutes before I open up for our stay and play group. If I'm late, there'll be grouchy toddlers everywhere.' She smiled broadly, showing a set of ultra-white teeth.

Sally Stevens wasn't much like Gina had imagined her to be. She'd imagined a mature woman, rotund and smiley, more like the one in *The Vicar of Dibley*. Sally was a lithe woman who exuded youth. Her wavy mahogany-coloured hair fell over the shoulders of her pinafore dress, which led to black opaque tights and a pair of chunky lace-up boots. Her pale face and dark eyes gave her a gothic appearance. The only thing that gave away her position was the white dog collar that she wore around her neck. She beckoned them in, pointing to the sitting room with her long black nails. A dog banged and barked against a closed door.

'Is it about the incident at the bus stop? I gave one of your officers all the recordings from the church CCTV.'

Gina shook her head as she stopped in front of the stone fireplace. The two settees looked comfy but they weren't staying long enough to sit. 'It's not about that, I'm afraid. It's about something far more serious.'

'Is it to do with all the commotion in the woods? I was walking my dog this morning and got turned back.'

The press were all over it and Gina had spotted the first mention of a body on their social media before leaving for the café. 'Yes.

A body was found in the woods last night and we're currently investigating, which is why we're here. Have you seen anything unusual recently, maybe over the past day or two?'

Sally let out a small huff. 'Only one thing, but it's Halloween. I don't know if what I saw was unusual for Halloween, which is why I didn't bother anyone. I normally get kids hanging around; sometimes I listen to them playing but only because it's quite funny. They tell stories about the dead coming out of the graves – one of them recites some stupid words or sits alone in the graveyard while the others look on from afar, usually laughing.' Sally smiled. 'These things either end with the poor kid who's undergoing the dare running away screaming or they sit it out and get a cheer. Once they all realise nothing is going to happen, they leave. The only thing they get is cold. It's Halloween tomorrow, so I'm expecting this to all happen again. I know it sounds cruel, but I sometimes turn my lights off and make ghost noises out of the downstairs toilet window to scare them. I have a weird sense of humour. It's all part of the fun and nothing bad is meant by it. It's theatre, that's all.'

'What did you see?' Gina was more interested in the unusual rather than the expected.

The young vicar scrunched her brow. The dog started to bark again. 'A figure in a long dark coat with a hood that covered their face.' She glanced at her watch. 'Come with me.'

Gina glanced at Jacob as they followed the vicar upstairs. Each step creaked in the old house. As they reached the landing, Gina spotted that one door was open, the door to the master bedroom. She followed the woman past the wooden four-poster bed and stopped at the window. As she stepped closer the floorboards felt spongy and the wardrobe rattled.

'It was from here. This is where I was when I saw the figure, just at the back of the graveyard. The dog woke me with his barking. It was about three in the morning on Wednesday. Jerry doesn't normally bark in the night so it had me concerned. We've had a few burglaries at the church in the past and I know I'm set back a little from the main building, but I do try to stay alert. Whoever was hidden under the hood looked up at me. Nearly scared me to death. I ducked behind the curtain and waited a few minutes before looking back out, then they were gone. I ran around the house in the dark, checking out of every window, but I didn't see the figure again. No one had tried to break into the vicarage as the alarm would have gone off. It was then I checked the CCTV. Whoever was out there had avoided the two cameras that we have. The one facing the front of the church that also catches the road and the one that covers the back of the church and the vicarage. There are no CCTV cameras on the graveyard, so I have nothing I can give you. It's a big area for two cameras but that's all the budget stretches to, I'm afraid.'

Jacob pulled his notebook from his pocket.

'Can you tell us any more about this person?' Gina leaned on the window ledge and tried to imagine how scary it would have been for Sally Stevens when she saw the figure. Living alone in this big house with its creaky floorboards would have heightened the fear.

She shook her head. 'No. From here, I couldn't really get much of an idea of the person's height and, well, the figure was covered in the huge coat so I couldn't even estimate their build. I don't know whether it was a man or a woman and I couldn't see their face, not even when they looked up. There are no lights out there at all and I recall it being cloudy, so the moon didn't even give off much light. Had it not been for the long coat material moving a little with the breeze, this person probably would have blended right into the night.' She glanced at her watch. 'I don't want to hurry you but if I don't get down there, I'll have a load of parents and children getting cold outside the church.'

'Before we go, do you know a man called Al who often hangs around the street. He has a crew cut and is approximately six feet?'

She shook her head, her curls bouncing as she moved. 'No. That description isn't ringing a bell for me.'

An image of the bell with no clapper inside sent a shiver through Gina. 'You've been really helpful. If you remember anything else or you see any strange people in the graveyard, would you please call me straight away?' Gina passed the vicar her card. 'Call me anytime, day or night.' If hanging around a graveyard in the early hours wasn't suspicious, then she didn't know what was. If it was kids playing around, there would have been more than one of them and three in the morning was late.

'I definitely will do. It'll be my pleasure.' The vicar paused and looked intently. '"Be sober-minded, be watchful. Your adversary the devil prowls around like a roaring lion, seeking someone to devour." Peter, chapter five, verse eight. I'm always on my guard and I'll call you if I see or hear anything else.'

Gina allowed that little speech to sink in and smiled. 'If it's okay, I'd like an officer to come by later when you have more time, to collect all the CCTV recordings for the past few days. You never know, we might just spot this person on another day at another time.'

'I have already looked but you're welcome to everything I've got.'

Jacob stepped out of the bedroom as Sally began to move towards the door. Gina trailed behind, having one last glance out of the window before reaching the landing.

'Jerry, shut up. I won't be long.' She glanced back. 'That dog hates me going out and leaving him. Separation anxiety.' They hurried downstairs and out of the heavy wooden door, back into the drizzle.

'Thank you. We'll be in touch.' Gina rubbed her hands together as the cold air hit them.

'You know where to find me.' Sally Stevens ran towards the back of the church, disappearing through the door ready to open up out the front.

'Shall we take a look around the back?' Jacob began walking around the house.

'Yes. I know the team are up to their elbows in it, but I'd like the graveyard to be secured as a potential scene. The night before we find a body buried alive in the woods, a suspicious individual was spotted at one of the potential entry routes at approximately three in the morning. It doesn't get any more suspicious. I'm going to call it in. Given the adverse weather, I'm not holding out for any evidence, but you never know. All it takes is that one little thing to be dropped and trodden into the earth.'

They reached the graveyard and Gina spotted a robin bobbing on a mossy bench. The tree's bare branches reached out, like bony fingers trying to nudge the robin as a gust of wind caught them. Gina shivered and wiped the misty raindrops from her forehead.

'It's creepy, isn't it, guv?'

She stared at the grave that Sally Stevens had pointed to. It was large enough to conceal a person should they duck behind it, but it was nothing unusual compared to the others. She held out her phone and zoomed in, taking a photo. 'Elsie Peterson, beloved wife and mother.' Gina did a quick calculation. 'Died at seventy-three, twenty-one years ago.' Something for Wyre to research, along with local undertakers and coffin makers.

Gina shivered. For a second, in her mind's eye, she saw a figure standing behind the grave in the early hours of a miserable night. 'I'm calling this in and we're getting back to the station. Graveyards give me the creeps.'

'I didn't have you down as the superstitious type, guv.'

'I'm not. It's just a graveyard, isn't that enough? It's full of dead bodies.' She turned and stomped away as she made the call. Death left a sour taste at the back of her throat. With each case, everything led back to one thing. The image of Terry taking his last breath as she watched him die at the bottom of their stairs all those years ago, seconds after she nudged him from the top.

She paused as she waited for Jacob to catch up. Did some people deserve to die? Terry had been a cruel, hateful person. Her mind flitted back to their victim. Had he done something so terrible that made him deserve his end? She gulped. Should she say something about the letter? Maybe she should tell Briggs.

'Hold on, guv.' Jacob caught up with her.

'I just want to get this memory stick back so that we can get our victim's image out there.'

Someone had to know who he was. Someone had to be missing him.

CHAPTER FOURTEEN

'Come on, Gladys, let's get you to the table. It's toad-in-the-hole today, your favourite.' Cherie steered the elderly lady and seated her by the other nursing home residents. As always, Gladys never answered.

Body aching like she had the flu, Cherie hurried to the kitchen. The table at the back that overlooked the garden was reserved for staff and it was time for her break. At least Christian couldn't have a go at her while she was at work. Getting out of bed with him at seven had been awkward. He'd huffed and puffed about what a trying day he was going to have. That it was her fault he was tired and stressed. He even went on about how they should cancel her dinner party on Saturday night. That had been it. There was no way she was cancelling her friends, especially now. She'd flipped and walked out. That's why her white tunic was creased and her hair looked like it had been styled by a hurricane. She'd pulled the leaves from her tangled mop earlier, when she'd clocked in.

'Can I sit here?' Sadie plonked a plate of toast on the table. 'Want some?'

Cherie smiled. A friendly face, at last. 'Thanks.' She took half a slice and began eating it. Thoughts of Christian could wait until she got home, where she'd then face whatever was coming her way.

'Can you believe, I ask the bastards about my pay rise and they fobbed me off again? It would take the bloody plague making a comeback for the powers that be to recognise our value and what we do, day in, day out.' She chomped on the toast and threw the crust at the plate, continuing to speak with her mouth stuffed. 'I really need the money too now Damien has been made redundant. I might start looking elsewhere, maybe go into private home care for the rich. Fat chance of that happening.' She let out a small laugh along with a few toast crumbs. 'You haven't heard a single word I just said. Are you okay?'

Sadie had noticed that something was wrong. Cherie glanced back and Sadie was shrugging at the cook. They'd been talking about her. She should have gone to the toilet and sorted her appearance out as soon as she arrived, but she'd been late.

'You're not normally late. It's okay, I covered for you. We bottom feeders have to stick together. Maybe one day, we'll actually rise up against the ruling classes.'

Cherie stared at her and furrowed her brow.

'Joke. I wasn't suggesting we walk out right now and start a revolution. Or was I?' Sadie snorted as she laughed and glanced back at the cook. The portly woman stirred a large pot of something that resembled custard, evident by the splats of yellow against the stainless steel splashback.

'Thanks. My alarm didn't go off.' That old excuse. Again, excuses weren't her forte. She'd proven that in the early hours of the morning.

'Oh well, these things happen. Rough weather out there. Yes, it's far too chilly for that revolution. I think I'll stay in the warm.' Sadie reached across and pulled a corner of a leaf from Cherie's hair.

'I am in a state. That's what you get for not setting your alarm properly.' *Grin your way through this.* 'Thanks for the toast.' She held the last bit up and popped it into her mouth.

'Well, if you ever need to talk—'

'I best get back to work.'

'You're still on break.'

Sod break time. She didn't need someone barely out of nappies offering to counsel her. She needed everyone to get off her back and act as if everything was normal. But it wasn't normal. Everything had changed. Her heart rate began to pick up. Nothing would ever be the same again. Her phone buzzed against her thigh. She scurried through the dining room and pulled it from her pocket as she ran along the corridor and out through the front door. She was still on break and she'd spend the last few minutes of it alone in the car park where no one would bother her. How hard was it to just be alone?

Just talk to me. I hate it when you shut me out like this and I'm sorry about your compact. C. xx

Like all the other times, Christian had mellowed. His need to fix and repair her was now shining through, along with the guilt of breaking her grandmother's compact. She smiled. Maybe things weren't so bad. The breeze whipped up a chill around her ears. Shades of orange and brown crispy leaves swished up in the corner of the car park before settling in an even larger pile against a skip. Sweeping it up would no doubt be one of her jobs.

She glanced at the message again. This week was just the beginning and she would need him onside should everything fall apart. Oliver and Bella were her world. She couldn't lose them. She couldn't lose her mind. *Keep focused, Cherie.*

I'm sorry, love. The compact doesn't matter. I was stupid and you saved me, again. I love you so much. Xxx CH.

Another lie to get him off her back. She wasn't even sure she loved him. Their marriage had been a little shaky for the past year since she'd stopped drinking herself into a stupor. She shook her head. She had to drop it for now. She had her friends coming over for dinner tomorrow night and preparations to make. A message from Marcus popped up on her phone.

Me and Penny had a huge row and now she's gone. She's not answering her phone. I don't know what to do. Can you try calling her? Marcus. X

With shaky hands, Cherie tried to call Penny but her phone went straight to voicemail. She threw it in her pocket, her mind wandering to the tension that would exist amongst them around the dinner table. She imagined Isaac making jibes about Penny being a drama queen as he slowly got drunk. His partner Joanna would hang on his every word like some lovesick teen and Marcus would be there alone as they all looked at the gap where Penny should be sitting. It wouldn't be the first time Penny had put Marcus through a couple of days of hell while she swanned off somewhere to be alone or maybe there was more to it. Marcus didn't normally contact her for help.

A tear rolled down her cheek as she gasped for breath. *Don't lose it. Forget the past, it's gone.*

She glanced back at the nursing home. Sadie was helping Sidney to walk with his Zimmer frame and one of the trainees hurried past with a mop. The pile of leaves were no longer her problem, neither was Gladys. She jogged to her car, got in and turned the key, knowing that the only consequence of this action would be her dismissal. Frankly, she didn't care. She couldn't face the rest of the day, not knowing that Penny had gone AWOL.

CHAPTER FIFTEEN

Gina slumped back in her office chair as she listened to DC Wyre on the other end of the phone. As the conversation came to an end, she checked her list. 'Can you check someone out for me? Elsie Peterson, died at seventy-three, twenty-one years ago. Our unidentified figure was lurking around behind this gravestone. It may or may not have some significance. I know you're busy with the undertakers and coffin makers but it might just offer us a lead.'

She ended the call and allowed the case to run through her mind as she tried to search for links that she hadn't already found. Watching the footage from the café while Jacob was in the room had sent her pulse rate soaring, now exhaustion had set in. Briggs may have only briefly touched her hand, but it would have been enough to get people talking. She inhaled, counted to three and then exhaled slowly. Pulling the letter from her pocket, she lay it on the table.

Gina,

Those who stand by and watch are as guilty as those who hurt people. They deserve to be punished and sometimes a person has to take things into their own hands. Can you remember how it felt back then? How it hurt? Does it still hurt? Do your dreams take you to places you can't escape from? Close your eyes, think back, take a journey through that tunnel, back in time.

I know. I know everything.

We are the same, I just need you to see that. I will show you, I promise.

I promise. She trembled as she held the letter and envelope that were in the clear plastic wallet. A million thoughts rushed through her mind. They were referring to her past, to Terry. She knew that much. *We are the same.* What did that mean? Was this person one of Terry's other victims from his past? He'd never mentioned any previous relationships to her, getting irate if she dared to ever mention the subject. *I will show you.* She felt her throat starting to close as she held back a sob. She could never escape her past. However hard she tried to let it go, it always came back for her. She knew she had to tell someone – and it had to be her superior. A shiver ran down her spine. No, it couldn't be anything to do with the current case she was working on. It was nothing. She threw the note to her desk.

There was a knock at the door. She placed a file over the letter and Briggs entered, taking a seat at the other side of her desk. 'Panic over.' He began to fiddle with the end of his tie.

She nodded. 'It seems that way. Only your back appeared on the CCTV. But you can't do that again.'

He paused and ran his fingers through his hair. 'I know. It was a slip up. It just felt so... natural.'

Gina cleared her throat and thought about breaking the silence with the news of her letter but then stopped as he went to speak.

'You okay?'

'Yes, why wouldn't I be?'

'Okay, onto the case. The press have our victim's photo and it's due to be released on the local news at lunchtime and, get this, the nationals are out there too.' He paused and linked his fingers together on the desk.

'Don't keep me waiting. There's more, isn't there?' She leaned forward, eyes widening as she urged him to continue.

His smile dropped. 'Lyndsey Saunders is back. She's been sent from Fleet Street to follow the story and she's teamed up with the *Herald* while here as they already apparently have inroads. I don't know where they got that from either.'

Gina slumped back and ran her fingers through her hair as she took in the news. The reporter who'd always tried to make a feature of her, who'd caught her at her worst, was back. Just when Gina thought she had gone for good. 'Damn it! Anyone but her would have been fine. If she comes near me—'

'You'll just refer her to Corporate Communications. Stay calm and don't say anything to her. Let Annie deal with her, that's what she's there for. Any updates?'

She moved her mouse, lighting up her computer screen. 'Yes, I was just updating the website before briefing the team. As you know, Jacob and I went to the café and the church. First things first, we came straight back and sent you the screenshot of our victim. After, I began working my way through everything that was said and updating the system. We have the start of a name. June, the lady who always knits at the café.'

He smiled. 'I remember June.'

'She said she's seen our man before. He hangs around the streets with a sleeping bag. I'm guessing he's homeless given that he smelled of smoke and looked so unkempt. I must admit, it didn't click when he came into the café. He just came across as angry. Now I think of it, he must have been hungry. I feel as though I should have slowed down a little and analysed that situation better.'

'Don't think that. He came in with a right temper and was scaring everyone in the café.' Briggs caught her gaze, then looked away.

'Okay. June also mentioned that she and Cyril have tried to speak to him before. She gave him some change and he said his name was Al. It's not much, but it's a start. I still can't get that moment out of my mind when I saw him at the back of the gardens on Monday evening. He was lurking around there and I can't think why. We really need to put out a search for those kids too but I know how hard that will be. Then, get this: our vicar, Sally Stevens, saw a person by a grave in the middle of the night on Wednesday.'

Briggs sniggered and scratched his nose. 'It's all sounding a bit *Halloween* if you know what I mean.'

She smiled. 'I know exactly what you mean.'

His phone beeped and he checked it. 'The press are already having a field day. First headline is in and guess who reported it.'

'Bloody Lyndsey Saunders. Go on.' Gina took a swig of her coffee.

'"Man Buried Alive – The curse of Cleevesford strikes again. More murders per square mile than Inner City London.'"

'That's a total lie!' Almost choking as she swallowed, Gina began to laugh as coffee almost escaped from her nose. She coughed a few times to clear her throat. 'What on earth? More murders than Inner City London. Curse – what the hell is she on about?'

He clicked on the article and shook his head. 'Looks like she's been speaking to the locals and our vicar, Sally Stevens. Apparently, Sally mentioned the figure in the graveyard and our Lyndsey has put two and two together and come up with a curse. If you read on, she mentions the ghost of a boy who buried a girl alive because she didn't love him – all backed up by the locals of course. In Lyndsey's words, all the dead girl ghosts come out to haunt the woods and get their revenge on Halloween. Anyway, that's ridiculous. Her reputation should be out of the window by now but people seem to lap it up. Thinking of other things, maybe it's a ritualistic killing or someone took the ghost story a bit too far.'

Gina rubbed her temples as she finished clearing the coffee from her windpipe. 'It all sounds ludicrous but we have to consider it. Our victim was buried alive with a bell. The bell didn't have a clapper in it. Our victim was never meant to be found. Imagine him in that coffin, pulling away in the hope that someone would come? This murder is so ritualistic. We found three matches and a matchbox. This case is warped. Coffins, matches, bells and clappers. It has odd written all over it. Ghosts – no. Someone is playing on the haunted thing and we need to find out who.'

'You're right. I just wish they'd concentrate on our victim more than sensationalising everything. Poor Al's photo is no bigger than one you'd use on a passport. I know it isn't the clearest but it could have been at least double in size. He's playing second fiddle to a stock footage photo of a creepy druid that has nothing to do with the case.'

'It's all about selling papers. Lyndsey doesn't care about people. She's shown that to be true in the past.'

Gina flinched as the office door burst open and Jacob entered. 'Guv, we have a lead on Al. One of the George Street residents called in, she's free to talk to us for the next hour before she starts work. She saw our victim on Tuesday of this week. He was arguing with a woman at the back of her house.'

'Just what we needed.' Gina smiled back at Jacob, grabbed her phone and stood. 'Get your coat.'

'One other thing, guv.' Jacob half-turned back to the door. 'What?'

'Social media has gone ballistic with the news of this murder. They are blaming ghosts, druids, cult members and Satanists. The list goes on. O'Connor is keeping abreast of it all just in case our killer is relishing being the star of his or her own show.'

'Great.' Briggs stood and nudged past Jacob. 'Keep me posted. I'll see you both later.' She wanted to call him back, tell him that she needed to speak to him about the letter, but Jacob was waiting.

Gina grabbed her coat from the back of her chair. She popped her phone in her pocket along with all the other rubbish that was building up inside it. 'That's all we need. All thanks to Lyndsey. I suppose at least with the public being panicked like this, everyone should be on their guard. It won't hurt them to be vigilant. Let's go and find out what our witness has to say. I want to know who Al was arguing with.'

CHAPTER SIXTEEN

I ring the bell that dangles from the wall of my cupboard. I stare at the photos on my wall and hit the bell. The ringing takes me back to a time I remember fondly. I fall into my seat and close my eyes as I think back to a time less complicated. I'm there. I can smell and hear everything, just as it was.

As I walk through the workshop, treading in wood shavings, sawdust and random screws, I feel a sense of peace. The click, click, clicking of a staple gun fills my head and the smell of varnish hits the back of my nostrils and throat. I can almost taste it.

I watch as my mother staples the lining into the casket, a deep red satin – like shiny blood. Bespoke and beautiful, she always says.

My mother thinks that the dead have souls and that they watch her while she works on their final resting place. She believes that these souls enter their coffins way before their bodies do. I shiver. I've never seen a soul, but you don't see souls – at least I don't think you do.

I stare up at the ceiling, imagining that the old man whose coffin my mum is working on is floating above. I trace a shadow with my finger, wondering if that's him or if it's just a shadow. It's nothing. My mother is wrong, I'm sure of it.

I look out of the window and hope that darkness falls quickly. Once it falls, we go home.

The staple gun comes to a stop. 'Beautiful. Dear Lord, bless this soul.' She makes the sign of the cross and smiles as she knocks one of the bells that are suspended from a frame behind her.

I'm not sure how I feel about God, about anything spiritual but I copy her and make the sign of the cross. There must be something. There can't be nothing. I don't know how I feel about there being nothing. It scares me. My mother always repeats something from the Bible when she's attempting to ward off evil. 'Your adversary the devil prowls around like a roaring lion, seeking someone to devour.' She smiles at the casket. 'The devil won't be devouring you, Mr Appleton.'

I lean back in my chair and stare at the photo in front of me. It's time to go. I snatch the clapper from the bell, breaking it clean off with my gloved hands. It is now prepared. What do I believe? Like my mother, I believe the devil always prowls and he's in us all, just waiting to be let out. I never thought I would open the door to the devil but there's no going back now. I close my eyes and channel my inner roaring lion. I need strength. We are one and the same.

CHAPTER SEVENTEEN

Gina walked slightly ahead of Jacob on the thin path along the bottom end of George Street. She'd only just managed to slot the car into a space on the road. The old-style lamps flickered as the trees swayed in the wind.

'Here it is. Number ten.' A chip wrapper blew past and settled in the gutter next to them.

The three-storey house looked like one from *Amityville* with its protruding dormer style window coming from the roof. Everything about the house looked rickety and a torn net covered the front window. Gina peered in. There was a light coming from the back of the house.

Jacob knocked the gargoyle tapper. 'Creepy.'

She had to agree. Ever since they'd found the body, everything felt creepy. A door banged, followed by another as a gust whipped up behind them. The neighbour's gate continued to creak and crash against the post.

A woman with short, ginger hair and a wide smile answered the door – not what Gina expected. She'd half-expected Lily Munster to answer.

Gina held up her identification. 'I'm DI Harte, this is DS Driscoll. Thank you for calling us Miss Hanson. May we come in?'

'Call me Celia – and of course. I have to leave for work in fifteen minutes, so we'll have to be quick.' They followed the woman across the tiled floor into the long galley kitchen. An old range stood to one side and a stained Belfast sink faced the window. A stack of washed Pot Noodle containers rested on the draining board and were threatening to topple at any moment. The door at the end of the room stood ajar, exposing the Victorian-style downstairs bathroom.

Gina inhaled the smell of bubble bath mixed with bleach. 'We'll try not to keep you too long. You told one of our officers that you saw this man around the back of your house on Tuesday?' Gina pulled the photo from her bag and held it up.

The woman nodded. 'I didn't think too much about it. We have a lot of problems around here so it was nothing unusual. There's an old access road that runs at the back of this street and it eventually reaches the high street.' Gina knew that to be the case. It was the same road where Gina had come across their victim, Al, only a few nights ago, although she'd bumped into him much further up. 'Some people drive up it to park their cars out the back and access garages, others dump things. I keep a look out. We're sick of people leaving old mattresses and bin bags by our houses so we take it in turns to keep watch. It was my turn on Tuesday night, that's when I saw him.'

Jacob pointed to the photo. 'This is the man you definitely saw. Is that correct?'

She nodded, her chin doubling a little as she scrutinised the photo. 'Hang on.' She opened a drawer stuffed full of oddments and pulled out a pair of glasses before placing them on. 'The photo isn't good but it's definitely the same man who was outside my back gate. I also took a photo from my bedroom when he was here. You can tell by his stance and what you can see of his features.' The woman pulled her phone from her pocket and scrolled until she found what she was looking for. She held her phone up.

Gina leaned in for a closer look. The photo was almost too grainy to see but the features matched their victim. The distance between the eyes and the length of the nose were a giveaway as was his ever so slight hunch where he leaned a little to the right. 'You said someone else was with him, a woman?'

'She came later. I was upstairs tidying the bedroom when I caught movement out of the corner of my eye. I was already on alert as I was on watch that evening, so I had no television or music on. Once I spotted him, I turned off the light and continued watching. I was hoping to catch him at something illegal so I could call you lot. At first, I thought drugs. He wasn't carrying any rubbish and he was lurking around, walking up and down as if he was waiting for someone. I took the photo quickly and hurried downstairs. I thought that if I went in the garden, I might hear something.'

'And did you?'

She nodded. 'I gently opened the door. My back gate was locked. I have several locks on it, so I wasn't worried about him coming in and attacking me. As I opened the door, I could hear him shouting. A woman spoke back in a hushed voice, but I couldn't work out what she was saying. He was shouting, "Stay away from me you stalking bitch."' She pulled a notebook from the side and flicked through a few pages. 'I know these to be the words I heard as I wrote them down at the time. There was a bit of shuffling and murmuring then my fence rattled and I heard the man scream in pain before the woman ran off. I hurried back inside, ran up the stairs. I was about to call you lot, then I saw him staggering in the direction of the high street. This happens a lot around here. There are always people arguing when the pubs close or when they're drinking, or taking drugs. We – the residents – have reported this on many occasions. To me, this was nothing unusual and the man went so I didn't call in the end.'

Gina could understand. She knew that they were underfunded and understaffed. Petty crime and antisocial behaviour were becoming impossible to eradicate and as far as she could see, the underfunding was set to continue. 'Thank you for taking such good notes. Have you seen the man before or since?'

'No.' She looked out of the window and scrunched her brow before looking back, revealing thick lines across her forehead. 'Not that I can remember. I don't think I have. If I have, I don't remember him.'

'What time did you see them?'

'It was around eleven thirty that night. I'd been back from work for about an hour. Sorry I can't be of more help.'

'You've helped us a lot. Here's my card. If you remember anything else, please call me straight away. Can you also email the photo you took?'

The woman began typing Gina's email address into her phone as she glanced back at her card. 'Done.'

Jacob finished scribbling a few notes before closing his notebook.

'I really have to get to work now. I hate the twilight shift but it's all they have available for me at the petrol station.'

'Well, thank you for your time. We'll be in touch if we need to ask you anything else. May we go out the back way so that we can take a look at the road?'

She nodded. The woman began unlocking the several locks that kept her back door secure. 'Can't be too safe around here.' She opened the door and slightly waddled towards the back gate before opening another mass of sliding locks and padlocks. 'Are you okay walking round the long way?'

Jacob smiled. 'Of course. Thank you for your time.' The woman smiled and left them with the sound of all the locks being replaced.

Gina walked up and down, taking in each rain-filled pothole and the masses of takeaway wrappers that had gathered along the line of gates. '"Stay away from me you stalking bitch." Those were the last words we know of that he said and the last time that he was seen alive was eleven thirty on Tuesday. Who was he talking to? We need to find this woman and hope that he was the only person she was stalking. Wouldn't life be easier if we knew who he was?' Her phone beeped. 'Email from O'Connor. We have four people registered as missing that match his description. Let's get back.' A knot formed in her stomach. She knew she should say something to Briggs about the letter.

A few hailstones began to bounce off the road. Gina stepped into a puddle and felt the freezing cold water seep through her boots and socks. She glanced back and imagined Al leaning against Celia Hanson's fence while getting vociferous with the woman who was potentially stalking him. In her mind, she could see a long dark coat, face hidden by the hood. She shivered as she caught Jacob up and turned towards the light glowing from the road.

CHAPTER EIGHTEEN

Penny leaned against the tree, waiting in the dark for Isaac. She knew why he'd chosen this spot to meet: it was convenient for him. She knew why he used another phone too: Joanna read all his messages. Penny never liked Isaac much and she had no doubts that he was going to enjoy telling her all about Marcus's affair. She wanted to kick the tree. How could she have not seen the signs?

Looking back on her own fling with a colleague, she remembered how well she'd hidden it at the beginning. Marcus could be doing the same. Perhaps he was having revenge sex; her fling had damaged his ego. She remembered his face that morning as she had picked a fight over him stifling her. (He didn't really stifle her; it was the news of his infidelity and not being able to say anything without evidence that was stifling her now.) She had shouted at him about how he always stank a little, how he never cooked and how annoying it was when he left the toilet seat up – all the squabbling couple clichés had come out. The argument had ended with the stupid dinner party. She wasn't going and that was that.

She didn't want to go to Cherie's dinner party tomorrow; she hadn't wanted to go last year, or the year before, but Marcus had made her. Never again – she was free of that commitment. It brought nothing but bad memories back.

She pulled her cardigan tighter as the air bit. The chill had her teeth chattering and her head was foggy. She hadn't felt so cold while walking but now, she wished she'd have driven and worn more layers. Time to think, that's what she'd thought when she decided to walk. She wasn't going home after seeing Isaac. Marcus could stew on his own for a day or two while she checked into a budget hotel and processed what she was about to hear. It wouldn't be the first or last time.

She reached into her cardigan pocket and pulled out her phone. It beeped three times and the light went out – battery dead. She exhaled a plume of mist and hugged herself to warm up a little.

The breeze caught a flimsy fence making it constantly creak and bang. She flinched as she reached it – their meeting point. The sound of feet dragging through the dead leaves on the ground caught her attention. 'Isaac? I'm over here.' With her phone now dead, she hoped he'd be able to follow her voice. In the distance the lights to the Portakabin went off and she saw the lights from a car vanish into the distance. A sense of aloneness washed over her. 'Isaac?'

The feet stopped rustling.

She stood on her tiptoes and tried to peer into the darkness, then the feet dragging started again.

Isaac wasn't answering. Was he enjoying the fear in her voice? 'Isaac, stop playing games, you dick.' She snapped her head to the right, hoping to catch him out but all she could see was the glow of a distant street light on a scurrying cat. The wind howled, circling her. It was as if the night itself could sense her foreboding. She pulled her work dress back over her knees, wishing that she'd just worn her jeans and a jumper. At least she'd worn her boots.

A dog barked in one of the distant fields, then the dragging noise came again. 'Isaac, stop it.' Turning, she caught sight of red and blue in the sky followed by a bang as the firework exploded. The dragging sound was getting closer and her breath quickened. As she went to turn, she saw the figure of someone wearing a long dark coat, their features blending in with the darkness. A prick in her neck caught her by surprise, then she was being dragged backwards, her attacker's hands clasped over her mouth.

She tried to shout, gasp for air, scream, kick, but her body was weighing her down. She couldn't breathe. She tried to open her mouth to bite the palm of her attacker, but the grip was too tight. Dizzy, chest pains – she was going to die. Her body now even heavier. She watched the sky above until her senses began to deceive her. The twinkling stars began to wink and smile. She closed her eyes and succumbed to the drug that was coursing through her veins.

'No!' she cried, kicking out as she opened one eye. Her fist crunched on what felt like wood behind some material. She went to reach out and her finger made a cracking noise. As she tried to lift her head up, it felt as though the darkness was spinning. Nausea – no, she couldn't be sick. She lay back down and cried out, 'Help!' It was no use, no one was responding. She licked her lips – salt from her tears – that's what she could taste. How long had she been here?

Her heart felt as though it stopped on an image of a person in a long dark coat, the hood covering their eyes, then a sharp pain on her neck. She trembled as she realised how stupid she'd been. Maybe the message hadn't been sent from Isaac. Had Marcus wanted to get her out of the way now that he had someone else? Who was that someone else? Was there even a someone else? Her head swam with questions, making her dizzier. She had to get out.

Her heart raced as she felt around for anything. She couldn't focus at all. There was no light coming into her box – it was a coffin. Sobbing, she tried to twist and turn but all she came against was solid wood and a cushioned top. She reached up and tore at the delicate material, pulling the hole until it was large enough to fit her wrist through. She slammed her fist into the lid; that too was as solid as it sounded. She screamed again, then an image of space and spaghetti came back to her. She was losing her mind. Teeth chattering, she felt for her cardigan; it was still on her back.

Her mind kept coming back to Marcus, it had to be him. One body found in a coffin, why not perform a copycat killing? She'd read the rumours online and the news. He'd get the house paid for on her death, the house he could never afford on his own. Tears slid down her cheeks.

She'd seen Isaac watching her as if he could throttle her in the past, but she was sure he had something to tell her. She pictured his ditzy girlfriend, Joanna, who did everything to please him.

She kicked out and hit the bottom of the coffin. Her worst nightmare realised. A few separate trickles ran down her feet and hands. She licked one of them and recognised the unmistakable metallic taste of blood. Her head banged as if it might explode. Pound, pound, pound.

There had to be a way out. She took a deep breath, but it didn't help. She gasped again and began to fight with the material above, banging and scratching. She checked her pockets for her phone then it hit her, her phone had died, just like she would. Her bank card! Maybe she could poke it in the hinges of the wood.

Cricking her neck as she tried to turn in the confined space, she reached into her pocket and all she could feel was a box, a tiny solitary box. She struggled to hold it in front of her. Using her fingers for guidance, she slid it open.

She lit the first match and had a quick glance around. String. 'Ouch.' She dropped the burnt-out match and reached for the string. She grabbed it and pulled. The bell had to be ringing. Someone would come.

She lit another match and the sight of her bloodied nails made her shudder. 'Help me,' she called. A dog walker had to pass. Trick or treating kids might wander through. A solitary walker coming back from a pub – anyone. Her eyes began to fill, no one came around here.

She lit the last match and her final thought came to her like a swift slap; she knew exactly who had sealed her fate. This was the moment she realised she was never getting out. 'No, don't let me die in here…'

CHAPTER NINETEEN

Cherie hid around the corner, behind Old Joe's house. She tried calling Penny again, but it went straight to voicemail. She took the miniature bottle from her bag and had the smallest of tastes. Her fingers, numb to the October chill, missed screwing the cap on, causing her to accidentally splash the cuff of her coat. She'd officially failed. Her dry spell had ended.

As Christian pulled around the corner, she retreated back to her hiding place so that his headlights didn't catch her loitering in the dark. She pressed her back against the cold brick wall and fished in her pocket for the pack of mints she always carried before popping one into her mouth. As the wind changed direction, she heard Oliver and Bella hounding their father about going trick or treating. Something she'd never allowed them to do despite Christian also pressuring her. The children hated that they weren't allowed to dress up and scrounge sweets from the neighbours, like their friends were.

She shivered as her front door slammed. As always, Christian dutifully picked their two up from the childminder's house on his way home from work as she finished later than he did. She checked her watch. If she got into the car and pulled up now, she'd still be forty minutes early and he'd wonder what was going on.

Her mind milled with excuses.

I wasn't feeling well. They let me go early as there were too many staff rostered on. I worked through my breaks yesterday as Sadie was off sick so they let me take the time today.

She ran his responses through her mind. She couldn't say she was ill, he'd only fuss and she didn't want that. On the other hand, he'd probably tell her to go to bed and he'd feed the kids. No – he'd cancel her friends coming over tomorrow. That couldn't happen.

Swallowing, she thought of work and how she'd let everyone down. She turned her phone back on and waited a moment for her notifications to come through. Seventeen missed calls and five voice-mails. She opened a text from Maureen, her supervisor, telling her not to come back again. There were several from Sadie with laughing emojis whooping her for making a stand against their non-existent pay rises. Maureen wouldn't call her on the home phone, she'd never given them the number. For now, Christian would be none the wiser.

'What you doing 'ere? You'll catch a chill.' Joe flung his back gate open further as he dragged his wheelie bin onto the path.

'I was just—' Just what? What should she say? *I was just loitering here until my husband went into the house. Then I was going to drive my car from behind yours and park it on my drive because I'm weird like that.* She stared at the rustling leaves, hoping that they'd cue her in, but nothing was coming to the front of her mind.

'Are you okay, dear? Do you want to come in for a cup of tea?' He hobbled to the kerb, dragging his bin as he awaited her answer. 'I don't charge for the tea.'

'Thanks for the offer but I have to get home. Maybe another time.' She left him standing and hurried to her car, unwilling to answer any more questions. She had to face home sooner or later and only being twenty minutes early would be fine.

She drove the car onto the drive and as luck would have it, Christian was looking out of the window with his hands poised to close the blind. If only she'd waited another minute.

As she entered, he was already there. 'You haven't just come home, have you?'

'What do you mean?' She knew what he meant but that silly question would give her a moment to think.

'You know what I mean. You just pulled in from the wrong side of the road. The side that leads to dead ends.'

Throw it back at him. 'Christian, you're stifling me. Don't do this now.'

'Do what?' He folded his arms, a frown appearing across his forehead.

'You know.'

'I don't. Where have you been?'

Oh, I just walked out from my job. I've spent half of the day going to places I shouldn't have gone to and the rest of it hiding out of the way so I don't have to tell you about my dismissal.

'I got let out of work a little early on the proviso that I deliver some leaflets about the upcoming fundraising raffle. We're hoping for a few donations for the Christmas fundraiser, you know, for the work to the garden at the home next year. I parked down the road so it'd be easier. I started from the bottom. Sorry, I should have messaged.' The lie had spilled out far too easily.

He turned and walked into the lounge. Bella and Oliver were sitting at the table at the far end, doing their homework. 'You should have messaged. You could have picked the kids up. They could have helped and it would have taken the pressure off me to rush.'

'I did think that but I looked at the weather and didn't want them to get a cold.'

'Dad, can you help me with my homework?' Bella beckoned him over.

He grabbed his glasses from the table and sat next to her before muttering something about what metaphors were and how they were different to similes. Today, she was in the clear but next Monday was another day. She was meant to be at work and she had no job to go to. Where she'd hide out then, that was something she'd have to think hard about.

As she placed her bag on the table, she pulled her phone from her pocket. There had been no more messages from the nursing home and no calls from Penny. She opened Facebook and clicked onto the *Warwickshire Herald*'s page and her body stiffened.

Breath quickening, she loosened her coat and leaned against the wall sucking in air. The more she inhaled the woozier she felt. She spotted the miniature in her bag, her fingers ever itching for a swig of its contents but she couldn't, not with Christian being in the next room. She wouldn't. She'd been a fool to buy it and an even bigger fool to take another sip. As soon as she had a moment, she'd hide it away. Out of sight, out of mind, like the other one she had as a backup.

Alex's face stared back at her from the screen and she wondered if her dinner party buddies had seen or read the news of his murder. Her phone beeped. It was a message from Marcus.

Have you seen the news? Keep calling Penny. I knew she had something on her mind when she was picking a fight. She must have seen this before me. Keep trying to call her. Marcus.

'You alright?' Christian walked over to her.

She deleted her messages and turned her phone off. She nodded as she removed her coat, burying her vodka-drenched sleeve under the rest of the material. 'I'm fine. It's just been a long day and I'm pooped.'

'I'm sorry I was so miserable when you came home. I should have asked more gently instead of charging straight in there.'

As he leaned in and hugged her, she spotted the woman who lived opposite with her little ghost and devil in tow. She fought the need to cry and roll up into a ball and hide under the kitchen table. All the running in the world wouldn't fix her problems, not with them flowing ever closer.

Some things should never be found and some secrets should never be told.

CHAPTER TWENTY

Gina leaned back in her chair and gazed at the four missing men on her screen and not one of them looked like their victim, not in any shape or form. She clicked the shutdown tab and waited for her computer to eventually go off before grabbing her coat from the back of the door.

Briggs entered as she was about to leave. 'Everything okay, sir?'

He nodded. 'I think so. Just watch yourself. The press are all over the car park. This one really has rattled them. They keep quoting people who think that they've seen ghosts of the killer farmhand in the woods. That's all we need, ghost hunters turning up all over the scene. They sure know how to scupper our efforts.'

She had to agree. So far, she'd ended three calls abruptly from reporters that had managed to obtain her direct number. 'We could do with them all going away and letting us get on with our job.' She grabbed her laptop.

'Are you doing anything later? Maybe we could get some food and go over the case?' He'd loosened his tie and his hair had kinked a little on the one side. They were all tired, that was a definite.

'I think I just need to go home, have a shower and get some sleep. Something tells me that this case isn't going to be solved without a few sleepless nights. I'm going to plan out what's next, in my head at least, then I'm turning in.' She saw the disappointment creeping across his face as his smile dropped a little. He was trying to get too close again. She saw the letter sticking out from under her pile of work. Now wasn't the time. She had to think on it, try to work out who could have sent it.

'Well, call me if you get a light-bulb moment.'

Gina waited until the sound of his footsteps had disappeared down the corridor before she headed out to the car park.

The hustle and bustle of news vans and reporters greeted her instantly and one face stood out amongst the many.

'DI Harte. How lovely to see you again.'

It was never a pleasure for Gina to be this close to Lyndsey Saunders. 'I thought you'd moved on to bigger and better places.' Gina dragged her laptop bag past the photographer and almost bumped into the news van. 'You know, this constitutes an obstruction.'

The woman shrugged. 'There are no double lines. It's not near a junction or on the pavement and other vehicles can get past.'

Lyndsey was right. The only thing Lyndsey was obstructing was Gina's movement through the car park. The reporter had changed since they'd last met. The same red lipstick reached each end of her full lips and the signage light from the station's entrance showed off her coppery bronze curls. The new colour made her look far more radiant than Gina ever could be. Her rain mac and patterned scarf screamed quality. Lyndsey really had gone up in the world. Gina only wished she'd stayed at the top and sent one of her minions out to get the scoop.

'DI Harte, do you have any suspects?' A spectacled reporter leaned over Lyndsey's shoulder.

'A press release was issued earlier today. I have nothing more to say.' She pushed Lyndsey out of the way causing her to wobble on her heels. 'If you want to ask any questions, please contact Corporate Communications.'

Lyndsey smiled. 'The curse of Cleevesford strikes again. Did you like that one? I take full credit. People love an urban legend and that ghost story is something.'

So, Lyndsey was behind that headline.

'Would you say that Cleevesford Police are the most incompetent in the country? So many crimes, so many murders, in such an itty-bitty town. Is the killer of this man going to be brought to justice before anyone else is murdered?'

Gina pushed another man out of the way and the photographer thrust her camera into Gina's face and the flash went off. She squinted until the green blobs that had formed in her vision had subsided.

'Is someone else going to be buried alive? You can't even identify the victim. Do you have any info on the motive or who might be behind this?'

Gina clenched her fists together. Already they'd taken her photo and she was being hounded all the way to her car. Lyndsey reached down and gently took Gina's wrist, pulling her back. Gina threw it off as hard as she could. 'Get off me.'

'The people of Cleevesford have plenty to say about you, poor little Gina.'

She paused and stared. 'Did you send a letter to me, at the station?'

'Ooh, tell me more about this letter you speak of?'

Gina turned and scurried across the car park, pushing through three more reporters before reaching her car. With shaking hands, she fumbled in her pocket for her keys.

'See you in the morning, DI Harte. Check out the papers, your mugshot might just be featured on the front page.' Lyndsey leaned over to the photographer and scrunched up her nose. 'As always, you do look lovely in photos.'

Gina got into her car and slammed the door, driving out and forcing all the reporters to part. Most times the press could be helpful, but in this case she sensed they'd be nothing more than a hindrance with their sensationalist stories and guesswork.

Briggs was looking out of the incident room window. He gave her a little wave as she drove off. This was just the beginning of this investigation and it was more than a nightmare, it was a personal night terror for her. A whirl of nausea and hotness flashed through her as she took another bend. She needed to get away from it all and clear her head.

As Gina drove along the high street, her phone rang. It was Briggs. She selected hands-free.

'Everything okay, sir?'

'We've just had a call from what may be our victim's mother. She recognised him from the press release. I'll email all the info across to you. She's in Spain, back tomorrow afternoon.'

'I'll pay her a visit after the post-mortem if I can get the address too.'

'I've just pinged it over with all the information we have.'

That was just the break they needed. She hit the steering wheel, whispering 'yes' under her breath. A tear slid down her cheek. A break in the case and a chink in her armour, all in the same day. What had the people of Cleevesford been saying about her? No one knew anything, or did they?

CHAPTER TWENTY-ONE

One, two, three. Matches – my gift to them.

I stare into a dark corner until my mind's eye becomes stronger. I see me, but not the me I see when I look at my reflection. I visualise the roaring lion and I know I'm doing the right thing. My plans have been simmering away for a long time. Only now do I get to follow them through. Finally, I am no longer invisible. There's only one person I need to see me for who I am – and she will. Someone has to understand me and be on my side.

My letter didn't arrive with the press today. I've no doubt that if it had, the newspapers would be full of it and DI Harte would want to know me. I wonder if she received her letter. I want to shake her and say, 'DI Harte, you are not safe. No one is safe. Terry showed you how vulnerable you really are. I need you to remember. Nothing good comes of letting a painful past go. Embrace it, let it be your strength, your fight, your edge. Wake up, DI Harte.'

I love the papers. The urban legend of the lovesick murdering ghost has been well planted. Let them think that if they want.

I close my eyes and inhale slowly.

I watch.

I wait.

I am coming.

These words are just for you, Gina.

I creep along the floor of my attic room, trying not to make a noise. Waking him up isn't an option I relish and I have too much to do before morning.

I press the handle down on the cupboard door at the end of the room and feel along the desk for my lighter. It's exactly where I left it. Lighting the candle casts a warm orangey glow into my secret office. This is where I will continue with phase two, then on to the next.

I owe DI Harte another letter so I best not disappoint.

If you think you're safe in your house, think again. No system is perfect and that includes yours. You know you're being watched but you can't work out if you're going crazy. Paranoia is a wonderful thing. It's lovely to see the patrol car passing every so often but don't think I haven't prepared for that scenario.

I can't send this one. I delete it from the screen.

Instead, I stare at the board. Penny smiles back at me. What a lovely photo she posted to Facebook for all to see and now I'm going to spoil that pretty little nose with a thick black cross through her face. Another one down. I think of Penny in that coffin, clawing away and gasping for breath. She might have thought I was out there as she screamed and cried but no one would have heard a thing and I certainly didn't stick around, I'm not a sadist. I just know she would have been screaming for her life, eating up all that precious oxygen. It sucks to be alone while you're suffering, knowing you're going to die.

Penny's long mousy hair is so pristine in the photo, not like it was last night.

I stare at the blank screen, knowing that I have to write something meaningful to DI Harte. I need her to sit up and take notice. I mean, she hasn't even responded to my first letter via the press. That was a huge mistake. I don't take kindly to being ignored, not when I have so much to say. Maybe it's time to shout louder.

I begin to tap away.

DI Harte,

I said I'd be in touch again. I know you believe that standing by and watching others suffer isn't okay. We must protect the innocent. Anger, tension, fear – they never leave. Scratching at the walls of your prison, knowing there is no way out, thinking you might die…

Maybe facing the fear is what it takes.

'Your adversary the devil prowls around like a roaring lion, seeking someone to devour.'

But sometimes your enemy isn't all they seem.

I place a sheet of paper in the printer and hit the button. It begins to jut out the other end and I cringe until it's finished. With every chug, I risk waking him up, and I can't afford to do that; but this needs doing and it needs doing now. DI Harte will love this one. I know she'll understand what is going on here. It's as clear as freshly polished glass. This may seem like a game but it's not. This is real and the consequences of every action are real.

Catching the page, I draw an equilateral triangle at the bottom. Time to ramp up the clues. 'I'm giving it to you on a plate, Harte.'

Everyone loves a puzzle. I place it in an envelope and pop a stamp on it. It's going straight to the *Warwickshire Herald*. I give the last two bells a nudge. There's no clapper in them to warn anyone of a presence. Silent panic, that's the only way to do it. I grab another box of matches. A pile of little sticks land in the drawer as I tip them out, all except three.

After removing my latex gloves, I flex my sweaty hands as I hear him calling for me in the distance.

I glance up at the next photo on my board and swallow. 'You're next.'

I close the door on my secret and then I step back into my role, the one everybody recognises. My highly practised façade. The me I've created to fit in with this world in which I don't belong.

'Be there in a moment.' I shake my clothes and smile at the mirror. That's better.

CHAPTER TWENTY-TWO

Now

Saturday, 31 October

Gina stood next to Jacob, shifting a little to see through the fingerprints on the glass that divided them both from the post-mortem room. Bright lights glinted off the stainless steel tops. The dripping of a faulty tap continued, plaguing Gina with its repetitive sound, the same sound that seemed to be annoying no one but her. Two hours had passed and despite all the slicing and organ removals, Gina felt her stomach grumbling away.

'Don't tell me you're hungry, guv?'

'Don't hate me. I couldn't face breakfast knowing we were coming here but now I feel sick because I'm hungry. Can't win.' She let out a small laugh as the chief pathologist leaned over and passed a succession of samples to one of his suited-up assistants. 'Is Jennifer off today?'

'No, I think she was working one of the other scenes until late. She'll be back in later. I left her in bed to catch up on her sleep.'

Gina glanced back at the cadaver. She'd watched them remove the bags from his hands and feet, take nail clippings and samples. Every orifice had been swabbed, bloods, tissue samples – the full works.

She gazed at the blue-tinged man lying on the slab. It had transpired their Al's full name was Alexander Swinton.

'Is his mother coming in to formally identify the body?' Jacob walked around a little, stretching his arms out, the bottom of his coat slapping the chair in the small viewing room.

'Yes, she wanted to. It would be the quickest way of getting his identity confirmed. From the photos she sent to us and the link to his Facebook profile, it looks like it's definitely him but we have to make sure. Our victim had no record either so we had nothing on the system that would have flagged up from his fingerprints or DNA.' She swallowed, not relishing being with the woman when she viewed her son's body.

'How old did you say he was?'

'Thirty-four.' She flinched as Jacob's coat caught her face. 'Can you stop pacing around?' She smiled.

He fell into the plastic chair and linked his hands in front of him. 'Sorry, I'm just getting a bit restless after sitting for so long.'

'How do you think he ended up in such a bad way?'

The chair creaked as Jacob leaned back. 'Who knows? Drugs maybe, relationship breakdown, lost his job.'

'Hmm, I hope meeting his mother will clarify that. Let's go over what we know from the post-mortem so far.'

'Go for it.'

Gina glanced at the pathologist. He continued working as the clean crime scene assistant kept stepping in to take more photos. The victim was respectfully laid out on his back in the sterile room. She shivered as the scales bobbed when the pathologist knocked them. Only an hour ago, the victim's liver had been weighing them down.

Gina's stomach was screaming for food but her throat tightened a little. She flipped back to the last page in her notebook. 'Male, white, six foot, blue eyes, various piercings and a tattoo. Piercing in his right eyebrow that has almost healed and a ring in his right nipple. Tattoo of a lion on his thigh. A lot of dirt under his finger-nails and ingrained on his hands. The smell of smoke oozing from his every pore and traces of ash in his neckline and his hair suggest he's spent a lot of time in front of open fires. Crew cut, blond hair. Track marks on his arm and groin. Screams drug problem.'

'Toxicology will tell us what he was taking.'

Gina nodded. 'Those results won't be back in a hurry. We know the track marks are a mixture of fresh and old. We need to contact all local drug services, see if he has been on a methadone programme. If someone was looking after his case, they may be able to tell us more about him.'

Jacob made a note.

'I just hope that the more we learn about him, the more we might find out about who did this to him.'

'I've never come across anything like this, guv.' Jacob stared at the corpse as the pathologist began to stitch him up.

'It's creepy, isn't it? We have to catch whoever did this. I checked social media this morning and there's a lot of scaremongering about the ghost that buries people alive. The press are really going to town on this one and Lyndsey Saunders is taking all the credit. She's right you know.'

'About what?'

'Cleevesford is a dangerous place to live. It used to be a desirable town and now house prices have dropped a little. This town has a sick feel about it and it's not getting any better. We can't let this happen to anyone else. It's just unthinkable.'

Silence fell between the two as they watched the pathologist remove his plastic apron and face mask.

A spark of an image flashed through Gina's mind. Nails on wood, clawing their way out. Blood, lots of blood and gritty tears, then the letter. The smell of fear, sweat and urine. The uncontrollable shivering as she took her punishment. Who knows about her past?

'Guv?'

She flinched. 'What?'

'We're being called through.'

The pathologist pointed to the corridor. She stood and followed Jacob, fighting the need to leave and inhale mouthfuls of fresh air. She wanted to get outside and run away, anywhere.

As her signal returned her phone beeped. A flood of messages came through at once and her phone rang. She looked up at Jacob. 'You go ahead. I'll catch you up in a moment.'

As he walked away, she accepted the call from Briggs. 'You need to get back to the station, now.'

'What is it?' Her stomach dropped and she felt a jitter running though her fingers.

'I'd rather you be here to talk about it. Don't talk to the press, don't talk to anyone. Just hurry.' He ended the call.

'Jacob.' He glanced back just as he was about to enter a side room with the pathologist. 'I have to get back to the station now. I'll get someone to come back and collect you as soon as I get there.'

He smiled and nodded. 'Okay, see you in a while. Is everything alright?'

'I don't know.'

She hurried down the corridor, signed out and ran across the car park, stopping to take a few deep breaths before getting into the car. She scrolled through her messages. Lyndsey Saunders's message flashed up.

It must be wonderful being star of this show. What do you know that you're not telling us, DI Harte?

She clicked onto the *Warwickshire Herald* to see a photo of her, the one that had been taken last night. Her hair covered half of her face and her hand had crossed one of her eyes as the flash went. Tired bags underneath the eye that everyone could see and chapped lips. Her appearance wasn't the most disturbing part. The text underneath almost knocked her sick. Her mouth watered and her throat tightened. She couldn't breathe. Gasping, she reached for the steering wheel trying hard not to faint, not to lose herself, not to cry. She couldn't believe what she was reading.

All she could see was a pinprick of light through each pupil. The light was about to go out. She couldn't inhale. Her throat was blocked. The pinprick was going, going, gone, along with her capacity to make sense. Where was she?

Gasping, her woozy vision began to return, like she'd just been resuscitated. But she was alone, just her in her car with her phone. She pinched her arm and flinched. That was real.

Her mind flashed back to a moment she had hoped to forget but it ran through her mind like a film being played out. She clawed at the wood, her fingernail stuck in a groove. Skin and nail parted, leaving the whole bloody thing sticking out. The past she'd left behind was set to never leave her alone. She'd felt death knocking on her door. The coffin killer had brought Terry back into her life and made that fact almost public. This morning she had been the cat, prowling for leads, now she was the scarpering mouse looking for a tiny crack to escape through before her past came out for all to see how weak she really was.

On the night Terry had locked her in the shed, he'd been watching – he had told her from outside, '*I watch*'. He'd enjoyed every moment. '*I wait*' – him waiting for her to learn her lesson. Answering him back wasn't an option. '*I am coming*' – that's when the real terror had started. The manic wide-eyed look on his face accompanied by an ecstatic grin had scared the life out of her.

Now, she slammed her hands into the car door, on the steering wheel, and she kicked at the brake pedal until she felt the skin on her toes dampen. She knew they were bleeding.

I watch. I wait. I am coming. Three short sentences that had been buried at the back of her mind were now all she could repeat in her head.

CHAPTER TWENTY-THREE

Cherie walked through the aisles of the corner shop once again as she searched for the herb section. For a moment, she stopped and stared at the wine and spirits. Her hand brushed a bottle of vodka, the clear liquid enticing her to buy it. Saliva spread across her tongue as she imagined swigging the liquid. Last night had given her the taste again, albeit a small one. That moment plagued her thoughts.

No. She dropped her hands and checked over her shoulder. Shame burning her cheeks; thankful that no one was looking. Christian had bought the wine for their guests and, as usual, Cherie would just tell them that it didn't agree with her as she filled her glass with flavoured water.

She didn't need vodka. Removing her hand from the bottle, she continued walking down another aisle. When shopping the other night, her mind had been elsewhere – it still was. She doubted it would ever return to normal. Something had been set in motion and she had to fix it. When her dinner party friends, Marcus and Isaac went out for a cigarette later, she'd get her chance to find out if they knew anything about Penny.

A devil mask stared back at her. She swallowed and stepped back, glad that after tonight Halloween would be over. The kids would stop knocking and her children would stop whining to dress up.

'Watch where you're going. You trod on my son.' The annoyance on the woman's face said it all as the knee-high boy began to screech the place down.

'I'm sorry. I didn't mean—'

One person turned around, then another and several more. All eyes were on her. She turned, pushing the door so hard it bounced on its hinges. She scarpered past the barking mongrel that snapped at her ankles until the lead snatched the dog back towards the post.

Soon she was away from the shop and heading for a tree-lined cut through towards the edge of the woodland. The earthy smell coming from the damp ground took her back to that night. She ran for the trees before leaning against the bark, hidden from the path. No one could see her like this, not a stranger, not Christian. He already thought she was losing it and turning back towards the drink. He couldn't know. All he should know was that as usual, like every year, her friends were coming over for dinner. It was a tradition they'd upheld since leaving school and they were her best friends. All would be fine, she told herself, but she knew in her heart that it wouldn't be.

She hit her head and slapped herself across the face. She didn't like them as much as she made out, but tradition was tradition. *Pull yourself together.*

Leaning back, she felt the roughness of the bark scratching her neck. She wanted to cower down and curl up next to it – hide.

Oregano. The one thing she'd come out for and she had failed to get it. She'd tell Christian that they didn't have any. He'd have to pop out to the supermarket while she started preparing the meal. She couldn't have stayed in that shop any longer with that bawling child and the staring crowd.

She almost slipped on mud as she took a step from behind the tree. One step after another, all the way home. Looking up, the grey clouds seem to swirl and fall. The treetops rustled, scattering wet across her cheek. A large bird squawked from a high branch, its beady glare meeting hers. Staring down, she followed the pavement, avoiding the little dips where the tarmac had come up over the years. Tarmac changed to slabs, halfway home.

Thud, thud came a noise from behind. A car engine revved up in the distance concealing the sound of whatever was catching her up. Then the car quieted down.

The footsteps were getting louder and louder. Heart pounding, she began to jog in her heeled boots. The end of the cut through was in sight but that was less welcoming than the woods. The back of the houses had long gardens. No one was out in weather like this, tending to their plants and pruning their shrubbery. No one would hear her scream. The wind on her back whooshed as her stalker closed the gap. *Run faster, just a little way to go. Then scream as loud as you can.* She aimed for a sprint then her heel caught on an uneven slab. Fighting to wrench it out, she skidded forward and plunged to the ground, landing on her arm. A sickening pain shot through her shoulder and bicep. Screaming, she turned to see his face.

CHAPTER TWENTY-FOUR

Cameras flashed and a boom pole almost clonked Gina on the chin.

'DI Harte, who is the killer?'

'You know the killer, don't you?'

'Are they coming for you next?'

'The public have a right to know what you're not telling us.'

Lyndsey Saunders stepped in front of Gina as she tried to exit the crowd of reporters, ignoring every question. 'You should talk to me, maybe then we could work together on finding out who sent this letter, but I suspect you already know. The more I delve, the more I'm finding. I know you better than you think.'

'What the hell does that mean? You sent me the letter, didn't you? Not the one in the paper. It feels like a threat you know, sending letters like that.'

Lyndsey smirked. 'So there definitely is another letter. My offer still stands. Let's work together on this. Show me the letter. Trust me.'

Gina nudged her out of the way. 'Stay away from me. If you cared about catching this killer, you'd have brought that letter to us before publishing it. Can't you see what you've done? Trust you – never!'

'I'm doing my job, DI Harte. The public deserve the truth, not a censored version of it. It is clearly in the public's interest.'

'You've hampered this investigation good and proper. The killer is loving what you did, so thank you for not helping.' Gina ran to the main door and hurried in, fists clenched and face reddening with a burning anger. She stood outside the ladies and shouted as she hit the wall. Seething, she hoped that she could calm herself, just a little, but it wasn't working. Her hands itched to hit out again until they bled.

Gina thudded through the fire door, straight to Briggs's office, knocked once and entered without waiting to be asked. She opened her mouth to speak but nothing came out. Pacing around the room, she stopped and stared out of the window, catching the end of a bus as it passed.

Redness crept up her neck. She scratched and tore at her skin until she almost drew blood.

'Stop. We'll catch whoever sent this letter to the press.'

Gasping for breath and fighting back a tear, Gina backed away from his embrace. 'It's like he's back. I can't escape – ever. Who's doing this to me? Why me?'

His gaze fixed on hers. 'They're playing with you and we will find them. You should go home for your own safety. We can get patrols to drive by regularly or even station someone at your cottage—'

'No, no and no.' She wiped a tear away. 'I'm going to be the one to catch whoever is doing this. I don't need to go home and calm down or back off or whatever else you think I might need to do. Look at me.' She paused. 'Yes, it's taken me by surprise, but you know what? I'm tougher than this. I won't be defeated.'

He steadied her towards the chair and pulled it out. 'Here, have this.'

She reached over to take his cup of coffee. 'Thanks, sir.' She took a sip and leaned back. 'Right, panic over. Think, think, think.' She tapped the side of her head and took a deep breath. 'I have a plan and I'm sticking with it. As soon as Alexander Swinton's mother is back at one thirty, I'm heading over there. At three, I have to take her to the morgue to view her son's body. Nothing has changed.' She could tell herself that as much as she liked, but things had changed. She swallowed and tensed up.

'Do you know why you were mentioned in our killer's letter?'

She shook her head. 'If I knew that I wouldn't look like this.' She pointed at her blank expression then snatched the newspaper. 'The press know how to stir. I wish they'd come here with the letter, at least to give me, us, the chance to prepare for its publication. What the hell were they thinking?'

'Sales, that's what Lyndsey thinks about. They love a bit of hysteria and threat.'

She nodded as she read it all again, stopping at the letter.

DI Harte,

This is for you. Trapped people, they claw, they plead, they beg. You begged, didn't you? Remember? Think back. Now I have your attention. Stay with me. I need you.

I know. I know everything.
I watch.
I wait.
I am coming.

'Do we have the actual letter?' She slammed the paper closed and gasped for breath as she fought back every wave of panic that was threatening to spill over.

'Wyre has gone to collect it. I do know it's printed in Times New Roman, twelve point font. It will be photographed and taken straight to the lab. My issue is, everyone at the *Warwickshire Herald* will have had their mitts on it. We need to go through this letter. What do you know?'

She placed her head in her hands. 'Why me?'

He sat down and took the newspaper from her side of the desk. 'There's no delaying what needs to be done. Talk me through it.'

'This person obviously knows me well. They know things that only I thought I knew.'

'Okay, that's a start.'

She leaned across and stabbed at the letter with her index finger. 'I watch. I wait. I am coming. Terry used those exact words when he locked me in the shed once – and during other times in our marriage. He'd taunt me with them. I don't know how anyone on earth could possibly know this. It's like he's back.' A tingle ran across her neck as she felt his invisible hands squeezing her windpipe. She winced as she remembered her ribs cracking. A swirl of nausea washed through her throat as the image of her nail peeling from her finger flashed through her mind. The dark days and nights and the boarded-up windows.

'Tell me, Gina. I need to know. For now, it will stay between us.'

'For now? That's helpful.' She closed her eyes, knowing that she had no choice in the matter. Her hands began to tremble. 'Terry locked me in a shed once, for a whole weekend. He kept coming and going between drinking binges, then he'd unlock the door to tease me, knowing I was too scared to fight my way out. He'd stand there, laughing and taunting, telling me that Hannah and he didn't need me. I'd hear her crying all the time from the house.' She wiped her eyes. 'He'd tell me he was watching me or watching the shed, that if I banged and made a fuss, he'd kill me. At times, I'd think he wasn't there, then he'd surprise me by whistling, reminding me that he was waiting for me to step out of line. He just couldn't wait for me step out of line so he could beat the hell out of me.' She let out a sad laugh. 'His last words filled me with panic. He told me he was coming and that I should brace myself. His words were, "*I watch. I wait. I am coming*".'

'I'm sorry to put you through all that again.' He hurried over and kneeled in front of her.

'And I did brace myself. All I could think of was that Hannah would grow up and not remember me if something happened.

I thought he'd hurt Hannah but he hadn't. After my ordeal was over, he dragged me back into the house and acted as though nothing had happened while I tended to my nail-less finger. He then told me why he'd done it. It was because I'd phoned one of my old friends from college. He'd redialled the number when he came home and her boyfriend had answered. I tried to tell him but—' She looked away.

He placed his hand on her arm. 'Thank you for sharing that with me. Listen.' He placed his other hand under her chin. 'You are DI Gina Harte. You are a brilliant detective and this is another puzzle and unfortunately, you are part of that puzzle. We are all going to solve this. Terry is dead, gone. He can't hurt you again.'

Gina looked away. Even in death, all Terry had ever done was hurt her. Just when she thought she was able to move on, he was back. 'Can you think of anyone who might know so much?'

She shrugged. 'There's his brother Stephen. He might be out for some sort of revenge after you threatened him in our previous case and there's his mother, Hetty – I don't think Hetty would know these things. He always gave off this false smiley persona when she was around. She didn't even know what Terry was like when it came to me. She had no idea how he punched, strangled and kicked me.'

'We have a murder where someone has been buried alive and this letter instantly takes you back to a time where Terry had locked you in a shed. They want you back there, in the moment. Question is, why? I hope I'm wrong, but it looks like our killer has chosen you for a reason. Let's consider Stephen. Obviously, I've met the prick and I can't say I like him. What are your thoughts?' He stood and sat on his desk beside Gina.

She shrugged and sniffed. 'I can't see it. Maybe we're looking for a link between Stephen and our victim. Stephen is ultimately a coward. Terry was the more aggressive brother. I could see Terry burying someone alive and enjoying it, but Stephen, however much I hate him, I'm sure it's not him.'

'Could he have got someone else to do it for him?'

'Murder an innocent man just to get to me?'

'No. It looks like our victim was taking drugs, maybe he got them from Stephen. He has got a past when it comes to drugs.'

The office fell silent. Gina knew that rattling Stephen's cage would further fuel the anger that Hetty and he harboured against her. 'It has to be someone else, someone Terry knew? It's not Stephen or Hetty; besides Stephen has been working up in Scotland for the past few months. Before you ask, yes I check out his whereabouts on Facebook. He's shacked up with some poor woman.'

'Then we're back to square one when it comes to finding the link. I'm sure this letter won't be the last, not now the press have made so much of it.' He pursed his lips together before speaking again. 'You shouldn't be alone at home.'

'I'm fine with the drive-bys. I have my CCTV, my alarm system, my deadlocks, double locks, gate locks.' She exhaled slowly as her cheeks cooled down. 'I'll be okay. The shock got to me but I'm not going to let this beat me. As far as this murderous freak is concerned, we're game on.'

'That's what I like to hear. If you sense any danger, you just have to call and I'll be there.'

She forced a smile. 'Is there anything else that will help with the investigation?'

'There is a postmark on the envelope. It was posted in Cleevesford.'

'As local as that. They didn't even try to hide how close they are – or did they come here just to post the letter? They know the woods, they know the area and I suspect they live locally. Why now? Any thoughts?'

He shook his head. 'Maybe talking to our victim's mother might give us something to work with.'

'There's something else. I received a letter yesterday. It was marked private and confidential. It's from the killer. I didn't link the two until I saw this one today.' She stood and pulled down at her shirt over her black trousers.

'What? You should have said something anyway. What does it say?'

'It's like they're trying to get me to remember my past and it mentions that they know everything.' She almost choked as she continued to speak. 'Whoever wrote it says we are the same. They want me to see that. I'm scared, Chris.' She gasped a sob and held her arm out as he moved a little close. 'I'm okay. I'll get you the letter. This is as personal as it gets.'

'Anything else, call me straight away. Don't sit on it. I won't mention this outside of us two at the moment. As the press don't know the content of this letter, it may help us catch the killer. I don't want any chance of it leaking in any way or form.'

She wiped a tear away. 'I might have confronted Lyndsey Saunders about it. I thought it was her and I was so angry. She has no idea what was written in it.'

'Damn it! Just keep a lid on the detail. Say nothing to anyone else. We don't know who's pulling the strings and, more often than not, it can be someone closer than we think. Also, we are assuming that this person might be a threat to you until something tells us otherwise. They are a threat to you. I need you to stay safe.'

Her gaze lingered on his for a few seconds longer. 'I'll call you later.'

As his door closed after her, her shoulders slumped. In her mind, she was screaming. She shook that thought away. What she needed right now was for everyone to see her as a capable leader of the investigation, not someone who was about to fall apart. Why had the killer chosen her?

CHAPTER TWENTY-FIVE

'Did you get the oregano?' Christian came into the hallway from the kitchen. The smell of fried onions filled her nostrils as she slammed the door closed.

Sweat poured from her forehead and her underarms reeked from the panic she'd endured. Her heart rate wasn't returning back to normal as quickly as she'd hoped – or was it anxiety? The man she thought was following her had simply removed his earphones and held out his hand. The jogger had then asked if she was okay but she'd stood and ran instead of replying. She grimaced. What must he have thought of her? No, she did the right thing. There was no such thing as being too careful. She was okay for now, but her time would come, she was sure of that.

'Cherie?'

She glanced at Christian as he wiped his hands on her apron. Catching her breath, she opened her mouth to speak. 'Yes, I ran from the woods. I heard something, it was probably just a bird but it made me jump.'

'You've hurt yourself.' He led her into the kitchen and helped her to sit at the table. His gaze felt interrogating as he focused on her hand.

'It's just a scratch.' She unzipped her bag and threw it on the table. 'Go on, I know you want to check. I haven't been drinking if that's what you think.' Be sober-minded, that was her aim from now on. To be sober-minded, she had to be sober. It was harder than it sounded when her body craved a drink.

There was no hope of him saying no to a search of her bag and simply trusting her. Her face flushed a little. She had already breached his trust when she took a sip from the miniature but that wasn't going to happen again. He reached into her bag and probed the items, pushing them around with his index finger. 'Come here.' He leaned over and hugged her. 'I just want to help you. We've got through so much as a family so I know whatever it is, we can get through anything.'

'I just fell over, that's all that happened. And no, I didn't get the oregano. They didn't have any.'

The sound of feet thundering down the stairs alerted Cherie to the fact that their children were about to enter.

'Mum, Oliver won't get out of my room and he keeps trying to take my iPad because he broke his. You're not having it, loser.' Bella burst in, her long black plaits dangling over each shoulder.

'No, it's not like that. Don't lie. You're just trying to get me in trouble.' Oliver stared at his mother. 'Is that blood?'

Cherie gave her children a reassuring smile. 'I just fell over on the way back from the shop but I'm alright. Oliver, if you broke your iPad, you can't expect your sister to let you use hers. We'll talk about this later.'

'But, I didn't mean—'

'Your mother said we'll talk about this later, now go upstairs and pack your overnight bag. Nan and Gramps are waiting for you both.'

Oliver made a loud huff noise as he left.

Bella shrugged her shoulders and followed. 'Loser.'

Christian took the first aid box from under the sink and opened it on the table. 'Hand.'

She placed it open and winced. The cut was deeper than she thought. He took a bit of kitchen roll and wet it before wiping the grit away and cleaning the wound. She flinched.

Her husband looked away. 'Yuck, I'd never make a nurse. Right, this might sting so brace yourself.' He squeezed the antiseptic liquid into the cut and put a plaster over it. 'Now, no ifs, no buts, I want to know what's going on. You've been acting weird all week but since yesterday, you've taken weird to a whole new level.' He paused. 'I can't help if I don't know what's wrong.'

She rolled her eyes and stared at him. There were things she couldn't talk to him about, elements of her secret outings that would end their marriage. It was already fragile and one more deception could shatter everything, especially one so big. Her stomach knotted as a flashback to the past filled her mind. All she could hear were taunts and sinister laughter.

'Cherie, out with it.'

'I… I lost my job.'

'You what? Why? How?'

'I just can't cope with the workload.' Another lie. 'I'm falling behind all the time. With the constant understaffing there's always so much pressure and I haven't been coping. It's my fault. I'll look for something else, first thing Monday. I'll do agency work, anything. I just haven't been coping. There, I've told you now.'

'You should have said something and maybe you could have taken some holiday or unpaid leave instead of working yourself up.' He closed the first aid box and threw it back under the sink amongst the cleaning products. 'I wish you'd talk to me more. I'm sick of you keeping important things from me.'

She didn't know where to look. 'I won't keep anything else from you, I promise.' She stood and hugged him.

His hands remained down. *Please hug me back.* If he hugged her back, she knew she was in the clear, for now. He reached around her limply.

She kissed him, hoping to feel some response but there was nothing as his cold lips brushed hers. 'I suppose we best clean up before everyone gets here in a bit.'

'Okay, I'll get started on tidying the lounge, you can carry on making the pasta sauce. I've browned everything off, it's just got to go in the slow cooker for a few hours.' He dropped the apron on the worktop and left her to it. Her phone beeped; it was another message from Marcus. She opened it up and almost choked on her breath.

I'm falling apart, Cherie. I can't deal with this any longer. I'll be coming alone tonight. Marcus.

She sent a reply.

We'll talk later, after dinner. Just try to keep calm, all will be fine.

She called out, 'We're one down tonight. Penny's not feeling well so Marcus will be coming alone.' For now, she wouldn't tell him what was happening. She had to work it out herself. She tried to call Penny again but, once again, her phone went to voicemail.

CHAPTER TWENTY-SIX

Gina exhaled a plume of white mist into the chilly afternoon air. Jacob followed her from the car towards the row of terraced eighties houses. A cluster of teens ran past, flapping around in black bin bags and topped with witch hats. The shouting and laughing disappeared with them around a corner. She swallowed and forced all thoughts of the letters to the back of her mind, for now.

They finally reached the row of houses that they were looking for. Red tiles covered the frontage, making them look as if the roof was on the front wall. Then Gina spotted the number they were looking for. At least thirty gnomes of varying sizes filled the tiny front garden, leading the eye to the plastic butterflies that were stuck all around the porch door. Gina checked the house number again. They definitely had the correct address. 'What's Alexander Swinton's mother's name again?'

'Eveline Peterson, guv.'

She rang the doorbell and listened as the sound of dogs barking came from behind the door. The owner shouted before opening it.

Gina held up her identification. 'DI Harte and DS Driscoll.'

'Bunty, shut up.' The bony woman picked up the miniature poodle and the boxer dog continued to bark.

From behind the front door, it had sounded like she had more dogs than she actually did. 'May we come in?'

The woman nodded. Gina could see how she was taking the news of her son's murder. Her creased clothes and inflamed eyelids gave her away. A slight tremble came over the woman as she lowered the poodle to the floor. Both dogs continued to bark until a much older man in a leather waistcoat came out. He led the dogs into the living room before shutting them in.

The outside of the house clearly reflected what the inside was like. The couple had more cabinets and shelves full of tat than Gina could take in, from models of hula dancers to toys collected from McDonald's Happy Meals. The hoard never ended.

'Come into the kitchen. We'll be able to hear ourselves speak in there.'

Gina and Jacob waded through the hoarded boxes of laundry powder and the recycling pile. The kitchen table was covered in dusty pots full of dying spider plants.

'I'm so sorry that we had to give you such terrible news, but it would really help us if we got to know a little more about Alexander,' Gina said.

The woman slumped into a rickety chair. 'He hated his full name. It was Alex.' Gina sat on the bench along the back wall so that Jacob could get in next to her. The warmth of the house and the smoke from whatever they'd been burning under the grill was almost suffocating. Gina coughed a little, trying to ignore the smell of rot that hung in the air while trying to see through the dispersing smoke.

'D'ya wan' a drink?' The man held a crud-infested cup up.

'No, thank you,' Jacob replied. Gina smiled, pleased that he'd read her mind.

He poured Eveline Peterson a brandy and held it out to her.

She took the glass and stared into the deep amber liquid, her head bowed, exposing white roots in her crimson red hair. 'I've read the papers today. I know what happened to him, I can't—' She stared into the glass and made a click noise as she swallowed. 'It's turning my stomach now.' She took another sip and winced. 'I don't normally drink.'

'We're definitely not judging you, Mrs Peterson.'

'Oh, stop with the Mrs. It's Miss, but I prefer Eveline. Peterson,' she said with a smile as she stared vacantly into her drink. 'Alex took his father's name when I had him but we never married. We were meant to, but he sadly died of cancer at a young age.'

'I'm sorry to hear that.' Gina tilted her head slightly.

'It was a long time ago. Gareth brought him up, didn't you, love?'

The man nodded and sat beside her. 'We did everything we could for him. Gave him whatever we could afford. I loved him like my own boy, he was my own. He even called me Dad.' The man looked to one side and scratched the dimple in his stubbly chin.

'How often did you see Alex?'

'Never.' Eveline began circling the rim of her glass with her finger. 'We had to sever contact for our own health. When he started taking drugs, we just couldn't cope with him any more.' She wiped her eyes. 'We should have done more.'

Her partner lay a chubby hand across her shoulder and pulled her towards him. 'We did everything we could. Don't upset yourself over that, love.' He kissed her on the side of the head. 'Eveline and I have been through a lot. We helped him so many times. He had a lovely wife and they had a beautiful baby boy, then he went and blew it all.' The man fiddled with a stray hair under his chin. 'After his redundancy things slowly got worse. He'd sit at home and fester all day, feeling inadequate as they struggled from hand to mouth each month. I mean, his wife had a good job an' all, but they both needed to work.' The man paused. 'We didn't know he had a problem before it was too late. He was already addicted to heroin. Nicky threw him out and he ended up here. It wasn't safe for him to be around the baby with him being on drugs all the time. He ran up debts and then the bailiffs took Nicky's car. 'Orrible times, they were.'

'So he came to live with you?'

Eveline nodded and wiped her nose. 'It was summer last year. We wanted to help get him off the drugs and we helped get him onto a methadone programme. We had a lot of hope until he strayed off the path again. He stole from us, used my credit card and got me into debt. He sold my dead grandmother's wedding ring. All that could have been forgiven but he became violent when he couldn't get his own way and started smashing the house up. We were scared of him – he kicked one of my dogs – and the neighbours fell out with us. It took weeks after we told him to leave for him to stop coming around. He threw a brick through the front window, poured paint stripper on our car, sent threatening messages. We couldn't cope. He was no longer my son. I didn't have a choice when I made him leave.' She began to sob. 'Maybe I should've tried harder to get him back on the drug programme, but he blew it and he didn't want it.'

'You did try 'ard, love. We did everything.'

She sniffled. 'And we failed, because he's dead.'

Jacob scribbled a few notes and Gina looked down. She could see the lines of pain etched into their faces. 'I'm sorry and I know this is hard for you. When did you ask him to leave?'

'It was last September. The last time we heard from him was in November of last year. We keep in touch with Nicky as we see little Joshua quite regularly. She'd have told us if she'd seen him.'

'We'll take Nicky's details after we've finished speaking, if that's okay? Do you know where he went after he left you?'

Eveline shook her head and blew her nose. 'He said he was getting as far away from us and Nicky as possible. He hated us all.'

'I'm sure that was the drugs talking.' Gina wanted to offer Eveline a bit of comfort. 'Did you know he'd come back to Cleevesford?'

'No. I know what he did was bad but if I knew he was back, I'd have gone out looking for him. We had no idea.' A few wisps of her red hair fell over her face as she hunched over the table and began playing with a spider plant leaf, wiping the dust with her finger from base to tip. 'I feel terrible as we'd started to live again. I'd convinced myself he'd made a new life and things were better for him. I lied to myself so that I could get on with life. Maybe I was being selfish but things got easier. We managed to laugh again, we went on holidays, we had fun, and all this time he was out there, suffering, and now he's been murdered.'

A lump formed in Gina's throat. The baggage this poor couple were carrying felt greater than her own. She couldn't imagine losing her grown up daughter, Hannah, in such a way. She couldn't imagine the heartache it would cause her and her young granddaughter, Gracie. Pushing that image out of her mind, she looked up. 'Is there anything else you can tell us? What was he like before all this?'

'He was always a handful. Nicky put up with a lot. He was a drinker and he was a bit of a wild child. He got into trouble at school for not doing homework, skipping classes and occasionally for minor scuffles. We hoped he would calm down. We're not aggressive in any way or form. I don't know where he got it from. When he met and married Nicky, we couldn't have been happier. He seemed calmer for a few years. He settled into a job at a medical supply factory on the industrial estate. We were so proud when he became a line supervisor. It doesn't sound much but it was a lot for him. For the first time in his life, he seemed calm and settled, then the baby came along. All was fine for a bit then redundancies were announced and, unfortunately, he was on the list. After that, all he could get was low paid, short-term agency work. He'd gone from a respectable salary to odd-jobbing for minimum wage. They'd cancel him some days, at the last minute. With every job rejection, he became more and more depressed. That was the start of it all.'

Eveline licked her dry lips. 'Can I see him now?'

Gina smiled sympathetically and nodded. 'Of course. We'll be with you the whole time. If there's anything else you think of to tell us or ask, just go ahead. Here's my card just in case you need to contact me after.' She passed her card over the table.

Something niggled Gina about Eveline but she couldn't think what it might be. She took another glance around the room, then back at the couple. No, it wasn't coming to her at all.

'I saw the news earlier. That letter from the murderer, it mentions you.'

A judder filled Gina's chest as her heartbeat began to ramp up. She now officially hated the press more than ever. Compromising their case was unforgivable. 'Yes, that's right. I'm going to be working hard on this case and I will find your son's murderer. One last thing, can you think of anyone else who might have a grudge against him?' *Please don't mention that letter again.* She loosened her clenched fists.

Eveline shook her head. 'Maybe the debt collectors and anyone else he may have stolen from. He'd fallen out with everyone in his life. The problem is, I don't know who any of these people are.'

Gina pulled her car keys from her pocket and kept glancing at Eveline. She was sure she hadn't met Eveline before but her mind was on full alert. There was something about the woman in front of her that gave her an overwhelming sense of déjà vu.

CHAPTER TWENTY-SEVEN

'Well, the morgue wasn't as bad as I thought it might be,' Jacob said as he offered Gina a cherry drop.

'No, thanks.' Gina paused as they pulled into Nicky Swinton's road. It was time to speak to Alexander Swinton's wife. Even though they hadn't been together any longer, Gina hoped she might be able to help.

'You look like your mind's whirring away.'

It was, in more ways than one, and she couldn't shake any of it. 'There was something about Eveline, something I can't put my finger on. Did you get the same feeling?' It was annoying her now. Normally her mind made links with ease, especially when it came to recognising someone. Maybe she was following the wrong links.

'I can't say I did, guv.' The smell of cherry came at her when he spoke.

'Why don't houses have numbers on doors any more? We're on the right side. It's an even number.'

Jacob glanced out of his side, squinting in the darkness. 'There. It has to be this one. Pull over.'

A street lamp caught a glint of frost shimmering on the top of a car. Gina pulled up next to the new-build semi and grabbed her bag. 'Let's see what his wife has to say. We know that Eveline Peterson called her earlier so she's clued up on what's happened. Let's hope that she can give us a breakthrough on this case. Whoever murdered Alex wanted him to suffer. Who hated him that much and why? Maybe Mrs Swinton knows.'

He crunched and swallowed his sweet before opening the car door, letting the frosty air in. Gina shivered as she hurried to the house, not wanting to get any colder than she had to. She heard a youth shout and several others laugh in the distance.

'Bloody Halloween.' A plastic skeleton dangled from the knocker. Gina tapped, trying not to disturb it.

Light seeped through the glass panel on the side of the door and the woman answered. Her long, brushed back fringe bobbed over the sides of her short hair as she removed her black-framed glasses and placed them on her head. 'Hello.'

'DI Harte and DS Driscoll. We were hoping we could talk with you.'

She nodded slowly and opened the front door. 'I've just got Joshua to sleep, so if we could speak quietly, that would be great.'

'Of course.' Gina stepped onto the mat and wiped her feet.

'Shoes off, I'm afraid.'

Gina and Jacob balanced on the tiny mat as they fought with their zips and laces. Mrs Swinton's house was a far cry from Eveline's. There was no clutter anywhere. Shiny wooden flooring led the way to the lounge. A tiny log burner filled the corner of the room and each log looked like it had been perfectly stacked. Gina sat on the two-seater sofa next to the copper pipe industrial lamp, allowing her gaze to be drawn to the crackling log on the fire.

'So, how can I help you?' Mrs Swinton sat in the peacock-coloured chair and crossed her legs.

'First of all, I'll start by saying that we're sorry for your loss.'

'Don't be.' The woman's angular features made her look quite stern and her lack of emotion added to it.

Gina cleared her throat. The woman in front of her didn't need or want sympathy.

Jacob took out his notebook.

'Mrs Swinton, can you tell us a little about your relationship with Alexander Swinton?'

She nodded. 'It's Nicky, please. I'm in the process of reverting back to my maiden name too. The less my son and I associate with the troubles of my now ex-husband, the better. For the purposes of us talking now, I'm still Swinton. Alex was my biggest mistake. I don't know what I ever saw in him. He was nothing more than a controlling drunk. Of course, I didn't see it at the beginning. He was funny, daring and, dare I say it, full of bold romantic gestures. I kept trying to make it work but he kept letting me down. His mother will tell you how he'd changed when he got the job at the medical supply factory but he hadn't. I gave him an ultimatum. Stick at a job or you're out.'

'What happened then?' Gina felt her face flush on the one side as the fire roared.

'He didn't get made redundant like she thinks. I told him to tell her that because I didn't want Eveline to be upset. She's so sensitive to the little things. I think, deep down, she was on tenterhooks, waiting for him to screw up. He'd been a difficult child and that continued into young adulthood. Anyway, he'd already had a warning for turning up at work stinking of booze and he did it again. They sacked him.' Nicky clasped her hands in her lap and stared at the fire. 'Can I get you both a drink?'

They shook their heads. Gina wanted a hot drink more than anything, but she didn't want to disturb Nicky Swinton's flow. 'No, thank you.'

'That's when things got really bad. It was mid to late last year. He became impossible to live with. His anger would scare Joshua. He'd put his fists through doors and he even flung a plate at me. He used to disappear on benders for days at a time and one time, when he was gone, I went through his things in the garage and found all the debt letters. Mostly short-term, high interest loans. There were credit cards that had been maxed to the full. I panicked and called him over and over again but he didn't answer or come home this particular time. He must've guessed I'd found them. That's when the bailiffs called and they took my car. The only thing we'd bought in his name was the car. They took the TV too as that was in his name. I tell you something, it felt like the end of the world that day.'

'Must have been worrying times.' Gina tilted her head to one side.

'They were. It wasn't all bad. The house was in my name. I bought this house before we met and I never added him to the mortgage – I will be forever grateful for that. I worked hard before I even knew him and I've almost paid the mortgage off. If I'd added him to the paperwork, all this,' she held her palm out, 'would have been used to pay off his debts and Joshua and I would have nowhere to live.'

Gina fidgeted in the seat and tried to create a small gap between her and Jacob as their legs pressed together. This wasn't a settee that a person was meant to lounge on, more style over substance. 'What happened when he eventually came back?'

'He was on something and I knew the problem was bigger than drink. He looked vacant and demanded to come in when he saw all his belongings bagged up on the drive. I'd changed the locks and that fuelled his anger even more, then I told him what had happened with the bailiffs and that I was so fed up of being let down. He pleaded for another chance. I couldn't put myself or our son through any more and, if I'm honest, I'd fallen out of love with him – that's if I ever was in love with him. He left.'

'Did he come back after that?'

Nicky nodded. 'Many times. He'd turn up at any hour. He scratched my new car. He'd shout through the letterbox and generally make a nuisance of himself. I rammed a broom handle through the letterbox into his stomach. He didn't come back after that.'

After all Nicky had been through, she still managed to defend herself with such confidence. 'Did you ever report this?'

She shook her head. 'No, I didn't want the fuss. Eventually he stopped coming so as far as I was concerned, it was all over. I picked up my life and rebuilt it. I'm still short on cash, but we manage. I had to get extra work for a while. Things improved and they continue to do so.' For the first time, Nicky smiled.

'What is it you do?'

'I'm the purchase manager at Arkel Bond Engineering over on Cleevesford Industrial Estate.'

The heat was taking all the moisture from Gina's sore lips. She unbuttoned her coat before she began to sweat.

'Did you know that Alexander was back in Cleevesford?'

Nicky Swinton stood and walked over to the fire. She drew the poker, opened the little window and prodded the log. 'Yes. I saw him.'

Gina leaned back into the cushion. It was possible that she didn't want her drug-addicted ex-husband back in her life causing trouble, but to what lengths would she go to ensure that never happened again? 'And where was that?'

'I wasn't sure it was him at first. I was driving and I saw this man hurrying down George Street. It was dark but he stopped under a street lamp and was fumbling in his pockets. I was being held up by a learner so I wasn't going fast. Then, I looked closer at him just as I passed. I knew it was him straight away. I then caught another glimpse of him in the rear-view mirror and watched as he cut through the old terraced cottages.'

Gina felt a slight surge of adrenaline running through her body. That was a route they needed to check out, see if it would lead them to something useful. She undid her coat a little more as her face continued to burn. 'Did you speak to him, or confront him?'

'No way. I didn't want him hanging around here again. I must admit, I couldn't sleep once I'd seen him. I was sure he'd come here for something, for money maybe, but he didn't. After that, I avoided driving up that road altogether. I thought no more about it until Eveline rang me up to tell me what had happened.' She paused. 'I couldn't tell Eveline that I'd seen him. She was so upset when she called me from the airport and I didn't need her telling me that I should have scooped him up from the street and brought him back into my home. I have Joshua to think of. He comes first.'

'So, let me get this right' – Jacob was catching up with his notes – 'you didn't see him again after that?'

She removed her glasses from her head and placed them on a side table, next to her book. 'No.'

'When was this?'

The woman grabbed her phone from the arm of the chair and began scrolling. 'It was Monday the twenty-sixth of October. I was driving to the childminder's house from work.' She scrunched her brow. 'I don't know why I felt the need to note that down in my diary. I suppose I expected him to cause trouble so keeping a log would have been the sensible thing to do. I vowed that if he came back, I would call the police this time. Our ties were well and truly severed and he hadn't lived here for over a year.'

Gina's mind went back to the night she and Briggs were in the café. Their victim had come in and caused a small amount of commotion. Then the kids had attacked another kid by the bus stop. She had chased them all the way to that row of cottages but they got away. Then, she had headed back and bumped into their victim at the back of the houses that lined the road. Last she saw of him was when he stood outside the accountants. Then he was gone. 'What time was this?'

'I worked over, so I would say about six thirty, or maybe nearer to seven. I don't know exactly.'

Gina glanced over. That would be about right. He must have gone that way after Gina had seen him outside the accountants.

'Thank you. Is there anything else you can tell us about him that might help with our enquiries? Did he have any enemies that you might know of?'

She threw her shoulders back and ruffled the curtains with the back of her head. 'I wouldn't know where to start. He owed a lot of money to people and caused a fair bit of disturbance around here. I don't think anyone on this road liked him. Do I think any of them would kill him? No, I don't.' She stared at the floor. 'There is something strange that I saw but it might be nothing. On the night I saw him, on the Monday…' She paused. 'When he stopped to rummage in his pockets, someone a few paces back ducked behind a car. I thought it was probably just teenagers playing about as Halloween was close.'

'Could you tell us anything about this person, anything at all?'

'They were more female shaped, wider hips than a man. It was so fast, I don't remember anything else. I just caught a glimpse but it did seem odd.'

A few minutes later, they wrapped up the conversation. Gina stood. 'Thank you. We'll keep you informed with what—'

'I don't want to know.' The woman swallowed and looked away. 'I'm managing to keep it all together now. It's been a hard year. My son and I just need to move on. Besides, Eveline will probably be told. When I'm ready to hear, I'll call her.'

'You have my card. If you do remember anything else, please call me.'

The woman nodded and showed them to the door, locking it behind them. As they reached the end of the path, Gina saw a teen dressed up in a cloak and a scream mask throwing custard on a car. He removed his mask. Gina bolted for the youth. 'Police!'

They had their Justin Bieber lookalike. The sound of footsteps scurrying off in all directions faded. His gang had deserted him. The boy smirked.

'You need to come with us. Criminal damage and causing alarm and distress is no laughing matter.'

He wasn't getting away this time. He slumped his shoulders and dragged his feet all the way to her car. Caught red-handed.

Maybe, just maybe, he disappeared in the same direction that Alexander Swinton did on Monday. And then there was the matter of this boy's attack on the other boy to deal with.

CHAPTER TWENTY-EIGHT

'Well, that was exceptional as usual.' Isaac smirked and scraped the dining chair along the tiled floor, standing with his cigarettes in hand.

'It's a shame Penny wasn't feeling too well.' Cherie knew that was a lie, but Marcus hadn't wanted Christian and Joanna to know about their argument.

'Bloody drama queen,' Isaac muttered. 'Do you mind if I pop out for a cigarette?' His intense stare meeting Cherie as he awaited an answer.

Cherie had barely touched her food. Each time she'd placed the slimy pasta in her mouth, it cloyed in her throat, and now the moment that was causing all her angst had finally arrived. 'Of course not. Go ahead.' She threw her serviette to the table. 'I might join you for some fresh air.' She wafted her top. It was time to talk. 'It's warm in here, what with the cooking.' She glanced at her water glass next to all the empty wine glasses. If there was a time she really needed a drink, it was now – desperately.

Christian began collecting the dirty plates, dutiful as always. 'I'll clear up and get dessert plated while we take a break. I'm stuffed at the minute.' He patted his belly, then he smiled and carried on, not suspecting anything was amiss.

Cherie knew that everything was amiss and for once she was glad that the kids had gone to stay with Christian's parents for the night. He'd reminded her that the kids could enjoy a little Halloween fun without her weird behaviour ruining it for them. Also, something was brewing and it wasn't good.

Marcus had seemed deep in thought as he'd pushed his pasta around the plate and Isaac had kept nudging him under the table as if to say, calm it down. Then Cherie had caught herself staring at Marcus. Isaac had also appeared to be deep in thought and had occasionally snorted through his nose as if suppressing a laugh. Cherie had felt the table judder as Marcus then kicked Isaac under the table. Tensions were definitely simmering over.

Joanna began collecting used serviettes from the table, passing them to Christian. 'So, how are the kids?' Relief washed over Cherie. She could leave Christian and Joanna talking while they all went into the garden.

Isaac grabbed his old bomber jacket and left the room with a cigarette dangling from his mouth, looking like he didn't have a care in the world. That was typical of him. Cherie always said that he never took anything seriously.

Marcus almost fell over the door frame.

Christian left the plates for a moment. 'You okay, mate?'

'I… I think so. It's the wine. I should have taken a leaf out of Cherie's book and stayed away from it. Nothing a bit of fresh air won't sort.'

Cherie's heart boomed away. She knew Marcus wasn't okay. Her so-called friend was getting too wasted. They'd all known each other a long time and Cherie could sympathise with Marcus. This was typical Penny – save it all up until it needed to escape in such a way that a trail of destruction had been left. It was the same when Penny told Marcus that she'd been sleeping with a colleague. He'd badgered her until she just blurted it out at a family party in front of his grandmother, but all that had happened years ago. Marcus had forgiven her and they'd moved on. 'Come on, Marcus.' Cherie grabbed his arm. 'Let's get some fresh air and have a catch up.'

'Good idea,' Marcus said as he wiped the sweat from his brow, just under his bleached hairline. 'Wait.' He leaned over and pulled a spliff from his pocket. 'I think this will lighten the tension around here. It will for me, anyway.' He began to half-stagger past her.

'No, it won't.' Cherie nudged him, hoping that Christian hadn't heard. The little smoke was something they'd always done when they'd got together as a reminder to each other that their secret had remained in the box for another year and that they all depended on each other's silence to keep it locked away. 'Put it away. You need your thoughts on Penny at the moment. What if she calls and you're stoned?'

'What's going on?' Christian leaned in as he walked across the kitchen holding the tiramisu. 'Is everything alright with Penny? I thought it was just a twenty-four hour thing.'

'It is. Penny's having a hard time at work too. Stress.'

Christian gave a sympathetic smile. 'Send her our love.'

Cherie brushed her hair from the corner of her mouth as her stare bored into Marcus's. 'I'm sure it's nothing that won't sort itself out.'

'Well, if there's anything we can help with, just shout.'

Christian, always wanting to help. All she wanted him to do was carry on faffing with his tiramisu so that they could talk. Marcus headed to the garden to be with Isaac, leaving Cherie standing in the doorway of the kitchen. 'I'll be back in five.' Christian had barely noticed her speaking as he turned back to Joanna and laughed at some anecdote she was telling him. Joanna then leaned over in her leopard print miniskirt to pick a piece of bread up and her auburn locks reached the kitchen floor.

'Cherie,' Isaac called.

'Coming.' She left them to it and hurried outside where they sat at the old patio set, passing the spliff around. Despite the wine, her friends suddenly seemed sober, like the evening had been nothing more than an act.

Isaac snatched the spliff from Marcus and trod it into the ground. 'Okay, which one of you sent the message? No games, just out with it.' The security light glinted off his nose ring as he leaned back in the creaky patio chair.

Marcus glared. 'I received one. It just says, I know everything.'

'Same,' Isaac replied.

Little did they know that Cherie was keeping some secrets of her own and she wasn't about to reveal her hand.

'Penny said I've been acting weird and I was when I received the message. I didn't know whether to say something to her so I didn't. She didn't mention that she had one but then again, she doesn't tell me much.' Marcus slammed his fist onto the glass table, sending the plastic potted cactus bouncing close to the edge. He exhaled plume after plume of white mist into the cold night as he seethed.

Isaac was grinding his teeth. 'You should have asked her. It's typical of you, Marcus. You're a self-centred prick sometimes.'

'What? Me? Penny walked out on me yesterday morning. I've got enough on my plate. You always did just think about yourself.'

Isaac flung a hand in the air for attention. 'What do we know? There's a freak killer on the loose and they killed Alex. He was our friend. Okay, he was a drug addict. He had problems and enemies. He's killed, then we receive weird text messages.' He stared at Marcus, then Cherie and not one of them cracked. 'Whoever sent these messages knows everything.'

'I don't know who I can trust any more.' Cherie tried to hide her trembling hands.

'Oh, shut up.' As Isaac's gaze fixed on Cherie's, her heart felt as though it was about to burst from her chest. She wasn't going to give him the satisfaction of seeing through her. She was sure that Alex's murder wasn't random. 'Let me see your messages.'

'I deleted mine,' Marcus replied. 'I know Penny has been looking through my phone and I didn't want to worry her.'

'I deleted mine too. I just thought it wasn't meant for me.' Isaac sat back with a grin across his face as if he thought he was clever by doing so. 'How about you, Cherie? When did you receive your message?'

She hadn't received anything, but she wasn't going to bring suspicion upon herself. Were they all lying about this message? Maybe it was a trap. For a second it felt as though their menacing eyes were on her, like they knew something but weren't letting on. 'It was about a week ago but I deleted it too. I didn't want Christian to see it.' She paused. 'So, who's lying? Isaac, don't play games with me. Did you send the message? I just need to know. It'll be all *haha, very funny*. A bit of a sick thing to do but then again, we know you're not normal in that sense.'

Isaac half-turned away. 'Shut up, Cherie.'

The stares continued. They knew she was lying.

Marcus broke away first and took a few steps towards the end of the garden. He glanced back, wide-eyed and with a deathly expression. 'I can't do this. I've had enough. I don't bloody well know why I came tonight. I should have stayed at home in case Penny came back.' He flung the gate open and stomped away, leaving it slamming on its hinges.

Cherie folded her arms. 'You have to go and see if he's alright.'

'You're serious? He's a grown man and he's on one.'

'Just go.'

'Are you lot coming in for dessert?' Joanna peered out of the door. 'It's chilly out here.' She glanced at the gate. 'Where's Marcus?'

'Just hold dessert. I'll see if he's okay, he wasn't feeling too well.' Isaac raised his eyebrows and headed out of the back gate.

'Okay. Shall I get my shoes?' Joanna bit her bottom lip.

'No, we've got this. He's just had a bit too much to drink.' Isaac kissed her and called out Marcus's name as he hurried along the path.

Cherie ran to the shed and grabbed her emergency bag, the special one she kept hidden under years of clutter and clutched it in her shaking hands. 'Tell Christian we'll be back in a minute.'

She closed the back gate as she left, hearing Isaac calling out for Marcus in the distance. She'd head the other way.

Cherie pushed past two teens. One was holding a glowing pumpkin and the other made her jump as he set off a banger. 'You know you kids shouldn't be out after what happened.'

'Whatever,' the lanky lad said.

'Have you seen a man come past? A bit drunk-looking, cardigan, bleached blond hair, about so tall.' She held her hand up, marking an estimate of Marcus's height.

He pointed. 'That way.'

Cherie took a deep breath. That way would eventually lead to Penny and Marcus's home by foot. It was the quickest route. He'd just gone home.

'Watch out for the creepy person in the black coat who was lurking around. We couldn't see his face but he was well creepy.' The shorter lad burst into laughter before throwing another banger in her direction.

They laughed at her flinching in response and a shiver ran through her. An image of a huge dark hood covering the tops of her own eyes came back to her. She peered into her emergency bag and clasped it shut before the lads could see what was in it. 'Did you see what they looked like?'

'Nah. They were just hanging around watching the gardens. He nearly shit himself when he saw the creep.'

The other boy slapped his friend. 'No I didn't. You're a prick, you are.'

'Did so! Don't suppose you've got any money. Trick or treat?'

Cherie ignored the cheeky pair and headed further away from the house. She had no idea who she could trust any more. She gripped her bag like everything depended on it. It had everything she needed in it, just as she'd planned if a situation like this arose. She had something she desperately needed to do and it didn't involve anyone at the dinner party.

CHAPTER TWENTY-NINE

'That's Nicola Swinton and Eveline Peterson interviewed. I feel as though we have a more rounded picture of our victim.' She let that thought dwell a little longer than she should have. Was she a victim, given that she was the chosen subject and recipient of the sinister letters? She bit her bottom lip, almost drawing blood. 'Any further questions on what I've just told you?' Gina waited as O'Connor, Wyre, Jacob and PC Smith finished writing their notes.

'Have we managed to identify our Justin Bieber lookalike?' Briggs entered with a drink in his hand.

Gina nodded. 'Yes, he's in interview room one. The good news is, he turned eighteen yesterday. His name is Logan Jones. I want to speak to him when I've finished here.'

Briggs took a seat around the table. 'What did you pull him in for again?'

'I witnessed him vandalising someone's car. Not exactly crime of the century but it got him in here so I can talk to him. He was one of the kids we saw picking on the boy at Cleevesford High Street, this past Monday. More than anything, I'm hoping he can help with our murder case but he can wait a short while. Any luck with the local drug addiction services? Did anyone recognise our victim's name?'

Wyre smiled. 'Yes, Alexander Swinton has a counsellor called Maurice Dullard. His details are on the system and he's more than happy to speak to us. He said he was deeply saddened by the news but there is one other thing: he saw our victim a couple of weeks ago. Mr Swinton wanted to refer himself back onto the programme which is why he'd got back in touch with Mr Dullard.'

'I'll head over to speak to him first thing. Great work on finding that out. Right, how are we getting on with identifying where our coffin may have come from?'

Wyre flicked over a few sheets of paper and pulled out a folder. 'So far, I've managed to collate a lot of information.' She pulled out several packs and passed them around. 'This is a list of all the funeral directors in the area and beneath it is a list of companies selling coffins on the internet. This was a huge task so I'm certain I haven't found them all but I'll keep ploughing on. There are hundreds selling coffins but only about twenty funeral directors within the primary catchment area we're looking at.'

'Have you managed to send a photo of our coffin to any of them yet? We obviously need to identify where it came from.'

Wyre nodded, her black fringe slightly obscuring the tops of her eyes as she bowed over to read her notes. 'Seven funeral directors have got back to us. None of them sell this coffin. The online coffin makers come from all over the world. So far, we've contacted over one hundred by email and we've had just over twenty replies. None of them sell or make this exact coffin either.'

Gina pulled out a print from the pile of paper in front of her and pinned it to the board. 'This email came just as we got back to the office. Keith has been going through all the items that were taken from the scene and that obviously included the coffin. We didn't see this at the time, but on the bottom end of the coffin, inside, there is a tiny engraving. Look close, what do you see?'

The detectives all leaned in and squinted at the printed photo. 'Is it a wolf, guv?' O'Connor said as he tapped his fingers on the table.

'It looks like it could be a wolf. I'm guessing this is the maker's mark. The coffin looks to be hand-crafted. This is a highly skilled piece of work. Start adding the word "wolf" to your searches. This is as good as the artist's signature. We just need to find the artist. O'Connor, how are things going with the door-to-doors and collection of CCTV?'

He stopped tapping his fingers and sat up from his slouch position. 'Still nothing that will help with the case. We're struggling to get any useful CCTV. Most cameras point at cars and drives. All I've seen are a few kids dotted around, knocking on doors in costume, but that's it.'

'Keep at it. We spoke to the vicar, Sally Stevens. She said she saw someone loitering in her graveyard wearing a long hooded black coat. On any of the CCTV, did you see anyone matching this description?'

He shook his head. 'No. Sorry, guv. Most of the kids were dressed in shop-bought costumes. A lot were accompanied by parents who were wearing the usual garb, coats, hats and scarves. There are so many, but I didn't see any long black coats with hoods.'

'Great work. Keep searching. We can't afford to miss anything.' Gina popped another pin in the map. 'This pin represents where Nicola Swinton claims to have seen our victim on Monday night, at six thirty. As mentioned, she drove past and saw him turn off by this row of houses.' Gina pointed to George Street, this time a little further up. 'Somewhere around here, she says she saw someone ducking behind a car when Mr Swinton turned. This suggests he was being followed. Mrs Swinton is also quite sure it was a woman but I think that's a long shot, given that it was dark and it happened quickly.'

'What's down that cut through?' O'Connor asked.

'As far as I'm aware, some land where kids play football, a park and another housing estate. PC Smith, I'll task you with researching this area a little better. We need to know where he went. Was he sleeping rough around there? Maybe he was hiding in someone's garage or shed. It's been wet and cold lately, he'd have definitely been seeking shelter. He smelled of smoke, look for evidence of bonfires.'

Smith smiled and jotted down a note. 'That'll be fun this close to bonfire night, but we can but do our best. I'll get on to it. I just saw PC Kapoor go past. Shall I fill her in?'

'That would be great, thank you.' Gina glanced back at Wyre. 'Did you find anything about the gravestone I gave you to research?'

'I'm still looking, it was a long time ago.'

Gina pulled out a note from her wad of pages. 'I know why Eveline was giving me such a sense of déjà vu. It was right under my nose all the time. Whether there's a connection, that's another matter completely.' She smiled as she shared her thoughts, leaving Wyre with a new lead to follow as she headed along the corridor to see Logan Jones.

CHAPTER THIRTY

'I'm sorry. I was a prick. Can I just apologise to the woman and maybe offer to wash her car? It'll clean up okay.' Logan Jones laid his scream mask on the table and ran his finger through his brushed-up fringe. Gina could only imagine how much hairspray it took to have kept it that way under a mask and hat. His Dracula-style cape was tied in a neat bow that skimmed his Adam's apple. Jacob cleared his throat as he headed up a witness sheet with all the boy's details.

'PC Smith will be here to discuss that offence with you after I've asked a few questions.' She wasn't letting him off the hook without so much as a ticking off and she also needed to tackle him about the incident on Monday night. 'As you may be aware, the body of a man was found on Thursday and I'd like to ask you a few questions.'

'What?' The boy stood, knocking the chair into the wall behind. 'I didn't kill anyone. I want a solicitor.'

'I'm not suggesting that you killed anyone. I'm hoping that you can help us with our enquiries, but it is your prerogative to have a solicitor present if you want one.'

The boy glared at her and shook his head twice, his brows furrowed before sitting back down. 'I don't know anything. I only know what Tilly told me.'

'Tilly Holden?' Gina flicked back to her note on the girls who found the body.

'Yeah, her and her mate found the coffin. It really freaked her out.'

Gina linked her fingers on the table and leaned in a little. 'I need you to go back to Monday, the twenty-sixth of October, around five thirty in the evening. My DCI and I saw you and several others physically assaulting a boy.'

'We were messin'. That's all. We all do it to each other all the time. It wasn't how it looked. He trod on my phone and thought it was funny. I wasn't layin' the boot in, I was just tryin' to scare him. That was all. We've made up since. You can ask him. Been best friends again since Tuesday morning.'

'What's his name?'

'Spencer Burrows. I don't know his address. It's all sorted, like I told you.'

Gina made a note with the intention of coming back to that incident after. 'You ran away when we came over and spoke to you.'

The boy shrugged. 'I panicked. You didn't see the build-up and I knew you'd jus' jump to your own answers and Spence was pissed off at the time. I didn't need the hassle.'

'I chased you down George Street. Where did you go after that?'

His shoulders slumped. 'Just walkin' around. We all met up at the park, even Spence turned up. If it was that bad, he'd have gone 'ome, wouldn't he?'

'Did you see this man on the corner of George Street or while you were at the park?'

The boy stared at the photo with his mouth open. 'Yeah, and I remembered seeing him. Tilly messaged me the photo the papers had printed and said he was the man they found in the coffin and it clicked.'

'What clicked, Logan?' Gina felt her feet urging to tap under the table as the tension of what he might say got real.

'Am I in trouble for not callin' in when I saw his picture on Facebook? I didn't call because we ran away from you and I didn't want to get into trouble.'

'We just want to know what you saw. This man was murdered and whoever did this is dangerous. We need your help, that's all.'

He leaned back and smirked. 'You're not trying to trick me or nothin'?'

'No, this isn't a trick. What clicked?'

'Flamin' hell. I'm not normally such a dick but the others were calling him names when he ran past so I joined in. It's not cool to stand out but I don't expect you to understand. We've seen him a few times. We call him baldy and tramp, normally. We badgered him until he gave us a few cigarettes. I just think he wanted us to do one.' Gina felt the tension forming in her neck. Logan was a regular bully, but at the moment she needed him to keep talking. 'I've been an idiot.'

'It's not too late to make amends for the things you've done and grow up a little.'

His cheeks were rosier now and he had more of a boyish look about him. He looked more like fifteen, not his eighteen years. 'I can't make amends with him, he's dead.'

'That one, no, but anyone else you've hurt, there's no time like the present to start being nicer.'

He nodded. Maybe some people could change. She genuinely hoped that Logan could. He was still so young and she didn't want him to become a regular face at the station. She didn't want him to turn into a Terry. She could see that there was still hope.

'So you called him names. Can you tell me anything else? Did you see anyone following him?'

He shook his head.

'Just going slightly off on a tangent, do you and your friends hang around at the graveyard?' There was still a chance that the person outside the vicarage was nothing more than a childish prank, designed to scare the vicar.

'No, I don't personally. Me an' my mates mostly hang around on the football field in the park. I remember playing dare with my friends at the graveyard, but that was when we were kids.'

Gina felt a smile forming behind her stern exterior. 'When you were kids.'

'You know, about fourteen, fifteen. We told scary stories about people being buried alive and their ghosts rising at Halloween.' He paused for a moment. 'That sounds bad with what happened. They were just stories – I think. Anyway, after we'd shit ourselves out, we'd normally run away after one of us pretended to see a ghost. That sort of stuff.'

'Going back to Monday, can you tell us anything else?'

'There is somethin'.'

'Okay.' Jacob glanced at Gina.

'Can I have some Coke or a Fanta in a minute?'

Gina nodded.

'He stays at this horrid place just off Beckett Street we call the tramp house, that's where some of the homeless gather and bed down. It's just a house that is fallin' apart and 'asn't been touched for a couple of years. We go there for laughs and we saw him arguing with a woman.'

'Did you see her?'

'No, we scarpered before she came out.'

'What were they arguing about?'

'She said he had ruined everything and to shut up. That was all I heard. Can I have that Coke now?'

'PC Smith will be here in a moment, I'll send it in with him. Thank you.'

'Can I go home in a minute? I've told you everything I know.'

'We need to check a couple of things first.' There was still his young victim, Spencer Burrows to look into. 'When you do go home, I don't want to see you here again.' She smiled at him.

'You won't.'

She jotted a note on her pad.

Who wanted Alex to shut up, and why?

CHAPTER THIRTY-ONE

Cherie pulled onto the drive and swallowed as she turned her headlamps off. Christian had probably been calling non-stop and she hadn't answered at all. She took a swig of water from the bottle in her glove compartment and got out of the car, leaving her bag in the boot. That could stay there. She hadn't taken her phone; that was her very valid excuse. As far as she was aware it was still on the patio table in the back garden, turned onto silent. He peered through the window, grimacing at her every move as she slammed the car door closed.

As she reached the front door, he opened it. 'Where have you been? The others have gone home.'

'I went looking for Marcus.'

'You came back to get the car and you didn't even pop in to tell me what was happening? I've been beside myself. Marcus came back, he left his coat. He still couldn't get hold of Penny.' Christian paused. 'So, where have you been all this time?'

She pushed past him and hurried out to the garden to grab her phone.

'I tried to call.'

'I left my phone when I left to look for Marcus. How was I to know he'd come back and gone home since?' She went into their living room and stared out of the window into the garden.

He followed. 'I can't deal with this? What the hell is going on?'

'What do you mean? I was worried about Marcus. He'd had a lot to drink and was beside himself over his row with Penny. That's all there is to it.'

He shook his head and pursed his lips as he spun her around. 'I'm sick of you treating me like I'm stupid. Even Joanna thinks something is going on between you, Penny, Marcus and Isaac. What aren't you telling me?'

'What aren't you telling me? You and Joanna looked a bit cosy. I saw you glance at her arse when she bent over.'

'Don't be ridiculous. This is just another of your attempts to deflect what we're talking about. Let's start again. What aren't you telling me?'

Her shoulders slumped. 'Look, I'm not hiding anything. We all go back a long way, that's all. You know that. They're my friends and I was just looking out for them. I'm worried about Penny. I know she's done this before but you just never know. She's not answering my calls at all.' She couldn't keep eye contact any longer. She looked away.

'You've been gone nearly two hours!' Christian grabbed the plant on the windowsill and smashed it against the wall. She flinched and took a step back. This wasn't like her usually mild-mannered husband, but she'd driven him to it.

He kicked the coffee table, then the door. His dark skin looked blotchy under the eyes. 'I can't stand this any more. I stick by you through everything, the moods, the drink problem. You lose your job, I support you. You repay me by lying and hiding things – it's sending me crazy. Nothing good has ever come from your secretive behaviour. Is there someone else? Huh.'

She shook her head and wiped the tears away.

'You wouldn't tell me anyway, would you? You'd let me think I was going mad for years, then I'd find out and then you'd still lie. That's what you do, over and over again. I'm running on empty here. Just tell me what's going on.'

She went to speak but then closed her mouth. 'I can't.'

'You can but you won't. Last chance or we're done.'

She turned away and stared at the photo of her family all together on the beach during happier times. It was all a lie, she was never happy. She wasn't capable of being happy.

'If that's how you want to play it, you can sleep on the settee.' He stormed out. Seconds later, a handful of blankets flew down the stairs and landed in a heap.

She exhaled and slumped into a chair. Grabbing her phone, she pressed Marcus's number. They had to talk and it couldn't wait. She opened the back door as quietly as possible and headed out of the back gate and down the path. What she had to say couldn't be overheard.

She glanced up at their bedroom window. The curtains were already closed and the light flickered off. She didn't know how all this was going to end. All she knew was that she needed to talk right now. If she didn't, she'd explode and that scared her more than anything.

CHAPTER THIRTY-TWO

'What are you thinking?' Briggs placed the pizza box on Gina's kitchen table. She didn't need him checking on her but given that someone was out to get to her, she appreciated that he'd dropped by.

'We have Eveline Peterson, her son Alex is murdered. Then we have the stranger in the dark coat at a grave marked with Elsie Peterson's name. Same surname. Wyre is looking into this. Whatever's happening seems to be personal in every way. I've read the forensics report from the scene. It was pretty fruitless given the awful weather so I'm not holding out any hope at all for anything more substantial to come back.' She opened the lid on the pizza box and took a slice to bite into, the stringy cheese stretching from box to her chin before snapping. It cloyed against the roof of her mouth. She chewed and chewed, suddenly not wanting to swallow the food. It was as if there was a stopper in her throat.

'If we're looking at this being personal, we need to know more about his friends and family. Did you speak to his wife yet?'

She took a gulp of orange juice to force it down and threw the slice of pizza back down. 'Yes, and now I'm concerned there was more to Mrs Swinton's story than she's letting on. Was she the woman at the derelict squat on Beckett Street? The woman apparently said that he'd ruined everything and to shut up. Had he ruined her life by coming back? Mrs Swinton said he hadn't turned up at the house since coming back. Then I get thinking, the way she describes everything, how he ruined her life at the time when he ran up the debts. Why would she want him to shut up? She seemed pretty open to me.'

'I see what you mean.'

'My mind is whirring away and it's not coming back with the answers. What isn't she telling us?'

He smiled warmly. 'It'll come. There's not enough to make the links as yet.'

She finished her orange juice. 'We're meeting at the squat at eleven in the morning, hopefully we'll come out knowing more than before we went in. Do you want a beer, maybe the powers of a light alcoholic beverage might get my cogs moving a bit faster?'

'I'll have a soft version if you've got one. Got to drive home.'

Their gazes locked and Gina broke away with a smile before grabbing the two beers from the fridge.

'How are you taking everything? This murder wasn't only personal when it came to Alexander Swinton, it's personal against you. That letter must be going through your head constantly.'

She swallowed and plonked the opened beers on the table. It was going through her head, twenty-four seven. Every thought of the letters took her back to her time confined in the shed, where the walls seemed to be closing in on her. She held her expression, not wanting to give her deepest thoughts away. Briggs couldn't see that she might lose it; he might take her off the case for the sake of her own mental health. That wasn't going to happen. 'Alcohol free for you.'

He gave a little laugh. 'It's quite nice.'

As she took a gulp, she shrugged. 'It is what it is, and I have to get on with my job. It scares me that someone has chosen me in all this, but it's also made me more determined to get whoever is doing this.'

He leaned over the table and gazed into her eyes. She could see that he wanted to kiss her so she cleared her throat and sat back.

'I suppose I should get going.' She didn't disagree with him. 'Your drive-by protection is due soon, at least we're keeping an eye on you. And you have my number if you need me.'

She nodded. She had his number, she had all her locks, her alarm system and CCTV. There was no way on earth anyone was getting through all her barriers without causing a commotion. The skin on the back of her neck prickled. A flashback to her lying in the dark shed, curled up against the cold scratchy wall in only her pyjamas, made her shudder. She had only been locked in a shed and that had terrified her with its boarded-up windows. She remembered the first few hours that went slower than the rest of the weekend. The icy chill in the air. She'd grabbed some plastic bags and old sacks to wrap herself in. Hours later, she found herself talking to no one, even making jokes; lucid dreaming followed by night terrors – maybe the effects of mild hypothermia and extreme fear. The thought of being locked in a coffin to the point of losing your mind, then death, didn't bear thinking about.

'Are you okay?'

She forced a smile. 'It's like Fort Knox here. I'll be fine.' Her locks protected her from intruders but they didn't protect her from the nightmares she knew she'd have that night. She glanced at the wall clock. 'The drive-by is due in ten minutes. You best grab some pizza and go. I don't want them coming by and seeing your car here.'

He grabbed one more slice of pizza and gobbled it down. 'I'm going,' he jokingly said with his mouth full. 'But one sniff of a worry, call me immediately.'

She nodded. 'You know I will.' And she would. She knew he'd come running without any hesitation. She literally trusted him with her life.

He placed a hand on her shoulder as they stood and rubbed it gently. 'I'll message you in a bit.' With that, he grabbed his coat, swigged the rest of his drink and left, pulling the door closed behind him. Gina hurried to the living room window and gazed out as he pulled away. She dragged the curtains closed and hurried to the front door. Alarm set, deadlocks on. What did the murderer want from her? The letter that the perp had sent ran through her mind.

Trapped people, they claw, they beg, they plead.

She knew how it felt to be trapped. She closed her eyes and saw the outline of a person. Was it the same person who was following Alexander Swinton along George Street? Had they been watching her chasing the kids around the estate? Maybe she'd just got in the way at that point and chosen her as a target. No – they knew too much.

You begged, didn't you?

Wouldn't anyone beg and plead if they were being buried alive? This part of the letter didn't alarm her too much. She walked to the kitchen and took a long swig of beer. Yes it did – it did alarm her. It was as though they were watching her as Terry locked her in the shed. A cold prickle ran across the back of her neck, like someone had reached over to touch her with icy fingers, just like Terry's when he was about to throttle her.

Now I have your attention.

She felt her hands start to tremble.

Only Terry knew about her being imprisoned in their shed, but Terry was dead. The dead can't come back to life and haunt the living. Someone knew her secrets? The wind picked up and a light whistle rattled the air vent above the kitchen window. She ran over to the window and pulled the blind down. Ebony burst through the cat flap, making her heart pound. She made a gap in the blind with her fingers and peered out. The foliage at the bottom of her garden rustled as the breeze burst through.

I know. I know everything.

She stopped still in the middle of the kitchen, holding her breath.

We are the same.

'We are not the same!' She snatched the beer bottle from the table and flung it at the kitchen wall, watching it shatter as the liquid drizzled onto the floor. The cat darted up the stairs. Maybe her only way to solve this was to finally face what she did in all its glory, especially if someone knew all her secrets.

Her deep sobs made her sound as if she were choking. She murdered Terry and now he was back to make her pay.

She stumbled up the stairs and hurried to her bedroom. Then as she went to close the curtains she noticed a spec of movement amongst the trees outside. She grabbed the curtains, closing them on whatever was out there. Back to the wall, she slid down onto her bottom and closed her eyes and all she could see was Terry.

I watch.

I wait.

I am coming.

Those words wouldn't leave her. *I watch. I wait. I am coming. I watch. I wait. I am coming. I watch. I wait. I am coming.* She closed her eyes and all she could see was Terry laughing at her as he grabbed her finger and threatened to bend it back until it snapped. He was sending her crazy. 'Leave me alone,' she yelled as she burst into tears.

CHAPTER THIRTY-THREE

Sunday, 1 November

I feel almost speechless as I stare at the screen. *Say something!*
I hit a random mix of keys in a temper and then it comes to me.

DI Harte,

We'd all like to feel safe but truth is, we're not. The worst thing is, imagining you are crazy. Even worse is, believing that you are.
They make you crazy, it is their fault.
We're not crazy. We need to stand up and roar, show them who we really are.

I draw another triangle at the bottom. Again, making it so easy for you DI Harte.

I look at her face staring back at me from the board and realise I've been grinding my teeth.

I truly am sorry for what I'm about to do. Innocent casualties weren't a part of my original plan, but the plan has changed. I feel ignored and that can't happen. The whole thing is too big to remain a secret forever more.

CHAPTER THIRTY-FOUR

Gina led the way through the tiny yard at the back of Cleevesford High Street, still confused by the false awakenings she'd had during the night. She stopped in front of the gate and checked the plaque. Maurice Dullard – MBACP. Several other business plaques were screwed to the wall, architects, surveyors and a financial advisor.

'Here goes.' Jacob went through and rang the buzzer next to the door. Above them, a bird flapped and a wedge of moss hit the ground. 'That was close. Why do I have an odd sense of foreboding this week?'

'I think we all do.' Gina stared through the pane of glass, wondering which one of the three floors Maurice worked on. Eventually the man came into view around the bend on the narrow stairs, carefully navigating his hefty weight down, one careful step at a time. The man huffed and puffed as he opened the door.

'DI Harte and DS Driscoll.'

'Come in, come in.' He inhaled and wafted his face with a sheet of paper. 'Such bad news about Alex and he'd been doing so well last year. Follow me. We're on our own today so it's rather quiet here. I only came in to talk to you and sort some paperwork out.'

'Thank you for seeing us at such short notice.' Gina followed him up at a snail's pace.

The man gasped and puffed with each step and stopped on the landing of the top floor to calm his breathing down. He pulled an inhaler from his pocket and took a couple of puffs.

'To top everything off, the stupid intercom doesn't work.' He inhaled deeply, twice, and his red face began to calm down. 'I must make a note to complain to the management company, yet again. Follow me through.' His brown curly hair crowned his head, sticking out a good two inches all the way around. The snowflake patterned cardigan he wore and his wide frame gave him a cuddly look. He was like a huge bear.

Gina entered his boxy little office. Maurice gestured for both of them to sit. The textured walls were painted in a soothing duck-egg blue and the subtle lighting gave a calm ambience. A couple of pictures containing inspirational quotes adorned the walls but were slightly wonky. Gina glanced at one as Maurice squeezed himself into his chair.

'It's all about the small steps that lead to the big changes.' Maurice smiled and pointed to the picture that Gina was looking at: the one of a toddler being helped to walk by a parent. 'Alex had been doing so well. I wish he hadn't left the programme last year, maybe then we wouldn't be having this conversation now. I did everything I could.'

Gina pulled out a few notes and Jacob snatched his pen from his coat pocket and tested it on a fresh page of his notebook.

'Can I ask why Mr Swinton stopped coming last year?' Gina pulled the wooden chair towards the desk.

He opened a folder full of notes. 'He lost his job and I couldn't get through to him. After he'd been doing so well, he'd started to take drugs again.'

'Can you confirm what he was taking?'

'There is such a thing as confidentiality.'

'Mr Dullard, your client has been murdered and we need to catch whoever did this to him.'

The man sighed. 'He was a heroin addict and he'd been on a methadone programme. I'd say the breakdown of his marriage wasn't helping. He'd lost his desire to continue. He didn't turn up to all our sessions and when he did, he was on the heroin. Not everyone that gets help becomes a success story but I didn't give up hope, I never give up hope. I told him that this door was always open but I never heard from him after the end of summer. I tried to call him but by then his phone never connected the call. He never read my messages. I always hoped he'd come back to me for help, and two weeks ago, he did. I couldn't have been happier to see him. He really wanted to change and I knew the time was right for him.'

Gina opened the calendar up on her phone. 'Could you tell me when this was?'

Maurice flicked through a few sheets of paper on his desk until he pulled out a scraggy notebook containing all his appointments. 'I know we're in the digital age but I much prefer good old paper and pen for my diary keeping.' He shifted the page to the right and squinted at the page. 'It was Friday the sixteenth of October, at one in the afternoon. That's when he came in.'

'How did he seem?'

Maurice pressed his lips together and scrunched his brow. 'Subdued.'

'And what did he say?'

'He told me he was desperate to get his life back on track, that he'd been stupid and thought he was losing his mind. He was trying to come off the drugs again, but without any help. He said he'd been crawling the walls and had succumbed to another fix. He was desperate. His emotions ranged from despair then to anger. Despair at feeling as though he was failing at going it alone and anger as he was an addict. He said I was his last hope when it came to seeing his child again. He knew he'd let his parents down and he wanted to make it up to them. He wanted to see his mum again but he said he wouldn't until he was clean and he could pay the money back that he'd stolen from her. He'd come back with fire in his belly. I really thought he was ready to try the programme again and I really wanted to work with him. There's no bigger satisfaction in my job than seeing someone come out of this at the other end and win the battle against addiction.'

Jacob sat back and leaned his notebook in his lap.

'Did he say that he'd seen his wife or son?' Gina needed to establish if Mrs Swinton was telling them the whole truth.

Maurice pulled his glasses from a pouch on his desk and put them on before scanning his case notes. The little dents in his nose were highlighted by the ray of sunshine that reached through the old sash window. 'He said he'd been to the house. When I probed him further, he said he wanted to knock on the door but he couldn't. Again, he said he wanted to get better before taking that next step. In his words, he wanted his boy to be proud of him and he knew he had to earn that. Also, his wife wanted nothing more to do with him. That was something he was trying to find a solution for.'

Gina noticed that Maurice had a warm smile. She could see why Alexander Swinton would have felt comfortable with him. 'Do you know where he was staying?'

Again, Maurice flicked through his notes. 'He said he was of no fixed abode. I made a note and it simply says "*squatting*". He didn't say where. I offered him some numbers to get help, but the council is stretched and that leaves a lot of people like Alex on the street. Unfortunately, he's not alone. There are many Alexes out there with barely any help and nowhere to go. You can see why it's so easy to give up.'

'Have you heard of a squat that the kids refer to as the tramp house?'

He shook his head. 'Should I have?'

'No. One of the local teens said they'd seen him at this particular place. That's where he might have been living.'

'Sounds about right.'

'Did Alex seem worried about anything else, other than the drugs? Did he mention any enemies?'

Maurice coughed a little and banged his chest. 'That's better.' He paused and bit his bottom lip. 'He rambled on a bit and said he thought he was seeing things. He thought a woman was following him. One minute he could see her, the next she was gone. He kept saying that it was while he was high. I didn't take too much notice as he went on to talk about the weird nightmares he was having. He spoke about being trapped and not being able to get out.' Maurice shivered. 'I should have asked him more. I saw the news reports, I know what happened to him. He knew this was coming and I thought it was all in his dreams. He said they were laughing at him and taunting him while he choked.'

Gina tilted her head slightly as she tried to fathom what might have been going on in Alexander Swinton's head.

'I don't know whether that was one of his dreams or whether something like this happened. He mentioned it when talking about dreams so I didn't worry too much. He said there was no going back. He kept repeating that phrase. I thought he meant going back to his mother or wife, but maybe there was more to it.'

Jacob kept his pen on the page, noting everything down.

'Did he try to contact you for another appointment?' Gina shifted her chair slightly to avoid the sun blinding her.

Maurice shook his head. 'I wish he had. I had another appointment booked for him but he didn't turn up. That was on Monday of this week. Before hearing about him on the news, I just suspected that he wasn't as ready as he'd said he was to tackle his problem. I had no phone number or address for him so I had to leave it at that.'

'Thank you, Mr Dullard. If you can think of anything else in the meantime, here's my card.'

The man smiled. 'Will do. Do you mind if I don't show you down?'

'Of course not. We'll see ourselves out.'

As they left the building, Gina glanced back up. The autumn sun shone over the tiled rooftop, casting a slight shadow of the chimney on the road ahead. 'I want to head over to the squat.'

'Smith's team went over last night and there was no one there.' Jacob opened the car door.

'I know but that may have changed. It's an old squat. Someone might be there now. We have to try again. Someone might have seen who Alexander Swinton was talking too. Logan Jones heard a woman talking to him – we need to know who that woman was and why she was there. She is key to our investigation.'

'Let's go.'

CHAPTER THIRTY-FIVE

A large rain cloud passed the sun as Gina pulled up beside the creepy old house.

'How long has it been this bad?' Jacob peered out of the windscreen.

'Too long by the looks of it.' Gina got out of the car and took a few steps towards the house at the end of the road, masked in unruly trees and shrubs. The boarded-up windows were partly pulled off. The mesh fence had been cut several times, leaving many holes big enough for a person to climb through. 'After you.' Gina smiled and allowed Jacob to enter first.

'So, the team were here last night and found nothing.' Jacob peered up at the house.

'Not a jot. There was no one here and with all the waste and rubbish, it would take the rest of the year to get into every nook and cranny.' Gina caught her hair in a prong of metal. 'Damn.' She tore a clump away to break free.

Her gaze moved from the main door to the damaged chimney, taking in the old red brick covered in moss and tangled ivy. She shivered as her stare stopped on the cracked dormer window jutting out through the roof. Flapping came from above and a crow flew from a large gap of missing tiles.

'What a state. Is it safe to go in?' Jacob reached the front door and gave it a slight shove. As expected, it didn't open. 'By the way, the back door is broken. That's how they got in last night.' He paused. 'Do we know why it's not taped off?'

'I wanted whoever stays here to come and go as normal. Last night was low-key and that's how we need to keep it. If the occupants of this place see the police anywhere near, they'll scarper and we need to speak to them. One of them might have seen the woman who was talking to Alexander Swinton. I did ask for regular checks and I know this should be in place now. Again, everyone is keeping back and out of sight. We can't afford to alarm anyone.' Gina walked in front of Jacob, pushing away the far-reaching bramble bushes that were getting caught around her middle and ankles. 'Ouch.' A thorn pierced her trouser leg.

'You okay?'

'Yes.' She kicked the brambles away and continued, stepping over the used syringe and the empty KFC bucket. 'The back garden is worse.' Branches entwined in branches filled every inch of the space, so high, it made the back of the house dark, it felt more like early evening than morning. Gina ducked to avoid the used condom hanging from the rattling branch. 'Watch yourself.'

She knocked at the door. 'Hello, Police.' Not a sound came from behind it. She placed a pair of latex gloves over her hands, gave the door a push and it opened slightly. 'Follow closely and don't touch a thing. The officers said there were sharps everywhere.'

Wrappers on top of wrappers filled the kitchen. Grime and dirt covered everything. Gina could taste the mould and fried takeaway food at the back of her throat with every breath. She pushed open the door to one of the sitting rooms and peered through. 'No one here.' Sleeping bags were thrown around in no order. A gust of wind clattered around the house and a waft of ash flew from the fireplace. 'It looks like they were using the fire to keep warm. Maybe this was where Alexander Swinton was sleeping.' She inhaled.

Jacob heaved slightly and stepped back towards the hallway. 'I can't be done with the smell of poo and sick. Bloody hell, it's bad in here. Someone will have their work cut out.'

The door to what was once a downstairs loo stood ajar and she knew exactly where the smell was coming from. She doubted that there was any running water. 'Let's head upstairs.' She pulled her shirt up a little to cover her nose. 'Hello, Police,' she called out in a muffled voice. 'We're coming up.' Each step creaked and the old carpet resisted her steps as it clung to the soles of her boots. 'I don't think there's anyone here.' She gazed around the last few rooms and they were much the same as the living room. 'Clear.' She hurried up to the top floor and took in the sight of the missing roof tiles. Her feet squelched on the rain sodden carpet. 'It looks like no one has been up here for a long time.'

'What was that?' Jacob held his finger to his mouth and they listened.

The cluttering sound from downstairs came again. 'There's someone there.' Gina turned to take the stairs and felt her foot slip on a damp path, sending her slipping down several steps on her bottom. 'Dammit.' She pushed herself back up, but it was too late – she heard the back door slam. 'They're getting away.' Jacob slipped past her and carried on running down the stairs. She half-hobbled towards the bedroom window and wiped the filth off the flimsy pane with her sleeve.

All she could see was a blurred outline at the very back of the garden, beyond all the brambles. The figure turned and ran. Jacob emerged out of the bottom.

She pointed and shouted out, 'They went that way.' Jacob pushed through the brambles and she only hoped he'd find the way out to the other end. She suspected their stranger already knew the best way through the garden and had made the cleanest escape ever.

'Stop. We just want to talk,' she called in hope that the stranger would turn around and come back, but in her heart she knew it was too late. Whoever had come to the house had gone. She hurried down the stairs ignoring her aches and pains. 'Jacob.'

Minutes later he came back from around the front covered in bits of branch. 'I was too late, guv. They got away.' He rubbed the fine cut on his hand. 'Bloody brambles.'

'We didn't have a hope in hell of catching them and they're not likely to come back now, are they?'

He shook his head.

'I know this is a long shot, but we need forensics here. They're not going to like this one.' She paused. 'I can't help but think that we've just let Alex's murderer get away.'

CHAPTER THIRTY-SIX

Cherie caught her breath as she slammed the door. Christian pushed past her and went to the kitchen.

'I just went for a run.' She followed him through and sat at the kitchen table.

'You never go for a run.' He stared out at the drive.

'I needed to clear my head.' The stitch in her side told her how out of shape she was. She had strength but speed was her downfall. She hadn't entered a gym for years and she'd never joined Christian when he went on one of his long treks, normally when they were on holiday. 'What time are we picking the kids up?'

'We're not. I said they could stay the week. My mum said she'd take them to school and they were happy with that. They can sense we're having problems and I don't want them upset.' He placed his palm on the worktop and stared at his wedding ring.

'I want the children back here. How dare you ship them off for the week without asking me?' She kicked the table leg and winced as her big toe cracked.

'How dare I? It's not me that's been caught with booze after you promised you'd never touch the stuff again. It's not me acting all weird and secretive and losing my job. You need to sort yourself out or you'll lose me and the kids.'

'I…' She closed her mouth. Say the wrong thing now and all hell will break loose. The last thing she had the energy for was a full-on argument and this was fast becoming one. 'You're right, about the kids. We need a bit of space to sort things out.'

'You. You need a bit of space. I'm alright. I'm fine and present and calm, and I've been trying my hardest to understand but you shut me out. I feel like you're playing me sometimes, manipulating me, like I'm nothing more than a game to you and I don't like that.'

She swallowed and played with the ends of her ponytail. 'I've been selfish, for that I'm sorry.' Gazing up at him, she hoped that he'd look at her like he used to, but all she saw was pity and anger in his face.

'Are you? You always say what I want to hear. I want you to be sorry. I want change, if not for me, for our children. They need a mother who's present, not one who's in a drunken daze, dribbling and waffling on about rubbish while she lies around stinking of sweat and puke. It scares them, did you know that? When you were drunk every day, it was me who lay with them while they cried. You won't remember – you were in a drunken stupor through it all.'

A tear welled up in her eye. 'You're right. I've been a bad wife, a bad mother and a bad friend. I should call Marcus again, see how he's getting on.'

'Yes, you should. They're your friends and that's what a friend would do.' He slapped the worktop with the tea towel and threw it on the draining board before stomping out and slamming the back door. She listened as the back gate bounced on its hinges. He'd gone out and she knew he wouldn't be back for a while.

She grabbed her phone and saw the seven missed calls from Marcus and called back.

He answered on the first ring. 'What took you so long? I haven't heard from Penny for another night. Something's badly wrong. What do I do?'

She stood and stared out of the window, watching a car pass by, then a woman walking her dog on the other side of the road. 'How would I know? She's done this before after an argument. Maybe you should just back off and give her a bit of time to cool down.'

'With what happened to Alex! You're telling me to sit on this? Normally she'd have called me by now after one of her walk outs.'

'Look, I don't know what you're meant to do. Do whatever. All I'm saying is it isn't the first time she's left you for a few days after an argument. She's probably pitched up at a Holiday Inn in a huff and she's making you sweat it out. That's the most likely scenario. Call the police if you want, tell them everything. Tell them whatever. I'm fast losing the will to live.'

Silence filled the room and Marcus didn't reply. He ended the call. She slammed her phone on the worktop and placed her freezing cold fingers over her hot throbbing head. With all that went on last night, she needed a lie down, maybe then she'd have the energy to deal with the mess she'd caused but it was all getting too much. She ran the tap and began washing the grime off her trembling hands, watching the brown water turn clear. She'd gone back to a special place and sat there, hoping that the ghosts of the past would finally stop coming, but they didn't. They were just getting started. She craved a drink, needed one. Blotting out the memories was all she wanted to do.

CHAPTER THIRTY-SEVEN

'Right, we've been through our findings at the squat and I've uploaded the notes from our talk with Maurice Dullard onto the system.' Gina drew a line from the photo marked up 'squat' to the edge of the board in green pen. 'Who was at the house talking with Alexander Swinton, and did they have anything to do with his murder? If not, did they know anything about the woman who our nuisance teen, Logan Jones, heard talking to him? Also, do we still have anyone watching the house in case this person comes back?'

PC Smith nodded. 'We have someone parked just on the edge of the street, keeping an eye on it. As soon as anyone enters the building, we'll get word.'

'Good.' Gina checked her notes. 'Maurice Dullard, Alexander's drug counsellor, mentioned that Alex thought he was being followed by a woman. Along with the report by his wife, Nicola Swinton, that she saw someone she thought to be a woman following him last Monday evening, I feel that this mystery woman is the key to solving the case. Just as a matter of following up on everything, has anyone contacted Spencer Burrows, Logan Jones's victim? It is possible that he saw something too.'

O'Connor scratched his ear and leaned forward. 'Yes, he confirmed that he and Logan are best buddies again and that they always fight. He wasn't able to tell us anything about Alexander Swinton. He says he wasn't with Logan near the squat so he had nothing to add.'

'Okay, great work. Make sure you follow up on the gang of kids. Maybe one of the others saw something. Any updates on coffin makers and coffin suppliers in the area?' Gina glanced across the table at Wyre.

Wyre twisted her pen in her fingertips and popped it on the table. 'Nothing that will further the case. No missing or stolen coffins, no orders that don't tie up with deaths that have been registered. Nothing on the engraving of the wolf. I feel as though I've reached a dead end with this one.'

Gina placed both hands on the head of the table and peered across at Wyre. 'Widen the net, contact those even further out. This coffin had to come from somewhere and we need to find out where. O'Connor, with regards to Nicola Swinton, will you look a bit deeper into her life?'

He nodded. 'Of course, guv.'

'I believe Logan was telling the truth about a woman being at the squat and I can't rule her out as being the woman who followed him there. We can't take her word for it that she just drove past, saw him then carried on driving. Maurice Dullard mentioned that Alex said he'd been to Mrs Swinton's house. He may not have knocked at the door but that doesn't mean Mrs Swinton didn't see him. She may have known he was there and, from that, she'd have seen him as a threat. Would she go as far as burying him alive to get rid of him for good? It's a rather elaborate way of killing someone.'

A moment flashed through Gina's mind. While looking out of her bedroom window the previous night, she felt that someone was watching. It was something she couldn't see or prove, but there was something off, maybe a hint of a shadow that shouldn't have been there, a slight movement that couldn't have been accounted for by the breeze or wild animals. Had Mrs Swinton felt the same? Had she then seen her husband and concocted a plan to kill him? She tried to hide the shiver that took her by surprise.

'Another thing to consider. The weather made it impossible for forensics to tell how the coffin had been transported to that part of the woods; most of the soil was sludge when we got there. Logic tells me some sort of trolley was used. How did our killer get their victim there? Either more than one person is involved or separate visits were made to the burial spot. One journey to dig the hole, another to get the coffin there and a final journey to transport or lure the victim to the coffin. Did our victim know his killer and turn up willingly? Was he drugged and led there? We won't get the toxicology results back for ages but this is something we should consider. Was he wheeled on some sort of trolley? There are still so many questions that need answering. This would be a mammoth task for one person but it would be doable.'

'Could one person still transport something as bulky as a coffin?' O'Connor stretched and leaned back.

Gina pulled out a printed photo from the wad of papers in front of her. 'Yes, I did a little bit of research. Someone could have used something as compact as a jack-style coffin trolley, they fold up nicely, the wheels are designed to tackle rough terrains. Awkward but doable.' Gina paused. 'Timing is crucial. This person had to be coming and going in the middle of the night. Although not the busiest of walking routes, there are people in the woodland during the day. I can only imagine that whoever planned this is a night owl. They had to be digging and transporting the coffin while there was no one around. No one has come forward yet. If a witness had seen anyone digging or moving a coffin in the woods, given what has happened, I'm sure we'd know about it by now.'

Gina stared at the board, flitting her gaze from the crime scene photos to the people they'd spoken to. 'What are we missing? Sally Stevens, the vicar – who did she see in the graveyard? Mrs Swinton – did she hate her husband enough to do this to him? I don't believe she did, but I don't want to rule that theory out just yet. She came across as being totally open when I spoke to her.

Getting a dead body to that location would be impossible for one person. He was either lured to the location or there was more than one perp. If he was lured, it would be someone he trusted. We still know so little.' She paused and stared at the question mark next to the squat before glancing at PC Smith. 'I can't believe we let this person get away. We're all depending on your team spotting one of the squatters coming back to the house.'

'Kapoor is there now. We will not be leaving this post, I can guarantee it. I'll take over when she's due a break.'

'Thank you. You're doing a great job. We need this mystery woman.' Gina glanced back at Wyre. 'Did you find anything more about Elsie Peterson's gravestone? Was there a connection to Alex Swinton's mother, Eveline Peterson?'

'Yes, Elsie is Eveline's mother and Alex's grandmother.'

Gina glanced at the board. 'Eveline was in Spain with Alex's stepfather at the time of his murder. That rules them out. Double-check their whereabouts. I want the flights checked with the airlines and I want to know that they were on the flights. I need to be absolutely certain that they were in Spain at the time.'

O'Connor nodded and made a note on his pad.

'I know it's a long shot but it's all we have at the moment. Have we had anything come back on the door-to-doors and press appeals?' She rubbed her tired eyes and grabbed her coffee cup. She almost spat it back out. The brown liquid was as cold as her fingers and certainly wasn't pleasant as it slipped down her throat.

O'Connor popped a fruit gum into his mouth. 'Nothing as yet. We still have a lot of reports of kids hanging around, people on the streets dressed up. The calls in response to the media's coverage have prompted a lot of people trying to tell us that Cleevesford is cursed by a woman who was buried alive years ago and never found. These types of unnecessary calls are clogging our resources up, if I'm honest. I did look into this so-called legend and it's rife on social media. Many a ghost hunter has reported seeing the ghost of a woman holding a bell with no clapper but there is no record of this type of crime being committed in these woods or indeed any woodland in this area or at any time since records began. It's nothing more than folklore, an urban legend the kids have developed over the years to scare each other.'

Gina's brow furrowed. 'Interesting. Our killer obviously knows of this legend too and is playing up to it. Keep an eye on social media. The "What's Up Cleevesford" Facebook page is definitely worth a close follow. It may be that our killer is a member of the group and is reading everything, enjoying being the star of the show. Keep a list of everyone who comments on or reacts to these posts.'

'Will do.' O'Connor reached into his mouth to pull a bit of sweet from the ridges of his teeth.

'Our victim had three matches in his possession. He may have already had these on his person at the time or he may well have been given them by the killer. If this is the case, why would the killer not have given him a torch? This is a long shot and it's not the most logical trail to follow but with nothing else to go on for now, Wyre, will you do a search on arson cases, local to this area over the past thirty years to start with? There is something about matches that make me shudder. They would've used up the oxygen in the coffin quicker; fire is dangerous. It's an avenue I want to pursue.' She shuddered as she thought of a meticulous killer digging the hole on one night, taking the coffin on another and then taking or luring Alex Swinton to his death, leaving him with three matches.

'Guv, you okay?' Wyre smiled.

'Yes, just thinking.'

Briggs pushed through the door. 'Gina, can I have a word?'

She nodded. 'Right, we'll convene again soon. Keep me informed every step of the way. Are you all okay with what you're doing next?' Everyone nodded and muttered in agreement. She left the room and followed Briggs to his office.

'How are you keeping?'

'Good. We haven't had any major breakthroughs and with the press on our backs, the pressure is mounting.' Gina glanced out of his window and caught sight of another media van pulling in.

'I'm fully up to date with what's on the system. I meant how are *you* doing?' He loosened his tie as he sat.

'I really am okay, sir.' Not this again. She could see what he was up to: he was questioning her mental state.

'Those letters, they keep going around my head. I couldn't sleep last night. You know how much I think of you and if anything happened—'

She smiled and sat opposite him. 'Nothing's going to happen.'

'I'm not taking no for an answer. I want a panic alarm fitted in your house. No ifs, no buts.'

'Okay.' It was a small thing and if it made him feel better, she could accept having a panic alarm fitted, in fact, she wanted one fitted. She swallowed as her anxiety heightened. The threat was real, both she and Briggs knew it.

'This killer knows things about you, personal things. I need you to think. Who else could know about you and Terry, I mean the most secret of details?'

Her heart began to hum and she placed her trembling fingers in her lap, out of his view. She couldn't hide the quiver in her voice. 'That's the thing, no one.' She knocked the chair over and stood, gasping for breath. She ran to his window and pressed her reddening face against the condensation on the pane as she breathed in and out. A member of the press glanced up, she moved away quickly. 'It's like whoever is doing this is in my mind.'

Briggs stood. 'You'll get through this, I promise.'

The only person who knew nearly everything about her past was Briggs. Had he been playing games with her? 'I've got to go, work to do and leads to follow.' She patted his hand and pulled away, not letting him onto her suspicions. If he had betrayed her in any way, she didn't know if her heart could take it. As it stood, he'd been the only person in the whole world she'd trusted with the details of her past. Had she made the biggest mistake of her life?

CHAPTER THIRTY-EIGHT

12 years ago

Halloween

I gasp over and over again as earth floods onto my stomach – cold, slimy, full of grit – and I fight the image of a clump of worms oozing out and finding all my bodily orifices. I want to go home and cuddle Miffy. I want to see my mum and dad, and I cry until I can cry no more.

'Stop,' I yell, but the earth keeps on trickling. I need to see. I need to anchor myself. At the moment, I'm flying in space on a cord clasped to a satellite and it's about to snap. I don't want to be set free, floating in an eternal sky with no end. My body never found, my sad end never known by anyone. Tears flood my face. I kick; it feels like one of my toes is broken. I don't care if everything breaks as long as I can get out.

Think! Seconds, minutes, hours? Which is it? How long have I been here and who is laughing from above? My senses are still working which means I have time. I feel the earth trickling and a splodge of wet follows. Soon, all the room in my coffin will be filled, taking my precious air with it. I gasp for air. I don't want to drown in rainy grit. I need to see what's happening.

I grapple around my hair, clumps of it tangling in my wet finger, pulling out and getting caught around my ears. It's in my eyes and mouth. I can taste a strand: it tastes earthy. My nose fills and my head is thick, my breathing is hard. It's happening. I'm going and there's nothing more I can do.

My finger catches the thin wooden stick and my heart feels as though it's about to burst through my throat. I have a match, another precious match. Trembling, I grab the box and strike.

Wide-eyed, I stare at the glistening worm, long and thick, not a little wiggler. Its huge anterior stares at me. I can't see eyes, I just know it's the head end and not the thinner bottom end. Its segmented body wriggles a little closer and I drop the match and the light is gone. I bat my hand in front of me, catching the worm. It'll find its way back when I'm gone. That's what it's come for. It smells how close my end is and it's waiting to take me.

My body will stiffen, then it will begin to rot from the inside, producing belching gases, then I'll be revolting. Maggots will get to me...

I can't breathe. My chest hurts. I'm having a heart attack. No I'm not, I'm too young, and I'm healthy. But shock. Panic. That can cause the heart to fail, can't it?

'You're killing me!' Through gasps, I manage to call out one more time but there is no answer, just the muffled laughter of my captor. Has my tormentor done this before? Will they do it again?

I can't... I can't... I can't... think. My sentence won't form. My chattering teeth. No sense made. My thoughts reaching out, no connections. Not connected. My mind – confused. Space, floating, dark. The cord has snapped.

Gasping and wheezing.

Can I hear? Only my own heartbeat.

It's going. Gone. Gasp.

CHAPTER THIRTY-NINE

Now

Sunday, 1 November

'Guv.' Jacob burst into her office. 'Uniform are on their way now – they saw someone coming back to the squat and they're bringing him in.'

She held the file up and flicked it. 'At last. I'm pinning my hopes on this person giving us something useful.' She ate the rest of the chocolate bar that was her lunch and grabbed her notebook. 'Let's prep the interview room.' Adrenaline coursed through her body.

As they hurried to the room, Gina felt her phone buzz.

'Are they here?' Jacob asked.

'Yes. Kapoor is bringing the man through now.' Removing her suit jacket, she placed it over the back of the chair. She passed Jacob a witness form on a clipboard and headed out to the main reception, meeting Kapoor as she reached the front desk.

'DI Harte, this is Michael Dowler.' Kapoor's squeaky voice aggravated the underlying headache that Gina had felt coming on since she'd started eating the chocolate bar.

'Mr Dowler, thank you for coming in. Follow me.' She massaged her temples as they walked.

The man stared at her suspiciously, his mouth twitching underneath his stone-grey beard. He opened his mouth, revealing a gap where his two front teeth once were. Gina estimated that he was in his late forties but living rough had aged him way beyond his years. The layers of torn puffer jackets made him look plump, but Gina could tell from how stick thin his legs were that there was no weight to him whatsoever.

'Is this about Al?' Gina struggled to hear his gruff voice; it was as if he needed to clear his throat.

'Alexander Swinton, yes. Thank you for coming in.'

He shrugged and wiped a clump of sleep from his left eye. 'Didn't have a choice, he was my mate.'

She opened the door to interview room one and pointed to the plastic chair. 'Please, sit. Can we get you a drink?'

'Tea, I'd love a tea.'

Gina poked her head out of the door and waved until Kapoor saw her. 'Could you please get Mr Dowler a tea, please?' The woman nodded and smiled. Gina sat next to Jacob.

'I'm Mike, just call me Mike.'

After going through the basics of the form the tea arrived. Kapoor knocked and placed the plastic cup in front of Michael Dowler.

'First of all, were you at the derelict house on Beckett Street yesterday, when we were there?'

He glanced back and forth between Gina and Jacob. 'Nah, I was in Studley, sitting outside a shop hoping to gain a few quid for food.'

If it wasn't their witness at the squat, who had come in through the back door before scarpering? 'Mike, is this the man you referred to as Al?' Gina slid the CCTV screen grab photo across the table.

The man took it and squinted a little as he held it closer to his face. 'That's him. That's Al. Do you know who killed him? I heard about what happened and I've been terrified that someone is coming for me as well.'

Gina shook her head. 'I'm afraid we don't as yet. We were hoping that you can help us. Can you tell us a little about Al? Were you friends?'

The man unzipped his puffer jacket a little and took a sip of the tea Kapoor had brought in. A smoky waft filled the room and dust motes danced in the ray of light that came through the tiny window. 'You wouldn't believe how nice this tea tastes.' The cup crackled in his grip. He placed it down and bit the corner of his filthy nail. 'Yes, I suppose we were friends. We looked out for each other – you have to when you're living on the streets. It's hard out there. The kids give us hassle. They shout and call us names and Al, he was far more vulnerable than me. When he'd had a fix he was good for nothing. He'd just slouch against the wall on his sleeping bag. I kept my eye on him, gave him food if I managed to get hold of a bit, things like that. I know he wanted to get his life back.' The man stared into the thin space between them. For a moment, Gina thought she'd lost him but then she spotted the money spider abseiling on a strand of web in front of the man's nose. He reached out and allowed the spider to crawl over his hand. 'Let's see if that brings me any money.' He let out a snort and threw the spider into the corner of the room.

'What did he say about his life and getting it back?' The only sound in the room was Jacob's Biro scraping across the page and the slight crackle in Michael's chest as he inhaled.

'He had a kid. He wanted to see his kid.' The man turned away and scrunched his wiry brows. 'I encouraged him to go back to his drug counsellor, to get straight. I didn't want him to turn out like me. I made some bad decisions and got into debt. I ruined my wife and daughter's life and now my daughter is at university and wants nothing to do with me. I'd do anything to go back.' The man licked his bottom teeth. 'That won't happen for me but I could see that Al had a chance. It wasn't over for him. I told him that he could change things and get back on track. I said he owed it to his kid to get straight and become the man we both know he could become and he was fired up for it. He went to see his counsellor but then something happened.' The man poked a bony finger in his ear and began to scratch.

Gina glanced at Jacob. 'What happened?'

'A woman turned up. I didn't hear what she had to say and he asked me to leave. I waited in the back garden and I could hear shouting. She was really going at him about something but I couldn't hear most of what she was saying. When she pushed through the back door she almost crashed into me. She looked livid. Most people stay away, most people are scared of us, but not her. She was on some sort of mission.'

Gina wanted to smile. Mike Dowler had seen their mystery woman close up. 'Did you hear any of the conversation?'

'That was no conversation, she was just ranting at him. He didn't have the energy to give much back on that day. It was one of his slip-up days. He spent most of it dribbling in a corner, dozing in and out of sleep. I heard her saying that he'd ruined everything and that he should crawl back under the rock he came from. He'd wanted to tell me something but he couldn't and after this woman had been, he refused to open up in any way. He was a man haunted by his past. I kept telling him he needed to face it, then he could move past whatever it was and get on with his life. Anyway, that's basically all I heard and he wouldn't tell me any more. Afterwards, he told me that this wasn't the first time she'd been and that she'd been following him. That's how she found out where he was staying.' Mike gulped down the rest of his tea.

'Can you tell me when this was?'

He shook his head. 'I can't remember. Every day seems the same and I get muddled, sorry. That's all I've got. I just can't remember.'

Gina tried to blink her headache away. 'You say it wasn't the first time he'd received a visit from this woman. Can you tell me of any other times?'

'I wasn't there during other times. He just told me that she'd been. I think it was over the past three weeks and only on a couple of occasions.' Michael sniffed and leaned forward, hunching himself over the table. 'Can I have another cuppa?'

'Of course. When we've finished here, I'll make sure you get some tea and biscuits. Can you describe this woman?' So far they had multiple visits by a mystery woman at times and dates that couldn't be confirmed.

'She was wearing a hoodie and leggings. It was also evening so I couldn't see too clearly. All we have at the house is the street light on the pavement and sometimes we light a fire. I think she had dark eyes and the bits of hair scraped into the hood looked to be dark in colour. She had a chin that pointed a little, just a little – or did I make that up. I'm just not sure, sorry.' He paused. 'Although, there was a harshness about her. She told me I stank and to move out of her way. I hadn't been at all rude to her, there really was no reason for her being so forward.'

Gina waited as Jacob caught up with noting the description. 'Is there anything else you can tell us that may help?'

'Al referred to her as either Shaz or Chez once. That must have been her name. I don't have anything else. Oh, she was wearing walking boots or heavy-looking trainers.' The edge of the man's eye began to tic.

'You've been really helpful, thank you for coming in. Does anyone else stay at the house with you?'

He shook his head. 'Not at the moment. It was just Al and me. Some of the others moved to an empty warehouse about a month ago but we preferred it there. It felt safer for some reason. We should have gone. Maybe Al would still be alive.' The man wiped his nose with the side of his finger. 'There was one other thing?'

'Go on.'

'I think when this woman was watching him one night, she might have been wearing a long dark coat with a hood. It had to be her as no one else had been around there so I'm guessing that they were the same person, although I might be wrong. This woman was just standing in the bushes at the back and I could feel her staring up at the window. Al came over. He wasn't in the mood and stuck his fingers up at her through one of the missing windows. He kept gibbering on that he was seeing things, but I saw her. She was definitely there. Again, I can't remember which day that was, but I think it might have been Monday gone.'

Gina thought back, that was the same night she'd seen him in the café.

'What time would this have been?'

'Late, very late. Probably close to midnight. The kids had been a pain in the arse calling us names, that's why I remember. I then slipped out for a bit, needed to get away but Al stayed behind. I walked the streets for a while and got back in the early hours of Tuesday morning. That woman and the kids were creeping me out. People are scared of bumping into us at night; what they don't realise is, we're the vulnerable ones. We're the ones who get abused and hurt.' He began tugging at something under the table and pulled a piece of chewing gum out. He pressed it down on the wood. 'Sorry about that.' He looked up with glassy eyes. 'I don't want to go back to the house, I'm scared. I'm going to be next, aren't I?' Shaking, the man hugged himself.

'When we've finished, I'm going to call the council emergency housing team and get you some help.' The council were going to officially hate her – with cutbacks and limited hostel spaces, they weren't going to be impressed at all. She knew that if she didn't take him off the streets, he could very well be right – he could be next. It was a risk she couldn't take.

'Thank you, thank you so much. I just need a chance, that's all. Just a little teeny chance. I won't screw up, I promise.'

She glanced at Jacob's notes. Now she had to work out how she was going to find this Shaz or Chez. Her stomach fluttered and not in an exciting way – in a sickening, nervous way. She cleared her throat. Now was not the time to dwell on whether she could trust Briggs, she had to get this description across to him, ready for the next press release.

Who was Shaz or Chez?

CHAPTER FORTY

Christian had taken his dinner to bed and he'd since ignored Cherie. The television above had gone off about an hour ago. She lay on the settee, staring at the ceiling with thoughts of Marcus running through her head. She'd really pushed him this time.

She glanced at her phone: three missed calls from Marcus. Her phone lit up again and this time she answered. 'What?'

'I'm seriously worried. I've called all the hotels and bed and breakfasts in the area. She hasn't checked into any of them. Something's happened.'

'Look, calm down. You call the police and tell them what?'

'I just tell them that we had an argument and I haven't seen her since. That's the truth.'

Cherie threw one of the scatter cushions to the floor and pulled the old quilt back. 'They'll blame you, you know. Husband has row with wife and wife disappears. She's just having another hissy fit like all the other times.'

He paused on the other end of the phone. 'Seriously, what have you become?'

'Nothing that you weren't already.' She wiped the bead of sweat forming at her brow.

'I don't know you any more.' He paused. 'Did you see Alex before he died? You know something, don't you? That's why you don't want me to go to the police. There's more to this than you're letting on.'

'You know why and I'm not going to explain it.' She clenched her fist. If he called the police, it wouldn't take long for them all to fall apart – they'd been unravelling ever since Alex had returned.

'How do I know you didn't hurt Alex?'

'How do I know you didn't? Or Penny, or Isaac? Please spare me the idiocy.' She let out a nervous laugh.

'Tell me what it is you're hiding, then?' He paused. 'Tell me, dammit? If you care one bit for Penny, you'll open your gob now. You know where she is, don't you?' She could hear him seething. If he was next to her, she knew she'd feel specks of spittle coming through his teeth as he awaited her answer.

Hands shaking like a branch in a storm, she ended the call. He was not going to be the one to break her. She had no idea whether she could trust him, or Isaac. A sharp pain flashed through her head. She dragged the quilt over her face and lay there in darkness as the oxygen slowly began to run out. Gasping, she threw the quilt back. That's how it felt for Alex and he didn't have the option of coming up for air. Her phone beeped and she opened the message.

After reading it, she knew her whole world was about to come crashing down.

CHAPTER FORTY-ONE

Now

Monday, 2 November

Hot and so sticky. Gina threw back her quilt and pressed her hand against her damp chest. Half asleep and half awake, she could hear the sound of her watch ticking on her bedside and then it faded again. Now she could see Briggs and Terry in her dream. Both laughing and overpowering her, moving in closer until she was suffocating under them. No longer able to breathe as their arms came down, they finally trapped her in the corner of the shed, then it lit up, flames consuming every part. The skin on her hand dripping like wax from a tipped-up candle.

A swift intake of breath fully woke her. As she grappled for the sweat-drenched quilt, she almost rolled off the edge of the mattress, crumpling the paperwork that Wyre had passed her as she'd left the station. She placed the list of names on the other side of the bed. Everyone who had been charged with any fire-related crime over the past forty years, from this area, was on that list.

The moon shone through the window, catching her bedside lamp and window ledge. She grabbed a tissue from her top drawer and wiped her chest and brow. It was just a dream. Nothing more. She was safe in her home. Reaching out, she felt for the panic button. It was still there, next to her watch. One press and she'd have the police here in next to no time.

With jellied legs Gina stood and walked over to the window. Getting to sleep had been a chore, not only had people been setting off fireworks in the distance but every thought of the day had been clogging up her mind. She gazed out of the window. The fireworks had long stopped and from what she could see, nothing seemed out of the ordinary tonight in rural Warwickshire, not like the other night. The shadows were exactly where they were meant to be and nothing was out of place. She pushed the window open and closed her eyes, enjoying the feel of the chilly breeze as it hit her sticky head. Terry and Briggs, her dream – it was knocking her sick. Her dry throat caught as she tried to swallow, urging her to grab the two-day-old glass of water and take a sip.

Her phone began to vibrate and her heart raced in time with it. In the darkness, she could see Briggs's name lighting up the room. Grabbing it, she held it to her ear.

'Sorry to wake you but I knew you'd want to be the first to hear this update. We have a man coming in, he says his wife is missing and, get this, they knew our victim, Alexander Swinton. Given what happened to Alex, he's worried something might have happened to her too. This may be nothing more than a coincidence but given that there's a link—'

'I'm on my way.'

'Are we okay, only you didn't say anything when you left the station? I thought we were going to go for a coffee after work.'

She inhaled and breathed out slowly. He had asked her to go with him after work and she'd reluctantly agreed. 'I know, I was just tired. Sorry, I should have told you but my head was killing.' That wasn't a lie. Maybe a half-truth would convince him.

'You didn't even call to cancel.'

'Sorry.' What more could she say? *Sorry, I don't trust you. What is your game? Is it to scare me into your arms so that you get me exactly where you want me? I learned a lot from Terry and I'm no longer the naïve young woman I once was. I'm not playing games like this any more. Not with you, not with anyone.* She couldn't even expose him if that were the case. She had too much to lose. Exposing him meant coming clean about everything. It meant giving up everything she'd worked for. It meant her daughter hating her forever and Terry's family finally being able to metaphorically burn her at the stake like she was some sort of poisonous witch who had taken the life of their perfect son. 'I... err... forgot. I went straight home to bed.'

'Something's wrong. Gina, talk to me.'

She forced a smile, knowing it would come across in her voice. 'I swear, there's nothing wrong. I'm going to have a quick shower and I'm on my way.'

'Can we head to the café after the interview? It should be open then. We need to talk and I don't want to talk at the station. We could get some breakfast there.'

Her stomach felt as though a mouse was burrowing in it.

'Please.'

She let out the breath she'd been holding, slowly and silently. 'Okay.' It was time to sound him out.

'See you soon.' He ended the call.

She had no idea how she was going to tackle her suspicions over coffee in the morning, but she had to say something. This tension couldn't carry on much longer, she couldn't stand much more. It was making her eyes itch and her heart bang. If he was responsible, she'd never trust anyone again.

'Focus, Harte.' She hurried to the bathroom and stared at her reflection. Half of her straggly brown hair had stuck to the sweaty side of the cheek she'd been lying on, and several pillow creases were imprinted on her face. 'Great.' She cranked the shower on and allowed the warm water and soap to wash away her nightmare.

CHAPTER FORTY-TWO

Gina moved her chair a little further away from Briggs. The strip light gave a slight flicker here and there, giving the pale grey interview room a creepy feel. Briggs marked a page up with the time, four twenty. She appreciated that he was stepping to the side and was still allowing her to lead the investigation despite his worries about her. She caught the side of his badly-shaven chin before glancing up at the man in front of her. 'Mr Burton, sorry to hear that your wife is missing. I'm just going to ask you a few questions—'

'Marcus, please.' He paused and bowed his head slightly revealing a thin patch in the middle of his almost white blond hair. 'You have to find her. We argue like any normal couple.' He fiddled with his wedding ring. 'That's a lie, maybe we argue a bit more – who knows. I don't know what everyone else is like. But this, her not contacting me at all, it's out of character. When we argue, normally she storms off and checks into a cheap hotel for the night, sometimes two nights, but then she comes home. When she does this, she always calls the next morning, mostly to have a go at me, but still, she calls, and I'm reassured that she's safe. She didn't call on Saturday. Either something's wrong or she's punishing me harder for our argument. I've called all the local hotels where I know she'd stay and she didn't turn up at any of them on Friday.'

'Firstly, can I take a description of your wife?'

He pulled a photo of a mousy-haired, pale-faced woman from his pocket. 'This is her. She's about five feet seven and has a slim build. She was wearing a black dress when I last saw her.'

Gina scraped her chair on the floor and got a little closer to the table. 'Thank you. May we keep this photo for now?' He nodded. 'Let's go back a little. When did you last see your wife?'

'Friday morning, during our argument. It was all over stupid things like me not pulling my weight around the house. She was right as always. Maybe I don't appreciate her enough. I could tell there was something else, but she wasn't saying. She did this a lot, trying to make me guess as to why she was angry in the hope that I'd confess. Thing is, I had nothing to confess to. She then began going on about the toilet seat being up and not wanting to see our friends on Saturday night.' He bit his lip and stared at the table. 'She was just being awkward, really. That hasn't got anything to do with it.'

Deflection, Gina could spot it a mile off. The flickering light was beginning to trigger Gina's headache again, or maybe it was the lack of caffeine. 'Hasn't it?'

'No, of course not.' He gave a warm smile. 'I just want her back home, with me.'

Gina knew there was more to his story. It seemed odd that he mentioned an appointment they had on the Saturday night. 'What was your relationship like?'

'Most of the time it's fine. We bicker a little, but doesn't every couple?' He paused. 'We don't always argue and the making up normally keeps us happy for a long time. It's quite routine for us. It wouldn't pay for us all to be the same. This time, it was different; she had something on her mind and she wouldn't come out with it. I could tell she wasn't happy with me but I don't know why.'

'What time did she leave?' Gina scribbled a few notes and Briggs caught up with logging the interview on a form.

'I didn't see the moment she walked out of the door as I went to work but I popped home at lunchtime and she was gone.'

'Did she take anything with her?'

'She always has her phone and her bank cards on her. I didn't see anything else missing but I probably wouldn't know if anything was missing. She has loads of clothes and make-up, there's no way I could tell.'

'Could she have gone to a friend or colleague's house?' Gina hoped this case was as simple as that and that Penny Burton would be found staying with a friend.

Marcus Burton pressed his lips together and sat up straight. 'She didn't really have friends whom she went out with. The only friends she really has are the ones we were seeing on Saturday night.' He scratched his nose. 'As for colleagues, apart from the annual Christmas bash, she never goes out with any of them.'

'What does she do for work?'

'She's in business development for a CCTV company. She travels around meeting clients here and there, but mostly she's office based. The company is located in Bromsgrove.'

'Can I take the names of the friends you said you were seeing and I'll need their address too? Where were you all meeting?'

She spotted him swallow and pause before answering. 'Fifteen Willow Way. The evening still went ahead, I still went to theirs for dinner. At this point, I wasn't overly worried about Penny leaving me. As I said, this happens a lot for us. We were invited over for dinner by Cherie and Christian Brown. The other guests apart from me were Isaac Slater and Joanna Brent.'

She made a note to get their addresses too when the interview was over. 'And how do you all know each other?'

'Does that really matter? My wife is missing. This is nothing to do with them.' Marcus's cheek dimpled as he ground his teeth.

Gina caught Briggs's eye. She knew that he too could sense that something was off about Marcus's response. 'As I said, we will need to look into who your wife might have contacted and a lot of people who are distressed or even angry might decide to call a friend. That's all.'

He flung his head back. 'I've already asked them. Never mind. Penny, Isaac, Cherie and I have known each other since high school. We've been friends since. Christian and Joanna are Cherie and Isaac's partners; we didn't know them at school but we've all become good friends. Every now and again, we all get together at one of our houses for a meal, to have a catch up and a drink. That's all.' The hum of Marcus's foot tapping on the floor made Gina's eyelids feel a little heavy.

'So, let me get this right. Penny didn't want to go to Mr and Mrs Brown's house on the Saturday and you argued about this.'

'Yes, but it's not how it sounds. She'd have argued about anything with me at that point. We rowed over nothing most of the time.'

Gina was far from convinced. 'We may be able to check on her whereabouts by seeing if she's used her bank cards and phone since. That may help us with locating her. We'll take those details off you before you leave.'

The man swallowed and the foot tapping stopped.

'Is that okay?'

He nodded and placed his elbows on the table as he leaned forward. 'I just want her found. I know she had another phone too, a basic pay-as-you-go. Years ago, she had a fling and I found it. I know she keeps it in her drawer under the bed, hidden behind all her old clothes. She doesn't know this but I regularly take a look at it. It helps me when it comes to trusting her. Up to a week ago, there hadn't been any communications on it for months and the only things on it from back then were messages from work and friends when she lost her phone for a few days. Oh, she did put the number on Facebook back then, much to my dismay, telling the world about her lost phone.' He paused in thought. 'I can check to see if it's gone.'

Gina remained silent for what felt like forever. 'That would be really helpful. You say you know Alexander Swinton. Could you tell me how?'

He scratched his chin and leaned back up once again. 'He was an old school friend. I haven't seen him for over a year, since he split up with his wife. I heard that he was taking drugs and had got himself into a bad way. News like that travels fast in Cleevesford. Anyway, we were all shocked when we saw his photo in the paper and when we heard what had happened.'

'How close were you to him?'

'Not close at all. As I said, we were friends at school, and not even close friends at that. I just knew of him, that's all. Sometimes we hung out and played football in the park. I didn't know him well.' He let out a titter. 'We used to rib him about his mum's garden gnome collection. She's a bit weird. He took it in good spirits though. It came as a huge shock to all of us when we heard what had happened to him. I suppose his murder might have been playing on Penny's mind; that may have been why she was really tense that night. I suppose given the way he was killed, we were all a bit tense. I don't think we're different like that, I think the whole town is tense. I mean, the person who killed him is still out there. Knowing what had happened to Alex just made me worry more about Penny.'

There was a connection between their murder victim and missing Penny, albeit not a recent connection, if Marcus was to be believed. Gina only hoped that Penny wasn't going to be next. She glanced down at the names on the page and one stood out. She wanted to know more about Cherie or Chez. Had Cherie been the Chez who'd been shouting at Alexander Swinton at the squat?

Then, she paused at another name. Isaac Slater, their junior fire starter going back twenty years. That name had been on the list she'd been looking at when she'd fallen asleep. She wanted to jump up and scream with joy. They had a break and her instincts had been right. At last she had a lead.

CHAPTER FORTY-THREE

Lucy's Café was vibrant in its usual way. Light, airy and the windows had returned to normal. No more looking out through artificial cobwebs. Lucy worked frantically behind the counter, trying to get bacon sandwiches out to the group of fluorescent-clad builders that were patiently waiting for their breakfasts.

Briggs slurped half of his coffee down in one go. 'I needed that. It's been a long night.'

The teenage girl who was assisting in the shop placed Gina's second cup down. 'Thank you. I've only got an hour. I'm meeting Jacob at Isaac Slater's address. Wyre was still trying to contact Cherie Brown as we left but so far, there has been no answer on her phone. If we can't get through, I'll turn up after speaking to Isaac Slater. I need to get to the bottom of what's going on.'

'Good call about pulling up old arson cases. At least we have a connection.'

'It was the matches. I mean who uses matches these days? Most smokers I know use a lighter. I even use one of those long lighters to start my fire off.' She blew her coffee and tentatively sipped but it was too hot. 'It might turn out to be a nothing thought on my part.'

'Or, it might turn out to be everything. Haven't you always said that there can be a clue in the smallest of thoughts?'

He was right; she always wanted to know everything, however small. And it was often the smallest of things that led to some of the biggest of breakthroughs. She smiled at Briggs, her only real friend, and a pang of guilt washed through her. She'd doubted him and she still doubted him.

'I can see your cogs turning.' He moved the cushion from behind his back and shifted in the seat a little.

Her smile dropped and her gaze met his.

'What?'

She felt a tremor in her knee. 'Only you know what happened between me and Terry.'

It didn't take long for his own detective skills to kick in. His warm expression turned serious. 'No, Gina.'

'Just humour me.'

'You think I could be involved? Seriously? I thought you knew me. I thought we knew each other. Have a real good think about what you're insinuating.'

She'd been thinking about it all night. No one else knew about what Terry had done to her. No one knew that he'd locked her away in their shed for the weekend. Had she mentioned that incident to Briggs in the past and not remembered? Maybe in the throes of a nightmare she'd cried out, revealing more of her past. They'd talked about so much, her mind was blurry with what he did and didn't know. 'I don't know what to think.' She daren't tell him that she felt as though she was losing her mind.

He reached into his pocket and dropped a ten-pound note on the table before standing and leaving. She knew she'd blown it. He didn't even look back as he stormed out of the door and headed down the path. That hurt. He'd never turned his back on her so coldly.

The crowd had thinned a little and Lucy came over to collect his cup. 'Is he okay?'

Gina picked up the note and passed it to Lucy along with a bit of change from her pocket. 'Yes, he isn't feeling too well. I'm sure it's nothing.'

Lucy snorted a little as she laughed. 'I hope it wasn't the coffee. Don't want to upset any of my best customers.'

'The coffee was lovely as usual. He just has a lot on his mind.'
That was true.

As Lucy turned to take the cup away, Gina recognised the
woman entering. The thickset boots with clanking chains around
the bottoms belonged to their local goth-styled vicar, Sally Stevens.
The woman waved across to Gina and headed to the counter.

Gina grabbed the coffee receipt and popped it in her pocket,
along with the little wrapped biscotti that sat next to her coffee.
There was no way she could force the biscotti down now.

As she headed to the door she turned. Were Lucy and Sally
talking about her? If they hadn't been, why were they still looking
in her direction? As she pushed the door open, Cyril nodded and
led the way through with his walking stick and June closely followed
him. He too stopped for a look. What was wrong with everyone?
She glanced at her reflection in the door as he passed her with a
warm hello. She didn't have anything on her face. Her hair was its
usual organised chaos and nothing seemed out of the ordinary –
except for everyone in the café. All of them were acting strangely
towards her. She shook her head. It had to be her. Just like she'd got
Briggs so wrong, she'd made something out of nothing in the café.

She glanced back. June and Cyril had taken their favourite
seats. He had his paper out in front of him and June had her
knitting in her bag. Lucy smiled as she served Sally. No one was
looking at her. A cold breeze caught her face and a grey cloud
pushed past at speed above her. The branches on the church
trees cracked and creaked, and she began to tremble under her
coat. Something was going on, something she couldn't put her
finger on. Maybe it was her, finally she was losing it and there
was nothing she could do to be rid of the uneasy feeling that was
stalking her. She turned and glanced back but there was no one
there except a lonely seagull pecking at a leftover kebab.

She sped up to a light jog until she reached her car. Staring
up at the church for a second, she held her breath. An image

flashed through her mind, a scene from *The Omen* film where the lightning rod falls from the church roof and impales the priest. Heart pounding, she got into the car and slammed the door closed as she glanced around. Breathe in and out, in and out. She couldn't convince herself that everything was going to be okay. It wasn't, she could feel it. Everything was as far away from okay as it could be and she had no idea how to fix it.

CHAPTER FORTY-FOUR

'You haven't been waiting too long, have you?' Gina ran towards Jacob's car outside Isaac Slater's house, disturbing the DS from his text. It was time to let her uneasiness go, for now. She had a killer to find and time was slipping through her fingers. With the press on their every move and first to criticise everything they were doing, she couldn't stop for a break now.

'Bloody hell. You made me jump.' He rolled up his window and got out of his car. 'I've only been here a couple of minutes. He's in by the way, I just saw Isaac walk past the kitchen window.'

'Great, let's go and sound our arsonist out.' Gina pushed open the old gate and headed to the front door. The quaint little cottage sat in the middle of its own acre of land. The grounds looked wintery dead, soggy and bare branched. In the distance she could just about make out Cleevesford, divided by the flyover and acres of asparagus fields. As she lifted the knocker, it almost came off the door. She placed it gently down and banged with her fist instead.

A man answered. The resemblance to his mugshot was still there but he had less hair on top and a couple of days' worth under his chin, not like the angelic looking sixteen-year-old that had set five allotment sheds on fire. 'Come in.' His mucky jeans were belted and his polo shirt tucked in.

They followed him through the narrow hallway, trying not to bang heads on the low ceiling. Gina knocked her shoulder on the door frame as they went through to a snug. The room had a tiled fireplace at one end and an old burgundy cottage suite surrounding it. 'Excuse the décor, my nan left me this place a few years ago. I'm still trying to do it up but you know what it's like trying to get the cash together. What's this about?'

'May we sit down?' The room was tiny, Gina felt as though she'd taken a bite of the 'eat me' cake from *Alice in Wonderland*, the one that made Alice taller.

'Yes, but I have to make this quick. I have to get to work.'

'What is it you do?'

'Builder. I'm working on the new housing development in Cleevesford and I can't afford to lose time.' He slumped in the chair that took him lower than it should have, once again adding to the weird proportions of the room.

'We've had a missing person's report come in. A friend of yours called Penny Burton.'

He stared into the sooty fire. 'The woman's a crazy.'

Gina didn't appreciate that term and she could tell instantly that Isaac thought he was funny by the smirk in the corner of his mouth. 'What makes you say that?'

'She's just a drama queen. She isn't missing, she's just choosing not to be found. She walks out on Marcus all the time. She'll be back. It won't be the first time this has happened.'

Jacob seemed to lean to one side and Gina noticed that the cushion underneath him only looked half stuffed. The room was playing with her senses, almost making her a little giddy and disorientated. With his elbow on the arm of the chair, Jacob scribbled a few notes.

'You also know Alexander Swinton, is that correct?'

He leaned forward, his shadowy eyes looking more like a smear in the half-light. 'What is this really about?'

'We have one murder victim and one missing person, both are known to you. We're just asking a few questions, that's all. We'll be asking your other friends the same questions. How did you know Alexander Swinton?'

He paused and picked a bit from the tip of his tongue. 'From school. I haven't seen him for years, so whatever tree you're barking up has nothing to do with me. I haven't seen Penny for probably a year.'

Gina spotted the matches on the hearth, the same brand that were in Alex Swinton's coffin. 'Can you tell me your whereabouts this past week, since Monday the twenty-sixth of October?'

'Am I a suspect?'

'We're just trying to find out where your friend is.' She felt her muscles tense, knowing that before long, Isaac would completely clam up and at the moment she had nothing to arrest him for.

'I am going to talk. When I've finished speaking, you're both going to leave and I know you will because I know how this works. We'll cut the bull. I have a conviction and you're looking into people with convictions first. Am I right? Wait, don't answer that. The answer isn't relevant.'

He wasn't wrong. He didn't know if it was his specific conviction that had made him such a feature in her mind.

'I burned a couple of sheds down when I was a little kid.'

He was sixteen and it was five sheds. Isaac was already lying.

'It was stupid and I regretted it. What I did then has nothing to do with now. I've kept a clean record since. This past week, I've been in every night except for the night I went to Christian and Cherie's house for dinner. My girlfriend, Joanna Brent, will confirm that. She lives here with me, and we were in together every night. We didn't go anywhere apart from work and home. That is all you need to know.' He grabbed a pad from an old magazine rack and scribbled on it with a couple of Biros until the green one started writing. 'Here's her number. She'll be at work now. Call away.'

He threw the page in Gina's direction and it landed at her feet. He stood and pointed at the door. 'Goodbye.'

Gina felt her face reddening. She wanted to interrogate him, haul him into the station, but having a box of matches next to his fireplace wouldn't be enough to do that. If his alibi checked out, they'd have nothing. A fleeting thought passed through her mind as she ducked under the door frame, following the man back through the corridor. His girlfriend may be able to give him an alibi, but primarily they were looking for a woman and maybe two people were involved. She needed to investigate further.

'Do you call your friend Cherie Brown, Chez?'

He rolled his eyes and exhaled. 'I'll give you this one for free, only Alex called her Chez and she hated it. She thought it sounded common and would always accuse him of taking the piss.' He opened the door and gestured for them to leave before slamming it behind them.

'That was the frostiest reception we've had in a while. What are your thoughts, guv?' Jacob headed towards the gate.

'He's cagey, he's definitely hiding something. He gives me the creeps. That can only mean we're getting closer to finding the truth. Any news on Cherie Brown?'

Jacob checked his messages as he leaned against his car. 'Yes. The station managed to get through to her while we were in the interview. She's on her way in.'

'At last!'

Gina glanced at her phone. A message from O'Connor came through. She opened the attachments. 'Marcus Burton gave us the login information for Penny's phone and bank accounts. I have the records here.' She clicked and waited for the files to load. As she scanned the dates and records, she swallowed and shook her head. 'This isn't what we needed right now. I'll meet you back at the station.'

CHAPTER FORTY-FIVE

Cherie stood on the path outside the police station. Several members of the press stood beside vans next to people holding cameras and boom poles. She gulped as she edged her way through. She recognised the one reporter, Lyndsey Saunders, the one who'd been writing what seemed like all the articles for the murder case. Cherie scurried past, knowing she would be hounded like mad had they all known she was being interviewed about Alex's murder.

She pulled her hood up and slid through, no one taking any notice of her at all. Breathing a sigh of relief, she hurried through the main door and waited at the desk. 'I have an appointment. DC Wyre called.'

'What's your name?' The desk sergeant smiled and looked down from his platform of a reception.

'Cherie.'

'Surname?'

'Brown.' She croaked the word out. Her throat was already beginning to stick.

'Take a seat, someone will be with you in a moment.'

She sat on the seat at the end of the row, as far away from the man who stank of whiskey and kept talking to himself. She prised her bag open and spotted the miniature bottle. That man could be her one day. She glanced over and smiled. He ignored her. At least she'd tried.

So this is what it was like inside a police station. Her first foray into such a building and she was being questioned about a murder. She forced her clenched hands open. Looking too tense wouldn't do her any favours.

Pressing her temples, she tried to massage her anxiety away. In her mind, she had huge gnarly knots all over her face and the only solution was to press them out. She glanced at her reflection in the back of the shiny computer screen. She looked fine, all normal apart from being scruffier than usual.

Tapping her feet, she felt her anticipation worsening. What would they want to know? What had Marcus said? She glanced at the last message on the phone, the one from an unknown number.

The truth has to come out, you know it does. I just need some time alone, to think, but I'm okay. Keep your phone on, I'll be in touch soon. Don't worry about me and don't tell anyone I've contacted you.

She swallowed and held onto her bubbling stomach. What was Penny playing at, not coming home and sending crazy messages?

She was entering this interview blind, not knowing what Marcus had said or if Isaac had said anything.

Alex had thrown up more questions that hung over her head. She should never have gone to see him. Her mind whirled between Marcus and Isaac as she wondered if one of them was capable of killing him. Isaac talked the talk and Joanna would back him up in anything he said if he needed an alibi and Marcus – what about Marcus? Neither of them wanted Alex to come back, and neither did she. She gulped. The thought of being buried alive was no longer a joke. It was a message and she had to work out who was sending it. Her mind briefly flitted to someone else, but she shook her head.

'Mrs Brown?' The woman with the bags under her eyes and slightly creased shirt called out. 'I'm DI Harte, thank you for coming in. Follow me.'

That was a name she recognised from the papers. That explains why the woman looked as though she hadn't slept. She headed along the corridor, into the dingy interview room, into the unknown. As she pictured her children and Christian finding out her secret, she knew she had to lie. She knew the outcome of this case was worth skewing with all she had. That couldn't happen. Christian, she could live without. Her children – now that hurt.

CHAPTER FORTY-SIX

'It is twelve fifty on Monday the second of November. Mrs Brown, I'm DI Harte, this is DS Driscoll. We just need to ask you a few questions about your friends Penny Burton and Alexander Swinton. The interview is being recorded and you are here voluntarily. Once again, thank you for coming in and assisting with our enquiries. Can I confirm that you are Cherie Brown?'

The woman nodded.

'For the tape, Mrs Brown nodded. If you could speak instead of gesturing that would really help.'

'Sorry.' Cherie cleared her throat and pulled the hood from her head, exposing her rat-tail hair.

'We've met before, haven't we?' Gina recognised the woman, although her hair had looked different, maybe a different colour. She'd also been wearing glasses. She normally looked a lot cleaner and tidier but there was no mistaking the fact that Gina had seen her on at least three occasions.

The woman shrugged. 'I don't think we've met.'

'You go to the café on Cleevesford High Street. Lucy's Café.'

'Oh, yes. I sit there and read sometimes. Sorry, I can't remember seeing you. Probably engrossed in my book.'

'That's okay. Right, let's carry on.' Gina went through the rest of her personal details and now the interview could start. The shine on Cherie's head looked damp and oily. Gina could smell her nerves oozing from her pores. Just a few moments in this room was making their person of interest sweat and itch. The woman scratched the back of her neck and her hands tangled in her hair. 'Your friend, Penny Burton, hasn't been seen since Friday morning. She was meant to be at your house on Saturday night. Can you tell me more about that and about your friendship? I'm just trying to get a sense of who Penny Burton is.'

The woman's nose began to run a little. 'Can I have a tissue?'

Gina slid a box across the table.

She took one out and wiped her nose. 'Everyone arrived around seven thirty as planned.'

'Everyone? Can you name them?'

She sniffed again. 'Isaac Slater, Joanna Brent and Marcus Burton. Obviously, Penny didn't come. Marcus said she was poorly but later told us that they'd had an argument and she'd left him.'

'How do you know these friends?'

'I know Isaac, Penny and Marcus from school. We all went to Cleevesford High.'

Gina knew that to be exactly what Marcus Burton had said. So far, so good. She allowed the room to become silent as she and Jacob looked at Cherie, knowing that her unease was growing by the second. A fleeting thought passed through her. 'Okay, tell me about the evening, from their arrival.'

Cherie exhaled. 'After settling in and a bit of small talk, we had dinner and caught up on what we were all doing. I could sense that something wasn't right with Marcus, he was upset that they'd fallen out. After dinner, we went out into the garden to smoke, Marcus was quite drunk at that point. We talked for a bit and that was it.'

'And after that?'

'Nothing. They went home and we went to bed.'

'Did Penny confide in you at all? Do you know what she and Marcus may have been arguing about?'

Cherie stared right across the table and shook her head. 'They never said. I'm sorry I can't be of any more use. I know they argued a lot and she often left him for a couple of days, that's why none of us were worried.' The woman stared again.

'Alexander Swinton. You knew him from school too, didn't you?'

She shrugged. 'I knew of him. I didn't know him that well, not well enough to call him a friend. I mean, he wasn't even an acquaintance.'

'Then why were you following him? We have a witness that puts you at the derelict house on Beckett Street late on Monday the twenty-sixth October.'

The woman opened and closed her mouth. Her gaze flitted across to Jacob then at the table. 'I wasn't there. That wasn't me. I was at home with my husband. Ask him.'

'And he'll be able to confirm that?'

She nodded. 'Am I under arrest?'

Gina wished she was. There was no way she could make an arrest at this moment in time without investigating further. The CPS would kick it straight out. She had a witness that heard Alexander speaking to a woman and he thought he heard him call the woman Chez or Shaz; that wasn't enough. If her alibi checked out, that would leave them with nothing. 'No, Mrs Brown, you're not under arrest. It is an offence to pervert the course of justice, which means if you are lying and we find out, you could be charged. It's a serious charge.'

'I want to go. I didn't do anything. I don't know where Penny is and I don't know anything about Alex's murder. I'm not perverting anything.'

'What aren't you telling us, Mrs Brown?'

'I want to leave.' Her fingers began to tremble.

'Mrs Brown, one of your school friend's has been murdered and another friend is missing. We're concerned for you too.'

'Don't be.' She stood and placed her hands on the table. 'I'm fine. I don't know what all this is about. I'm upset that my friend is missing and, as I said, I didn't really know Alex. My condolences go to his friends and family. Now I just want to go home to be with my husband and children.'

'Is there something worrying you?'

'No, no...'

'You're shaking.' Just a little nudge. Cherie Brown was on the verge of saying something.

'Yes, I'm scared. I'm scared that the person who killed Alex is still out there. We're all scared. The whole community is scared.' She grabbed her bag from the floor.

Gina passed her a card. 'If there's anything else you can think of or you need to speak to me about, please call anytime.'

The woman snatched the card from her fingers. 'I want to go. I have to get out of here.' She began to gasp and back up against the wall. 'I can't breathe.' She slid down the wall and cowered in the corner, violently trembling until she began to hyperventilate and sob.

Gina hurried around to her and kneeled beside her. 'Jacob, can you open the door?' Jacob hurried to the door and pushed it open. 'It's okay, Mrs Brown, you're safe.'

The woman gripped her chest and began to steady her breathing. Gina knew a panic attack when she saw one and what had happened to Mrs Brown couldn't be put on. 'I'll show you out. Interview terminated at fifteen minutes past thirteen hundred hours.' Jacob pressed the button to stop the recorder. Something was literally scaring the life out of Cherie. 'Jacob, call a first aider.'

Cherie gasped again. 'I'm okay. I'll be fine,' she paused, 'but I am scared. I just don't know who I'm scared of? I'm scared of what happened to Alex, since I read about it. I just can't stop thinking about it. It's like it stays with me, day and night.'

'Cherie, it's important that you answer me. Is there anything else you're not telling us? A man has been murdered.'

'I don't know anything. Do you think I'd be like this if I knew what was going on and who was behind it all?' As the woman threw Gina's card into her bag, Gina spotted the miniature bottle of vodka. 'Call my husband, he can confirm my whereabouts on the Monday you were asking about.'

Gina offered her a hand and helped her up. 'We will, thank you.' As Gina heard the woman hurrying down the corridor, she stared at Jacob. 'What the hell just happened? We need to look into Cherie Brown immediately. Everything about her behaviour is all wrong and what is it with this case? Nothing is making sense.' Gina slammed her palm onto the wall.

'I feel your frustration.' He dropped the folder onto the desk and fell into the chair.

'We need an arrest. I can't walk back through the path of reporters tonight without something positive to share. Did you see what they've been writing? They're tearing us apart. No, they're tearing me apart.'

'Yes, they don't seem to mention how overstretched and under-funded we are and they seem to like using the word "incompetent" a lot. They forget that we need evidence or the CPS will throw it straight out. Oh, and they like blaming the ghosts of Cleevesford Woods. They're revelling in the theatre of it all.'

'Damn it! This mess has to end. Call a briefing, now. We need to pool our theories and maybe look for some new ones. Mrs Brown knows something and so does Isaac Slater. They know Alex too. We're close, so close.'

CHAPTER FORTY-SEVEN

'Gather round.' Gina pushed the chair out of the way and stood at the head of the table. Wyre and O'Connor came from their computers and grabbed chairs, along with PC Smith. Jacob picked up his bottle of water and sat opposite. 'First things first, has anyone managed to contact Joanna Brent?'

Wyre smiled. 'Yes, she has given Isaac Slater an alibi for every night over the past couple of weeks. She said he never goes out on his own and they're in every night after work and they went shopping once, together. She said she has the Asda receipt if we want to see it.' Wyre shrugged and continued. 'I also called his place of work but I couldn't get an answer so I've left a message.' O'Connor passed a packet of biscuits to Wyre. She shook her head and passed them on to Jacob.

'Thank you. As soon as this briefing is over will you also do an alibi check with Christian Brown? Cherie, his wife, has just told us that she was with him all night on Monday the twenty-sixth of October; that was the night our witness says he heard a woman arguing with Alex Swinton. I want to know if there was any way she could have been out. I also want us to look further into Cherie Brown, she's keeping something back about the case. I want to know everything about her. Another way to look at this is she may also be in danger.' Gina glanced back at the board and drew a ring around four names. Isaac, Penny, Marcus and Cherie. 'They were all school friends and they knew Alex. Both Marcus and Isaac say they barely knew him, Cherie claiming to know him even less. O'Connor, Wyre?'

'Yes.' He placed the biscuit he was about to eat on his paper-work.

'I want you both to investigate them closely and any other links that flag up, I want them forwarded to me straight away. Take any alibis amongst this group with a pinch of salt. The investigation of them doesn't close because one person confirms they were with another. What aren't they telling us? That's where our focus should lie. Any thoughts?'

The room went silent.

'There's the obvious.' Wyre scribbled a few notes and stared at them for a moment. 'They were all in on killing Alex and now they're sitting tight, hoping that we can't prove a thing while they all vouch for each other's whereabouts.'

O'Connor swallowed a bit of biscuit and continued. 'Any number of them or any combination of them could be working together. We've also established that Alex's elaborate murder could have been planned and set up by one person, even though it would have been difficult. We have no leads on the coffin or coffin makers. No useful witness accounts or CCTV evidence.' He put the rest of the biscuit in his mouth.

Jacob leaned in. 'Or none of them did it.'

Gina paused. 'That would throw us back into having nothing. They're all acting suspiciously. If none of them did it, I can guarantee that at least one of them has the information that could lead us to the killer. Whatever they're concealing, I want it.' Gina placed her hand in her pocket and felt the biscotti from earlier that morning. Her stomach began to rumble a little. She let go of it and grabbed a biscuit from the table, crunching as she stared at the board. 'I know it's early, but are Alex Swinton's toxicology results back?'

'No, guv.' Wyre flicked over to another page. 'And not likely to be back for ages.'

'Damn – I don't know why I asked. I suppose I just live in hope. Apply some pressure. Put a fast track on it. Do whatever it takes. What are we missing?' She swallowed, knowing full well that any chance of getting toxicology results back so soon was little to none. It was time to address the one thing she didn't want to speak of. 'The letter that was sent to the papers.' As agreed, only she and Briggs knew about the personal letter. 'This person wants my attention and they've got it. Why haven't they made contact again?' She felt a shiver under her hairline. 'I hate to say it but they haven't contacted me again because they haven't murdered again. Or have they? We still have no word about Penny Burton's whereabouts. Talk to me about Penny's bank and phone records.'

Wyre did her jacket button up. 'Since the Friday she went missing, there have been no transactions on her debit or credit card. As for her phone, she hasn't texted or called anyone. We don't have the details of previous messages, only numbers. She did, however, have another phone and her husband, Marcus Burton, has confirmed that she had taken that phone with her when she disappeared. It's a pay-as-you-go and not registered. I've applied for the content of her contract phone and that should be with us soon.'

'As soon as you have it, please forward it to me. I want to see her messages in the run up to her disappearance. So far, we have this. She leaves on the morning of an argument with her husband. Her behaviour is classed as normal behaviour by her friends and her husband, Marcus. He was only concerned when she still hadn't got in touch the next day. She doesn't have any other close friends that he knows of, so where is she? She didn't check into a hotel. It's like she's vanished.' Gina walked over to the window. 'We need to put out a press release. Give them Penny's photo. We need to find her. I won't lie, I'm worried for her, which is why I've taken the decision to ramp things up. Whether she's a suspect or a potential victim, we need her found. Whatever it takes. Smith?'

'Yes, guv.' The PC undid his jacket and exhaled as he leaned back.

'Given what happened to Alexander Swinton, I need you to organise a search of all woodland in the area. Get the dog team out. If Penny is out there somewhere, she may not have long, unless we're too late. It's been nearly three days since she was last seen.' Gina swallowed. Finding another shallow grave with a body in it was the last thing she wanted. 'Just because some of her friends aren't worried, it doesn't mean that we shouldn't be. We have one murder; I don't want there to be another.' The emptiness in her stomach caused it to flip. If Penny was out there, she wanted her found. Enough time had already been wasted with the days it took to report that Penny was missing. Those vital hours could never be regained.

As the meeting came to a close, she spotted Briggs passing. 'Hey, can we talk?'

He looked blankly at her, no warmth in his expression as he ground his teeth. 'Look, let's leave it for now. Let me know how you get on today.'

'Sir—'

It was too late. He was already halfway back to his office.

CHAPTER FORTY-EIGHT

Cherie gripped her phone to her ear. 'What aren't you telling me, Marcus? What did you tell the police?' She scurried along the path and broke down, just as she turned off the road, away from the police station.

'I didn't tell them anything apart from that Penny was missing. What the hell did you tell them?'

'Nothing.'

He paused on the line as she sobbed into her hands.

'Shut up with the blubbering, for heaven's sake. Pull yourself together.'

She wiped her eyes with the sleeve of her hoodie and glanced around. An elderly man with a walking stick passed her.

'Are you still there?'

She kept her eye on the man as he shuffled past. 'Yes. I'm just cutting through Windsor Close at the back of the police station. The press are everywhere. I don't know what to do.'

'Say nothing. Do nothing. Just go home.'

She hung on to the call, neither of them ready to end it. A breeze caught her hair and sent a shiver down her neck. It might only be lunchtime, but it felt as though night was looming fast. The weight of the message she'd received was bearing down hard. 'Have you heard anything from Penny?'

'No.'

'I have. She's not using her own phone.'

'I know her spare phone was missing. I told the police about that. That's the one she used to cheat on me with that bastard.'

A cat jumped from the fence behind her, making her flinch. 'What was that?'

'Nothing. Just a cat.'

'You really heard from Penny?' He paused. 'What did she say?'

'Bear with me. I'll read it to you. "*The truth has to come out, you know it does. I just need some time alone, to think, but I'm okay. Keep your phone on, I'll be in touch soon. Don't worry about me and don't tell anyone I've contacted you.*" I shouldn't have told you. I didn't even tell the police.'

'Whatever. We don't need to involve the police any further than we need. She's totally losing it.' She heard his lips slap before he continued talking. 'Shit. That can't happen. I wonder if she's been in touch with Isaac, telling him the same crap.'

'Do you think she might have?'

'I don't know. Maybe she never sent the message. Or maybe she's going mad and playing with us. Too many maybes.'

Cherie swallowed and checked up and down the street again. Every window looked dark. Behind that darkness, she imagined eyes watching her. 'Could Isaac have sent the message?'

'There's something you don't know. No one knew apart from me, Isaac and Penny. Penny has slowly been falling apart so Isaac threatened her. He told her that if she talked, she'd be the next person to see the insides of a coffin and I stupidly backed him up on that one. I didn't mean it but we needed to shut her up. It was just an empty threat, nothing more. You know I wouldn't hurt Penny, don't you?'

The thoughts of Marcus threatening his wife like that ran through Cherie's mind. She also knew them all too well. People don't change that much. She doubted she'd changed either and that was the scariest part. 'I don't know anything any more. You basically both threatened to bang Penny up in a coffin?' Darkness began to swell and a few drops of rain fell onto her nose. She glanced up at the windows, from one end to the other, then around and around until she lost her footing and stumbled. Her breathing quickened.

'If you think I'd do that you can just do one! Don't call me again.'

'Wait, don't you dare hang up on me.'

She paused and kept the call open.

'Imagine if sweet, loving Christian knew exactly what you did? Imagine your children's faces when they see their mummy for who she really is. You'd never see them again – ever. Shut the hell up. You say a word and I will make sure the world knows exactly who you are, just maybe you'll see the insides of a coffin next.'

Her gasping became deeper but she couldn't get enough oxygen. The world was fading. She slid to the ground, cowering and shaking as she ended the call. She needed it all to go away. Maybe she could run. She could go home, pack a bag and get on a train to anywhere. She could empty their savings and start again somewhere. Her children would be better off without her anyway.

She shivered and cowered until the panic passed. This wasn't new. All those years ago, she had panic attacks, but time heals and she'd said goodbye to them long ago. Like an unwelcome friend, they were back. Her phone beeped. She read the message.

I'm joining the kids at my parents' house. Don't call me, don't message. Sort yourself out. C.

He'd left her. There would be no chance of him verifying her whereabouts when the police rang. She only hoped that he hadn't woken up when she'd sneaked out of the house to confront Alex one last time. Her thoughts flashed back to what the teen boys said on Saturday night, about there being a person watching them from afar. She hadn't imagined the person at the back of the squat when she'd left Alex, the one loitering in the long dark coat. She glanced around again, gaze flitting left and right, up and down, then back again.

She would now have to go back to the house and be alone with her thoughts. Maybe it was for the best. She glanced at the message she thought was from Penny. It had to be her. Marcus was wrong. That threat from Isaac had made her run away. It had been weird with Penny not being at the dinner party. Their annual Halloween get together had always been a reminder of the secret they were keeping and the high stakes involved in cracking but now it was more than a reminder. Each one of them was under threat. They'd successfully scared Penny and now they were working on her.

She hit reply on Penny's message. It was time to do the right thing, regardless of the consequences. She replied.

Penny, please call me. Please. Let me help you. Cherie.

Would Penny truly trust her enough to text again? Was it even Penny? She leaned against the fence, shaking and shivering, sweat dripping down her forehead as she imagined Isaac reading the message she'd just sent.

'Are you okay there?' A woman leaned out of her bedroom window. One of the voyeurs had come out from behind dark glass and reached out. She ignored the woman and carried on down the path, hurrying towards where she'd parked for free on one of the residential roads.

Images of the figure in the long dark coat by where Alex was staying ran through her mind. She had been wearing something almost identical back then. It was just like her coat. Same pinched in shape. She'd worn it over her Dracula's bride costume and it had looked like it fitted in with the theme so well at the time. That coat was a part of her costume. It was as if she was haunting herself, but this other person had been real. Were they real? Did she imagine the conversation with the teenagers?

Rain fell harder, splatting on her hood, seeping through the material. Chilled to the bone, she reached the car and got in. As soon as she got home, that coat she had kept in the loft for all these years was going on a bonfire. It would be gone, once and for all, along with her fear. Burn the lot. Burn it all. Burn the memories. She pulled the little bottle of vodka from her bag. As soon as she got home, it was hers. Stuff it, she'd stop on the way back and stock up on wine. There was no one left to try for, not even herself.

CHAPTER FORTY-NINE

Jacob's voice crackled through the hands-free but Gina couldn't make out what was being said as she drove down the snaking Warwickshire roads in the dark. She thought of her home and how cold it would be when she got back. She'd sit and pore over the case notes and slowly her thoughts would turn to those letters and what they were doing to her. She realised she was gripping the steering wheel.

'I can't hear you. I'll call you when I get home. Hello, hello?' It was no good trying, he'd gone. All she knew was that the dog search had finished for the night, ready to resume in the morning and so far, nothing had been found. She exhaled. That wasn't a bad thing. She also reminded herself that so little ground had been covered. Some of the officers were going to continue under torchlight for a while but they wouldn't be able to keep that up for too long. If Penny was out there somewhere, she hoped they'd find her.

Her throat contracted. Whether the sheer panicky thoughts of someone else in a box caused that reaction or whether it was the severe lack of food in her system, she didn't know. No breakfast and no lunch, that was the sum of the meals she'd had – none. All she'd had was a couple of biscuits. A wave of nausea crept from her throat to her rumbling gut. There was a block of cheese and a packet of crackers waiting for her back home. She'd refuel while she cranked up the laptop for the evening.

The press had almost stopped her completely as she'd left the station and Lyndsey's final words were like a punch to her gut.

'Do you know what people in the village are saying? They know all about your past. How your husband beat you senseless. You should talk to me, put your side over. People love to hear a real-life story especially when it's embroiled in the case of the coffin killer. Talk to me, DI Harte. I can help you.'

It wasn't Briggs who sent the letter. Somehow, everyone seemed to know her business, her secrets. She almost let out a small cry as she thought of them all finding out her big secret. Maybe she was safe in the knowledge that the circumstances surrounding Terry's death were undiscovered, as Lyndsey wouldn't have been able to hold back on reporting that if she knew.

The press had left several messages on her mobile, and her office phone had rung constantly. They all wanted to know the same thing. Why hadn't they made any arrests? Was the coffin killer slipping through their fingers? Would the coffin killer strike again? The coffin killer – that's the name they'd settled on. Did her past have anything to do with the coffin killer choosing her?

Another snaking lane led to yet another as she got deeper into the heart of her rural village setting. On a clearer day she'd see her house in the distance, but not in the dark. As she trundled around a bend, taking it slowly, she saw a car in a verge, the glint of her own headlights on its bonnet, catching her eye. There was movement in the darkness. She pulled up on the opposite side of the road, grabbed her phone and got out of the car. No signal. She walked a little further and held it up. One bar.

'Hello.'

A voice came from the side of the car. 'My baby, please help my baby. I'm hurt but I'm okay. It's just my ankle, I can't walk. Please tell me my baby is okay.'

'Police, I'm checking in your car now. Stay still in case you've broken anything.' She checked her phone again but the signal had gone again.

The baby seat was empty and the changing bag had opened out everywhere. Milk splattered the back seat and the interior light was out. She felt around for anything and not a cry or breath could be heard. Panic rose in her chest. No, not tonight. She couldn't find a dead baby, she just couldn't. She grabbed her phone, using it to light up the car. Her gaze caught the rear-view mirror then her stomach sunk. There was no baby. She pressed a number, any number on her phone and it made a connection. As she turned to defend herself from the person whose face was half-covered by the black hood, something struck her hard.

The last thing she heard was Briggs's voice. 'Hello… Gina. Are you there?' Then her fuzzy vision lost the last bit of light, the stars in the sky were gone. She felt a prick in her neck. Sinking… she was sinking into uselessness. She tried to force her eyelids open but the sheer pain of the blow to her head and… the drug? Woozy, this was more than a blow to the head.

CHAPTER FIFTY

DI Harte, this should help you remember. I need you to remember how it felt…

I hit the clapper-less bell with my gloved knuckle; it's ready for its intended. The dull clunk brings a tear to my eye. Every bone in my body aches. I press on my arm: yes, yes the bruises are still there. Even though they come of their own accord, it's still hard steering a wobbly body into a coffin. They still fight me with the little bit they have left to fight with. The exhaustion I feel is unreal. My face is flushed even though a frost has formed over the past couple of hours. I've never worked so hard but the work has only just begun for phase three.

One more to go then my work is done. The aggressor and the bystander have gone. The only one left is the instigator. *You were more than just the instigator but that is what I remember you for. I thought you were my friend.* Hurrying back to my car, I easily drive it out of the ditch. It was never as bad as it looked from the road but DI Harte, the hero, had to stop and check. She'd never forgive herself if she'd driven by without checking that everyone in the car was okay. I stare at the matchbox and three matches that sit on the passenger seat. This is it. After this one, I'm out, gone. I won't be here to bear the consequences of everything I've done. My departure is all planned and I won't be coming back. I'm going to fly and be free to not have to relive another nightmare.

DI Harte, she only wanted to save the baby and I tricked her. It was so easy, knowing her the way I do, and I didn't have to wait around too long, thankfully. She wants to help, always helping people. Always catching the bad ones. She's a hero but I know her pain and now she knows mine – every last bit of it. Then again, she already knew, a little reminder was all she needed, and I sure gave her that tonight. *I am you, Gina, and you are me. We are one and the same, I just need you to see that.*

Fight, DI Harte. You didn't that last time, when Terry locked you away. You gave up like a little mouse. Now that mouse must become a lion.

I imagine her tear-soaked face. *DI Harte, do you still choose to be a victim? I decided to no longer be a victim and you must do the same. I've prepared you for this moment. You're ready, Harte. Time to fight.* A tear rolls down my cheek. In another life we could have been a lot closer.

I pack the clapper and matches in my bag and carefully place them next to the syringe. I'm all prepared and ready to go. Final phase, here I come.

I've done all my watching.

I'm more than done with waiting.

Instigator – I am coming for you.

CHAPTER FIFTY-ONE

Briggs stared at his phone. He'd tried to call Gina back but her phone was ringing out. He toiled over their last few words. He shouldn't have walked away, he should have given her his time and put his anger aside. She was scared, he should have seen that, scared and paranoid, knowing that some killer was making things personal.

His anger was nothing more than love disguised. He knew that and he wondered if she really knew that. He shook his head. He didn't even really know if she trusted him at the moment. He tried again. No answer.

'Sir.' Jacob stood in front of his open office door.

'Everything okay?'

'I don't know. Guv was meant to call me back but she hasn't. She was heading home and it's not like her not to do as she says. I keep calling and it keeps ringing out or going to voicemail.'

'There are a lot of spots in the area where you can't get a signal.'

Jacob scratched his five o'clock shadow. 'There is that. I think this case is just making me a bit paranoid. I think it's making us all feel a bit grossed out. I'll keep trying her. Maybe she's stopped off at the shop to grab some food or a takeaway.'

'Yes, that's probably it.'

Jacob turned to leave as Briggs tried to call her again. Something didn't feel right. Could it be that she was angry with him for turning his back on her when she left? Maybe that's all it was.

But Jacob, why wouldn't she answer his calls? His chair scraped on the floor as he hurried to the incident room.

Wyre was just about to put her coat on. 'Right, got to get to the gym. See you tomorrow, sir.'

'Wait. Have you heard from Gina since she left?'

'Should I have?'

'Don't worry about it.' He went to leave.

'Is everything okay?'

He nodded. 'Of course. I think she's on her way home. Jacob can't get hold of her. I'm sure she'll call as soon as she gets home.' It was still early and she'd only left the office about an hour ago. No, she always calls back.

'Catch you tomorrow.' She waved and did the zip up on her coat before leaving.

He slumped at the main table, alone with only the buzzing of the strip light for company. A few raindrops scattered across the window. He grabbed his phone and tried again and again. Maybe he could annoy her into answering. Not his usual style but worry was driving him to it. Her voicemail kicked in. 'Gina, call me ASAP. I just want to know that you're safe. Jacob said you haven't called him back yet. Call me.' He placed the phone face down on the table and put his head in his hands. Everything was falling apart. He wanted to know that Gina was safe, go home and snuggle up to his dog and pour a glass of whiskey by the fire.

His phone rang. 'Gina?'

'Sorry, sir.' It was Jacob. 'I was going to head off home but I'll stick around until she's home and calls me.'

'You're worried too.'

'It's stupid, isn't it? Guv hasn't been gone that long but I can always get her on the phone.'

'It's not stupid at all. Something isn't right. If you hear anything at all, let me know. Make sure a drive-by passes her house again, and tell them they need to do it now.'

'On it, sir.'

He ended the call and linked his hands together, staring at his shimmery reflection in the smeared dark window.

CHAPTER FIFTY-TWO

Gina wiped the drool from her cheek. 'Hello,' she stuttered. As she opened her eyes to darkness, she felt her body swaying. *I'm dizzy, just dizzy.* She gripped what was in her hand and it made a rustling noise. Dropping it, she reached up and to the sides. Every now and again, she would slip back into the room with no way out, but she was fighting the drug with all she had. Her senses were coming back, but not fast enough for her to get a grasp of reality.

'No!' She hit and kicked the box that surrounded her. The top was soft and velvety as it glided along her fingertips. The sides, also lined. Choking, she gasped hard, but her lungs felt devoid of any air. A chill worked its way from her shoulders to her feet. She tried to inhale but nothing worked. Her throat was closing up. Was that damp she could smell? As she went to gasp again, a little bit of air got through. Not much, not enough. She wheezed and pounded on her chest with her fist, knocking the top of the coffin with each hit.

Breathe, breathe.

Hyperventilating, she reached for the soft material above and began pulling and loosening it until she felt it tearing around the edges. More of it pinged away from the sides and her breath came back a little. She pulled at the material again and the clump of it fell to her chest. As light as a feather but its presence, as heavy as iron when she couldn't inhale deeply. Shivering away, she managed to tangle it in her fingers and around her one hand. Reaching up, she could feel more wood. It was just like Alex's coffin.

Head pounding and throat dry, she tried to squeal as tears fell down her face. She was once again scared little Gina, locked in the shed with no way out. But it hadn't been like this. Maybe with a lot of fight, she could have broken the wood and climbed out at any time, but fear had kept her a prisoner in the same way that fear had kept her with Terry. Scared of what Terry would do to her if she tried to escape. Another life had been her responsibility at the time. She knew he could have killed her and she always wondered what might have become of Hannah. He'd taken everything with his mind games, controlling behaviour and violence. She'd had nothing left to fight with. She had no idea when he'd been waiting and watching and he'd reinforced that uncertainty at every given opportunity. As far as she'd been concerned, he was always there. Always waiting.

She kicked the wood and held what little of her breath she could. There was no sound, but then again, Terry never made a sound. *I am watching.* Stalking like a hunter waiting for its prey to move. That's how Terry operated. Whoever had her trapped in this coffin knew that. They knew too much. They knew Terry.

'Are you enjoying my little surprise, Gina darling?' Terry's voice sounded like it was next to her. It was in her, around her, everywhere.

'Leave me alone.'

'You thought you were safe, in the clear. Let me tell you something, I always win. You know I do. You can't get away from me, ever. I always told you that.'

He would never let her go, however hard she tried to leave him behind and start afresh; he was always there, crawling through her thought passages. His laughter filled the box and the darkness was closing in. Pitch-black darkness.

She shuffled against the side of the coffin away from his tyranny, but she bumped into something soft.

'See, I'm everywhere.'

She jerked and shuffled to the other side, like a snake slithering sideways but with less finesse. Reaching out, she could feel the material that she'd pulled from the top of the coffin.

'Miss me.'

Screaming, she held her arms over her head. She'd been drugged, she knew it. 'Go away. Get off me.'

A few seconds later, the coffin was silent except for the sound of a hooting owl. Her heartbeat ramped up again and the sound of blood pulsating through her head silenced the owl. She had heard the owl; that was the important thing.

With trembling hands, she pulled out a small box from her pocket. She knew exactly what it would be. Shaking it, she listened to the three matches hitting cardboard. As she slid the tiny box open, the smell of sulphur hit her nostrils. She struck and for a few seconds, she could see the horror of her situation. The coffin killer had come for her. Alexander Swinton had not got out alive. She wasn't going to get out alive. She struck another match and felt a fresh tear sliding down her cheek as she saw the hopelessness of her situation.

Closing her eyes, she imagined herself to be locked in the shed again.

In her mind, she wrapped her jumper around her elbow and jabbed the wooden panels that Terry had nailed across the shed windows, hoping to crack them and the glass behind them. After tearing them off with her bare hands, she felt freedom as the glass shattered and she could climb out. She grabbed a knife from the kitchen, and if Terry got in her way, she'd jab him with it. What next? She would run to Hannah and grab her from her cot. Then she'd sprint to the road and flag a car down. She had to imagine her victory. That's what would have happened. She could have stopped his tyranny there and then. She could have found a way but fear had held her back, and love. She swallowed. Whatever punishment Terry had bestowed on Gina, she had loved him once and she couldn't let go of that person she'd met at the time, the same person who would break down and beg for forgiveness and claim she was his everything.

Her fingers gripped the last match as she remembered the moment she had pushed Terry to his death. For a split second, she saw the old Terry. That's what had hurt so much. She wiped her tears away. 'If you ever loved me, Terry, really loved me, you'd never have hurt me so much.'

She lit the last match and stared ahead open-mouthed. How had she missed that?

CHAPTER FIFTY-THREE

Cherie placed her key in the door and felt the emptiness of what was once a bustling family home. The first thing to hit her was the cold, the second was the vacuous feeling of loneliness and she was to blame. She exhaled and a plume of white mist led the way into the chilly hallway. She grabbed another coat from the peg, putting it on over her hoodie as she switched the light and heating on. 'Christian,' she called. She knew there wouldn't be an answer. Why would there be? She'd driven him away.

Hurrying through to the kitchen, she slammed the bag of shopping onto the kitchen table. Shopping – she wasn't sure she could call it shopping. She pulled out the litre of vodka and two bottles of red wine. Unscrewing the vodka, a tear slipped down her cheek as she placed it to her lips and felt the warmth of the liquid slipping down her throat. It no longer mattered that it was cold. It no longer mattered that Christian had left her and it no longer mattered that there was a chance she'd never see her children again. Everything was going to come out and there was nothing she could do to stop it, not now the divisions in the group had been caused.

Maybe, just maybe, she'd been recognised as she discreetly sat and watched, trying to pluck up the courage to speak up and say something. She shook her head. No, that hadn't happened. What was happening came down to Isaac or Marcus or even Penny.

Her finger hovered over Isaac's number on her phone. No, she couldn't call him. Not after the conversation she'd had with

Marcus. Who to trust? That was the big question. Isaac – no. Marcus – no. Penny – who knows? Joanna – had Isaac said anything to Joanna? Maybe he'd kept his secret from her like she had from Christian. Maybe he hadn't. Maybe Joanna was in on all this with Isaac, doing all she could to protect him. Maybe they were all playing with her head.

The only thing she could trust was the alcohol in front of her. She could rely on it to make her forget and to fill her heart with all that she was missing. After an initial hit from the vodka, she unscrewed a bottle of red and took a swig. The merlot was mellower, full-bodied and flavoursome. 'I have missed you, you beauty.' She swallowed a bit more and leaned her head against the wall.

The light coming from the hallway led her eye to the windowsill. The photo of Bella and Oliver filled her with a flush of love that warmed her up. Their chocolate-brown eyes and bright smiles stared back at her. Bella's long black plaits and freckly, coffee-coloured skin made Cherie want to reach out and hug her, drink her in as she smelled her hair. She gulped down some more wine. A quarter of a bottle gone, just like that. The table shook as she slammed her hand down.

She stood and balanced on her wobbly legs, then shuffled to the photo and held it close to her heart as she sobbed. The effects of the vodka and wine were kicking in quick. The room swayed a little – she was just at the slightly merry stage. During her pre-alcoholic stage in life, this is how she'd start a night out. But now, this is how she was going to start a big night in. If she was to sleep, she needed a drink and she needed to sleep. She needed the chance to dream of her children and her life before the past popped in for a visit and ruined her future. If all she could have were dreams, then that was what she'd have to settle for.

Taking one step at a time up the stairs, she turned off the landing light and headed to her and Christian's bedroom. Her unread book lay flat on her bedside table, the one she hadn't been able to concentrate on while sitting at the café, hiding at the back in the shadows while she watched and waited. *Crime and Punishment* – she hadn't even got through the first chapter. As she'd sat in the café, she'd pondered over what to do. She should have revealed her motives sooner but as always, she was too late and the person she needed to speak to wasn't often there when she was. Besides, that person would no longer recognise her. They had barely known each other.

It was too late to fix anything, too late to save her family and too late to save herself. The only thing she had control of was her spiral into descent and this she was doing her own way.

The quilt was all ruffled on the side where Christian had slept alone the night before. As she went to pull a curtain, she stumbled and dragged it along with the rail. 'Damn.' She placed the wine on the windowsill and dropped the curtain to the floor. Movement caught her eye. She stared beyond the back garden and saw someone in a long black coat. Similar, if not the same as the one she'd failed to get rid of and, for that, it still haunted her. She glanced back and the figure had gone. Maybe the only thing she'd just seen was a vision of herself. It was that creepy coat again. She would get rid of it but not now, tomorrow, or it would haunt her forever.

She grabbed the wine and sobbed as she reached Bella's bedroom. Slipping off her shoes, she got into her daughter's bed. She lay there in the darkness inhaling the citrusy scent of her shower gel, the one Bella loved. A long black hair lay on the pillow. She held it up and ran her fingers down it before allowing it to slip and fall to the floor. She grabbed the bear that had been Bella's favourite since as long as Cherie could remember and hugged it closely as she brought the wine to her lips once again, a drizzle slipping down the side of her mouth.

An image flashed through her mind. A stick poking through cut flesh and laughter as salty tears dripped down the girl's neck.

She could see her black coat reflected in that girl's eyes as she held the torch in her direction.

Marcus and Isaac would love it if she lost the plot. Maybe they were now seeing her as the loose cannon of the group but it was one of them, not her, and she'd get to the bottom of it all once she'd sobered up.

Her phone beeped, lighting up the darkness. She frowned and finished off the wine before closing her eyes. It could wait. She stared at the wine and felt her car keys in her coat pocket. There was one thing that couldn't wait.

CHAPTER FIFTY-FOUR

A split in the wood, just around her waist area – Gina could see it. The match burned down, catching her finger. 'Ouch.' She placed it in her mouth and sucked it to take the sting away but all she could taste was dirt and grit. She spat it away and felt in the darkness for the split.

There. She remained still and silent. That was definitely the sound of an owl. Then her phone began to ring but the coffin hadn't lit up. She was in a shallow grave. She felt the adrenaline pumping as she pushed, cutting into her finger as she prodded the gap to drive it apart.

Punching and hitting it, the split finally crunched. A shower of earth thudded onto her midriff. She reached behind and caught the end of a piece of string. If Alexander Swinton's murder was anything to go by, she knew what was at the other end. A bell without a clapper. She tugged it but something was different. It dinged away with every pull. Whoever had buried her had not wanted her to die. 'Help.' Someone had to hear her. Her phone went again. It wasn't too far away. It had to be close to the coffin. Another spurt of muck slipped through the split as she probed the hole further. The gap was widening. She only hoped the grave was shallow enough to escape from.

Kicking and punching at the whole box, she hoped something would give soon.

'Help!'

Maybe the person who trapped her was waiting and watching. *I am waiting. I am watching. I am coming.* She stopped and tried to steady her breathing, listening for clues. Nothing. Not a sound. Her phone had stopped ringing. Had her attacker ended the call or had the caller stopped the call?

Gently, she popped a second finger through the gap in the wood and continued to drive it upwards. A cold drop of water landed on the tip of her little finger followed by the chill of air. Rain. She was only buried a couple of inches under the earth at most. The tiny drop turned into a downpour. Frosty water started to drip like percolating coffee through the hole. Then the drip, drip, drip, turned into a stream. She was going to drown.

Panicking, she hit and punched the weak spot and felt one last creak of resistance. The box gave up as her fist emerged through the wood and soil. As she pulled her fist back down and punched again, the splinters dug in. A tear trickled down Gina's cheek as the sting turned into raw hot pain.

She imagined herself stuck in the shed, listening to Hannah's cries coming from the house, then she roared as she snatched her arm back into the coffin and punched again. Dead people don't come back to life. Terry was gone and no one in her life was as scary as Terry had been to her. She was ready for whatever was waiting for her outside her coffin and she wasn't going to die tonight, not without a fight.

She pounded again and again, each time more wood breaking away. Muck, water, soil and grass began to spill in, but she felt something magical – air. She gasped and smiled as she finished breaking the wood by her head. Jerking up, she emerged through the thin layer of earth and laughed as a sheet of torrential rain slashed against her face, washing the dirt away. A clap of thunder boomed through her ear. A fork of lightning flashed in the direction of her house. It was as if Terry himself was here and was trying to scare her back into the box. *Not this time.*

With bloodied arms she reached out and lifted her stiff upper body out, where she fell open-mouthed into a puddle, the stench of manure making her gag. Her phone lit up again, just ahead on a clump of grass. She dragged her stiffened body through the sludge and snatched the phone.

'Chris.'

'Gina, where have you been? I've been calling for ages. I know we had words but… maybe we need to speak. Can I come over?'

Gina rolled onto her back and smiled at the dark sky above. She was alive and no one else was there. 'I need help, now. Send an emergency crew and forensics to Bramble Lane, on the way to mine.'

'What's happened?'

'I'll tell you when you get here. I can't speak.' She gasped for breath and drank the raindrops that kept landing.

'Gina.'

'I haven't got the energy to talk. They'll see my car. Just get here now.' She dropped the phone and lay there shivering with her hands in her pocket. Something rustled. She pulled out the biscotti and a handful of receipts and smiled as she let them go in her pocket. She wasn't hungry, not right now.

Why her? Why this? Her own manic laughter filled the night.

The first letter from their killer. The words now meant more than ever before.

We are the same. I just need you to see that.

She knew exactly why this had happened to their killer and it was nothing to do with Terry. Terry's torturing ways was merely their common denominator. *You have my attention alright!*

CHAPTER FIFTY-FIVE

In the distance, Gina could see blue lights flashing. She struggled to her feet and slid along the ground to her car, trying not to slip. The rain turned into a slight drizzle before almost stopping. Her car door was still open, just as she'd left it, but the light was no longer on. The battery had obviously gone flat. Hands shivering, she stepped into the driver's side and closed the door, hoping to warm up a little. As she pulled the last of the splinters from her hand, she glanced out of the window. The other car had gone. She'd been so close to catching the killer and she'd let whoever it was go without even seeing a face or taking a registration plate number.

She'd fallen straight into their trap. Placing her hand back into her warm pocket, she felt a piece of paper with her fingertip and pulled it out. It was larger than the usual receipts that normally filled her pockets and bag.

The blue lights were getting closer.

She turned her phone light on and squinted to read the tiny writing on the faded sheet of paper from a notebook. Gina dropped it on the passenger seat and leaned over, not touching the page again. It appeared to be a diary entry.

1 November 2008

Dear all of you.

I'm no longer the person I was yesterday. I have been reborn as a hollow image of my former self. Hope has gone. Love has gone. I have gone. I want to feel something but I can't. Do you know how it feels to feel nothing? I haven't even cried. Why can't I cry?

What you took from me can never be returned. It is a part of me, a slice of who I am. I'm not going back to that school, ever. You will never do this to me again.

To my aggressor. Why me? What did I ever do to you? Your cruelty knows no bounds. I pity everyone in your life. My wounds are testament to how evil you are.

The bystander. You could have got help at any time but you stared at me throughout. Humiliation overload! You could have done the right thing, but you chose not to.

Finally, the instigator. You noticed me leaving the party and you couldn't help but throw fuel on the fire. My so-called new friend! Following me out, taunting me, forcing me in a direction I wouldn't choose to normally take. Pick on the school newbie, why don't you? I wasn't allowed to walk back through the woods – Mum and Dad would never have allowed that. That's when I realised that you'd planned this all along. It was probably meant as a Halloween joke originally, but the joke took a sinister turn, didn't it? How did you all get so carried away? I'll tell you how, because of you, the instigator. A suggestion here, a remark there, which led to more than any of you had planned. You enjoyed every moment of it all.

The bystander shouted out that what you were doing wasn't a part of the plan but you both carried on and the bystander continued to keep watch, alongside two others in masks. You all had a choice in this, you could have stopped at any time, but you didn't and I paid the price.

That brings me back to my main question. What did I ever do to you? Nothing.

I will never be fixed and I will never be free of what you put me through, and I will never forget. Never!

One minute I think I should tell someone, the next I can't. If I tell, everyone will know the details and that scares me more. I don't want people to know what you all did to me. I want to go back to my old school. I want to go home. Today, I am going to ask Mum if I can stay with Nan. I'm going away for a while. I need to think, get my head together, decide how I live with this or what I do about it.

A large tear plopped onto the back of Gina's hand. She flinched at the tap on her window. PC Smith smiled and Kapoor was just getting out of the car. 'Alright, guv. We got here as quick as possible.'

Gina pulled an evidence bag from the glove compartment, turned it inside out and bagged the letter up. One last thing caught her attention through the plastic. On the back of the page was a triangle. The top point had a doodle of a tree next to it, the point on the left had a doodle of three tiny houses next to it, two of them without roofs. The last point had a question mark next to it and a picture of a little ghost. Her mind whirred: if the woods represented Alex's body, what did the houses and the ghost represent?

'There's another body.' Gina gulped. 'I think it will be Penny Burton's.'

'What?'

Gina held the bagged letter up as an ambulance parked beside them.

Briggs's car skidded to a stop behind hers and he ran out from his car. 'Are you okay? What happened?' Gina stared at him, unable to speak. 'Gina, are you alright?'

She forced a smile and looked up at PC Smith. 'Can you keep the letter safe? It needs to be booked into evidence ASAP.' He nodded and left Briggs with her.

Gina knew she wouldn't be going home or anywhere else for ages. Samples from her body would be taken, she'd have to make a full statement and that would take hours, her car would be impounded for further sampling. 'I know why I was chosen, it's in the killer's letter. As soon as forensics get here, they need to cordon off that side of the road, the cut through to the field and the coffin. I was buried alive.' Another tear slipped down her cheek. She turned away from Briggs, not wanting him to see her weeping.

'It's okay. You're safe now.' He placed a hand on her shoulder. How could she have ever doubted him? Briggs had not sent the letter to the press. Her mind had just got the better of her.

'I'm sorry.' She wiped her eyes. 'Have a look at the letter that I just gave to Smith. It's a diary excerpt from a very distressed person, a victim of an assault. They know I'd understand how they feel. How they know this, I have no idea. Probably the same way Lyndsey Saunders and everyone in the town seems to know.'

'What?'

'I'll fill you in when I can get my breath back. That's what I was calling the station for while I was driving. I was hoping to sound Jacob out first, just fishing to see if he'd been called by the press, then I was going to call you.'

'Okay, is there an immediate lead in all this, the diary you mentioned?'

She nodded. 'There's a triangle drawn on the back of the letter. One point has trees on it; I'm betting that it represents the woods. Another point has three little houses drawn on it, except two houses have no roof. We need to check out all derelict and crumbling buildings. We need to go back to the squat. This is a big clue. A house with no roof. The roof of the squat is damaged and it is at the end of a row of three houses. Whoever is doing this is giving it to us on a plate. We just need to focus.'

'But the other houses on that row have roofs.'

'I know. It's the best I have and it has been a link to the case.'

'I'll call it in, get someone over there to search the house and the area.'

'We're looking for a buried coffin and hurry. Penny might still be alive. Get the dogs to go over the grounds.'

Briggs turned and hurried over to PCs Smith and Kapoor. They both hurried back to their car and radioed for assistance. Gina spotted the forensics van pulling up and stepped out of her car. 'Whoever did this to me may have been in my car.'

Keith slowly straightened his stiff back out and nodded. 'I'll be over in a minute.' He hobbled around to the boot of the van to get his kit.

She grabbed her bag and stood at the roadside. 'I need to go to the squat. I need to be a part of this.'

Briggs hurried over. 'You are not going anywhere. You are heading back to the station. You know the procedure. For heaven's sake, you've just come into contact with the coffin killer. We'll need your clothes, swabs, nail clippings, the lot. Your hands are bleeding.'

'Were bleeding. It was just a couple of little splinters, that's all. I need to be there, I know this person better than anyone.'

'No arguments or I'll have to take you off the case. Go back and get checked out and cleaned up. If we find anything, you'll be the first to know. Don't leave until I get back. You can't go back home alone tonight.'

'Says who?'

'I can't force you into anything, but I'm scared for you. Take this seriously, you were buried alive tonight!' He gave her a pleading look. 'Please don't go home. I can feed your cat and I can drop you at a hotel, at someone's house or lo and behold, you can stay at mine. I have a spare room.' He wiped the tear from her eye.

He was right. It was too risky to go home. 'I'll see you at the station later. I'll need a lift back.' She knew that neither of them would be going home that night, with all that was going on. She'd grab an hour in the family room on the couch.

'Get in my car.' He gave her the keys.

She took them and hurried, grateful of the warmth as she got in. She closed her eyes and imagined the drawing of the triangle one more time. It was a perfect little triangle and that couldn't be a coincidence. The third point had been marked up with a question mark. Was there another victim?

CHAPTER FIFTY-SIX

Now

Tuesday, 3 November

'Lola… Lola.' Tracy popped the purchase orders into a tray and pushed open the door to the Portakabin, scanning the makeshift car park for her missing young dachshund. She glanced back; the two older ones were curled up in their baskets, far too sensible to be out on such a chilly damp day but she had let Lola out for a pee. Being a pup, Tracy didn't want to risk her messing on the floor, especially as she hadn't stocked up on cleaning supplies. That was another job on her ever-expanding list. She glanced at her answerphone: twelve messages. She'd get around to that after she'd finished all the other urgent jobs like ordering the next batch of materials.

In the distance, she spotted her husband coordinating the builders on site. This development was going to be the making of them after investing everything they had to build it. Thirty detached homes on an exclusive gated community with security at the entrance, just what the wealthier people of Cleevesford craved. Safety, luxury and comfort. They were offering it all and at least twenty had been reserved after they'd completed the show home.

She glanced back at the board as she contemplated making some toast for breakfast. Every contractor had turned up today except for the one she wished they hadn't included in the project.

Isaac Slater. For two weeks he'd messed them around by turning up late and leaving early, and he'd even dropped a brick from height, narrowly missing a labourer. That had been his final warning. The last thing they needed was bad press when it came to health and safety. She walked over to the board and drew a ring around his name. He'd blown every chance. From now, he was officially off the job. Grabbing the phone, she tried to call him once again but like the other times, the call went straight to voicemail. Maybe he'd left one of the many messages. She shook her head. That would be a first.

'Be good for Mummy.' She removed her coat and a dog lead from the back of her chair and left, shutting the other two dogs in. As she trod the sodden earth below, she felt a bit of damp oozing through the tear in the side of her old work boot. Her tangled blond ponytail had begun to come loose and her straggly hair blew into her mouth and stuck to her face. She zipped up the body warmer underneath her coat and shivered.

Glancing back and forth, trees at the one end, fast-moving building works at the other, she called out again. This time louder. 'Lola, come to Mummy. Lola.' In the distance she could hear the clattering of tools being carried in the wind.

She dredged through the turned-over earth that would at some point resemble a lush flower bed and she spotted her little mischievous dog in the distance barking and wagging its tail. 'Lola you little shit, come here now.' That dog was going to get obedience lessons sooner rather than later. 'Come on, Lola. Don't make Mummy tread in all this.' Tracy frowned as she took another step. It was no use hoping that the dog would come to her. 'Come on, girl.'

The dog began to yap and run around in a circle. It's long body catching up with its front legs, little tail wagging away.

'Bloody hell.' Tracy persevered through the sludge until she reached the most exclusive row of three detached houses on the estate. She glanced up at the roofs on two of the houses that still needed some work. Plastic sheeting rattled as the breeze picked up and a gust of dried leaves whipped into the air. 'Lola. Come here now.' Tracy removed her hair band and retied the stray strands away from her face.

The little dog looked like it was laughing as it refused to obey her command. Stepping past a pile of roof tiles, she hurried to the dog as it yapped at the fence.

'Get here now.' She reached down and clipped the lead to the dog's collar. 'You naughty girl.' She leaned forward and the dog licked her nose. Tracy couldn't be angry for too long. She stroked the dog's head and began to pull it back towards the Portakabin, but the dog refused to budge as it continued to bark at the fence.

Something wasn't right. She knew her newest member of the pack was a handful, but she and Fred hadn't seen her acting like this before. 'What is it, girl.' One squelching step after another led her to the low fence. She peered over. There was nothing but brambles. As she went to turn, something shiny caught her eye: a bell hanging from a branch. She edged in closer and saw there was string coming from the top of the bell that led to what looked like a clearing. She looped the dog lead over the low fence and cocked one leg over, followed by another. As she went to push past the brambles, her coat caught and held her back. 'Sodding hell.' She released the coat and continued, taking what looked like a bit of a trodden path into the thicket.

She gave the bell a little knock but it didn't sound. Her gaze followed the string until it settled on a mound of earth. Heart pumping, she kneeled and began scooping away the soil. She'd been reading the news this past few days. It had been dominated by the coffin killer. She only hoped the killer hadn't struck again but the signs were there. It was no good, there was too much earth and her hands kept getting caught in pieces of bramble and pine needles. Little cuts started to ooze blood. She reached into her pocket, but her phone wasn't there. She'd left it on her desk after trying to ring Isaac. 'Damn.'

A rattle came from beyond the shrubs that backed onto a lane. She paused and held her breath. 'Hello?'

The dog began to whimper from the other side of the fence. She caught a glimpse of the long black coat and that led her eye to the bottom half of the figure. 'Hello?' Her last word sounded like a croak. A loud rustling sound came at her as she turned. She screamed as loud as she could, but she knew that no one would hear. The houses that were being built at present were right at the entrance to the road.

As she stood to run, her foot caught in an entanglement of branches in the spiny undergrowth. She was going down and fast and there was nothing she could do. She closed her eyes and hoped that she would be spared as her bare hands landed in a clump of stingers.

CHAPTER FIFTY-SEVEN

'You didn't find Penny at the squat. Damn. Where is she?' Gina stood at the front of the incident room in the standard issue grey tracksuit that had been given to her by the medical officer after her clothing and samples had been taken. She picked at the dressing that covered the thicker scratch on her arm. It hadn't quite needed stitches; that was something she'd been grateful to hear.

PC Smith popped his hat on the table and rubbed his eyes where the dark bags had taken over as the most prominent feature on his face. Kapoor sat next to him and yawned as he spoke. 'We searched the grounds at the back and all up and down the road. Unfortunately we only found four shopping trolleys and a load of fly-tipped household waste. Oh, and several dead rats. Not what we'd hoped for. The dogs didn't sniff anything out either. We didn't stop there: we went through every bin store and tree filled patch on and beyond the street. Not a thing.'

Gina pointed to the triangle that had been drawn on the back of the diary excerpt. The one she'd blown up to A4-size and pinned to the board. 'This is a puzzle to our killer. They have given us a triangle. I'm guessing each point represents a victim, given that the top point is of the woods and that's where Alexander Swinton was found. The point to the left, I'll call it point number two, has a little drawing of three houses. Just a simple square for the houses and one with a triangle roof. I see it as a house. Two houses without roofs. What kind of house wouldn't have a roof?'

Jacob finished chomping on a sausage sandwich. 'Flat-roofed houses. There are a few in Cleevesford. No, let me think, they're maisonettes or flats. Or…' He put the sandwich down.

Wyre interrupted. 'Houses that are still being built.' Her smile filled the room as she dropped her pen to her pad.

Gina pointed and grinned. O'Connor smiled back. Given that she'd washed in the station toilets and felt like a dog's dinner that had been sitting in the sun for a day, she knew that Wyre had hit onto something worthwhile. 'I'm betting on that. Don't let me stop you looking into flat-roofed buildings though. We are looking for a building with a roof, next to two without. The drawing is simple but specific. Can you get onto that immediately?' She smiled at Smith.

'Of course, guv.' He scraped his chair across the floor and gestured for Kapoor to follow him.

'Oh, and thank you. I know you have both been out all night and you're tired. I know it's a lot to ask…'

'But we need to catch the person or people who are terrorising Cleevesford. We're totally on board.' Kapoor's high voice and enthusiastic expression filled her heart with joy. The team were giving their best to the case regardless of how little sleep they'd had, including her. Smith and Kapoor grabbed their hats and did up their fluorescent coats as they left the room.

The rest of the team glanced at the board as the room fell silent. Jacob went to open his mouth.

'If any of you ask if I'm alright, I'm going to flip. If I wasn't, I'd go home, okay?'

They all nodded.

'Right, what's next? The diary entry. This screams revenge. Whoever is doing this is hurting right now, hurting from something that happened in the past. As we've had no word from Penny Burton, nor have we found her yet despite the press release, I'm considering her to be the next victim. Given the amount of time she's been gone, I'm not holding out much hope.' Gina swallowed. For a moment she felt a sense of panic flash through her. She was back in the box with a lit match, believing that she was going to die in that very box. O'Connor went to speak. 'Yes, I'm alright.'

'I wasn't going to say anything, guv.' O'Connor held his hands up and smiled.

'You were tempted.'

'You got me.'

Her serious expression broke into a smile. She couldn't be angry at her team for being concerned. 'Smith and Kapoor are currently looking into what site the house drawing could represent. The triangle; the woods, three houses and the final drawing. A question mark with a ghost next to it. I have no idea? It's around Halloween so a ghost is relevant. A ghost doesn't represent a place like the other two.'

'A haunted house, guv.' Wyre leaned forward, her black straight hair resting on the tabletop.

'I'm not bringing the supernatural into this investigation but where around here is considered to be haunted by people who are into that sort of thing, by people who have those beliefs?'

O'Connor tapped his pen in a drumming motion on the edge of the table. 'The woods. Didn't the girls who found the first body say that there was a ghost story attached to those woods? Something about ghosts of the past who were buried alive and now roam on Halloween, scaring people.'

'But we have that area in our sights. It's cordoned off and it's being watched.' Gina frowned. It would take a brave killer to dig another grave and transport a coffin into place under our noses, let alone kill someone there.

'They'd come back full circle if they ended up back at the woods.'

Gina pointed to the board. 'But this is a triangle. Not a bad starting theory but we need more suggestions.'

'The squat looks like a backdrop for a horror film. Maybe it's that and we missed something.' Wyre began to twist the bottom of her pen away as she pondered that thought.

Gina ran her fingers through her hair, half-trying to brush it a little. 'Again, we're all over it and we'll be keeping an eye on that location. Just digressing, any more news on Nicola Swinton?'

Wyre flicked to another page. 'She has an alibi later that night: her new lover. She was reluctant to say anything but eager to put herself in the clear.'

'Great.'

PC Smith hurried through the door. 'Guv, we've had another report of what looks like a grave. It's on a building site close by and get this, I asked if there were any houses nearby and the woman, Tracy, said it was behind a row of three. When I probed a little further, it turns out that two of them have roofs that still need working on. Uniform have already been dispatched.'

'We need a full team down there immediately. Wyre, call Bernard, get forensics on it straight away.' Gina removed the zip up top. 'I'll grab a smarter jacket and my trainers then we'll go. Anyone got a spare pair of trousers in roughly my size?'

Everyone shook their heads.

'That was a long shot. Did you say the woman's name was Tracy?'

PC Smith nodded. 'Yes, Tracy and Fred Salter own the building company.'

Gina shivered as she headed along the corridor. 'I recognise the name of the company. It's where Isaac Slater works. Did we hear back from them?'

Wyre shook her head. 'I've tried to contact them a few times and no answer, so I left a few messages. It was on my list to actually pop in today.'

'Another grave, another body. Looks like our killer has struck again. We have to jump on this now. The coffin killer strikes again, I can just see it in the papers. Satanic cults, burying the living.'

*

The woman from admin came in with the post. 'Oh, here you go.'

Gina took the envelope from her; as before it was marked private and confidential. She ran to her office, put some latex gloves on and began prising it open as carefully as she could. She grabbed her phone and hit Briggs's name. 'Come on.'

'You okay?'

'I've had another private and confidential letter. It says, "DI Harte. We'd all like to feel safe but truth is, we're not. The worst thing is, imagining you are crazy. Even worse is, believing that you are. They make you crazy, it is their fault. We're not crazy. We need to stand up and roar, show them who we really are." This person is standing up and roaring. They want us to acknowledge what has been done to them. I can't let this be about me, I just can't.' Her voice began to crackle. 'The others are going to see these when all this is over and the evidence is compiled. I have to get used to the fact that my private life will no longer be that.'

'I can't protect you from that, Gina. I wish I could, but you need to put all these thoughts aside right now and work on catching this person. They feel they know you and that might mean you know them. Let that help you.'

She shook and wiped her eyes. 'You're right. I'll speak to you later.' She glanced out of the window and Lyndsey Saunders gave her a slow wave. Her life as she knew it was soon to be over.

CHAPTER FIFTY-EIGHT

Cherie grabbed the kitchen chair and flung it against the worktop. This is what it felt like to lose everything. If her family had gone then so would the house. She grabbed another chair and flung it into the garden. Not content with it landing in one piece, she picked it up and smashed it onto the patio several more times until it split and broke. She ran to the shed and grabbed her emergency bag. There in the corner sat another one of her hidden bottles. When she'd been out after the dinner party looking for Marcus, this is what she'd done, drank some of her hidden stash then eaten several mints before returning home. It was a bit of a blur.

She snatched the empty bottle and stormed back into the lounge, smashing it into the television, along with the two empty wine bottles. She grabbed the vase her mother had bought her on one of her birthdays and dropped it from height onto the coffee table. Shards landed everywhere. She kicked what was left of the little table over. What was the point of anything? She had blown the lot. At least her family might apportion some of her behaviour to a breakdown should they take the mess she was making into consideration.

Running into the kitchen, she grabbed hold of the mug tree and flung it at the microwave, followed by the coffee and sugar jars. The whole room looked like an explosion in a coffee factory. She kicked the doors, leaving muddy prints on everything. Exhausted, she fell to the floor and sobbed like never before into her sticky hands. She could show them her real self. It would be easier in the long run for the kids and Christian to hate her. It would make moving on easier for them.

She pulled her phone from her pocket and stared at the message. Why should she be there for Penny? Why? Penny had caused all this with her little stint. On the other hand, Penny was the only one still speaking to her; she needed to cling to that. When she tried to call the number back, Penny's phone had been switched off. Her friend didn't want to be traced or found if she was scared for her life.

Maybe Penny had tried to talk to Marcus and Isaac before she had messaged Cherie. One of them had to be trying to kill her, to shut her up. If only Cherie could persuade her to shut up but in a nicer way. Her one last chance came with turning up at the meeting point in the message. A chance she couldn't blow. Everything else was lost but not this, this was her chance to make things right. Maybe she and Penny could do the right thing for once. That was what scared Marcus and Isaac the most.

A flashback to the previous night filled her mind, of her driving badly through a red light. The rest was a blur. She'd come back with more wine though, evident by the third empty bottle she'd found next to the bed.

She could still turn things around by facing the consequences; that option still had to be on the table. Everyone's shock and hatred filled her mind: the one reason she'd remained silent. Now, it seemed irrelevant. Her children and husband were gone. *Her husband.* The words rang in her head in time with the pain from her hangover. She'd taken Christian for a fool with her lies and she'd inwardly laughed as she won him over every time. She caught her reflection in the stainless steel kettle that lay on the floor, dotted in damp coffee granules. If Christian could see her straggly hair and mascara-streaked face, he'd know he did the right thing by leaving. If he was close enough to smell the staleness of her breath, he'd recoil just as he'd been doing for a long time. She was way beyond fixing.

Wiping the tears away with her sleeve she knew what she had to do next on this dark and gloomy morning. She had to take a couple of paracetamol, get freshened up as much as she was able and prepare to meet Penny. At least she'd find out what was going on.

Her legs shook as she stood and walked to the stairway. She grabbed the old black coat and began to shred it with the scissors. As she hacked through the material, she hoped that it would finally stop haunting her.

CHAPTER FIFTY-NINE

In a daze, somewhere between hallucination and reality, I grab the cord and drag my weary body back towards the satellite. As I watch Earth from the skies, what I see becomes blurred and then I feel nothing but water. That's when I snap out of my weird dream. I notice the cold liquid filling up my box and then I remember. I'm buried alive. The laughter from above booms out, throbbing through my head. Scratching around, I feel the matchbox and the final match on my chest. I must have left them there when I was lucid. One match; that is all I have left. One measly match.

As I inhale, my chest lets out a crackly wheeze. I'm fading fast.

Strike, and once again my confined world is lit up. It's a far throw from my vision of being in space where I'm hanging on by a rope but I'm free still.

The match runs down. I'm sure my finger burned as the fire reached the end of the wood but I can't feel anything. My whole body has stiffened. A tear escapes my eye as I think of rigor mortis. It's coming for me. I wheeze again. This time I don't panic. There's nothing more I can do apart from accept my end. I'm at peace. I haven't hurt anyone, I don't have unfinished business.

Then I think of the person above, laughing. I do have unfinished business. I manage a weak murmur. 'I'm going to come back and haunt you. You just wait and see. I'm going to haunt you all until you wished you were the ones in a box.'

I remember falling and hitting my head, but there's more. I remember who and how and why. It's flooding back. Great, my biggest moment of clarity has hit when I'm in no position to do anything. I'm at the mercy of whoever's up there.

CHAPTER SIXTY

Now

Tuesday, 3 November

Gina headed over to where forensics and uniform had congregated. A short dog sniffed at her ankle. She leaned over and stroked its long body as she continued over the rubble and mud. The three houses struck her. The symbol on the back of the diary extract had been as accurate as it could be. If that one was accurate and the woods had been accurate, what was with the ghost and question mark? That one was certainly more symbolic.

'Ah, DI Harte. We're certainly being kept busy this week. I've had to cancel afternoon tea. The girlfriend's not happy at all.' Bernard tucked his beard into the cover and pulled his forensics suit hood over his thinning grey hair. As he walked closer, his height almost blocked out what was ahead.

'I'm sure our victim would apologise if they could. Saying that, do we know if there is a victim as yet?' A part of her hoped that this was nothing more than a sick joke in response to what the papers had reported.

'Jennifer and the rest of the team are already on it. There is definitely a body. It seems our coffin killer has struck again.' Bernard handed her a couple of crime scene suits. 'One for you and one for DS Driscoll.'

'I didn't know you had a girlfriend?'

'I didn't tell you. We met on a dating site a couple of months ago. I decided it was time to put myself out there again.'

'Ah, nice one.' Gina glanced back and watched as Jacob ran. He might resemble Action Man when still but he looked quite awkward at speed. 'Thanks.' As she started to slip it over her tracksuit bottoms, Jacob ran over and grabbed one too.

'Sorry, got stuck in temporary lights.' He grabbed a suit and began pulling it over his trousers and coat. He waved at Jennifer and she waved back. 'Do we have another body?'

'Afraid so.' Gina turned back to Bernard. 'Any description as yet? I need to know if the body is Penny Burton's.'

He glanced back and caught Jennifer's attention. 'Is the casket fully open yet?'

She shook her head, removed a glove and held up five fingers.

'Should be able to answer that question in five minutes. When I was over there, we'd managed to prise the box open a little but one of the hinges had stuck. The team were trying to ease it so that we can open it fully. The body will be ready for formal identification sometime later.'

'I see. Anything else you can tell us?'

'Only that it's looking exactly like the one in the woods, but this time we have had less rain to contend with so I'm hopeful of a better outcome on the forensics front. It's early doors at the moment so not much to report, I'm afraid. We also have a few members of the team going back and forth with uniform searching for anything that the killer may have left behind. I can tell you that a trolley was used to get the coffin into place as there are wheel marks, quite thick tracks. There is sign of smaller wheel tracks on top of the larger ones. I would say it is a fold-up trolley so would easily fit into any vehicle. I have some ideas of what would be used so I'll send you a photo of it in an email later.'

Jacob finished zipping up his forensics suit. 'Transporting the coffin would be another matter. We are talking a long car or a van.'

'Yes. Ah, it looks like Jennifer is ready for us to go over.'

Gina was grateful she hadn't eaten too much, only taking one of the muffins that O'Connor's wife had baked. She caught sight of a woman watching from outside a Portakabin and realised how she must look in her spare suit jacket and the dowdy grey tracksuit bottoms that had been given to her after her clothes had been bagged for evidence. Her unruly hair and scratched face were an accurate show of how her evening had gone. At least the trainers were comfortable.

'Alright, guv?' PC Smith lifted the outer cordon to let her through and she followed Bernard carefully over the small fence until she reached the metal stepping plates. Her shoes clunked on each one. Pushing through the brambles, she could see the clearing now.

A small trodden mud path led in from one of the walking routes. She knew that there was a road and a car park close by. This location would have been much less of a challenge for their killer than the woods. She leaned in and peered at the corpse. Mouth open, eyes closed. It was, without a doubt, Penny Burton.

'That's our missing woman.' The body lay still, her mouth almost contorted in fear. Her toes and fingernails bloodied from scratching her way out. Gina closed her eyes, tuning in to her own fear only a few hours ago. She felt her chest tightening as she remembered trying to claw her way through the hole, not knowing if she would die. 'Thanks, Bernard.'

She walked off, leaving Jacob and Bernard talking about the body. Staring back at the three houses, she tried to take her focus from being trapped in the coffin back to the case. They had found Penny. She could only hope that the murderer had slipped up this time. Her mind bounced from one theory to the next. The dinner party crew. Isaac: she didn't trust him. The wolf carved into the coffin. What did a wolf mean? Ghosts, the squat, the kids all dressed as creepy figures, long black coats and bells.

Marcus: he and Penny were having problems and he definitely wasn't telling all.

She hurried back to Bernard. 'Is there an engraving in the coffin?'

Bernard nodded to Jennifer.

She kneeled down on a plate and leaned in, moving the woman's feet a little. The clean CSI zoomed in with the camera and took a photo before walking over to Gina and showing her and Jacob the image on the display.

Jacob screwed his eyes and they both moved in closer. 'That looks a little bit less wolf-like than the last engraving, guv. The artist has improved. It could be a lion. Look at the carving marks; they're a little more defined than on the last engraving. It's a lion. Does that look more like a lion to you?'

Bernard nodded.

'You're right.' Gina paused as she tried to recall what the vicar, Sally Stevens had said to her. '"Be sober-minded, be watchful. Your adversary the devil prowls around like a roaring lion, seeking someone to devour." It's from the Bible.'

'I didn't have you down as an expert in the Bible.'

'I'm not.' She went blank as the letter she'd received that day came back to her. You need to stand up and roar. Another lion reference. 'It's just this verse stood out to me. Sally Stevens said it the other day as we left the vicarage. I remembered thinking about it after; it gave me the creeps and it was such a weird thing to say. It's more than just a coincidence. We have to go back and speak to her. She knows something. As soon as we're done here, we're heading over. Will you call it in? We need the team to check her out and we need some backup. Wyre and O'Connor can drop whatever they're doing and head over. What does a graveyard have?'

Jacob shrugged. 'Gravestones, trees, death, corpses.'

'If you believe such a thing, maybe ghosts? She even mentioned the kids telling ghost stories when we spoke. The person who put me in a box was a woman, I know that much from the faint voice I heard.'

Jacob turned to Jennifer. 'I'll see you at home.' He grabbed his phone as he followed Gina back towards the outer cordon where they climbed back over the fence.

'Give me a call or message me if you find anything,' Gina called back to Bernard as she slipped under the cordon.

The little dog ran over on its short legs, wagging its tail before squatting and peeing on Gina's trainer.

'Lola! Lola!' the woman called as she caught up and lifted the dog into her arms. 'Sorry about Lola. She's overexcited by everything that's going on.'

Gina flicked the wet from her shoe. 'That's okay. I know what has happened has been a shock, but can we come in and ask you a few questions?' She also had a few about Isaac and why Tracy hadn't returned their calls.

She nodded. 'Of course. Come this way.'

CHAPTER SIXTY-ONE

Gina stepped into the Portakabin and instantly felt the warmth. She yawned, feeling the need to sleep.

'Please, take a seat. I'm Tracy. My husband, Fred, and I own the company and this is our development.'

Gina sat and Jacob pulled up another chair from next to the cupboard door.

'Can I get you a drink? The coffee's already made.'

'Yes, that would be lovely.'

The woman poured out three coffees and passed them out. 'I don't have any milk or sugar.'

'Thank you. Just how I like my coffee.' Gina was looking forward to this coffee. 'With regards to the body that you found, have you seen anything suspicious over the past few days?'

The woman shook her head. 'I can't say that I have. I generally finish between five and seven, and the development is fenced off from the roadside. I can't remember. I don't walk around checking everything before I leave.'

'How about by the three houses at the back?'

'Again, no. We haven't worked on those for a couple of weeks and as you saw for yourself, that area is quite set back and secluded.' The woman paused and stared at the paperwork on her desk. 'I don't know how this is going to affect our sales and our own home is at risk if these houses don't get snapped up. This is a disaster.'

There was nothing Gina could say to reassure the woman. Forensics would be all over the area for days, weeks even. And then there was the public. Would finding a body at the back of the three most exclusive houses on the estate affect sales? She was sure it would. 'I'm sorry that this has happened to you, but a woman has been murdered and we have to find out who did this.'

'It's the second one isn't it? It's the coffin killer.'

Gina couldn't deny it. It would have been obvious. Enough details had been reported in the press for anyone to make the connection. She shuddered as she thought of what the papers would be reporting later that day.

'I did say something to the officer who arrived first but I blurted it out and it sounded like my mouth was running away with me. I'm much calmer now, thankfully. It really scared the life out of me. There was someone there when I found the bell and I caught sight of a person standing back in the bushes, but just a glimpse. They were wearing a black coat that fell below the knees. A hood covered their eyes.'

Jacob began to take notes. 'Height?'

'I can't say. I mean it would be a guess. I don't know.'

Gina finished the coffee as Jacob continued. 'Did you see the bottom of the face?'

'Sort of. It looks like they had a bit of mud on their cheek.'

Jacob leaned in, his tie touching his knee. 'Were the hands exposed?'

'No, they were dark too.'

'Dark?'

'Gloved.'

Jacob smiled, putting Tracy more at ease. 'Is there anything else you can think of?'

'No, I was scared. Whoever it was started to come my way but I turned and ran back here. By the time I reached the door, I glanced back and they'd gone. I locked myself in, called my husband who was project managing the site down by the entrance and then called the police. I should tell you something else. I touched the bell and the string and I started to dig up the earth with my hands. I did tell the uniformed officer that.'

Gina leaned back a little in the chair as Jacob caught up with the notes. 'That must have been frightening for you. One of the team will come to take elimination prints from you in a while.' She glanced around the room. There were piles of paperwork everywhere, along with health and safety notices that clogged up the wall. Hard hats and yellow jackets were stacked up next to a room marked with a toilet symbol. The phone was flashing every few seconds. Her gaze led her to the noticeboard and one name stood out. 'Isaac Slater, he works for you.'

'He did. I left a message on his phone this morning telling him not to come back. He's not the most reliable of builders. Turns up late, doesn't put a full day in and this puts the project back. Today he didn't turn up and I snapped. What's this got to do with him?'

'We left a message on your phone to call us back.'

Tracy glanced at the flashing light on the office phone. 'Sorry. I'm struggling to keep up.'

'Could you tell us a bit more about him? What was his timekeeping like last week?'

Tracy pulled up a spreadsheet. 'Not brilliant. It's all over the place. Last Monday—'

'Is that the twenty-sixth?'

'Yes. He turned up in the morning but about two in the afternoon Fred wanted a word with him, but he'd left site and not told anyone. The following day, we asked him where he'd been and he said he had to go to the dentist and forgot to tell us. He was late the day after too, that was the Tuesday. He looked like he'd been on the drink – scruffy and hungover looking. On the Wednesday I have him marked down as leaving early again. Thursday: not in until eleven. Friday: he was meant to do a half-day but left at ten in the morning. This week has been the straw that broke the camel's back. When he didn't turn up again this morning, I lost it and left him an angry message. There are plenty of builders looking to earn the good money that we pay. I'd rather give one of them the job.'

'Thank you.'

As they left the Portakabin, Gina turned to Jacob before he got into his car. 'Not only did Isaac lie to us about his whereabouts on the Monday, his girlfriend Joanna Brent confirmed that he was with her after he finished work at six. Was she lying too? Did he go home early or did he go somewhere else? Maybe he was busy digging a grave or moving a coffin. Does he have a van?'

Jacob flicked through his notes. 'He certainly does.'

'Call that one in too and have him brought into the station for questioning. After the vicar, we need to speak to him as a matter of urgency. I'll message PC Smith about Tracy's elimination prints.'

'I'm on it.'

As she went to get into one of the pool cars, her phone rang. It was Briggs. 'Hello.'

'You need to check the papers. I have the full letter from the killer here. I'm about to email it through to you. There's also another little perfect triangle at the bottom of the letter but that wasn't published in the article.'

'Thanks.' She opened the file and read the letter.

I said I'd be in touch again. I know you believe that standing by and watching others suffer isn't okay. We must protect the innocent. Anger, tension, fear – they never leave. Scratching at the walls of your prison, knowing there is no way out, thinking you might die… Maybe facing the fear is what it takes. 'Your adversary the devil prowls around like a roaring lion, seeking someone to devour', but sometimes your enemy isn't all they seem.

It made her shiver as she read her name at the top, then she saw the same Bible verse about the lion at the bottom of the page.

She needed to get to the vicarage now and she needed to know what Sally Stevens knew. The lion on the casket was one thing but a direct quote; that was something else. The clues had been there all along.

CHAPTER SIXTY-TWO

Gina hammered on the vicarage door, hoping that Sally Stevens was in. She hadn't answered when they'd called ahead.

Jacob followed her past the church and across the grass. 'Anyone in?'

'She hasn't answered.' Gina rushed to the window and stared through. The large lounge was empty. 'I'm worried.' She ran to another window, then another, before slipping along the side of the house and peering through the kitchen window. It was so dark with the clouds above and Gina struggled to see in. She wiped the glass with the sleeve of her jacket and peered through again, making out the dining table and the centre island.

A woofing noise came from across the graveyard and a large Cairn Terrier bounded over.

'Sally,' Gina called, but the woman didn't answer.

'I wonder where she is.' Jacob started to head over the grass, slipping between the graves, then a faint voice came from the right.

'This way. Sally?' Gina ran as fast as she could, jumping over the smaller gravestones before clearing a large tomb-like structure and seeing Sally kneeling over an empty grave. It was the grave of Elsie Peterson.

The woman turned, her black lipstick a striking contrast to her pale face. 'Someone did this in the night. I was just about to call you.'

I am watching, I am waiting. Gina leapt over the mound of earth and began to search the area. The killer obviously liked to watch. They'd been at the building site earlier that day. She ran and ran through the trees and around the grounds but there was no one in sight. Her breath short, she bent over and took in a good few gulps of air. There was no one lurking. A tree shook. Gina took a few steps towards it. 'Police. Come out now.'

No response. She stepped a little closer and the tree shook again. Heart beating like it might burst from her chest, she took another step then the bush parted. A magpie escaped and squawked as it flew off. She ran into the bush, parting the shrubbery. There was no one there.

'Anything, guv?' Jacob caught up.

'No, nothing. I just thought for a moment that whoever dug that grave might have waited around, making sure we turned up. They certainly like playing games.'

'Sally Stevens has migrated to her dining room. I left her there with a cup of tea.'

'Great, let's find out what she knows.'

As they headed past the grave, Gina couldn't help but stare at it, drawn in by the dark painful death that it represented. 'I wonder who this grave was for.'

'Guv, I found a shovel leaning up against the house. I know we can't be sure but I wonder if Sally dug this hole.'

'Call for backup and we need another forensics team. That grave is now a definite scene, especially as the grave belonged to a family member of our first victim, Alex.'

'They're totally snowed under but someone will have to come here to secure the scene. I'll make the call and meet you in there in a moment.'

Gina left him at the doorway and entered the house. Sally wrapped her black cardigan tightly around her bust as she stared at the floor. The dog lay under the table, its head resting on her black boot.

'Sally, are you okay to speak?'

She nodded. 'This has unsettled me. Ever since that person was standing in the graveyard, I've been a bit creeped out and now this happens.'

'When did you spot that the grave had been dug up?'

'About forty minutes ago. I was taking Jerry for a walk and I spotted the earth piled up, then I saw the gaping hole. It almost reaches the coffin, I'm sure. The worst of it is, I didn't hear a thing. It must have been in the dead of night when I was asleep.'

Gina sat next to her at the large oak table. 'Did you walk past that grave yesterday?'

'Yes, in the evening when I came out with Jerry.' The dog whimpered and cocked its head. 'It was dark but I take a torch out with me at night. No one had been digging at that point.'

'And what time was that?'

'Around eleven. Jerry had been disturbed by the fireworks earlier on as he always is around this time of the year. He'd been a bit scared so I waited for them to die down which is why I was out so late. I didn't hear or see anything odd.'

'What time did you get back?'

'Oh, about quarter past. I just stood amongst the graves while Jerry ran around sniffing grass and cocking his leg up.'

Jacob entered and stood in the doorway. 'Forensics will be here shortly. We'll need to cordon off the grave area.' He took a seat next to Gina and pulled out his pad.

'That means that this grave was dug between eleven fifteen last night and…' She looked at her watch. 'Ten thirty today.'

'I've been in the kitchen most of the morning. I work at the island. Today, I was paying the bills for the church. If there had been someone digging in the distance, I'm certain I'd have seen movement.'

Gina leaned over and stroked the dog's head. 'What time did you start work?'

'About eight fifteen.'

Gina nodded and Jacob amended the time on his notes.

'I have to ask something else. Remember the last time we spoke to you, you quoted a passage from the Bible?'

Sally frowned. 'I quote a lot of those. You'll have to enlighten me.'

'Be sober-minded, be watchful. Your adversary the devil prowls around like a roaring lion, seeking someone to devour.'

'Ah, yes, Peter, five:eight. I remember now.' Sally stretched her arms in front of her then picked up her tea.

'Why did you choose that one?'

'I don't know. I suppose I was scared after seeing that person in the graveyard. I was just reminding myself that the devil is always there, testing us, and that we should be watchful.' She furrowed her brow. 'It's odd. It's not one I normally use but someone said it to me recently. Maybe it was one of the parishioners, one of the parents or one of the people we help at the AA meetings. That's why I remembered it.'

Gina felt her fingers begin to twitch with excitement. She wasn't totally letting Sally off the hook right at this moment. There was still the matter of the used shovel leaning up against her house but there was something about Sally. She couldn't believe the dainty vicar who ran mother and toddler groups and joined people in matrimony could be the one committing the coffin killings. She'd come across the coffin killer herself but identifying that person would be near impossible from what she'd seen. All she knew was that she'd heard a woman's voice. 'Think. Can you remember when it was said or in which group?'

She shrugged her shoulders. 'No, I wish I could. Is it relevant to the case?'

Gina cleared her throat. 'I can't say anything just yet as it's relating to an ongoing investigation. All I can say is we need a name. One more question, how did the shovel end up against your wall? Is that where you leave it?'

'What shovel?' Sally took another sip of her tea and moved a strand of hair from her mouth.

'The one against the back of your house.'

She stood and looked out of the window. 'I have no idea how that got there. It's not even my shovel. I'll confess to not having any gardening tools, we have a gardener for all the church grounds, but he hasn't been for two weeks. That shovel wasn't there yesterday. I don't want to stay here.'

The woman rubbed her eyes. Gina could understand her fear. 'Forensics and uniform will be here soon. I can make sure that after we've left someone drives by and keeps an eye on the church and vicarage. Would that help?' Gina knew the budget would be blown but at the moment, she wanted Sally to be reassured that they could protect her. She swallowed. Maybe she wasn't safe. 'Do you have anyone you could stay with?'

'My sister lives in Redditch. I could travel into work from there. I'll call her and write her phone number and address down for you, in case you need to ask me anything else. I don't want to stay here at night, not at the moment.' The dog made a whining noise and lay back on her boot. 'Yes, Jerry. We're going to stay with Auntie Elaine.' She patted the dog's head.

Gina's phone beeped. She checked the message from Wyre.

'We have to get back to the station. Please try to remember who mentioned that verse about the lion, we really need to know who said it.'

Sally stared at the wall and scrunched her brow. 'The more I think about it, I'm sure it was on the Sunday a couple of weeks ago. I have a list of names somewhere. I'm doing a charity run to raise money for the roof in a couple of weeks and I was taking names of sponsors. I think the list might be at the church but I'm not sure. Can I get back to you when I've found it? I'll start searching when you leave but there are so many nooks and crannies, it could take a while.'

'Please do. Call me as soon as you've found it.' Gina placed one of her cards on the table as she reread the message on her phone.

After Gina had guided an overworked Keith from forensics in the direction of the hole and shovel, she led Jacob back to the church car park. 'We're onto something. That message was from Wyre. They've just been to Cherie Brown's house, the one who hosted the Halloween night dinner party. Her husband has called saying he arrived home this morning to find their house wrecked. She's missing. We need to get over there now.'

CHAPTER SIXTY-THREE

Cherie stared at her phone. *Meet me at the haunted pond. You know, where we used to tell scary stories when we were kids. No one can know you're coming. I have to tell you something and it can't wait. Someone is trying to hurt me and I know who. Hurry. Penny.*

Cherie turned her phone off, glad that Christian could no longer ring. She took a swig from the bottle and stared at the sky as she leaned back on the bench. She inhaled the stench from the murky old pond. This was where she was meant to be: the hangout. A place where the adults could never find them, set back from the estate by the nature pond that had long given up on nature. It was home to trolleys and plastic wrappers. They'd called it the haunted pond on account of Penny thinking she saw a lady in the lake ghost emerging from an upturned bike. They'd all laughed at her back then. No wonder Cherie hated Halloween with all the fear it brought with it.

She fell to the floor on her knees, bending to see the underside of the bench.

Cherie loves Isaac. It was still badly carved in the wood. She'd also tried to carve two cats – love cats, but no one else could tell what they were. She'd fancied Isaac back then but not now. For a short while she thought there might have been a spark but then Joanna came on the scene. Besides, she'd been in the middle of her alcoholic turmoil and her marriage had been shaky – a bit like now. She tipped the bottle of vodka down her throat as she remembered the ghosts of her past. This had been their

Halloween meetup place all those years ago, before heading to the school disco.

She got back up onto the bench and glanced through the overgrown weeds. No one was coming; besides, it might not even be Penny. Anyone could send a text from a burner phone, she knew that much, but curiosity had overwhelmed her. She had to come and put an end to all this nonsense once and for all. Who? Marcus, maybe. Isaac – yes. Should she be worried? No. If it was Isaac, he had brought her here for a reason. It was the only place they'd kissed. Their one and only encounter as teens. Only he knew about the kiss and they hadn't spoken about it since. There's no way she'd kiss him now.

She huddled up and lay on the damp wood. No one was coming. Not a soul. She turned on her back, taking in the granite clouds as they sped by. Shivering, she zipped up her hoodie, just as a sheet of rain began to fall.

Planting her feet on the earth, she felt her knees wobble as her vision deceived her. She'd had too much to drink. Maybe if she could just get back to her car. She could turn her phone back on and if another message didn't come through, she could sleep the drink off then drive home. As she stepped in the mud, she almost slid along the edge of the pond into the scum. She let out a little laugh. 'That was close.'

A rattling noise came from the bushes. 'Penny, Isaac – I came.' She half-expected one of them to appear but there was no one. She took a few steps forward and parted the brambles before continuing. That's when she saw the hole in the ground filled with a coffin. She turned to run and bumped into the hooded figure in the long black coat. As she gasped for breath, a hand came up and injected her swiftly before removing the hood.

'I… I destroyed that coat,' was all she could murmur.

'You destroyed me too, but I'm back.' The voice wasn't meek, not like she remembered.

She should have known. She had been recognised despite trying to disguise who she was as the woman before her watched on. Her disguise hadn't worked that well. She now knew that this woman had also been at the squat while she'd been trying to send Alex packing. 'You've been at my house, watching me on the night I had everyone round for dinner.'

'When I saw Alex after all that time, I then noticed you and wondered how I didn't recognise you before that moment. Yes, you've changed but not that much. Not so much that I wouldn't recognise such evil. Did you all like my messages? I thought that would get you all going.'

Cherie went to punch her, but the woman reached for her fist and pushed her back. She stumbled onto her bottom, trying to grip anything as she went down. Her fingers dug into the mud and stone but everything was slimy.

The skies above were beginning to whirl into the trees. What had she been injected with? She never saw things like this when she'd been drinking?

'A little bit further.' The voice boomed in her ear, repeating that line over and over again in different voices. She heard Penny saying it, then Isaac, then Marcus followed by Christian and her children. The face in front of her morphed into her own and she backed into the coffin to escape the monstrosity. Sliding a little further, she felt her body drop as she landed in the box. Stiff with fear, the next thing she saw was the lid closing.

No one ever comes here. This is where we come to hang out. We can share a drink without being caught. We can hide from everyone and have a good time.

No one was coming. Maybe she was destined to forever haunt the pond, the new lady in the lake. Maybe the ghost Penny had seen was Cherie coming back from the future, warning herself of what was to come. As the drug took hold, she imagined that she was trapped under a layer of scum, ingesting pondweed as her lungs filled with rancid fluid. She reached up higher and higher but all she could do was sink. She was going, whirling into a huge sinkhole, down the plug and all she could hear was the woman's laughter. That's when she knew it was too late. She'd walked into a trap.

CHAPTER SIXTY-FOUR

Gina and Jacob hurried to the door. She knocked hard.

Christian Brown answered. 'I don't know what's happened here.' He ran his hand over his head and left the door open as he went into the lounge. 'I just came back to get some clothes and I saw this. I can't get hold of Cherie. I've tried to call but her phone is off. I don't know what to do. I shouldn't have left but it got too much. I... I...'

'Mr Brown, shall we go through to the kitchen?' The living room was covered in glass, not a safe place to sit and talk.

'It's not much better in there.' He stood for a second before pushing through and opening the kitchen door. Coffee granules covered everything in the room but there was something else that bothered Gina more. The black material on the worktop, torn and cut to shreds. The only thing she could identify on it was the hood. 'We can't touch all this. We need to go out to the car.' As she turned, the back of the door was smeared in ketchup and she made out a finger drawing of what looked like a ghost.

The man looked like he might cry or scream in frustration, but he kept calm and followed them out to the car. 'Can you call the station and update them. We need forensics here as well.' She knew they were stretched to the limits and she could tell by Jacob's grimace that he thought that too. They had a huge team at the building site, a part-team at the graveyard and now this. It was all kicking off at once. She opened the car door for Christian and closed it once he'd got in. She turned to Jacob and spoke in a hushed tone. 'Did you see that cut up coat? Possibly our long black coat?' She glanced at the oncoming police car.

PC Kapoor pulled up and two officers got out. 'Alright, guv. We got here as fast as possible.'

Jacob nodded to Gina. 'Right, we need to seal the house off. Put a cordon up and someone needs to stay on sentry duty and wait for forensics. You could be waiting a long time.'

'We're on it.'

Gina got into the driver's seat. 'I'm so sorry, Mr Brown. We are deeply concerned about what has happened in your house given that two people your wife knew have already been murdered.'

'What? I thought there was only one, Alex.'

'There's been another and I'm afraid the person seen at the location of that murder was wearing a long hooded black coat, just like the one that is shredded in your kitchen.'

'No, no, no, no, no. Are you saying my wife did this? She may have problems, but she's not a killer.' He wafted his hand across his face as he took a few deep breaths.

Gina turned the key in the ignition and opened the back window and an icy breeze drove a few raindrops onto the back seat. 'We're not saying your wife did this, but you can see how it looks. We need to bring her in and ask her what happened. Your wife has become a person of interest. I'm so sorry.' Gina was trying to keep him calm and keep him on side. Cherie was more than a person of interest. She was very much a suspect and at the very least, the key to solving the case.

'Damn. Why did I not do more? She's been struggling. I should have been there but no, I walked out and took the kids.'

Gina wiped the sleep away that had formed in the corner of her eye. 'Can you tell me what you mean by struggling?'

Jacob got into the back passenger seat and smiled over the headrest as he pulled out his pad. 'Carry on.'

'Over the past few days Cherie hasn't been herself. She's been drinking again.' He paused. 'I thought she'd recovered, as an alcoholic, but things have been getting worse. She was coming and going at all hours. She thought I didn't hear her leaving the house in the night. She'd go out in the car and try to convince me that she'd been nowhere and accuse me of getting at her. Then I'd find drink bottles in her bag.'

'Did she ever attend any AA meetings?'

'She did back then, they were at the church on the high street. Anyway, with her drinking, I knew it was all happening again. There was something else?'

'Go on.' Cherie had been going to AA meetings at the church. Had she been back over the past couple of weeks? Had she attended a service and planted a Bible passage into the vicar's mind?

'On the night of our dinner party, last Saturday, Marcus, Cherie and Isaac seemed to be casting weird looks over the table. I felt a couple of kicks by my feet and the room had gone silent a couple of times. They all knew something. Then, while Joanna and I were cleaning up, the others went in the garden to smoke. Marcus seemed really upset but I later found out that Penny had left him, which in my book explained it, so I didn't think any more of it. The kids stayed at my parents' house on Saturday and I joined them yesterday. I need to protect my children from whatever's going on, from their mother. She walked out on her job too, that just showed how badly things were going. I just want her to get better. I want to go back to how we were before she started drinking again.' He stared out of the window like a broken man, shoulders slumped. 'She didn't kill anyone. She wouldn't hurt a fly. I mean, she cared for old and vulnerable people for a living.' He shook his head and scratched his chin. 'At least, that's what I wanted to believe. I've been so stupid.'

'Tell me what you mean by that?'

'Last week she walked out on her job. She said she couldn't cope. There were far more than the pressures of working at the care home on her mind.'

Gina retied her hair. 'Why did she start drinking?'

'I don't know. There wasn't an incident that I can recall and she hasn't mentioned any traumatic events. She doesn't talk to me much. I think something happened between her and her friends. Isaac, Marcus and Penny. That is just my theory. They all seem to have some insider club thing going on and they do this nudge, nudge, wink, wink thing. She's also quite terrified of Halloween and goes mad when trick or treaters knock, but she insists on having her friends over every year on the date she fears. I don't get it. I really don't know my wife at all.' He leaned back and stared at the roof of the car as he ground his teeth.

Gina shuffled a little to get comfortable, moving her knee from right under the steering wheel. 'The ketchup on the back of the kitchen door. It's outlining a simple picture of a ghost. Can you tell me anything about that?'

He sighed and shook his head. 'No.'

'It means nothing to you at all, in any context.'

'Only that she was scared of Halloween and that included ghosts, ghouls, vampires and anything else horror.'

Taking a deep breath, Gina knew she had to broach the subject of him not going back into his house until forensics had taken all they needed. 'I'm sorry to have to tell you this but your house is now a potential crime scene. We have found remnants of a hooded black coat and a drawing of a ghost, which are both relevant to our current investigation. We need to search the house for further evidence. Do you have anywhere else you could go until we call you?'

He leaned back. 'Go ahead. I need to get to the bottom of it to preserve my sanity. Something's happened to her, hasn't it? She's next, isn't she?'

Gina couldn't rule out that possibility. 'We can't say as yet but we're hoping your house may contain the evidence we need to find her.'

He pulled a bunch of keys from his pocket, removed two and handed them to Gina. 'Front and back door keys. Oh, and here's the garage.' He passed the last one over. 'I'll be at my parents' house. I have nothing to hide in there.' He pointed to the house. 'If Cherie does, then it's time for it to come out. Can I go now?'

'We'd appreciate you meeting one of the team at the station to give a formal statement.'

'Okay. I'll drive there now.'

'Thank you.'

'There's one more thing. Cherie thought I couldn't hear her on the phone when she was in the garden but she was talking to one of her friends about Alex living in some squat. They all knew where Alex was. I should have said something when I'd heard of his murder but I never thought for one minute his death could have been anything to do with the people I open my home too and cook dinner for. I didn't give it a second thought. But now, I don't know who to trust.'

'I don't suppose a triangle would mean anything to Cherie?'

'What, like the shape?'

'Yes.'

'No, she probably wouldn't know the difference between an equilateral and an isosceles. She used to bunk maths classes at school if she could. She even struggled to help the kids with their maths homework if they asked her.'

'Thank you.'

Cherie was missing and given the circumstances, she had to work on the fact that she was in a box somewhere, the next in line to die – or was she the killer waiting to pounce? It was time to crack Isaac, the one who'd been lying about his whereabouts for the past week. Her phone rang.

'I'll finish up here.' Jacob smiled.

She stepped out of the car. 'O'Connor.'

'Guv, we've had a call about the carving in the coffin. You're not going to believe this.'

CHAPTER SIXTY-FIVE

'Mr Slater, this isn't just going to go away.' Gina was fast losing patience with Isaac, she could see Jacob was too as he rolled his eyes after another 'no comment' and they both had better things to do.

The tiny room stank with the waft of smoke that was coming from his battered-looking bomber jacket every time he moved. 'We'll go over some of the questions again. Does a ghost mean anything to you? Could it represent a place?'

Location three on the triangle was still a mystery and the only clue they had as to where another body might be buried. She felt her fists clenching. He knew how important it was that she had this information and he was purposely holding back, that much she could tell.

'I'm saying nothing. Why should I give you all the rope you need to hang me when I didn't do anything?' He leaned back and gave her a wry smile. His stare was quite fixed and it made Gina want to turn away but she wouldn't.

'You lied to us about where you were on Monday the twenty-sixth of October. Why?' Gina checked the time. Half an hour had gone by and the man hadn't answered a single question. 'Why?'

He leaned back and rocked the chair, smirking as he stared at the ceiling.

'Your friend, Cherie Brown, is missing and we know she was at the squat on that night too, late that night. We know she was having some sort of argument with our victim, Alexander Swinton, and soon after he turned up dead. Where were you in all this?'

He continued to smirk. 'Were you keeping lookout? Were you aiding and abetting? Were you in the garden wearing a long black coat? You can see how it looks. Your partner, Joanna, even lied for you, telling us that you were with her all night, but you weren't, were you?' Gina leaned in and stared at the man. His gaze met hers and his smile dropped. 'What's going on, Mr Slater? Did you lure Alex to his death? Did you dig the grave?'

'I didn't do anything.'

'It's not looking like that from here.'

He paused, his gaze once again piercing Gina's, but she remained focused until he broke away. 'Okay, I was with Cherie but it's not what you think and I wasn't wearing any long black coat. I don't even own a coat of that description. I just needed to talk to her. She called me and told me where she'd be. I didn't do anything and I knew when his body turned up that this would happen.'

'What?'

'You lot. I want a solicitor.'

One more chance, he was clamming up. 'Your other friend, Penny Burton, was discovered dead this morning at the building site where you've been working.'

'What?' He seemed to be breathing faster through his nose, letting out little snorts every time he exhaled. 'She can't be dead, she can't. Why Penny?'

'That's what we're trying to find out. We've been talking to your boss, a lovely lady called Tracy, and she tells us that you've seemed a little distracted of late.'

'That stupid cow. You're barking up the wrong tree, seriously.'

'What tree should we be barking up?'

He rubbed his eyes and exhaled. 'I don't know.'

'Why are you lying to us, Mr Slater?'

He shook his head and grinned. 'No, no... I'm not falling for this. I. Want. A. Solicitor. Read my friggin' lips. Get me a solicitor, now!' He slammed his hand on the table, his eyes wide.

She met his stare. He could be the one who was sending all the letters that were driving her mad. It was personal.

'Why—'

'No comment, no comment, no comment.'

'Interview terminated at eleven twenty.' Gina threw her pen to the table and left the room, Jacob following a few seconds later. 'Organise a search warrant for his house. O'Connor or Wyre can lead that one. I need to take five.' She could feel her face warming and her hand clenched the rubbish in her coat pocket, scrunching up the old receipts in her fist.

'I'll wait for you in the incident room and I'll chase up Mr Slater's solicitor. We need answers.'

'I doubt we'll get anything more than "no comment". Not now. We've lost him.'

'He hasn't walked out though.'

As they parted, Gina hurried to the ladies and ran the tap. She lathered her hands up, washing away the stench of murder. She stood back, taking in her reflection in the smeared mirror. She turned to the side and checked out her profile. After all this was over, she was going to have a long bath and an early night. She pulled the rubbish from her pockets and dropped it next to the sink, sick of it being there all the time, filling up her pockets. As she went to throw it in the bin, something stopped her, just a word on a page. She grabbed the tiny piece of paper and nearly broke the door off its hinges as she moved like a hurricane towards the incident room. O'Connor ended his call. Wyre turned from her computer screen and Jacob stopped writing on the board.

'I know who did it.' She held the piece of paper up and laughed. 'All this time, but why? Get your coats on. Isaac Slater can wait. I know Cherie Brown's life is on the line. I don't know why but that's something we can work out later. The ghost symbol, that's where she is.'

'Gina? What's happening?' Briggs stood in the doorway.

'I'm ready to make an arrest. Cherie Brown's life is in danger and we don't know how long she's been missing, which means the clock has already started ticking and we don't know how long we have left. We might already be too late.' She had all the evidence they needed. She stared at the board and her attention was drawn to the copies of all the letters. The very clue to solving the case had been under her nose the whole time. 'How long did we say that the average person had when they are buried alive in a coffin?'

Jacob scoured the boards for that bit of information. 'Approximately five and a half hours, guv.'

She did up her coat. 'No time to waste, then.'

CHAPTER SIXTY-SIX

The weird whirling trees had merged into night in the darkness of the coffin. The drug had brought Cherie's children's voices to her ear and their faces to her eye. Her head pounded and her dry throat craved water. The pitch-black darkness was suffocating her along with the lack of air.

'I'm sorry,' she cried as tears streamed down her face. 'I came to talk to you, that's all. I was a coward and I'm sorry. Every time I saw you I wanted to say something but you didn't seem to notice me until that day when Alex turned up. Please give me a chance to be a better person.' Her nose filled as she choked on her words. She pressed the last match between her fingertips. It was like back then. Her abductor had given her exactly what she had given them, nothing more; nothing less. If only the police had released more details, they could have all worked this out rather than turn on each other. Three matches – just saying those words gave her the chills.

She lit the last match and looked through the torn material at the top of the coffin. There were no cracks in the wood, not like the box that they'd thrown together all those years ago, in fact, the box had been a large garden tool storage chest that Marcus's dad had made to store hoes and forks in. Their victim had been petite back then, making her fit perfectly. The coffin she was staring at was a professionally made coffin, made just the way their victim's father made them. *Come to a party, it'll be fun. You're new. Come meet the others.* She hadn't told the newbie of their plans to initiate her into their group but it had all gone wrong as they got carried away. She dug her own nails into her neck, punishing herself with the pain.

The match burned down and out, leaving nothing but the smell of sulphur and less of the precious oxygen she was breathing and she sobbed. Her heart rate sped as she screamed again. 'I'm sorry.'

A voice bellowed from above, sounding robotic through the soil. 'Say it again.'

'I'm sorry.' She fidgeted and flexed her legs. Someone had heard her. She could get out of this. As she waited in silence for the earth to be dug away and the box to open, she was then faced with her end as another thud of earth rained down. She lay there thinking of Bella and Oliver as the news was broken, that their mother was a victim of the coffin killer. She only hoped the truth of her own past would remain buried with her, Penny, and Alex. Death was the better option rather than her children knowing what a real-life monster she was. She was sorry, for everything, but the sorry had come too late. Maybe in some cases, sorry would never be enough. When she had seen Isaac kiss her captor at the party back then, that had been it. She knew she had to make the girl pay and what she'd brewed up was more than just the initiation that they had planned. A joke turned sour.

She sobbed as she delved further, remembering their victim's eyes staring back at her, pleading for an end to it all. Those eyes were what mattered now. Her final moments would be dedicated to that person while she took her punishment. Justice was being served.

As she wheezed on the inhale, she accepted the fatigue that had replaced the shivering and smiled as she slipped into another world, that of her sitting by the ghost lake with her vodka. She was sinking it all, every last drop, with a smile on her face.

CHAPTER SIXTY-SEVEN

'Where's Lucy?' Gina shouted as she leaned over the counter at the café. She held her identification up as she pushed to the front of the queuing tradespeople. The teenage girl passed a takeaway coffee to the man in the overall.

'Erm, I dunno. She doesn't tell me where she is when she's not working.' She wiped her hands on her apron and nodded an apology to the couple who had just come through the door and taken a seat.

'How about Lucy's father? Bill Manders.'

'Oh, the old man. He's not here either. They're probably at home as they're not on the rota for today. They don't work every day.'

The hum of people had dropped to silent as Gina stood there. She glanced around then back at Jacob. 'Keep trying to call her.' He nodded and stepped outside to make the call. 'Can we talk, around the back?'

One of the other overall-clad men in the queue sighed and stormed out of the café, leaving two women in paint-splattered overalls. 'I don't know. I'm kinda busy.'

'This is urgent.'

'Are they okay?' Her false lashes made a little batting noise every time she blinked.

'I don't know. May we?' Gina held her arm out towards the storeroom.

'Just take a seat everyone, I'll be around to take your orders in a minute. Sorry, guys.' She removed her apron and led Gina through to the staff area.

'Lucy's going to go mad if we get loads of shit reviews on Tripadvisor because of this.'

'I think Lucy has more to worry about than her Tripadvisor reviews. When did you last see Lucy or Bill?' Gina leaned up against the open pantry door.

'Yesterday. Bill came to lock up but Lucy wasn't with him. He said Lucy hadn't been feeling too well. With hygiene regulations and working with food, they asked me if I'd work for the rest of the week and left me with a key to open up. I'm only part-time, you see. What's going on?'

Gina swallowed. 'That's what we're trying to find out. How has Lucy seemed this past week, when you did see her?'

'She puts on a big smile for the world, but I know she's not right. I've caught her sitting right here, staring at the walls. One day, she didn't even hear me talking to her. Maybe she wasn't feeling too well then.'

Gina checked her watch. There was no point delaying. Maybe Lucy's house held the answer. With a life at risk and Lucy being their main suspect, they were going in. Gina caught sight of all the handwritten memos on the wall. It was the way she wrote an 'e' that gave her away. The same half an eight 'curly e' was on the handwritten order in Gina's pocket. That 'e' had been the same in the diary excerpt left in her car, and the notes on the board in front of her confirmed that it was Lucy, but why? Gentle, friendly Lucy. The happy, smiley woman who serves coffee and brightens everyone's day up, the woman who runs a café with her lovely father, Bill. It was now time to find out. 'I best let you get back to your customers. Sorry for keeping you.'

'I hope everything's okay.' The girl fed her apron back over her head as Gina hurried back to the street where Jacob was ending his call.

'Call for backup. Let's get to Lucy and Bill Manders's house in Stoke Prior.'

*

The three-storey Victorian gothic house stood back at the end of a long, winding, tree-lined drive. Weeds grew up from the old tarmacked drive and what was once a fountain was now covered in oak leaves, the basin filled with old bricks and moss. Gina hurried out of the car and took the five steps up to the grand front door as Jacob followed. She zipped her protective jacket up, ready for what might come their way. Ivy had all but covered the front of the house concealing most of the old brickwork. She pulled the vine away from the doorbell and revealed a broken plaque. First word unknown, second word carpentry and she bit her lip as she saw the carving of the lion underneath, a lion that was far more accomplished than the attempts on the coffins. She banged hard and opened the letterbox. A spindly spider fled for its life, attaching its web to Gina's hand. She flinched and shook it away. 'Lucy, Bill, open up. It's DI Harte. Gina from the café. We need to talk to you.'

'They're either not in or not answering, guv. I'll head around the back.' He left her at the front, knocking.

She moved back, taking one step at a time. Everywhere she looked, it felt as though the house was watching; its imposing size and proportions were threatening in their own way. A flurry of crispy leaves drifted down as the wind howled. This ghost symbol had to be referring to this house. She'd never seen a creepier house in all her life. It made the squat look like the Wacky Warehouse. The smeared windows reflected stony skies and wavering trees, that same smeary mess distorting everything in the natural world. Gina tried to tiptoe on the drive but the main windows at the front were too high to peer through. She caught sight of a little window at the base of the building. It was a cellar. She leaned over the cast iron railings and peered through, all she could see was a dust-covered workshop full of shelves and tools. Full bin bags filled one end of the room.

Another two cars pulled up. Wyre and O'Connor got out of one and PCs Smith and Kapoor out of another.

Smith zipped up his jacket, checking that his baton and stab proof vest were all in place. Gina did the same. It was getting real. 'More backup is on the way, guv.'

She nervously smiled. Fear and excitement coursed through her veins. 'I'm heading around the back with Jacob. Keep an eye out here. Don't go in until I say.'

They nodded while getting into place, either side of the front door. Smith gripped the Enforcer.

She hurried around the building, which revealed a large expanse of open farmland. 'Alright, guv. There's a large shed just over there. Follow me.' She hurried over, stepping on the uneven slabs that led to it. 'You can see through the window. There are reels of red material, just like the lining in the coffins. It's leaning up against that corner.' Just short of pressing her nose against the glass, she managed to peer through the grime. Despite there being loads of wood and material stacked up, there was no sign of a person in the shed.

'See there?'

Jacob leaned in for a closer look. 'It's a dust outline. It's the size of a coffin or a stack of coffins. And next to it, a fold-up trolley that has no dust on it at all.' A trail led from the door to the spot. It had been put there recently.

'What the hell? We're going in. Cherie might be in that cellar or buried on these grounds but I can tell you something, we can't lose another person to the coffin killer.'

They ran across the long-overgrown garden, taking a shortcut straight through. Stingers and brambles pierced the tracksuit bottoms that Gina was still wearing. She flinched as pinpricks of pain attacked her ankles and legs.

She nodded to Smith who stood poised with the Enforcer. 'Police. Stand back, we're coming in.' On the third strike, the solid door bounced open. Gina hurried through the old tiled hallway, taking in the grand staircase and large stained-glass window ahead. She turned to what appeared to be a library and felt a shiver run down her back as her gaze locked on the body in front of her.

CHAPTER SIXTY-EIGHT

Gina crouched down to check Bill's pulse but he was cold. His stiff wrist and the curl in his index finger told her that rigor mortis had set in. 'I'd say he's been dead between two and six hours.' That much she knew. The bluish tinge to his greying skin, with a backdrop of floor-to-ceiling bookcases gave her the creeps. She looked away from his open mouth. 'The coffin maker, dies in the library with a cord around his neck.'

She stood and hurried back into the hallway. 'Lucy, it's the police. Come out. It's over, Lucy.' They all waited for an answer. She took a few more steps into the kitchen. The old range stood at one end of the room. 'Wyre, you take the lead upstairs with Kapoor and O'Connor. There are two floors. Jacob, Smith, you come with me. We're heading down to the cellar.' As they crept around the house in their teams, Gina pushed at the cellar door but it was locked.

'Clear.' Wyre leaned over the bannister. 'There's no one upstairs. We'll call the body in.'

'We need to get into that cellar. Let's get the Enforcer on it.'

As Smith poised himself, Gina called out one more time. 'Lucy, Cherie, we're coming through now. Stand back.' No one answered. Gina swallowed and took a deep breath as the wooden door split on the first blow; the second had the door open. Smith pulled the tangled light cord but the cellar remained in darkness. Gina brushed past him with her pocket torch as she took the first few creaky steps. 'Cherie, it's DI Harte. Make a noise if you're down here.' She heard a scuffle.

As she reached the concrete floor, a bit of light came from the tiny window she'd peered through while standing on the drive. The dirt, coupled with a stormy dark day, still made it difficult to see too far ahead. She could make out the racking. Wood panels of all different sizes were haphazardly slotted into shelves, dusty like they hadn't been touched for years. As Gina passed them, a flurry of dust motes danced in the light.

She heard the same scuffle coming from a pile of bin bags. Beckoning Smith and Jacob to follow, she turned the corner to see an old sack moving. She grabbed a thin piece of wood and lifted the edge of the sacking, disturbing a bag full of wood shavings that spilled everywhere. The rat escaped from the pile and scurried between her legs, making its escape.

'Bloody things.' Jacob let out a startled cry.

Gina hurried over and lifted the sack. There was nothing but more wood. She threw the strip of wood to the floor and let out a frustrated roar. 'Where the hell has Lucy taken Cherie Brown?'

'Guv,' O'Connor called her from the top of the house. 'Come here quick.'

She nudged between Jacob and Smith and ran up three flights of stairs until she reached a narrower flight.

'Up here, guv. In the attic.'

Taking two steps at a time, she gasped as she entered the room with the door at the end. Wyre was poring over a board, a bit like the ones they used in the incident room. There were photos of Alex, Penny and Cherie on the main board; each of them had black crosses through their faces. Then there was another board beside it. Gina stared at a photo of herself, but her face had a red ring around it. Her heart rate started to rev up. Copies of the letters to the press were stuck underneath. She spotted a few old articles in the local papers that involved the cases she'd worked on in the past and the one of her receiving an award while in uniform. Lucy had been delving deeply into her life. A map was stuck to another board, a pin in the woods, a pin in the building site and one more pin. 'Where's this? Anyone know this location?'

O'Connor pointed his torch at the board and squinted as he looked a little closer. 'It's about a mile from the park, off the edge of a housing estate. The woodland here is sandwiched between an estate and the bus route. It's quite the danger spot really. It should have been fenced off years ago. There's a pond, a dirty old pond there.'

'Brilliant, O'Connor. Look at that last pin.' She grabbed a ruler from the desk. Each line, equal in length, the angles looked to be the same too. Something Christian Brown had said to her clicked. It was an equilateral triangle – not an isosceles or right-angled. These locations had been chosen with precision. 'We had the burial sites under our noses all this time – simple maths. Wyre, stay and wait for forensics. Get a search up and running of the grounds just in case we're wrong about the pond. Cherie could still be buried here and I want you to take the lead on it. Get some dogs in too; it's a large area to search. We have to go. Now!'

Her phone rang. It was Briggs. 'We know where the body is, sir.'

'The old pond off Cobble Lane?'

'How did you know?' Gina shrugged her shoulders at the team.

'Isaac Slater just decided to tell us on the advice of his solicitor. He said you asked about a ghost in the interview. The kids used to call it the haunted pond, something about a lady in the lake.'

'We're heading straight there now.' She ended the call.

Wyre turned to leave the attic room. 'Stay safe, all of you. I've got this.'

'Right, what are we all waiting for? A life is at stake!' Gina raced down the stairs and back to her car, hoping it wasn't too late to save Cherie.

CHAPTER SIXTY-NINE

Gina glanced at the message that flashed up on her phone. 'Sally Stevens now remembers who mentioned the passage to her. We already know it was Lucy but at least she's confirmed that.' She rolled her eyes as she passed Cherie Brown's car, heading along the thin path. As she pushed the spindly branches from her face, she spotted the old pond. 'Here it is. Cherie,' she called.

A branch flicked back, striking Jacob across the cheek. 'Ouch.'

'Sorry.'

He dismissed it and smiled. 'I think I can cope.'

'It's as revolting as I remember it, guv.' O'Connor caught up, his jacket done up to the neck. 'We used to play here as kids, gather jars of tadpoles, things like that. It was always horrible. I doubt anything could live in it now looking at the state of it.'

'Look.' Gina hurried to the weather-beaten bench and saw an empty vodka bottle. 'Cherie?' she called again, louder. 'Search the area. Search everything. Smith, you head around the pond, see if you can safely get to the other side.'

'Wait for me.' Kapoor caught up with Smith who was doubled up and panting.

'Both of you start searching along here.' She pointed to another little path. 'The road runs along this way.'

O'Connor looked up. 'Yes, there's a stile at the road so people can cross. Lucy Manders may have parked there and came this way.'

Gina glared at the ground with its sprigs of brown grass poking through the dense mud. 'Wait, Lucy came the way we came. Those are trolley wheel prints. There's no way she'd get a coffin on a trolley over a stile.' She stood to the side of the line and followed its direction. 'Stay back.' Gina crept along the bank, almost sliding towards the edge of the pond. Her heart rate sped as she almost slid into the frothy scum that had gathered over one end of the pond. 'Tread carefully. We don't want to disturb the imprints and I don't want any of you to end up in this pond.'

As she took a few more steps, she continued along the wood-land covered pathway, pushing through more trees and shrubs until she bumped into a bell, suspended from a tree. 'Here.' She ran forward.

'Dammit.' Jacob began fighting with the cord as the bell clunked against the bark. 'I walked straight into that. 'No clapper, like all the others.'

She ran to the mound of earth, hands pushing through as she scooped it away.

The others hurried past and began helping except for Kapoor. 'There's a couple of shovels in the car, guv. We came prepared for this.'

'Go get them, thank you.' As Kapoor ran off Gina felt some-thing wet and soft wriggling beneath her finger. Her one creature fear: the earthworm. She flinched and let out a sharp cry as she slid back in the mud, shaking her hand over and over again as she stared at it in terror. Smith ignored her and continued to scoop.

Jacob shuffled over to her on his knees. 'Have you hurt yourself?'

'No, I'm being stupid.' She took another breath and got back into the soil, scooping it out. 'Don't stop, we're against it. We can't lose Cherie. Please be alive.' With closed eyes she continued. What she couldn't see couldn't hurt. She listened to the grunts and groans as they all began to tire. A flick of earth hit her face.

She opened her eyes to the sight of Kapoor, pushing back through the bushes. 'Here they are.'

Gina grabbed one and Smith grabbed another. 'Stand back.' With every shovelful she threw over her shoulder she thought of the time she was trapped in the shed. She wished that someone had come to her rescue and taken her and Hannah away from it all. All she wanted to do was open that coffin and show Cherie that she'd made it, that she'd live.

As she continued to shovel the earth, she called out. 'Cherie, shout if you can hear me. It's DI Harte, you're safe now.' She felt her eyes welling up as no answer came. What she was going to find in the box was another body. 'Jacob, have the paramedics arrived yet.'

He stepped aside. 'They should be here any moment. In fact, I can just about hear the sirens.'

'O'Connor, head back to the road and bring them here. Cherie. Help is on its way.' There was no response. Gina's muscles ached with every movement and as the rain began to patter, it mingled with the sweat pouring from her head and the grit in her eyes. A flash of an image crossed her mind. The roof of the coffin with the red satin material. The feeling of claustrophobia and imminent death. *Loneliness – no one misses you, no one is coming and no one can hear you.* Her head was fit to burst with emotion as her body shook. 'Can you take over?'

Jacob took the tool from her and continued where she'd left off. He and Smith dug a shovelful of earth in turn until Jacob's tool clanked against the coffin.

'Hurry. Cherie, can you hear me?' Gina kneeled down as the digging continued. A moment later, she could see wood, beautifully polished wood. She held her hand up to stop them digging, then she reached for the coffin, grimacing as she flicked a worm aside. Delving further, she felt for the clasp to open the casket and smiled as she gripped it. She closed her eyes and took a breath as she lifted the lid.

'There's no one in here!' The only things in the coffin were an open matchbox, three burnt-down matches and a piece of string that had been threaded through a tiny hole in the coffin. Gina fell onto her bottom as rain dripped down her face. Her phone vibrated in her pocket. Briggs was calling. 'Hello.'

'Gina, you have to get to the carriageway bridge, the Cleevesford Flyover. We've just had a report of a woman matching Lucy Manders's description standing on the edge with another woman. Uniform are about to arrive on the scene and traffic police are in the process of rerouting cars and putting barriers up, but you have to be there. You know this woman and she likes you, I know she does. Get there now.'

CHAPTER SEVENTY

The wooziness passed as blood coursed through Cherie's body. For a second, she visualised her body cracking as she hit the concrete below. She flinched and opened her eyes. She hadn't been dreaming. They were still on the Cleevesford Flyover. She shook her head, trying to clear the fuzziness away.

One minute she'd been in a coffin, the next here on the dual carriageway bridge. She couldn't remember getting out of the box but then snippets of her staggering through trees kept coming back. Her soaking wet legs reminded her that she'd slipped into the stagnant pond. The journey from the pond to the bridge were completely missing, that's all she could remember.

'Lucy, how did I get here?' The woman ignored her. 'Please, you can stop this. I have children that need me. I need them.' Cherie sobbed as the woman glared wide-eyed at the road below. Blue lights ahead blocked any further traffic from passing through. 'I'm sorry, I really am. I can make it up to you.'

'I should have left you to die in that coffin but you know something, Cherie, it wasn't enough for you. I thought you were my friend. I trusted you back then when you took me to that party.'

'I know and I hurt you. I'm truly sorry. You weren't meant to kiss Isaac. I lost it, I'm sorry.' The road below became blurrier. Maybe it was the vodka she'd consumed earlier, the drug she'd been injected with, or the lack of air in the damn box that the lunatic beside her had trapped her in. 'I'll do anything to make it up to you, Lucy. Please, just give me a chance. We don't have to keep reliving the past. We can move on from it.'

Tears streamed down the woman's cheeks. 'What did I ever do to you? I was just the new girl. That was my only crime. You barely knew me, how could you hate me that much? Okay, Isaac kissed me once but that was it.' She paused and stared at the sky with glassy eyes. 'Since that day, I've had to live with all that baggage while you all carried on with your merry little lives. You're married, you have children. Bella and Oliver.'

Cherie began to hyperventilate. 'Please don't hurt them.'

'Me, hurt them? I'd be more worried about you hurting them after what you did. I saw a version of you that you probably don't want the world to know about. Does your husband know the real person behind the mask you wear? If not, he will after this. I've left everything written down in a notebook, in the van. Everything you did to me is in that book. I'm finally ready to tell my story even though every word I wrote down felt like a stab to the heart.' She paused and smirked. 'It looks like death is a good option for you. You pay for what you did to me and you escape seeing your children look at you in a way you never thought possible. They will hate you but you know something, I bet they'll go easier on you because you died. Or will they? Whatever, you won't be there to see how much they all despise you.' Lucy laughed through her tears, a brown curl falling over her red-rimmed eyes.

The notebook. She had to get Lucy off her and get the notebook before the police arrived. She could push Lucy over the edge, claim it was self-defence or suicide and have everyone feel sorry for her, including her own family. Christian would come back home with the children and he'd be none the wiser. She'd go back to AA to deal with her drinking, start again. Get another job. Whatever it took, she'd do it. She reached for the railings but the world began to spin as she looked back. *Get a grip, Cherie. You can do this.* As she went to grip the railings, she felt a tug at her wrist. Rope – binding her and Lucy together. Blood pumped around her body, thudding in her head and ears. *What next? Think, think.* She couldn't hear the sirens any more. She was going to faint or maybe she was going to be sick. Her stomach rolled as she gripped the railing with the other hand. The metal was getting slippier as the rain got heavier.

'I knew you'd try to shake me off. I really am prepared for everything. We're doing this together, Cherie. I've killed three people, but you know something, when all this comes out, the world will see what you all did and that you deserved what you all got.'

Mind awhirl, Cherie thought of Alex. It was now obvious that Lucy had killed Penny and used the messages to lure her to the pond. If only it had been Isaac. Everything would now be okay. She knew Lucy had sent the original messages that the others mentioned. Her old friend had been meticulously planning her revenge for a long time. Who was the other victim? She was still alive and Lucy had only mentioned Alex and Penny. Who was the third?

'You're thinking hard and your maths is right. Three people and it will soon be five, if I count myself and you.' Lucy paused and wiped her tears away. 'I can see your pea brain whirring around. Who's my other victim? I wanted to kill the other two that were with you on that fateful night but you know something, I never knew who was behind those last two masks.' Lucy let out a huge laugh as more tears spilled out. 'Seeing as you didn't ask, the other one was my own father. The reasons are no concern of yours but let's just say this, he turned out to be a big disappointment. All I can say is that people who stand by and do nothing are as guilty as those committing the crime.' She shrugged. 'What is a concern of yours is, if I can kill my own father, I will have no problem killing you. When I look at you, Cherie, all I feel is hate and fear and anger. Time may tick by but a person never forgets how you made them feel, which is why we are going together, now. I'm looking forward to it. You can embrace it too.'

Cherie felt the tug at her wrist, gulped and closed her eyes.

CHAPTER SEVENTY-ONE

'Lucy, you don't have to do this.' Gina took one tiny step towards the woman in the long black coat as she was about to let go of the railing, which Cherie also gripped with one hand, her eyes still closed. 'Can I come a little closer, so that we can talk?' She held her palm up to Jacob to keep him right back. One wrong move and both women would be dead.

A flood of tears streamed down Lucy's face. 'I like you, a lot, I always did. This piece of shit doesn't deserve anything. I've left you something in the van. Everything is in the notebook. I wanted you to have it. I knew you'd understand. It had to be you, Gina. Only you would understand.' Her lower lip trembled as she held back another sob.

'Please, Lucy, just let me go.' Cherie tried to loop her elbow under the rail to get a better grip, but the gap was too small to feed her arm through.

'Tell her what you did. It's confession time.' Lucy stared down at the road.

'I can't.'

'Tell her!'

'What do you need to tell me?' Gina took another half-step forward but she was still too far away to make a grab for anyone if the two women were going down. Cherie shivered in what looked like soaking wet leggings. Lucy's coat was open and reaching out in front of her as if it was beckoning her to follow it over the edge.

Cherie screamed as Lucy teased her by leaning forward a little. 'Okay, years ago I hurt Lucy, I hurt her badly.'

'Tell her how.'

A tear streamed down Cherie's face. Gina took another step.

'Get back.' Lucy's wide eyes stared at Gina. This woman knew so much about her, she knew about Terry, and Gina needed to understand how much she knew and how, if Lucy took Cherie over that edge, she'd never have her answer.

'Years ago, my friends and I locked Lucy in a coffin at Halloween. It was meant to be a prank and it went too far. I was jealous because I saw Isaac and her kissing at the party. When I recognised her at the café, I kept going back to apologise, but every time I just couldn't do it. I wanted to, but you didn't recognise me and you looked so happy, Lucy. I didn't want to bring up the past and make you sad again.'

'You mean you were a coward. Tell the lovely detective what happened after you dug me up from that horrible box. She wants the details from your mouth.'

'Please, Lucy. You've written it all down. I can't—'

Lucy tugged again and Cherie screamed out. 'I guess I'm in control here and I'm giving you no choice in the matter, just like you gave me no choice back then when you buried me in a box with only three matches for company.'

'I hurt Lucy.' Cherie sobbed and almost choked as she continued to blurt out her darkest secret. 'We got her out of the coffin and we threw things at her – stones. Alex whipped her with a branch as we teased her about her dad being a coffin maker. We said they were like the Addams Family.'

Lucy wailed as she listened to what Cherie was saying. Gina took another half-step, still not near enough.

'How long did this go on for?'

'I don't know. Lucy, I am so sorry. Please forgive me. I was so horrible back then. I should have stopped it.'

'But you didn't, you suggested that he do all those horrible things, didn't you? I still have the scars. I remember the blood smearing over my arms and legs. You disgust me, Cherie. You! Now your husband and children will know just how evil you are. I have noted all the details of your torturous little rampage against me. Alex listened to you, he did everything you told him to do like some stupid puppy. You could have said, *okay we shut her in a box, joke's over. Let's all go home*, but no, that was just the start of the two hours that ruined me as you laughed and pitched in with suggestions on how to punish me more. I could see Penny wasn't comfortable, but did she help? No, she just stood by and watched, just like my coward father did all those years ago.' Lucy glanced back at Gina.

Cherie looked away. 'I did all that, I did it.'

'Are you ready to go?' Lucy glanced back at her. 'There's nothing left for you, not now. Just like me, your life has been ruined too.'

Cherie let go of the rail and closed her eyes. Lucy took a deep breath.

'Lucy, it doesn't have to end like this. I heard everything and you wanted me to hear, didn't you?'

Lucy began to rock back and forth against the railings.

Gina's stomach jumped with every move. The mud had seeped through her tracksuit bottoms and they were now sticking to her knees and thighs, tightening as they dried a little. 'You wanted me to know how you felt, didn't you? That's why you trapped me in a coffin. I felt the fear, the panic and, believe me, I've felt what it's like to be humiliated and hurt. We can talk about this, Lucy. It stings, doesn't it? There can be life after something so terrible and I'm sure when everyone knows what happened to you, the courts will be lenient.' She hoped they would, but in reality Gina had no idea how sentencing would go down or how a jury would react to the case. At the end of the day, Lucy had murdered three people and was threatening to kill a fourth. 'Please, Lucy. Let her go and step back over the railings, then we can talk about everything. I'm here to listen. You know me from the café. You know me better than I know you. I saw your room, in the attic. You didn't want me to die, you wanted me to notice you and be there to listen. You chose me because you know I'd understand and all you wanted to do was remind me of what it was like. I'm sorry I'm late, but I'm here now.'

Lucy snatched a pair of scissors from her pocket and brought them up to Cherie's chin.

The woman opened her eyes and flinched as the metal traced her neckline. Lucy swiftly brought the scissors down to the cord that bound them and snipped it in the middle. 'You now have to live with the fact that everyone will know what you did; your husband, your friends, your neighbours, your poor children. At least they are no longer in danger from the likes of such a cruel, abusive person.'

'I'd never hurt my children—'

'Save it. I'm not listening. I'm now free to not have to listen to your bullshit. Before I change my mind, go. Go live with it. By the way, I sent a copy of my notebook to the press too. It should arrive in the post tomorrow and the world will know why.' Lucy wiped away her tears with the arm of her coat. 'You know something else, I'm done with crying.'

Cherie edged away but stopped.

'What are you waiting for? Are you thinking of jumping? If I was you, I'd jump. Tempting, isn't it?' Lucy taunted.

As the wind began to howl, blowing the fine raindrops into Cherie's face, she edged forward slightly.

Gina took another step. 'Cherie, stop. You don't want to do this.'

'I think she does, Gina.'

Cherie's bottom lip began to wobble. She sobbed as she went to climb over the railings. 'I can't.'

'A coward to the end.'

As the woman cocked one leg over, her hand slipped. Gina stepped forward and grabbed her arm. 'Come on.'

Lucy slid away from her.

'Cherie Brown, I'm arresting you on suspicion of the attempted murder of Lucy Manders. You do not have to say anything, but it may harm your defence if you do not mention when questioned something which you later rely on in court. Anything you do say may be given in evidence.' She glanced over to Jacob and waved him across. 'I've arrested Mrs Brown. Please take her to the ambulance to be checked over and get her taken in for questioning.'

Gina took a step closer to Lucy. She knew that the charge may not stick due to the circumstances of the confession, but she'd work that one out later. 'Let me help you, please step over the railings.' Lucy held her hands out in front of her. She went to touch the railings but snatched her hand back out of the way.

'I don't know if I want help. You've done enough. Just make sure she pays for what she did, will you? Don't let her walk.'

'Please, Lucy—'

'Please, Lucy,' the woman mimicked. 'That's all *she* said, and the others.' She paused and cocked her head to the side. 'They were all so easy to lure to their death. Alex would turn up anywhere for a fix. Poor Penny thought Isaac was about to tell her about Marcus's affair. There was no affair. Cherie thought I was Penny. Without question, they all turned up right where I needed them.'

Gina swallowed.

Lucy shook her head a couple of times. 'Look, I'm sorry for what I put you through. Like I said, I needed you to know exactly how it felt. When you're interviewing her, take that feeling and use it. That's what she put me through all those years ago, then there was the torture. You know all about that, don't you? I didn't need to show you how that felt, not with what Terry did to you.'

A tremble began to form at Gina's knees. She turned her head slightly. 'I do, and it's horrible, so horrible I wonder how I'm going to get through some days but somehow I do. You will too, Lucy.' She paused as her dry mouth stopped her from continuing. 'I can also tell you that you can live with what happened, you can get through this. Maybe you can even help others one day.'

'I liked you when you came into my café and once I'd heard what happened to you, I knew you were the one. People like Terry, they deserve to die; that's why I killed my father. He wasn't the nice man he made himself out to be.'

Gina felt the pressure of needing to be alone so that all her own tears could escape. 'Did he hurt you too?'

'He didn't hurt me, Gina. He hurt you. He used to drink in the pub with Terry when you lived in Birmingham all those years ago. When you started coming to the café, he told me about Terry and the things he'd said about you when he was hammered. I know he locked you in a shed. It's not a coffin but still, it must have been scary. I know back then that everyone at that pub talked about your bruises. All those people in the pub that knew what he was doing to you did nothing. You can imagine how disappointed I was in the man who brought me up. He gossiped about you in the café when you'd left, telling the other customers about your horrible ex-husband and they were all happy to listen, to take it all in. He even told the press a few little things and that made me sick. That was private stuff, not to be shared with our customers or anyone.' She swallowed. 'You know what clinched it? He knew and he could have helped you, just like Penny or any of the others could have helped me to get away from Alex and Cherie. They chose not to, and they had to pay, just like my father. There's a price to pay for silence, especially when that silence caused so much harm.'

A tear streamed down Gina's face. When she killed Terry there was no premeditation, but she still killed him. Lucy had gone one step further and planned it all to make them pay. 'Lucy—'

'Don't speak. Before you ask, I'd been planning this for years. I wanted to hurt them but I didn't know where Alex was. He had to be the first. I knew when I wanted to open a café that it had to be back in Cleevesford, where it all started. When I saw it was up for rent, it felt like it was meant to be.' She paused. 'I also built more into that stupid urban legend, about the ghost in the woods. The kids came in for cake all the time and they thought it was brilliant and, stupidly, they believed me. I thought it would get back to Cherie and freak her out, but it didn't. She came in to read at the café but I could tell her mind wasn't on the book. I didn't even know it was Cherie at that point. Then when Alex came in, it was as if the light had been turned on. I saw that woman with the book was Cherie. She didn't disguise herself brilliantly, but I'd failed to notice her until then. Her hair colour had changed and so had the style. It was short back then. The glasses placed a barrier against her eyes but when I caught sight of her on that Monday, I knew straight away.' Lucy's hair blew back as a gust caught it. 'I enjoyed playing mind games with them, digging up Alex's nan's grave, sending messages, following them around and creeping them out.' Lucy stood on the thin ledge and lifted the arms of her coat like a dark angel.

Gina felt her heart judder. 'Lucy, please lean back.'

'I'm sorry I drugged you. I've been taking ketamine for years to dim the pain. It was only a tiny dose.'

'It doesn't matter, Lucy. Please just grab the rail.'

She shook her head. 'Do you know how good this feels? I'm free. I'm going to fly with the birds. For the first time in my life I'm just me and that's enough.'

'You are free now. You're free because the truth has come out and your abuser has been arrested. Let justice be your freedom. Let me help you.' Rightly or wrongly, if Gina could get Lucy off that ledge, she was going to be there for her after sentencing.

'Those coffins, the three of them were mine, Dad's and my older brother Ricky's. He's in the army, we barely see him. They were the last three Dad made before retiring from the business. He said he kept the best for us. I had a go at engraving them but my attempts weren't good.' She paused and made a windmilling motion with her hands. 'This feels so good.' Rain began to fall heavier, drenching her hair and saturating her coat. 'I don't care about coffins. I believe nothing happens when you're dead. It's just the end. He wasted his time. Had he spent more time helping the living, I'd have respected him more. He didn't help you, Gina.'

'Sometimes people don't know what to do, Lucy. He might not have felt he could help.' She wished someone had reported Terry back then, but she wasn't going to tell Lucy that, not now. 'I forgive your father, maybe you can too. If you step over, we can go into my car where it's warm and dry.' Gina took another slight step.

Lucy stopped abruptly. 'Stay right there.'

Gina held her hands up. 'Okay. I'm not moving.' The rain fell heavier and began cascading down Gina's face.

'I wasn't going to bring Cherie here but she kept shouting from the coffin and I hated her even more. I wanted her to suffer more horror than the others. I mean what's worse than facing the thought of death once? Facing it twice.'

'Why did you let her go?'

'The world loves a hate figure. Her life won't be worth living once the newspapers publish everything. I think she's getting what she deserves. In prison, they hate people like her. A day won't go by when she won't have to watch her back. When she comes out, her precious children won't want to know their mum. I'm pretty sure she'll need a new identity.' Lucy turned to face the sky, mouth open as she cried out. 'I can't face it.'

'You can, Lucy.' Gina reached over. 'Please take my hand. You were a scared young girl and what they did to you was awful. The world will see your side of the story.'

'I shouldn't have gone to that party.' Her face formed a pained expression as she trembled.

'It was their fault, not yours. You were a girl and you went to a party; you did nothing wrong. They abused your trust. They were in the wrong.'

Gina reached for Lucy's hand. Lucy turned, her chest heaving under the coat with every sob. Her hair stuck to her face. Lucy held out her hand. As Gina went to take it, she lifted it, twisted her body and fell back, arms spread out, her coat flapping in the wind. Gina noticed one thing: a light smile on the woman's face.

CHAPTER SEVENTY-TWO

As Lucy was about to hit the ground Gina turned away, unable to look. She felt her chest heaving and she couldn't control herself. She'd lost Lucy but saved Cherie. She fell to the road onto all fours, then sat in the wet, crying, until Jacob ran over.

He put his raincoat over her shoulders. 'Come on, guv.'

'I tried to get her to climb over the railings. I thought she was coming.' Her speech turned into a jumbled mess and she struggled to breathe.

Jacob wrapped his arm around her as he helped her up and walked her to the ambulance. 'There's nothing more you could've done.'

Maybe that was true, maybe it wasn't. Everyone failed Lucy, even her father. She wished she'd known Lucy before and, maybe then, she could have helped her.

'You did all you could, guv. I know you're punishing yourself now but none of us could have done any more.'

She gave Jacob a slight smile as he led her into the ambulance and went in with her. 'Jacob, thank you. I'm sorry for blubbing.'

He smiled. 'No need. I feel like blubbing myself, but you can thank me with a pint when this is all over. We should all have a drink at the Angel Arms now slimy Samuel Avery has gone. Anyway, that's for later. Cherie Brown is at the hospital being checked over but we should have her back at the station soon. You'll have enough time to change out of those wet clothes and grab something hot to drink.'

Gina took a deep breath. *Cherie Brown, it's about time you told me everything. I want the accessories to the crime, the masked people that Lucy couldn't identify but who must be Marcus and Isaac. I want you to relive every gory detail.* She already knew who they were, but Lucy died not knowing. She wanted to see Cherie squirm as she forced her to relay the details. She would get revenge for Lucy, but it would be through the courts. She had to nail the confession or the woman could walk.

CHAPTER SEVENTY-THREE

Gina wrapped her cardigan around her body, still feeling the chill of the earlier events of the day. The young solicitor shook her head and Cherie refused to speak once again. Jacob caught her gaze and leaned back in his chair. Wyre was interviewing Marcus Burton at the same time that O'Connor was interviewing Isaac Slater. Which one would crack first? A confession while being dangled over the top of a carriageway bridge wouldn't be enough.

'As I said before, I only said those things because she was going to kill me. I didn't do anything. It was Alex. Back then, when I tried to run away, Alex said to come back or it would be me next. He threatened me so I had to stay.'

'I've read the notebook.'

'So, she was mental, she made it up. You saw her.' Cherie grinned as she bit her bottom lip.

Gina had pushed her hard, been soft, tried to be sympathetic when she spoke of peer pressure and how hard it is for a person to go against their friends, but nothing had worked.

'I work as a carer. I'm a mother and a wife. Could I be all that if I was such a monster?'

Gina knew she could. Behind Cherie's smug grin, she knew she was speaking to someone who was cruel and calculated. She'd seen it in Terry, first-hand.

There was a tap at the door. Jacob spoke for the benefit of the tape as Gina stepped out.

'What is it?' she asked.

O'Connor grinned. 'Before we interviewed Isaac Slater, his girlfriend Joanna Brent asked for a word so we spoke to her first. She confirmed that he'd made her cover for him. She said he'd been acting oddly for a couple of weeks, drinking too much, getting into trouble at work for not going in. She'd find him at home in a stupor and he'd murmur about a girl they'd all hurt years ago. He said it wasn't his fault. He was just told it was a prank and then it got out of hand. He said Alex and Cherie tortured the girl and because he was there too, they'd blamed him, so they'd all kept this secret. The next day he said it was all a load of drunken rubbish. She said she couldn't keep it to herself any longer.'

'And?'

'When we interviewed him, he cried like he couldn't wait to get it out of his system. He fully described what Alex and Cherie had done to Lucy.'

'Let me guess, it matched up to what was in Lucy's notebook?' She clenched her hands together in hope.

'Exactly, and the details of that notebook have not been released anywhere, as yet. Briggs is on to the press at the moment, pleading with them to not publish it straight away, just to give us a bit more time with follow-up questioning. It hasn't arrived in the post either, so they definitely don't have the details.' A grin spread across O'Connor's face.

'I could kiss you right now!'

'Mrs O wouldn't approve. Jacob said drinks are on you down at the pub, I'll take a beer instead.'

She playfully slapped his arm. 'I'm definitely buying everyone's drinks when this is over. While I'm pushing her, get onto the CPS and relay what we have. I'm hoping it will be enough without her confession but I don't want to get this wrong. I know Lucy was our killer but I feel I owe it to Lucy to get this right. She suffered a lot in her life, carried the burden of what they did to her, they need to pay too.'

'I'm on it now.'

She dropped her smile and reopened the door.

Jacob started the recorder again. 'Interview continued at twenty-one-hundred hours.'

'Cherie, I'm not going to mince my words. We have a full witness statement and the person who gave it described everything that happened in Lucy Manders's notebook having never read it. You've got nowhere to go now, Cherie.'

The woman kicked the table leg and bit her lip. 'That bitch. She could have just moved on with her life. She tried to kill me. What we did to her was nothing in comparison.'

'On the contrary, what you did to her was everything. It started this whole chain of events. You don't get to do all those things and expect the victim to give you a free pass. It's now time to face up to your crimes.'

'I was stupid, only a kid.'

'You were sixteen, above the age of criminal responsibility. You buried Lucy alive and you assaulted her. You buried her in the ground knowing it could kill her. You threw stones at her and whipped her with branches. You tortured her for nearly two hours.'

Tears trickled down Cherie's cheeks. 'What now? Will my husband and children be told? I don't want them to know what I did. They can't know. Surely they need protecting.'

The solicitor stared at her notes on the table and whispered in Cherie's ear.

'You'll be charged and you'll attend magistrates' court, where you'll be referred to crown for trial by jury. Now is your time to do the right thing and face up to it.' Gina closed her folder and leaned back in her chair. The case was over. She could now go home, take that long-needed bath and dwell on how she was going to tackle a night out with the department.

*

She hurried along the corridor, heading to the kitchen. Briggs was leaning up against the counter waiting for the kettle to boil. She closed the door. 'I really am sorry about what I accused you of. Do you forgive me?'

'You were under a lot of stress. Of course I forgive you. Do you want a coffee?'

She shrugged and he smiled as O'Connor burst in. 'Make one for me, will you? I think we've all earned this drink. Oh, by the way, sir, drinks are on guv tomorrow.'

She shrugged and nodded. 'I guess they are.'

EPILOGUE

Now

Friday, 13 November

The best way Gina could remember what Lucy had been through would be to move on with her life. That's one thing this case had taught her. Gina wasn't sure if that was possible, but her current frame of mind said it was at this precise moment. Right now, she was going to forget all her problems and live for now – but there was one thing she had to do first.

Her phone rang. 'Sir?'

Briggs paused and cleared his throat. 'Do you want the good news?'

'I would love some good news.' She smiled, glad that another case hadn't come in so soon.

'The journalist, Lyndsey Saunders, she's been taken off the story and sent packing. Publishing that letter and your name could have hampered the case. Corporate Communications put a complaint in and, well, they're investigating. I'm just sorry that your name had to be dragged through the papers. Are you okay? Are we okay?'

She smiled, even though a few specks of rain were drizzling down her forehead. 'Couldn't be any better, sir. That's made my day.' She paused. 'Look, I have to go.'

She stared up at the church and walked through the open door.

As she went to end the call, he spoke. 'Where are you? Fancy a coffee somewhere?'

'I'll have to get back to you on that one. Speak later.' She placed the phone in her pocket as she glanced at the flower and candle display that took pride of place on the altar.

Gina flinched as the door behind her creaked. 'DI Harte. Good news about making the arrest. It's been all over the news.' Sally Stevens clunked over to her. 'What do I owe this pleasure? Come to join the church?'

She shook her head. 'I'm not a believer. I just wanted to come in and enjoy the peace.'

'That's allowed. We welcome anyone here. Take a pew and make yourself at home. It looks like we're on our own. Do you want a cuppa? I was just making one.'

Gina nodded. 'Thank you.'

Gina closed her eyes, taking in the silence. Even with her eyes closed, she could tell she was occupying a vacuous space. The musty smell hit her but it was also comforting. It reminded her of her childhood. Her mother's sideboard used to smell the same. A tear slid down her eyes, she suddenly missed her mother and everything lovely about her life before meeting Terry. She missed Lucy, the woman she knew so well but for so little time. Since the case, the toxicology results from Alexander Swinton's blood had come back. He had been lured to the location, just like Lucy had said. She didn't have to carry anyone anywhere. They all came to her. After a search of Lucy's house, Penny's burner phone had been found and all the messages proved that Penny had first been lured by messages from Lucy and then Lucy had used Penny's phone to draw Cherie in. Lucy must have been watching Penny for a long time to get that number, the one Penny had shared with the world on Facebook when she'd lost her phone.

In her mind, she pictured Lucy sweating as she dug those holes in the dead of night. Such determination to achieve what she set out to do. An image of her falling back over the bridge flashed through Gina's mind and she found herself weeping.

'Are you okay? Wanna talk? You don't have to believe to talk.' Sally sat next to her and passed her a cup of coffee.

She shrugged.

'The newspapers hit you pretty hard but they've moved on. It's now all about the killer.'

'I'm grateful of that.' She paused. 'You heard the rumours that Bill Manders had been spreading. I could tell from the way you looked at me. You know, I thought I was going mad.' She let out a little laugh and wiped her eyes.

'I heard them but I didn't get involved with any gossip. That's not what I do.'

'What exactly was he saying? I need to know.' Gina leaned back and stared at the wooden roof. Large ancient-looking chandeliers hung from the ceiling.

She cleared her throat and placed her drink on the floor. 'Bill used to live near you and Terry, and he used the same pub that Terry was always in. He said Terry was drunk one night, buying everyone drinks and that he'd mentioned locking you in the shed. Apparently, Terry also said that he often had to punish you to keep you in your place.' The vicar placed a hand on Gina's arm. 'I'm sorry he did that to you. It must have been hard back then with a baby.'

'Can you please go on?'

'One night, Bill was apparently going to report Terry and he claimed he was going to try to catch him in the act, so he followed him home from the pub. He heard you screaming from the shed and he said for some reason he couldn't do it. I think the thing that irked Lucy was him saying that he thought he shouldn't interfere between a man and his wife, so he did nothing. I saw Lucy's face when he said that, but I didn't click. I didn't think for one moment that Lucy could have been the killer.' Sally brushed her hair from her face with her fingers.

'So Bill was a bystander in my torture. It's so hard to trust people sometimes, especially in my job. Thank you for being so honest.'

'I think the truth is important, however hard it is to hear.'

Gina smiled. 'The press only mentioned vague things. As they say, I'm yesterday's news and let that continue.'

'I'll drink to that.' Sally held her mug up and Gina tapped hers against it.

Gina pulled out a tissue and wiped her nose. 'That verse. "Be sober-minded, be watchful. Your adversary the devil prowls around like a roaring lion, seeking someone to devour." That's true of life in general, isn't it? There is always someone prowling and we need to keep up our guards. Sometimes, you can't see them coming.' Lucy never saw what was coming to her. 'At the end of the day, if they want to devour you, they will, and you won't be able to do a damn thing about it.'

'You can be sober-minded and be watchful.'

Gina glanced up, unable to think of an answer.

'I know. What a load of tosh. I'm not into victim blaming. These manipulators, sociopaths, narcissists; they ruin lives and their victims are blameless. They give their trust, their love to these people and it's abused. We can't always see the devil coming but maybe we now live in a better society in which people can speak out more. Show these people up for who they are.'

Gina passed the cup back to the vicar. 'Thank you for the chat and the drink. You know, it would be lovely to carry on this conversation sometime if you could be friends with an atheist.'

Sally laughed. 'I would love to spend a few hours having philosophical conversations with you while we get through a bottle of wine. Come and see me again, soon.'

'You're a good egg. I'll catch you again and we'll have that chat.'

As Gina stepped out into the biting wind, a crow squawked and the breeze howled around the churchyard. She spotted the café across the road. It had been boarded up. She smiled; for the first time in a while, she felt unburdened. Lyndsey Saunders had tried to make her life a misery – again – and she'd failed. Now Lyndsey was paying for her wrongdoing. Lucy was getting justice and Gina knew she'd be there to attend her funeral when the body was released.

She closed her eyes and tried to remember how it felt to be trapped in a coffin. Her heart wasn't pounding. She stepped on the icy path, trying not to slip, and knew it was time to turn over another page. The white tinge of frost on everything looked beautiful. The crow was now edging along a branch. That creature was proof that life could survive anything, even these temperatures. She could survive anything – and she would.

She was going home, throwing some logs on the burner and having a glass of wine in Lucy's memory.

A LETTER FROM CARLA

Dear Reader,

I'd like to start by saying a big fat thank you to you for choosing *Their Silent Graves*. I hope that you enjoyed reading it as much as I enjoyed writing it.

If you'd like to be kept up to date with my news and new releases, sign up to the following link. Your email address will never be shared and you can unsubscribe at any time.

www.bookouture.com/carla-kovach

I wrote this book from a strange place and that strange place was lockdown! It's like we've all gone through this weird time of loss and fear and I suppose it kept my mind busy as I wrote during those days, especially after losing my father just as we were told to stay at home. If you've suffered any losses or illnesses during this time, my thoughts wholeheartedly go out to you and your families.

When it came to this particular story, I knew I had to set it around Halloween. It's that smoky, dark, dismal time of the year when our imaginations are allowed to run away with us. It's okay for us to enjoy spooky films and for our children to dress up in creepy costumes. It's fun, it's theatre, and, for some unknown reason, one of my favourite times of the year.

I hope you enjoy my Halloween-set offering as much as I love Halloween.

If you loved *Their Silent Graves*, I'd be grateful if you'd leave me a review on Amazon, Apple Books, Google or Kobo. I also spend a fair bit of time on social media and I enjoy chatting with readers. Please pop along and say hi.

Once again, thank you so much for reading *Their Silent Graves*.

Carla

 CKovachAuthor

 CarlaKovachAuthor

carla_kovach

ACKNOWLEDGMENTS

I'll start off by saying that behind every book is a team of people who bring the whole package to life and, for those people, I'm extremely grateful.

My editor, Helen Jenner, is an absolute star. I love working with her and I'm always appreciative of her input. She helps me to shape my manuscripts in ways I wouldn't have thought of if left to my own devices. I look forward to working with her again on the next book. Thanks, Helen! I'm in awe of your vision and all the hard work you do to make my work shine.

The Bookouture publicity team are amazing! Noelle Holten, Kim Nash and Sarah Hardy are all brilliant. I don't know where they get their zing from, but I'd love some please. Thank you so much for making publication days wonderful.

I'd love to send this next thanks to the other Bookouture authors for continuing to be a huge support. I really do appreciate you all.

This next group is special in every way: bloggers and reviewers. I'm so grateful for all that you do, especially during the blog tour and around publication week. You are all amazing people and it's touching that you have chosen to read and review my work then share your thoughts for everyone to see.

There's always so much I don't know. I've no experience at all of working in a police station, which is why I'm so grateful to DS Bruce Irving for giving up his time to answer my police related questions. Thank you, Bruce.

I have to give a big mention to my lovely beta readers. Apart from my editor, they are the first to cast their eyes on my book. Huge thanks to Brooke Venables, Vanessa Morgan, Su Biela, Derek Coleman and Anna Wallace for all that you do. Long may our friendships continue.

I'm always in love with my covers and I have Toby Clarke and Helen Jenner to thank for those. I'm totally bowled over by them.

Another thank you goes to Bookouture's Peta Nightingale for keeping me updated. It's always lovely to be contacted by her. Thanks, Peta.

Lastly, mega thanks to my husband, Nigel. Thank you for all the coffees and biscuits while I'm racing against a deadline. You're also my sounding board when I need to talk things over or work out niggles in my story. I often ask you to read bits of my manuscript while you're trying to work or watch something on the television and you never moan – haha. Thank you.

Lightning Source UK Ltd.
Milton Keynes UK
UKHW011306280322
400723UK00003B/718